BOOKS BY DARYL GREGORY

Pandemonium

The Devil's Alphabet

Raising Stony Mayhall

RAISING
STONY
MAYHALL

RAISING
STONY
MAYHALL

DARYL GREGORY

BALLANTINE BOOKS / NEW YORK

A Del Rey Books Trade Paperback Original

Copyright © 2011 by Daryl Gregory

Published in the United States by Del Rey Books,
an imprint of The Random House Publishing Group,
a division of Random House, Inc., New York

DEL REY is a registered trademark and the Del Rey colophon
is a trademark of Random House, Inc.

Gregory, Daryl.
Raising Stony Mayhall / Daryl Gregory.
p. cm.
ISBN 978-0-345-52237-5 (pbk.)—978-0-345-52238-2 (ebk.)
1. Zombies—Fiction.   2. Mothers and daughters—Fiction.
3. Brothers and sisters—Fiction.   I. Title.
PS3607 R48836R35 2011
813'.6—dc22   2011010016

Printed in the United States of America

www.delreybooks.com

1 3 5 7 9 8 6 4 2

Book design by Susan Turner

For the sisters, Robin and Lisa

And the kids, Emma and Ian

Are you sleeping,
Are you sleeping,
Brother John?

2011
Easterly Enclave

It is traditional to end with the Last Girl, the sole survivor, a young woman in a blood-spattered tank top. She drops her chain saw, her sawed-off shotgun, her crowbar— these details differ—and stumbles out of the ramshackle house and into the light. Perhaps the house is burning. Dawn glows on the horizon, and the ghouls have been defeated (for now, for now—all happy endings being temporary). Perhaps she's found by her fellow survivors and taken to an enclave, a fortress teeming with heavily armed government troops, or at the very least gun-toting civilians, who will provide shelter until the sequel. Perhaps this enclave is located in Easterly, Iowa, about sixty miles northwest of the ruins of Des Moines. Perhaps the girl's name is Ruby.

That's her sitting in the high summer grass, head tilted like a painter. She is twenty-three, and wears her dark hair short, which on these postapocalyptic mornings can be a real time-saver. She's lived in the enclave for a little over a year, since the start of the second outbreak, and on most days, even through the icy winter, she's ridden her bike out here to the Mayhall farm, to watch for movement amid the blackened timbers where the house once stood. She is always disappointed. Out here, nothing moves but the wind.

Often she totes books with her. Sometimes she reads from a thick, five-ring binder jammed with typed pages, and at other times from the old-fashioned girl's diary she inherited, a thin book with a cloth cover of green and pink plaid, whose lock she opens with a safety pin. Mostly, though, she sits and thinks. She has a plan, this girl. And today is one of the red-letter days in that scheme.

A rider approaches, pedaling down the long gravel drive, a middle-aged woman with steely hair pulled into a fierce ponytail. Her aunt Alice. "Are they coming?" Ruby asks.

"Should be here within the hour," Alice says. "Thought you'd like to know."

"Ride out to the gate with me," Ruby says. Alice frowns; she is a woman with Things to Do. "Oh come on," Ruby says, and puts her arm around her. "You know you want to." Side by side, they could be taken for mother and daughter. Both are tall, with strong noses and high cheekbones. They are beautiful.

They ride down the drive to the highway, then head toward town. The enclave consists of twenty square miles of flat farmland, old housing divisions, and a few boarded-up stores and fast-food restaurants that used to make up Easterly. The clean zone is enclosed by two rings of fences topped with razor wire and spotlights. Good for keeping out the shambling hordes of last year, and good now for keeping out the federal government—the *illegitimate* federal government, people in the enclave say.

The road is flat and makes for easy riding. Ruby is anxious to reach their destination, but it is very hot and Alice, a doctor, will not be rushed into heatstroke. It's nearly an hour before they reach the southern guardhouse and its lobster trap of inner and outer gates. Sheriff Tines comes out to say hello, and he and a few of the guards stand around chatting with the women. Not for long; within minutes a man in the high tower calls down that a truck is approaching.

Ruby can't see anything on the road, and then she makes out a mercurial blob shimmering through the haze of heat. The truck gradually slows as it approaches the outer gates, where the federal troops are stationed. The helmeted and dark-visored guards briefly inspect the cab of the truck, as well as the yellow backhoe being towed on the trailer, then allow truck and trailer to pass into the no-man's-land before the inner gate. This movement signals a transfer in jurisdiction, and an entirely new bureaucracy springs into action. Civilian guards, without uniforms but with guns even larger than those carried by the federal officers outside, sweep forward and demand that the two men in the cab exit the vehicle.

The driver is a burly Korean man. He steps down slowly, then sees the women and walks toward the fence in a clump-ing gait. Both legs have been removed below the knee, and the prosthetics don't fit well. The guards yell at him to stop and be searched, but he laughs and waves them off.

"So you found one," Alice says.

"Did you doubt me? Did you doubt me?" the man says, laughing. "Found it at a place in Ankeny, with plenty of diesel, too. I claimed it as an unscheduled donation to the enclave. How you doing, Ruby? You girls didn't have to come out here and meet me."

"Not much going on today," Ruby says. "We really appreciate this, Kwang."

"Don't you worry, we'll find him," he says.

"Come on, Kwang," one of the guards says, making his name rhyme with *clang*. Even though Kwang's lived here almost his entire life, Iowans can't seem to get his name right.

"Gotta do the bite check. 'Less you want us to do it out here in front of the ladies."

Kwang laughs. "I don't think they could take the excitement. You all want a ride back to the house?"

"We've got our bikes," Alice says.

"Awfully hot for pedaling," Kwang says. "Come on, you can throw 'em up on the trailer and ride in the cab. I've got air-conditioning."

Ruby touches Alice's arm. "It's only polite to keep him company," she says. It's been a year without many things, but at the moment, perhaps air-conditioning feels like the greatest loss of all. There's generator power in the enclave, but it's strictly rationed.

"We shouldn't be wasting fuel on that," Alice says. But of course they shouldn't be wasting fuel on this project at all. It was Ruby who pushed this idea, who convinced Kwang to find them a backhoe for the excavation, who convinced her relatives to hold a funeral. Her determination to carry out this plan is a mystery to them, but they're indulging her.

Fifteen minutes later, after Kwang has passed the bite check, the women climb up into the cab with him; his co-driver has decided to hang out at the gate awhile and shoot the shit.

Traveling by vehicle, even a slow-moving semi, makes it obvious how tiny the enclave is. Someday, maybe soon, they'll have to expand, push back the fences as the population expands. There are pregnant women in Easterly.

Kwang nods to their right, at a patch of untended field. "That's where your mom found him, right, Alice?"

"About there," she says.

"Who?" Ruby asks.

Kwang says, "Stony and his mother."

"Wait, slow down!" Ruby says. She leans across her aunt,

and presses the button to roll down the window. "How come you've never pointed this out to me?" She'd traveled this road a hundred times with Alice.

Kwang slows the truck to a crawl. There's nothing to mark the exact location. Ruby says, "There ought to be a cross or something. A monument."

"It was about there," Alice says.

"There?" Ruby asks. It's just a patch of grass.

"Your grandmother was driving us home through a snowstorm," Alice says.

PART
ONE

CHAPTER ONE

1968
Easterly, Iowa

I t was a wonder she saw the dead girl at all. The first winter storm of the season had rolled in well ahead of the forecast, and Wanda Mayhall drove hunched over the wheel, squinting through a shrinking ellipse of clear windshield at a road being erased by drifts, and singing in a high, strong voice. The wind buffeted the Ford Falcon station wagon and threw snow across her headlights, making a screen of white static. She sang "I Will Meet You in the Morning," a belter of a hymn that would keep her three girls from worrying.

And there, at the edge of the road, a dark lump on the white snow.

She thought it was a downed cow, or maybe a dog. Then, a moment after her headlights had swept past, she thought she'd seen a glimmer of yellow. Something about that wink of color made her think, *Rubber rain boots.*

She pressed on the brake as hard as she dared. Still the car slewed, and the two girls in the backseat squawked excitedly. Alice, her oldest at thirteen, braced herself against the dash and yelled, "Mom!" Ever since her father died, Alice had bestowed upon herself all the privileges of an adult, including the permanent right to ride shotgun and criticize her mother's driving.

Wanda put the car in reverse and slowly backed up, her eyes watching the rearview mirror for headlights barreling out of the snow, until she reached the spot where she thought she'd seen the dark blot. She left the car running and the lights on. "Don't get out of the car," she told the girls.

She walked around to the rear of the station wagon. The wind whipped at her skirt, and icy snow bit her ankles through her nylons. Typical Iowa snowstorm, raking the empty fields at fifty miles per hour. A few feet from the taillights the dark closed in; she could barely distinguish gray field from pitch-black sky. She should have taken the flashlight from the glove compartment.

Then she saw the lump, perhaps ten feet from the road. She stepped off the shoulder and instantly plunged into snow up to her shins.

It was a girl, not more than seventeen or eighteen. She lay on her side, half buried in the snow, her arms curled in front of her. She wore an imitation rabbit fur coat, a dark skirt, black tights, and yes, yellow rubber boots. Wanda pulled off one glove and crouched in the snow beside her. She pushed the girl's long brown hair from her face and touched a hand to her neck. Her skin was the same temperature as the snow.

A light illuminated them. "Is she dead?" Alice said. She held the big silver flashlight. Of course she'd remembered it; Alice was as levelheaded as her father had been.

"I told you to stay in the car," Wanda said.

"Chelsea's watching Junie. Who is she?"

Wanda didn't recognize her. Maybe she was a runaway, trying to make it to Des Moines. But how did she get way out here, sixty miles from the city? And what killed her—exposure? A hit-and-run driver?

The girl's arms were wrapped around her stomach. Wanda had a bad thought. She put her hand on the girl's shoulder and tried to push her onto her back, but only moved her a few inches; a drift had formed against her, holding her in place. Wanda pulled on the girl's arm—it felt heavy, but not stiff—and moved it down to her side. Then she tugged up the hem of the jacket.

The infant was wrapped in what looked like bath towels. Only its tiny gray face was visible, its eyes closed, its lips blue. Wanda made a low, sad sound. She worked her hands beneath the child, her hand cradling its neck, and brought it to her chest. It was cold, cold as its mother.

Alice moved closer to her, and Wanda put up a hand—the girl didn't need to see this. The dead girl's pale shirt and dark skirt were stiff with frozen blood. Her black tights, she realized, were crusted with it.

Alice stepped forward anyway, frowning. She didn't scream, didn't panic. She looked at the girl, then the baby in her mother's arms, and said, "We have to get them to the hospital."

"Oh, honey," Wanda said. She'd witnessed a few kinda-sorta miracles in her years as an RN, but there was no hospital on earth that could help this baby now. She held it to her and got to her feet. Then she carried it back to the station wagon. Alice said, "Shouldn't we bring the girl?"

"We'll come back for her," Wanda said. The mother she could leave, but she couldn't imagine abandoning an infant, even a dead one.

When they reached the car she made Alice get in first, then put the baby in her arms, as gently as if it were a living child. The younger girls leaned over the seat back, amazed. "You found a *baby*?" Chelsea said. She was seven years old, Junie only three and a half.

Alice said, "It's not—"

"Sit in your seats, all of you," Wanda said, cutting her off. The last thing she needed was three hysterical girls. She wouldn't allow herself to cry, either.

She eased the station wagon into the lane. In all the time they'd been pulled over not a car had passed them in either direction. The closest telephone was their own, a couple of miles away. She'd have to call the police, or maybe the fire department, and tell them where to find the girl.

Then Alice shouted and Wanda nearly slammed on the brakes. "Alice, you can't—"

"Mom!"

The baby's eyes were open.

After a moment Wanda said, "That happens sometimes." She used her nurse voice. Maybe Alice would believe her if she used the nurse voice.

"It's *moving*," Alice said.

One of the towels had come open, exposing a little gray hand. Wanda looked at the road, back to the child. Its tiny fingers flexed.

Wanda felt a stab of panic. Suddenly she had a dying newborn to save. She couldn't floor it; the Falcon would never stay on the road. "Hold him up to the heater," she said. "Her. It."

The ten minutes to the farm seemed to take forever. The baby's arms shifted feebly under its wrap, and its lips moved silently. Alice talked to it the way she talked to Junie after a bad dream: Don't you worry, little one. Don't you cry.

Wanda drove up the lane and didn't bother to put the car in the garage. She killed the engine and took the baby from Alice. "Help the girls out," she said.

"Chelsea, carry Junie in," Alice said, and followed her mother into the house. With one hand Wanda plugged the kitchen drain and turned on the warm water. The baby looked into her face. Its eyes were the color of clouds before a heavy rain.

"We have to treat it for hypothermia," Alice said.

Wanda had long ago ceased to be surprised by the things Alice knew. "That's right. Now go get me some towels."

Wanda unwrapped the child. Ah, a boy then. He was blue-gray from top to bottom, with a black umbilical cord a couple of inches long, and a tiny gray penis. Dark hair with a bit of curl to it. She stirred the water in the sink, decided it would do, then lowered him into it.

Chelsea dragged over a kitchen chair so she could see. Junie climbed up with her and wrapped her arms around her sister's waist. "We should name him," Chelsea said.

"He's not ours to name," Wanda said.

The boy seemed to like the water. He kicked his legs, waved his arms. He still hadn't made a sound. Then she realized that his chest wasn't moving. No: hadn't moved. The boy wasn't breathing. Junie reached out to touch him. "Get down, girls," Wanda said. "Down!"

She'd never been this scared caring for a patient. She decided she had to treat his hypothermia and breathing at once, so she cradled him in the water with one hand and pinched shut his little nostrils with the other. Then she bent her lips to his. Gentle, she thought. New lungs were fragile.

She puffed a bit of air into his mouth. His chest rose a fraction, dropped—and stayed down. She breathed into him again, and again. After a minute she put her fingers to his neck. No pulse.

He gazed up at her with those cloud-colored eyes, perfectly calm. His hand came up, seemed to reach for her face.

And in that moment she made her decision. If it was a decision. If she had any choice at all.

"Mom?" Alice said. "Is he okay? You want me to call the hospital?"

"No. No hospital." Alice started to argue, and Wanda said, "They're snowed in. Nobody could get here anyway. Please, put the girls to bed."

Alice managed to get the girls into their pajamas, but none of them would stay out of the kitchen. They watched as Wanda worked, and soon she was sweating like a long-distance runner. After a half hour the baby was no better and no worse for all the forced resuscitation. In fact he seemed to like it. The air she gave him he turned into gurgles and sighs and whines. His first sounds.

"We have to call the police," Alice said.

"We're not going to do that." Wanda lifted the boy out of the water and his arms waved as if he wanted to get back in. "Not yet."

Alice lowered her voice. "You know what he is. One of those things from that night." Alice was old enough to read the paper, to watch the evening news.

"Those were all back east," Wanda said. "And they're all gone now." The president told them the creatures had all been killed—or whatever you called it when you destroyed their bodies. And if the police found out about this boy, they'd destroy him, too.

At some point Junie had climbed up on the chair again. She softly patted his head. "Lit-tle babeee," she sang to him. "Little old babeee."

Then the boy's chest rose, and he let out a long sigh.

"He's learning to talk," Chelsea said.

"He's just making noises," Wanda said. Though how did he learn *that*? His ribs moved again, and his mouth made a breathy whistle. Wanda put her ear to his chest. She heard nothing but her own pulse in her ears. Maybe he could learn to pump his heart, too.

And then she thought, Oh no, I can't do this. But of course she'd have to.

"Girls, I have something important to say," Wanda said. She lifted Junie onto her hip. "Alice, Chelsea, give me your hands." She made them place their palms atop one another's on the boy's head, *a laying on of hands,* just like the deacons did for someone who was terribly ill or troubled. Concentrated prayer.

Alice said, "What are you doing, Mom?"

"We have to make a solemn promise," Wanda said. "An oath." She took a breath. "We cannot tell anyone about this boy."

"Why not?" Chelsea asked.

"Nobody," Wanda said. "For a while at least. Can you promise that? Junie?"

"I promise," Junie said. And Chelsea said, "I won't tell a soul."

"This is a mistake," Alice said. "We should call the police." Chelsea yelped indignantly and Alice said, "Fine. I promise."

Wanda leaned down and kissed the boy's forehead. "Our secret," she said.

Her mind raced. She did need to call the police, to tell them about the dead girl. She'd say she thought she'd seen something out there, wasn't sure what. She wouldn't mention the child.

"We should name him Gray," Chelsea said.

"He's not a cat," Alice said. "We shouldn't name him anything."

"We'll call him John," Wanda said, surprising herself again.

"That's it?" Alice said. *"John?"*

"Brother John," Chelsea said.

The boy looked up at them. Then he blinked. He hadn't blinked before.

"A boy like this," Wanda said, "is going to need a normal name."

That first night, a Saturday, Wanda took the baby to bed with her, but he refused to sleep. He lay there, gurgling to himself, waving his arms and kicking his legs. Wanda eventually slept, for what seemed only minutes. The boy never settled down, but neither did he cry. Near dawn she picked him up and carried him to the living room, where she rocked him until the girls awoke. Wanda called in sick to the hospital, and sat back, exhausted, as the girls took turns holding him. He stayed up the whole day, never napping, hardly ever shutting his eyes.

Feeding was also a problem. He often smacked his blue lips and worked his toothless mouth, but he turned his face away from water or milk. She was afraid of what he might be hungering for, but that day she taught him to swallow formula, and a few hours after each feeding he'd spit it back out. She doubted he was digesting any food at all.

After supper she hauled the crib from the basement—Junie had only stopped using it a year ago—and set it up next to her bed. The boy refused to sleep in it. She sang to him and rubbed his back, but after a half hour of leaning over the rail she gave up and brought him to bed with her again, where he cooed and squawked and fidgeted until morning.

On Monday she called in sick a second time, and again on Tuesday. She couldn't afford any more absences, but neither could she deposit the boy with the old woman who watched Junie. On Wednesday morning she told Alice, "You now have mono. You'll be out for two weeks. Chelsea will bring home your schoolwork."

"This isn't fair!"

"It's temporary."

Wanda learned to fall asleep to his noises and movement, and grew used to his cool body next to hers. He spent the night experimenting with new sounds. Eventually he discovered a kind of cry that would get their attention, a long, high-pitched wail that would cease the instant Wanda or one of the girls picked him up. No tears—there were never tears—and he never seemed too upset. He simply liked being in their arms.

The morning Alice was supposed to go back to school, Wanda dressed the boy in a special onesy she'd sewn from an old bathrobe. She threaded a leather belt through the back loops and fastened him to the inside of the crib. Alice was appalled. "He's not a *dog*." Wanda swallowed against the steely taste of guilt and said he'd be fine. She'd run home at lunch to check on him, then as soon as Alice got home from school the girls would let him out, got it?

John seemed unperturbed by the new arrangement. He didn't recoil from the onesy harness when she slipped it on him. Every morning he was happy to be tied down, and every afternoon he was happy to be let loose. They played with him, fed him, and he spit everything back up. He refused to die, and refused to grow.

If he'd shown the slightest sign of distress she would have been forced to take him to a doctor. She'd worked at the hospital for years, and she trusted several of the nurses and even a doctor or two, but she didn't think any of them could have, or would have, kept this secret. To them the boy would be a danger, a disease carrier. The government said that all the victims of the outbreak had been destroyed, but newspapers still reported sightings of the walking dead out in Pennsylvania and New York, and the grocery store tabloids ran stories every week about the hordes of unnatural creatures waiting out there, ready to attack. Alice brought a *National Enquirer* home one day, her eyes red from holding back tears, and slammed it down on the kitchen table. The cover showed a gray man with a bullet hole through his head.

"Those pictures are fakes," Wanda told her. "They do that all the time." She was holding John in her arms, and he seemed excited to see Alice.

"Does it matter?" the girl said. "This is what they'd do to him." Wanda hugged her daughter, and John squirmed between them. "What are we going to do, Mom?" Alice had made a complete turnaround since the night they found John. Once she decided that she was protecting the baby from the world instead of shielding her family from the devil child, she appointed herself chief concealment strategist.

But Wanda was the adult here. Ever since the cancer took Ervin, the *only* adult. "I'll think of something," she said.

Somehow they had to keep the boy's existence a secret. They'd been lucky so far. The body of his teenage mother had been recovered from the side of the highway, declared a Jane Doe, and cremated (because every corpse was being cremated as quickly as possible that year), without any mention of a missing baby. And fortunately, Wanda's house was set back from the road, surrounded by corn and soy fields, so there were no neighbors to peek through their windows. The rare visitor could be seen coming down the lane in plenty of time for them to take the baby into the back bedroom.

Alice, enforcer of secrecy, policed the younger girls. She quizzed Chelsea almost daily to see if she'd told anyone at school about John. And even Junie, who saw hardly anyone during the winter except when she went to the babysitter or they all went to church, understood that he'd be taken away from them if anyone found out. Alice read to the girls from *The Diary of Anne Frank,* which Wanda thought was inappropriate, but it did seem to get the point across: Junie asked her if they were going to put John up in the attic.

They were coping. They were keeping the secret. And then came the day in April that Junie snuck John out of the house and carried him across the road to see the calf that had been born that week.

Wanda was walking back from the barn when she saw the strange car in the driveway. A skinny, black-haired man leaned against the front bumper, smoking a cigarette. The front door of the house was open.

Wanda dropped the bag of cat food she'd been carrying and ran. When she was a few yards from the car she slowed to a fast walk and said, "Hello? Can I help you?"

The man was Oriental—Wanda couldn't tell if he was Japanese or Chinese or what. He said nothing, but waved toward the house, then took another drag on his cigarette.

Wanda went inside, then froze at the kitchen doorway. A woman, foreign like the man outside, sat at the table, cradling John in her arms. Beside her stood Junie and a boy who looked five or six years old. His hand was on John's chest, and the baby was gripping one of his fingers.

Junie saw her mother and screamed, "It was an accident!" Then she bolted for her bedroom.

The stranger woman watched her go, and then said something to her son in another language. The boy said, "This is my mom, Mrs. Cho. She says she's sorry for going in your house."

"That's all right," Wanda said automatically, though her heart was pounding. She came forward, holding out her arms for the baby. The woman nodded and transferred John to her.

The boy said, "That girl? She was walking by herself along the road. We almost hit her."

"I'm so sorry," Wanda said. "Junie knows she's not supposed to go in the road."

The woman nodded as if she understood. She was made up as if going to church: bright lipstick, curled hair, a blue polka-dot dress, high heels. Her son was dressed in shorts and a button-front shirt.

"We just bought a house," the boy said. His English was better than Junie's. "Down the road. There are mice inside, but my dad's going to kill them."

"I'm sure he will," Wanda said. They had to be talking about the Allen house. No one had lived there since the widow died last year. "I'm going to put the baby down for his nap. Can you tell your mother that? And say thank you for watching out for Junie."

The boy spoke to his mother in that other language—Korean, she guessed. They exchanged some words and then the boy said, "She apologizes again, but she has to ask something." He hesitated, then said, "She wants to know if your baby needs, uh, help?" He asked a question of his mother, and she spoke a few soft sentences. "Medicine help?"

Mrs. Cho looked at her, her expression calm. Wanda couldn't figure out if she knew what John was. Had she heard about the outbreak last fall?

Wanda said, "No, no help needed. But thank you. He has a skin disease. Poor circulation. Do you know that word? *Circulation?*"

Mrs. Cho stood and smoothed out her dress. Then she touched John's head. "Good baby," she said.

The boy reached up to John, and the baby grabbed his finger again. "I think he likes me," the boy said.

The next morning, John had grown, Wanda was sure of it. She retrieved the cloth tape from the kitchen drawer and measured him from crown to foot. She weighed herself on the bathroom scale, first with John in her arms, then without. Then, even though she knew the numbers by heart, she got out the paper tablet and checked the figures she'd written down the night she'd found him—numbers that had not changed in all the weekly measurements that followed.

He'd grown three inches. And he was nearly a pound heavier.

That afternoon she made a red velvet cake, told Alice to take charge of John and Junie, then put Chelsea in the car and drove a quarter mile down the road. The Allen house was still as run-down as it had been when the widow had died, but the lawn had been mowed, and once Mrs. Cho had welcomed her inside, Wanda saw that they'd scrubbed the floors and walls and had already set up household. Wanda was disappointed that there were only a few Korean decorations in evidence: a floral print tablecloth with colors too bright for the Midwest, two exotic-looking candlesticks, and a book with pictograms on the cover that she thought—she hoped—was a Bible.

Mrs. Cho accepted the cake while her son translated. "Could you tell your mother that we'd love to have you come over and play?" Wanda said.

"You could help feed the cats," Chelsea said. "We've got a barnful."

The boy, whose name was Kwang, was obviously excited, but he watched his mother's face carefully as she considered the offer. Finally she spoke. Kwang said, "She wants to know about the stone baby. No, not stone. You know . . ."

"The stone baby is doing just fine," Wanda said. "He is no danger to anyone."

It took the boy almost a minute of talking to pass this on. Wanda had no idea what all he was telling his mother. But eventually she nodded.

"Yes," Mrs. Cho said. "Thank you. Tomorrow."

Kwang showed up the next day, and the day after. With each visit, Stony grew. Within a few days he was walking. The next week he was talking. By the end of the summer the two boys were exactly the same height and weight, and they were hardly ever out of each other's sight.

CHAPTER TWO

1974
Easterly, Iowa

he day they created the Unstoppable, they decided to test him with an air rifle, a bow and arrow, and a knife. They started with the air rifle.

Like most of their experiments, they decided to conduct this one inside the barn, away from the eyes of Stony's mom and sisters. Stony stood up against the wall, wearing a red ski mask with a *U* drawn in Magic Marker on the forehead. Kwang took up position about ten feet away. He pumped the rifle five times, thought for a second, and pumped it again.

"Don't go crazy," Stony said.

Kwang said, "Put your hands down."

"You're going to hit me in the face."

"I'm not going to hit you in the face. Besides, you're the Unstoppable."

"I hate that name. Unstoppable what? It's like calling the Hulk 'the Incredible.' "

"We talked about this! Just 'Unstoppable.' Like 'the Thing.' Now put 'em down."

"I can see right down the barrel. If you just—" A soft *pop* and the BB struck Stony just above the Adam's apple. "You jerk!"

"Shut up, you're fine. Did it hurt?"

"You hit me in the *neck*."

"But did it hurt?"

No, it didn't hurt, not really. Stung a little. Or maybe it was only the idea of it that stung. Pain was like that. It slipped away when he wasn't paying attention.

Stony pulled off the mask, then looked at the rafters while Kwang inspected his neck. Stony's skin was a brownish gray—the color of last night's pork chop, his sister Alice said—and dry as paper. "I can't tell where it hit," Kwang said. "Nope, no damage."

"Good," Stony said. His mom told him not to come home with any more scars. He carried a half-moon of stitches on his shoulder from where he'd fallen onto a metal sewer pipe last summer. (Kwang was chasing him.) And just last week the lawn mower had thrown a rock into his right thigh that left a dent the size of a half-dollar.

Kwang said, "Let's try the bow and arrow." Stony made a face and Kwang said, "What, you're wimping out on me?"

"I don't think criminals use bows and arrows."

Kwang shook his head. "What, you want to go right to knives?" He picked up the bow and one of the steel-tipped arrows. "This? This is just a warm-up. It's nothing."

"Why don't we shoot a few at you, then?"

"Hey, you're the invulnerable one." *Invulnerable.* A comic book word. Kwang owned two cardboard boxes loaded with comics—*The Teen Titans, The Mighty Thor, Tales of Suspense,* and that was just the T's—which he allowed Stony to read or touch only according to a strict set of rules, rules that only Kwang understood or would share. He'd let Stony read, say, issues 51 through 62 of *The Invincible Iron Man,* but not 63 or anything after. "What are you going to do when he comes after you?" Kwang said. "You want to know you can take it, right? Besides, I'll only shoot at your leg."

"I know that if somebody comes after me with a bow, I'm running."

Kwang paced off a dozen feet, turned. "You have a *super-power*," Kwang said. He notched an arrow and pulled back the string. "And with great power—"

The barn door banged open, smacking Kwang, and Junie said, "There you are."

Then Stony was on his butt and Junie was screaming. Stony looked down. The shaft was buried an inch deep in the left side of his chest, straight through the red *C* in his blue Cubs shirt.

"That was great!" Kwang said.

Stony shook his head. "Mom's going to kill me."

But Wanda Mayhall had taught her girls early to keep secrets, not realizing how easily their skills could be used against her. The sisters had formed an inner circle around Stony, a force field of Everything Is Fine, designed to keep their stressed-out mother from going off the rails, and to keep Stony out of sight of the world.

Junie was shorter than Stony by several inches, but she was technically older than him and took her big-sister status very seriously. She grabbed him by the wrist and hauled him toward the house, yelling for Chelsea. During the school year it was Mrs. Cho who watched him while his mother worked, but during the summers his sisters were in charge, and with Alice at work it was Chelsea who was the next-highest-ranking officer of the sorority.

They found her on the back porch in the rocking chair,

bare feet up on the railing. She was thirteen, a teenager now, and had declared that she was not just stuck in the house *with* her siblings every day, she was in charge of them. She'd spent most of the summer screaming at Junie and Stony, reading Carlos Castaneda books, listening to KRNQ, and talking on the phone with her girlfriends. Mom checked on them whenever she could break through the busy signal, effectively pinning them all to the house. Stony thought this was only fair, since he was *never* allowed to leave the farm.

It was the number-one commandment in the list that had been in effect his entire life: Hide. Never leave the farm, never answer the phone, and never let a visitor see you. Only the Cho family was exempt. His mother had told him about the disease he was born with. She told him how some ignorant people would say he was dead, even though he obviously wasn't, and think he was contagious, even though he definitely, definitely wasn't, and that's why he had to stay hidden.

When Junie, Stony, and Kwang walked out the back door, Chelsea quickly closed the magazine she was reading and placed it facedown on her lap. Then she noticed the arrow sticking out of her brother's chest. "What did you *do*?"

"It was an accident," Stony said. The old family joke.

Chelsea put the magazine away in her hemp purse, then made him sit down. Wincing, she put her fingers to the hole in his T-shirt.

"Don't rip it," Stony said. It was his number 14 Ernie Banks shirt.

"You are such a doofus," she said. She lifted the shirt up over the shaft and pushed the cloth under his chin. There was no blood—he'd never bled in his life—but she still made a disgusted face. The shaft was buried in him like a reed in the mud.

"Should we pull it out?" Junie asked.

"No! That would make it worse."

"Well, you can't just leave it in there," Kwang said. Wrong move. The girls turned on him, telling him it was his fault—which was mostly true—and finally drove him from the house. Then they started yelling at Stony.

Chelsea said, "Geez, Stony, he shot you in the *heart*. You could have *died*." This caused Junie to burst into tears.

"It's okay, Junie," Stony said. "It doesn't hurt." Though that was weird, come to think of it. Shouldn't something like that be a little painful? Mom said his disease made him different from everybody else, and he could do things other people couldn't. But still, the heart was kind of important, wasn't it?

"We need Alice," Chelsea said. Alice was always the one who stitched and repaired him. But she was working at the Tastee-Freeze in Easterly and wouldn't be home until supper, the same time as Mom.

"Let's just snip it off," Stony said. "I'll hide it until Alice can get it out."

They retrieved their father's big metal toolbox from the barn. Ervin Mayhall had enough tools to fix anything, except maybe cancer. From the pile of formidable instruments they chose a pair of pliers that looked like hedge clippers. Stony lay on the dirt floor holding on to the base of the shaft near his chest, while Chelsea clamped down and twisted the pliers. He could feel the arrow tip twisting inside him but didn't want to tell her to stop. Eventually she managed to gnaw through the fiberglass shaft. The remaining stub still made a pup tent of his shirt.

"We can't cut any more or we won't be able to pull it out," Chelsea said. She was dripping with sweat. The air in the barn was stifling.

"Maybe you could wear a coat to the dinner table," Junie said.

"No, tell her I'm eating at Kwang's," Stony said. "I'll hide out here until you can get Alice."

That became their plan. At 4:30, a half hour before Mom's usual arrival time, he went back to the barn, scattering the near-feral barn cats. Only a few minutes into his exile, Junie came out with a stack of Hardy Boys from his room. She was nine; he was five years old but looked and acted ten. She both mothered him and looked up to him. Though she wasn't a reader herself, she approved of his appetite for books. Stony didn't think there was much to admire there. He was a boy who didn't sleep, in a house in which no TV was allowed. What else was he going to do with all that time?

"Anything else, Brother John?" she asked.

He thought about telling her that he'd read the Hardy Boys at least two times each, but he didn't want her to feel bad. She was just trying to be nice. "I'm fine," he said.

"Okay then." She kissed him on the forehead, in the same way that their mother kissed all of them, and hurried out.

For a while he flipped through *The Secret of the Old Mill*, looking at the illustrations, and then he remembered the magazine that Chelsea was reading on the back porch—the one she'd been so careful to hide from the little kids. That had to be more interesting than Frank and Joe tracking down counterfeiters. He snuck out of the barn, keeping low so he wouldn't be seen from his mother's bedroom window, and ran, crouched, for the back of the house. Chelsea's multicolored purse was still on the porch next to the rocking chair. If he stood up he'd be in direct view of the kitchen window. He dropped to elbows and knees and commando-crawled across the lawn: the Unstoppable, evading Agents of Hydra. When he reached the porch he slipped a hand through the slats and pulled her purse to him. The magazine was folded up inside. He took it out, a *Time* magazine with a gray photo of a battlefield on the front, and stuck it into his back pocket. Mission accomplished!

He started to crawl back, then decided to risk a peek inside the kitchen. He slowly rose, head tilted back, until his nose cleared the railing and he could look into the window. His mother and sisters were at the table, just starting to pass around the baked spaghetti. He hated to miss dinner. Not the meal, that was just food—no, *foodstuff*, a word he'd picked up from a box of Commander Calhoun FishStix. He could taste food, but he had no taste: he never knew what dishes were good or bad until his sisters or Kwang pronounced judgment. *Delicious, spicy, yummy* were colored toothpicks he stuck into whatever appeared on his plate and remembered for next time. Chocolate, according to Chelsea, was the best food ever invented. Mrs. Cho's kimchi was the worst ever, unless you ate with Mr. Cho and heard him grunt happily through a plateful. Stony didn't want to offend Mom or Mrs. Cho, so he decided early on that he should *really like* everything put in front of him, and the way you proved you really liked something was to chow down. He taught himself to chew chew chew, letting his gut fill up like a lawn mower bag, and then later he'd slip out to the bathroom and throw everything up. He'd long since stopped thinking of this process as weird—it couldn't possibly be weirder than pushing poop out your butt—but it was time-consuming. He kept up the pantomime because he loved sitting around the table with his sisters and hearing them talk about best friends and former best friends and the biology teacher with Jack Lord's hair, and he loved the way his mother smiled to herself when he told her he liked the burnt spaghetti noodles at the edge of the casserole dish.

Junie suddenly glanced out the window and saw him. He

froze, and then Junie turned back to the table and announced at the top of her voice, "We forgot to say grace! Everybody close your eyes."

He ducked down, laughing silently, and then crept back to the barn with his prize.

Kwang somehow figured out that Stony was in the barn. A little after five, he sneaked through the big doors and climbed up the ladder to the loft.

"Hey, are you okay?" he said. "Did they get it out?"

Stony sat with his back against an ancient bag of seed, staring straight ahead at nothing, the *Time* magazine open on his lap.

"Look, I'm sorry I shot you, okay? I promise I won't do that again."

Stony seemed to focus on him for the first time. "I—I think I'm . . ."

"What? Is it hurting?"

Stony handed him the magazine. On the cover was a black-and-white photo of a field full of bodies. In red letters it said, "The Fifth Anniversary." Then in black letters below that: "Can It Happen Again?"

"Look at the pictures."

Kwang flipped through some of the pages, and stopped at the two-page spread that showed a grassy field full of corpses. Men were tossing bodies into a huge bonfire. "Wow, there were a lot of 'em."

"*Zombies,*" Stony said. He'd never said the word aloud before, didn't really know what it meant. "A lot of zombies."

He took the magazine from Kwang and flipped to another page. "There were thousands and thousands of them. They were all over New York and New Jersey and Pennsylvania and some other places. They killed tons of people. They didn't tell you about how big this was in school?"

"Maybe. I don't know. In social studies we haven't even gotten to the Korean War yet." Kwang said nobody knew about Korea. All the kids at school thought he was from Vietnam. "So what's the deal? There were a lot of dead people."

"Kwang, they killed them all. Every one of them that had the disease."

"I thought they sent them to a hospital or something."

"That's what I thought. That's what Mom told me. But there never was a hospital. They just rounded them up and shot them and burned them."

"Geez," Kwang said. Together they looked through the pictures again. Then Kwang said, "Does your mom know?"

Stony stared at him. "Of course she does—they all do. My sisters, your family. Everyone's been hiding this from me my whole life."

"It's not like you're very old."

"Shut up." Stony got up from the floor and walked to the loft door, which was slightly ajar. He could see his mother's station wagon in the lane, and the beater pickup that Alice drove. The Hardy Boys would call it a jalopy. "If the police found me, they'd kill me."

"They can't kill you," Kwang said. "You're the Unstoppable." Stony made a disgusted noise and Kwang said, "No, this is what you're training for! When they come for you, you'll be ready."

"Stop it. This isn't a joke."

"Look, they only killed those other guys because they went crazy and ate people. You don't want to eat people, do you?"

"Not you. You probably taste like spiced cabbage."

"See, then nobody has to be careful around you."

"Careful?" Stony said. "Who told you you had to be careful around me?"

"Nobody."

"Who?"

"Nobody! My dad maybe."

"What? When?"

"He used to say it all the time. Mother made him stop."

Stony felt sick. "I thought your dad liked me. He lets me watch him work on the cars."

"He doesn't like anybody, why would he like you?"

"Okay, fine! Just—get out, okay?"

"Come on, Stony."

"Get out!" Stony spun and shoved Kwang in the chest, knocking him backward onto the floorboards. The magazine flew out of his hands.

"Don't you get it? They're *hunting* me." Stony picked up the copy of *Time*, then stepped to the edge of the loft. "And when they find me, they'll kill me."

He stepped off the edge. Twelve feet of air, then the hard smack as his feet struck the packed dirt. He felt no pain, but the shaft in his chest vibrated like a tuning fork.

He ran.

Once they started looking, it didn't take them long to find him; they just followed the trail that connected the Mayhalls' grassy, overgrown fields to the Chos' faltering corn rows, a dirt highway Stony and Kwang had scraped out for Tonka trucks and army tanks. Stony was holed up in the windbreak of trees that marked the border of the farms, a strip of woods where two summers ago he and Kwang had built a fort out of discarded plywood and Sheetrock. Stony heard his sisters' voices in the distance, then looked out to see the beam of the flashlight jerking toward him. He placed the magazine against the wall and covered it with a square of cardboard.

Since leaving the barn he'd decided to run away, then decided to stay, changing his mind a dozen times. His family had lied to him. They'd treated him like a baby. He obviously couldn't trust them. And wasn't he the Unstoppable? He could run all night, hide during the day, and cover hundreds of miles without tiring. The only thing that kept him from running away was the complete lack of a destination.

The flashlight beam played across his face. Alice knelt down in front of the fort, Junie behind her. "Don't be scared," Junie said.

"I'm fine," Stony said.

Alice shined the light on his chest, and prompted him to lift his shirt. "What the *hell?*" she said. "You were shooting *real arrows?*"

"Just at me," Stony said.

"Well, that's okay then." She studied the wound. "I could probably pull that right out. But then we might tear something internally. We need to stitch you up, kid."

"All right. Whatever you say." She'd fixed him up a dozen times before. He didn't know what he'd do when she left for college. In a few days she'd be gone to Iowa City. Who'd repair him then? Not Chelsea, that's for sure. She was too squeamish. Probably why she didn't come out with them tonight. "Can we do it out here?"

"Uh, no. We've got to sew you up from the inside out. We're going to need lots of light. And Mom's going to have to do it."

"What? No!"

"Sorry. Let's go."

He didn't try to argue further. Once Alice decided something, she couldn't be budged. As they crossed the field together he asked, "Alice? I'm dead, right?"

"You're not dead, John."

"But I'm not alive."

"Of course you're alive. You're running around and hiding in ditches, aren't you?"

"Stop talking to me that way! You know what I mean."

Alice stopped walking. "You should have this conversation with Mom."

"She's just going to tell me the same things she always does—I'm very special and God loves me and please don't go outside. I need someone to tell me the truth."

She looked out into the dark fields, lips pursed. Moonlight and shadow carved her angular face into something ancient and severe, an Egyptian sculpture. Mom said Chelsea was the pretty one, but it was Alice whose face he studied, that he loved most.

"Here's the truth, John," she said finally. "We don't know *what* you are. Those people from the outbreak are nothing like you. They wanted to attack and kill people, and you wouldn't hurt a fly."

"Maybe that's because Mom found me so early."

"That's another thing—I'm pretty sure the living dead aren't supposed to grow. They don't start out as babies and turn into kids."

"Really?"

"Pretty sure. So whatever it is you are, you're not one of them."

He didn't know if this made him feel better or worse.

"So does that mean I can die?"

"Kid, you just took an arrow to the heart." She gripped

his hand and started walking. "If you can die, I'm highly confident you won't be checking out tonight."

"Where is it?" his mother said under her breath.

Alice leaned forward, tilting her head to stay out of the path of light. She held a set of tweezers in each hand, keeping the wound open while their mother worked on the internal tissue.

"Where's what?" Stony said. They'd already removed the arrowhead, so it couldn't be that. He lay on his back on a beach towel spread on the kitchen floor. He felt pressure when his mother poked and tugged inside him, but he was otherwise comfortable. Only the bright light bothered his eyes.

"Nothing," his mom said. "Lie still." She'd been furious with him, of course. Stony didn't mention that his sisters had conspired to hide the wound from her, and in return they didn't mention that Stony had allowed Kwang to shoot at him. It was, they said, an accident.

Alice said, "It's like . . . meat. Solid meat, all the way down."

"Wait a minute," Stony said. "You can't find my *heart*?"

"I'm sure it's in here somewhere," his mother said. "How do you feel, John?"

"I'd feel better if you could find my heart."

"He's fine," Alice said. "He's always fine."

His mother sighed. "Well, it's not like it's ever pumped or anything. All right then, let's get the fishing line and close up. Are there any of the old wounds we should fix up while we're here?"

His wounds never healed. In fact, they only grew larger as he grew. Stitches popped, even those made from the high-test

line his mother used. They repaired him like a rag doll with
too much sentimental value to throw out.

He closed his eyes and let them tug and cinch and fasten
him back into shape.

Later, he would think of the next few months as the Summer
of Terror. He didn't tell his mother or sisters that he'd seen the
Time article, but he thought of it constantly. No matter what
Alice said, he knew he'd die someday. And he knew how. The
police would find him, and then they would shoot him, and
then they would burn him.

While his mother and sisters slept, he walked the house.
Occasionally he would lie down, impersonating a normal person, but his mind would thrash and root, his thoughts tangling
into each other like blackberry vines. Sometimes he'd try to
distract himself with the Little Big game: He'd stare up into the
dark and convince himself that the ceiling was impossibly far
away, that he was a speck, an ant in the middle of a huge bed.
And then, abruptly, he was gigantic, a mountain range under a
dark sky, and the floor was miles away below him. If he relaxed
into it he could keep the scales flipping for minutes at a time.
Years later, when he picked up a novel titled *Little, Big,* he
thought, Hey, somebody else knows about this! But of course
the book turned out to be about something else entirely.

One morning his mother asked him why he looked so
tense. Did he look different? He tried to remember what his
face felt like before he understood that the world was trying
to kill him. He told her nothing was wrong and she let it go
for the moment, but he could tell she was studying him. Then
one night she came out of her bedroom at two or three in the
morning and found him sitting on the floor in the middle of
the living room, staring out the picture window. He was

watching for flashing lights, listening for sirens. He started
when he noticed her standing there.

"Talk to me, my son."

But of course that was the last thing she should have said.
He couldn't just talk when she told him to. Impossible.

"No one's out there," she said.

"I know."

She crouched beside him and stared out the window with
him. "No one can hurt you here, John," she said. "This farm is
mine, and it's yours. It's our mighty fortress. No one gets in
without our say-so, I guarantee it."

"You can't promise that," he said. "No one can promise
that."

"Oh yes I can." She stood up and walked purposefully
into the kitchen. He was curious, but he didn't get up. Thirty
seconds later she was back, holding a five-pound bag of flour.
Then she opened the front door and walked outside.

He thought, Mom's gone crazy.

He got to his feet and walked to the door. His mother
stood on the lawn in her bare feet, cradling the white bag.
"Come on," she said. She tugged open the top of the bag,
reached in, and then sprinkled a bit of the powder in a line at
her feet.

"What are you doing?" he asked.

"'God sits above the circle of the earth,'" she said. "And
we're all safe inside it." She began to walk in a circle around
the house, scooping a handful of flour from the bag and tossing it before her. Stony followed her at a distance. Is this the
kind of thing they did in church? They'd never let him go, of
course, but if it was like this then maybe it was more interesting than he thought.

"Everything in this circle belongs to us," she said. "Come
on, say it. Everything in this circle . . ."

He laughed. "Belongs to us."

By the time they reached the front of the house again the bag was empty. His mother turned it upside down and shook it over the lawn.

"There," she said. "The walls are up." A fuzzy circle of white surrounded the house.

"What if somebody digs underneath them?"

"Don't be silly," she said. "This is a magic circle. Now come on, my feet are about to freeze off." She put an arm around his shoulder. "I know you can't sleep, John, but you can lie down next to me for a while."

He didn't believe in magic circles, of course. He knew that the government wouldn't be stopped by a border of baking material. No, he'd need his own defenses, his own fortifications. In fact, he could start working on them tonight.

Or maybe not tonight. His mother snored lightly beside him, and her arms were warm.

CHAPTER THREE

1978
Easterly, Iowa

very August was a betrayal. Alice drove back to college. Junie came home from Kmart with new binders, plastic zip bags packed with colored pencils, protractors, compasses—shiny weapons for a war in which he was not allowed to enlist. And then one morning Chelsea and Junie and Kwang would be gone, driven away in a crowded yellow bus to their new classes, new teachers.

New friends.

The August he and Kwang were fourteen, the year Kwang went to high school, was especially cruel. Out of nowhere Kwang had developed an obsession with football. Two weeks before school began, he started practicing twice a day with the high school team, abandoning Stony to his sisters. Chelsea, though, was hardly ever home. She'd *fallen in love* with a greasy-haired eighteen-year-old named Alton, and since he wasn't allowed to come to the farm, Chelsea spent most of the time at the lake with him, or in his Chevy Malibu. That left Junie, who since joining the youth group at the Baptist church only wanted to talk about Jesus.

His mother tried to make him feel like he was starting a

new year, too. As usual, she'd gone to the mall in Des Moines and bought him new gym shoes and a couple of pairs of jeans. The first day of class, Junie said a prayer over breakfast: "Bless us Lord for this oatmeal, and watch over us during the day, and bless our teachers" and on and on until she was almost late for the bus. Chelsea walked out to the end of the lane to be picked up by Alton. His mother kissed him on the cheek and left for work. And then he was alone.

He thought about going back to his bedroom to read, or heading down to work on the cellar. But if he stayed home, Mrs. Cho would only come looking for him. Finally he trudged across the field.

Mrs. Cho greeted him with a hug. "First day of the year. A very big day." She went through the textbooks and study guides he'd brought with him—his mother purchased them each year from a used bookstore in Des Moines—and commented on each of them. "Ooh, calculus, very advanced. And American literature! That's good for us both."

His mother called it homeschooling, but Stony knew what it was: babysitting with books. He would churn through the assignments his mother and Mrs. Cho made up for him, and then start in on any homework Kwang and his sisters left lying around. He corrected math problems, filled in the blank spots in worksheets, proofread essays, finished extra-credit questions. Only Alice's college textbooks, the ones she'd brought home because she couldn't sell back, provided any challenge.

He was forced to create his own electives. He picked up an advanced degree in reruns (unlike his mother, Mrs. Cho considered television an important educational tool), with an emphasis in Dick Van Dyke and *Hogan's Heroes*. But he also began to study car and small engine repair—Mr. Cho's business. In Korea, Kwang had told Stony, his father had been an engineer who worked on turbines for hydroelectric dams. But Mr. Cho had moved his family from Pittsburgh to Iowa because he wanted to become a farmer. This, even though he knew nothing about crops, owned no equipment, and did not have enough capital to seed a garden patch. Also, he did not like working outside. Eventually the side business he started in order to keep food on the table while he killed food in the fields turned into a full-time job.

"My sister wants to save my soul," Stony told Mr. Cho one afternoon. Stony had dismantled a Toro engine down to the screws and laid out each part on a white sheet. It looked like a crime scene. Mr. Cho had said the engine was beyond repair, though not in so many words. He communicated primarily in grunts and scowls.

Stony said, "Do you know that word, *soul*?"

Mr. Cho did not answer; he was stretched out under a Chevy Vega that needed new brakes. Stony had never forgotten what Kwang had told him in the hayloft. The fact that Mr. Cho thought they should be careful around him didn't make him want to avoid the man. The opposite, actually. Stony wanted to prove himself trustworthy, and at the same time, to hang around someone who thought of him as dangerous.

"The problem is," Stony said, "I don't think I have one."

"Socket," Mr. Cho said.

Stony picked up the socket wrench from the toolbox and squatted to hand it to him. Mr. Cho tilted his head to look at it, then said, "No! Nine-sixteen."

Stony walked back to the tray of socket heads and started to fish through them. "The Bible's not much help. A lot of resurrections, but those people come back to life, you know? Their bodies don't stay dead."

Mr. Cho reached up and impatiently slapped the fender of the Vega. Stony wondered, when Mr. Cho lay there with his legs sticking out like that, did he ever think, That dead boy could bite me?

Stony snapped the nine-sixteenths head into place and put the wrench in his hands. "It seems to me that if I'm already dead, then my soul went to heaven or hell or wherever it was supposed to go. There's nothing left to save."

Mr. Cho grunted, though probably that was just because he was struggling with the bolt.

"On the other hand," Stony said, "maybe what happened is that my soul never left like it was supposed to. It was *prevented* from going to the afterlife. So, there's no use trying to save it, because some other rules are in effect. I'm in purgatory."

"Shut up now," Mr. Cho said. "Fix lawn mower."

At night, after his family had gone to sleep, he worked on expanding the cellar. His mother had given him permission to dig a new floor to provide some headroom and to double the square footage. He'd already gone well beyond that. A crawlspace extended under the entire house, and he'd dug almost to the cinder-block walls in every direction.

The work was tedious, but he'd learned that he had a talent for manual labor. He could let his mind wander and work for hours without realizing it. He thought about the state of his soul. He thought about the Cubs. He thought about his body, and why he didn't get tired, and how it was that it could move at all.

He couldn't find himself in any of the science books he'd been reading. He knew how bodies were *supposed* to work: Lungs inhaled, alveoli transferred oxygen to red blood cells, the heart pumped blood to all the cells. But while he could inhale and exhale, his heart didn't beat, and there wasn't any blood for it to pump anyway. If the cells didn't receive any oxygen, they couldn't do any work. Muscles couldn't contract, neurons couldn't fire. He should be as inert as a lump of clay. Yet he moved and talked. He grew. He had feelings and ideas. He thought things such as, How am I thinking this?

He'd found only one textbook that mentioned the outbreak of 1968. Alice had brought home a book called *Government and Society* that spent a measly three pages on it. The outbreak struck on October 1, and by the end of the next day, between 35,000 and 72,000 people were dead, depending on whether you counted people who were dead before the outbreak began and had to be killed again. The article was mostly about how the event changed federal disaster preparedness plans. It didn't even talk about what caused the disease, what the living dead were, and what the government would do if they found more of them. It was as if the whole thing were all over and he didn't exist.

Useless.

He began to think that his mother and sisters were deliberately hiding the truth from him. What he needed was free rein at a library, a few hours in the stacks without his family looking over his shoulder. Since that wasn't possible, he went to his next-best option.

"Here are the topics and keywords I'm interested in," Stony said, and handed Kwang the sheet of notebook paper. He'd waited at the Cho house until Kwang came home, and made sure to pass him the list when Mrs. Cho wasn't in the room. "Next month is the tenth anniversary of the outbreak, so there should be *something*. Check out everything you can find in the catalog. Whatever's not on the shelves, write down the title and Dewey decimal number."

"How do you know about Dewey decimal numbers?"

"I'm not an idiot. How many books will they let you check out?"

"I don't know, five? I really don't have time for this tonight. Me and the guys—"

"What guys? The *team*?"

"Yeah, they're on the team. What does that have to do with it?"

"Nothing. I just didn't know that hanging out with them six hours a day wasn't enough for you."

"All we're doing is going to Brett's house for a bonfire."

"Bonfire. Are you kidding me? *Bonfire?*"

"What's the matter with you? You're acting all weird."

"Forget it. I'll find some other way. Have fun with your Nazi friends."

"What?" Kwang put up his hands. "Never mind. I'll get you the books, okay? But it'll have to be tomorrow after practice."

Stony stomped back across the field through the high grass, thinking dark thoughts. He'd just passed the property line where their old fort stood when he noticed a white van stopped on the highway.

He froze, suddenly sure that he was about to be captured. They'd grab him, shoot him, and burn him.

He crouched, then ducked behind a sapling, watching, and tried to calm down. Stupid, so stupid. When he was younger and shorter, he couldn't have seen the highway from any point on the path. The track of dirt ran parallel to the road but was set back several hundred yards; a slight roll in the land provided a bunker that had before this year kept him hidden from sight the entire way. Now that he was taller, he'd have to be more careful.

He could see just the top of the van and the driver's-side

window. He couldn't make out a face behind the glass. The vehicle sat there thirty seconds, a minute, and Stony paged through one nightmare scenario after another. Would they shoot first, or try to capture him "alive"? Would they come at him with nets like in *Planet of the Apes*?

Finally the van moved. He watched it roll slowly away, and when it was out of sight he sat down. He was shaking. Why was he shaking? He wasn't some dog in a thunderstorm, some frightened baby. He was the Unstoppable. He stared at his hand and in a few seconds the trembling subsided. There. He didn't need fear, he needed anger. After several minutes he stood up. Take that, coppers! Then he crouched again and ran toward home.

He'd reached the back door when heard Chelsea inside the house, screaming *"You don't even try to understand me!"*

Another fight then. It seemed like there was one every couple of days since Chelsea had turned sixteen.

Against his better judgment, he walked inside. His mother and Chelsea stood face-to face in the middle of the kitchen, with Junie hunched against the refrigerator, watching them. Mom's face had gone rigid—never a good sign—and while tears welled in her eyes, she seemed determined to keep them from falling. Chelsea was raw and outraged, awash in tears. Junie was the worst. She wept silently, like a great-grandmother remembering a childhood tragedy.

Three women, three different ways of crying, Stony thought. He'd lived among them his entire life, and it seemed like he'd spent most of that time in a state of bafflement. "Is this about Alton?" he asked.

Chelsea screamed at him to shut up. His mother screamed at Chelsea to stop screaming. Stony put up his hands, turned slowly, and walked back outside.

He went around to the side of the house and pulled open

the cellar door. Junie came running out after him and threw her arms around him, sobbing. He didn't try to move. He'd learned years ago that when Junie seized him like this, there was nothing to do but stand there until she released him. She could go from bawling to screaming at him in seconds flat. He fought with Junie much more than he ever fought with Chelsea or Alice. Partly this was because they were together more often, so fights were bound to happen, in the same way that most car accidents occur within seven miles of home. Partly this was because, as he'd tried to explain to her, Junie was an erratic personality. And partly this was because, as Junie explained to him, he was a jerk who used phrases like "erratic personality" and thought he was smarter than everybody else.

So he let her hang on him and waited for the tears to subside. She was so much shorter than he was. She took after the women on her father's side, Mom said: short and curvy, which in Mom Code meant that Junie would get fat if she didn't watch it. Alice and Chelsea were tall, lithe, and dark; their fairhaired, fireplug sister looked to be more of an adoption case than Stony. Stony had the same dark hair as his older sisters, the same thin frame. His skin tone just happened to be grayer.

A few minutes later she said into his shoulder, "Chelsea wants to spend the weekend in Chicago with Alton. There's an Allman Brothers concert or something."

"Is she crazy?" Stony said. "Mom's never going to go for that."

"She told me she's going to run away," Junie said.

"Mom or Chelsea?"

"Stop it. She says she's going with Alton out west." She let him go, then patted the damp spot she'd made on his shirt. "She's changing her name to Amethyst or something, and they're going to follow the Grateful Dead around."

There was a joke there, but he let it pass. "That's never

going to happen, Junie. Besides, nobody gets to run away before I do."

Junie yelped. "Don't even *say* that!'

He ducked into the cellar door. He'd laid down reinforced plywood ramps over the cement stairs, then had kept extending the ramps as he dug deeper under the house. Junie followed him down. "I feel like everything's falling apart," she said. "Mom's all alone, you're angry all the time—"

"What? I'm not angry." But what he was thinking was, Mom's all alone? But of course she was. Kids didn't count. But she couldn't get married again, not with a dead boy hiding at home. How could she even date—he'd have to hide in the barn while she made him dinner. He was ruining her life.

"Oh, you're angry all right," Junie said. She pulled on the chain to turn on the single lightbulb. "Just look at this place." The ceiling was eight feet high—or rather, the floor was eight feet low—and the new walls extended far into the dark.

He said, "What does the basement have to do with anything?"

"You're down here by yourself, digging at all hours. You've got to be mad at somebody." She walked over to a stepladder, picked up the hacksaw that was lying on top of it. Sawdust covered the ground. "What are you cutting?"

"Old barn wood. For the ramps. Don't tell Mom."

She shook her head and put down the saw. She walked around the perimeter of the room. He'd decorated a little, and furnished the place with found furniture: an old couch Kwang had rescued from the side of the road, a couple of rusting lawn chairs. But it still looked like, well, a hole in the ground.

She stopped at the north wall, where he'd tacked up an unfolded refrigerator box. Taped to the cardboard was the huge Kiss Alive poster that Chelsea had given him for his

birthday two years ago. "I'm worried about you, Brother John. It's like you're digging your own grave."

"Don't be silly. It's more of a mausoleum."

She walked back to him and gripped his hand. Her skin was hot. "I'm serious, Stony. Have you thought about what we talked about?"

"A little bit." He'd thought about salvation a lot, actually. Eternal life, his immortal soul, how Jesus had died for his sins. Though why some sacrifice was necessary was never explained. *For God so loved the world that He gave His only begotten son.* It seemed to Stony that there was no need for God to send his own son off to be tortured and killed, just so God could bring him back to life and *prove* that he was his son. Why not just forgive their sins himself? He was *God.* Was he so petty that he needed some kind of payment, or else he'd burn all of humanity in hell? Jehovah, he'd decided, was kind of a dick.

He liked Jesus, though, and not just because he rose from the dead himself. It was because after he resurrected Lazarus, he wept. He knew it was a bum deal. You were already in heaven, Laz, but your sisters wanted you back. Sorry, man. Jesus also resurrected the widow's son, then the twelve-year-old daughter of a guy who ran the synagogue. If Jesus wept for them the Bible didn't mention it. Maybe because they were kids, their whole (version two) lives ahead of them.

"You're not listening to me," Junie said. She'd been talking earnestly at him for several minutes.

"I was, I was. I was thinking about resurrections. You know there are eight of them in the Bible? Elijah had one, and Elisha had two, if you count the guy who was tossed into his grave when the Moabites came through—"

"The what?"

"They were trying to bury a guy, and the marauding

bands from Moab attacked, so they tossed the body into Elisha's grave, and as soon as he touched his bones, bang, he was alive again."

"Stop it stop it stop it. You always do that, start talking about the crazy stuff you read."

"This is from the Bible, Junie."

"I'm talking about *you,* Stony. God has a plan for you. He brought you back and put you in Mom's arms. That *means* something. You just have to accept what he's offering you. I can pray with you if you want. Right now, you can ask Jesus into your heart."

He thought about saying, I don't have a heart, but that would have started her crying again.

"Junie, I appreciate what you're trying to do, but—"

"No you don't."

But he did. She sincerely thought that he was going to hell without her intervention. If she loved him, how could she not try to save him?

"You keep praying," he said. "And I'll keep thinking."

He came home one day in late October to find a shoe box on his bed, with a note inside from Chelsea. She said she'd taken all the dollars from his coin bank ($42), but she was leaving him her Sony Walkman and ten cassettes, including two albums that she knew he coveted, *Boston* and Fleetwood Mac's *Rumours.* She signed the note "Crystal Rain."

Mom went down to the police station in Easterly to report that her daughter had run away; if she called the cops, she said, they might come out to the house, and she couldn't risk that. Just in case they came back with her to investigate, he went down to the cellar. He wasn't worried about Chelsea. She'd be back as soon as the money ran out or she figured out what an a-hole Alton was. He put on the headphones and blasted "More than a Feeling" while he looked through the latest selection of books Kwang had found for him.

.The Easterly Public Library's meager collection had grown thin. After the initial bonanza of anniversary books, Kwang was down to the dregs: a medical book with a few pages about symptoms of the disease; a book on cemeteries, which really had nothing to do with the living dead at all; and one thin paperback. He turned it over. *The Head Case: A Deadtown Detective Adventure.* The cover art featured a gray, bony hand holding a .45 automatic.

A thrill ran through him. *Deadtown?*

He skimmed the first page, expecting the worst. And then he realized that it wasn't about killing the walking dead—the *hero* was dead. He read the first chapter, and the second.

> *"Drop the piece, Gore." That was Maurice, the head on the left.*
>
> *"Why not?" I said. I thumbed on the safety, and tossed the gun onto the couch. "You've got me outnumbered."*
>
> *Delia was staring at them. Or him. Maurice and Harold made pronouns difficult.*
>
> *"Delia, meet the Stitch Brothers."*
>
> *"What happened to them?" she asked.*
>
> *"Little accident with a chain saw." I didn't mention that I happened to be holding it at the time.*
>
> *"My God. I've never seen anything like this." She didn't seem disgusted so much as fascinated. "Are they together permanently, or can they come apart?"*
>
> *"Hey, lady," Maurice said, "we're standing right here."*
>
> *"Forgive her, boys. She's new in town."*
>
> *"Oh we know she's new," Maurice said.*
>
> *Harold chuckled. "Oh yeah, we know." Harold didn't have the brightest head on their shoulders.*

"Funny thing is, they're not even brothers," I said to Delia.
"They're just very very close.",

"Fun Time is over!" Maurice said. *The gun in their right
hand waved in the direction of Delia's hatbox.* "Hand over the
brain."

He didn't look up from the book until the door slammed
upstairs. He'd forgotten to turn over the cassette an hour ago.
He pulled the earphones from his ears and ran up the ramp,
then into the house.

Mom was furious, madder than he'd seen her since last
Halloween. Junie sat at the kitchen table, bearing the brunt of
it again. "All they wanted to talk about was if Chelsea was on
drugs!" Mom said. She banged down a mixing bowl and
started clearing the sink. "They said they wouldn't even arrest
her if they *found* her—or him!"

Stony waited as long as he could before interrupting.
"Mom—Mom. Have you ever seen this book?"

She spun on him. "Did neither one of you even *think* of
doing the dishes while I was gone?"

"It's about zom—"

She knocked the paperback out of his hands. "Don't you
use that word!"

He stood very still. Junie didn't move.

Mom turned back to the sink and twisted the hot-water
faucet. Stony picked up the book and went back outside.

Kwang met him in the backyard. "Did you ask her about
trick-or-treating?"

"Not a good time," Stony said. He showed him the book.
"Are there more of these? The library has to have more of
these."

* * *

Jack Gore, the words on each back cover proclaimed. *A hard-bitten cop bitten hard.* Gore had been turned into one of the walking dead, but instead of being shot and burned after the outbreak, he'd been taken to a walled city located somewhere in the Midwest. Jack was like Stony: dead, but not one of the mindless monsters the newspapers and magazines had described. And he *solved crimes.* In *The Head Case,* a human woman tries to smuggle in a human brain in a jar, to sell at Deadtown's black market. "But it's not just any guy's brain," Stony said.

"Whose is it, Abby Normal?" Kwang asked.

"You have to read it."

"Just tell me, jerkwad."

"Okay, this woman, Delia? She stole *Einstein's brain.* Except they don't know if it's really his, or a fake. And there are all these people who want it, and Jack Gore is caught in the middle between the cops, these undead gangsters, and these guys called the Stitch Brothers—"

"So which is it? Real or fake?"

"I'm not telling you *that.*"

There were four other Deadtown books listed inside the front cover, all by C. V. Ferris. Stony made Kwang promise to go back to the library and ask for them. "We have to find him," Stony said. "He *knows.*"

"Who what?"

"Ferris. The author. I think he's living dead."

"Uh . . . no."

"But he can't just be making it up—it's too much like me! See, the outbreak made all the dead crazy for a while, and then they, like, recovered."

"There's no such place as Deadtown, Stony. There's no prison city out in Indiana or wherever they took all of you after the outbreak."

"You don't know that."

"Stony, you know what they did to them. You're the one who showed me the pictures."

Stony was annoyed. When did Kwang become the sensible one?

Kwang said, "You didn't ask your mom yet, did you?" Halloween was tomorrow night. Last year, Stony had dressed up in a rubber Nixon mask and sneaked out to meet Kwang. He made it as far as the Cho house before his mother's clairvoyance kicked in. She came squealing into the Cho driveway, and hauled him home before he could collect a single treat.

"I better not," Stony said. "You remember how she freaked out last time. And she's having a hard time right now." Two weeks had passed and they still hadn't heard from Chelsea. Every day Mom went a little crazier with worry. "I think she's having kind of a nervous breakdown," Stony said. "Last night she went to bed right after supper and never got up."

"That's perfect," Kwang said. "She'll never know you're gone."

"Not tomorrow. She's going to be on high alert."

"Well fine, if you're too much of a wuss . . ."

Stony burned to go. If he didn't, Kwang would just meet up in town with his football friends. That's it, end of friendship. And next year, Kwang probably wouldn't want to go out at all. He'd already made noises about being too old for trick-or-treating.

"Meet me at the fort at seven," Stony said.

Finally he decided, What could she do, ground him?

He conceived a two-part plan. Part one consisted of begging. He explained that he'd be dressed as a mummy, wrapped head to foot, and that no one could possibly see anything. That they would only go to five houses. That Junie and Kwang would cover for him. (Junie said, "What? No! I'm going with the youth group.") He promised that he wouldn't even *speak*—Kwang would do all the talking.

No, his mother said, as he knew she would. No, no, absolutely not.

He argued for a good fifteen minutes, even raising his voice (which he hardly ever did), while his mother grew more and more angry. What's gotten into you? she kept saying. He almost bailed out on his plan then. Mom was still on edge from Chelsea's disappearance, and it didn't seem fair to hit her when she wasn't at the top of her game. Then he thought of Kwang taking off without him, and he played his trump card.

"I'm going out," he said. "And you can't stop me."

Her face went white. "What did you say?" Her voice, Stony thought, was like a knife sliding between two ribs (*Head Case*, chapter 4).

He took a breath. "I said—"

"Go . . . to . . . your . . . *room*."

He stopped fighting. He turned and marched toward his bedroom, his mother two steps behind him. He walked into the room and before he could slam the door his mother slammed it for him. He tried to think of what his sisters would say, and finally yelled back, "Fine!" Then he loudly and conspicuously locked the door.

His bedroom was a converted pantry, a tiny room with one broom closet for his few clothes, and enough space for a bed and a dresser and a small writing desk. By his mother's design, there were no windows. Maybe it was a bit paranoid to think that anyone could see into the house this far from the road, or that strangers would sneak up to the house and peek in, but he'd never objected. He was comfortable in the dark.

He sat down on the bed. He stared at his hands, the floor, his shoes. He thought he heard his mother crying, but maybe that was Junie. After thirty minutes, nobody had checked on him.

He went to the closet, opened the door, and knelt. He pushed his shoes out of the way, then worked his fingers into the holes he'd bored into the rightmost floorboard. He lifted, and a two-foot-square section of floor lifted away.

"You are such a jerk," Stony said.

Kwang laughed. He wore torn clothing smeared with dirt. He'd painted his face white, then darkened under his eyes, blackened his gums. He'd even made a fake red wound on his forehead. He moaned, lifted his hands.

"And I do not look like that," Stony said.

"No, you look worse. Are you ready?"

He wasn't, quite. Kwang helped him finish wrapping and taping. Weeks ago Stony had come across two rolls of white crêpe paper in the hall closet, which had triggered the mummy idea, but that went quickly and he'd had to supplement with toilet paper. The tissue would not stay together. He stood still while Kwang used silver duct tape to reinforce his back and legs. Last Stony wrapped his head, leaving an inch-wide gap for his eyes.

They hit the first five homes in quick order, then kept walking toward town, where the houses were closer together. "These are full-size Snickers," Kwang said after one house. "Do you know how rare that is?"

He didn't, but he was happy anyway. Their pillowcases grew

heavy, despite Kwang eating constantly as they went. Stony didn't care for candy—he didn't care much for anything, food-wise—but he loved the idea of *loot*. Each Three Musketeers and pack of Smarties was a sign of accomplishment; each Chunky a medal of honor. Even the lesser treats—popcorn balls, hard candies, caramel corn—were valuable for the weight they added to his bag.

Stony's mummy costume had begun to shred, especially around the hands and feet, but none of the other trick-or-treaters (little kids, mostly) and none of the parents answering doorbells had asked him any questions or even looked at him curiously. Kwang said "Trick or treat," Stony moaned, and the adults handed over the candy. It was foolproof.

They were walking along the two-lane when a white pickup pulled up alongside them and slowed. "Hey, Kwang!" The voice made it rhyme with *clang*.

The guy in the passenger seat was a teenage boy, maybe a junior or senior. Four other boys squatted in the bed of the truck.

Kwang stopped. "Hey, Brett."

"What the fuck are you supposed to be, a white man?"

A boy in the back said, "I can't believe you're trick-or-treating, man."

"Hey, I've got two pounds of candy," Kwang said. "What the fuck do you got?"

Stony looked at Kwang. Whipping out the F-word, talking in some tough-guy voice?

"We got a lot better than that!" the kid in the back said. He lifted a beer can. "Get up in here, boy."

Kwang glanced at Stony, and must have seen something in his expression. "That's okay," Kwang said. "He's gotta get back home."

"I said, get the *fuck* in the *truck*!"

Kwang laughed, shook his head, and started to climb up on the bumper.

"Are you crazy?" Stony said, keeping his voice low.

But Kwang was in the bed of the truck now. The boys grabbed his pillowcase from him and started going through it. "Pixie sticks!" one of them yelled.

Another said to Stony, "Hey, Toilet Paper Man. Are you coming or not?"

Kwang looked back at him, his face blank. Your choice, Stony. And Stony thought, This is a mistake. He did not like these muscle heads, and he didn't trust them.

He climbed in.

Someone handed him an Old Milwaukee. Kwang already had one in his hand. Stony watched in disbelief as his friend pulled the tab, pushed it into the mouth of the can with a practiced gesture, and took a big gulp. The pickup lurched forward. Stony took a sip of the beer, frowned at the sour taste, and kept it in his hand.

For the next hour they cruised around the streets of Easterly, shouting at kids and passing other high schoolers in cars. Nearly half of them seemed to be dressed as the walking dead. The pickup's driver didn't seem to be taking them anywhere in particular. Stony had studied maps of his hometown and the surrounding area, and he recognized the names of streets, but he could not stop staring at everything they passed: the split-level homes, the paved driveways, the Pontiacs and potted plants and lawn ornaments. Nothing was completely alien—newspapers and books had told him what to expect of the world—but each sight was accompanied by an inner *a-ha,* the satisfaction of a tourist checking off items from his guidebook. And all these kids! Each of them a classmate in the parallel universe high school he should have attended: his chemistry lab partner who could do a dead-on Chewbacca; the stoner he traded jokes with in the parking lot; the girl with the braces that he asked to Homecoming. They would have signed his yearbook. *Stay cool, Johnny!*

No wonder Kwang was growing tired of him. Even these yahoos in the truck were better friends than some dead boy haunting a few square acres of farmland. The boys called him Klang and Krang and Kwanto, and he called them by their nicknames, and everybody called everybody else asswipe and douchebag and faggot. They couldn't seem to stop punching one another. And Kwang was one of them. He fit.

"Hey, TP." The beefy boy, whose nickname was either Torque or Turk, squinted at Stony and said, "Who are you again?"

"I'm from Belgium," Stony said. The boy frowned. Stony said, "It's in Wisconsin."

The boy nodded as if suddenly remembering the place. "You know, you can take off your costume now."

"That's okay. Where I come from, it's a rule that you have to keep your costume on until the next morning."

"Shit, really?"

"Well, it's more of a guideline than a rule."

But the kid was staring over Stony's shoulder. "Hide the beer!"

Blue and red lights flashed behind them. Stony turned, still not understanding, and then the panic struck like a black sledgehammer. He saw the squad car and thought, The police have come for me.

Stony looked to Kwang, but he was jamming a beer can into the center of the spare tire—all the boys were frantically hiding evidence. The pickup pulled onto the shoulder. The squad car parked behind them, leaving its lights on. Stony watched helplessly as an officer climbed out of the car. Stony thought, I am still in disguise. Do nothing, say nothing.

The cop flipped on a big flashlight and said, "What are you boys up to this evening?"

Brett and the driver of the truck had stepped out of the cab. Brett smiled and said, "No good, Officer Tines."

The driver said, "We were just riding around. Seeing the costumes."

"Uh huh." Officer Tines shined the light over the faces. The beam seemed to rest on Stony's face longer than the others, and he resisted the urge to close his eyes and scream.

"Everybody out," Tines said. "And hand over your IDs."

The boys began to climb down, and Stony followed, trying not to rip his costume further. What road were they on? They were somewhere on the north side of town, in a neighborhood of new, larger houses cut into the cornfields. That would put him how far from home—four miles? Five?

Officer Tines went down the line, collecting licenses and school IDs. Stony had nothing. He needed to run, but he couldn't move. And then the cop came to him.

"I . . . I don't have my ID with me," Stony said.

Tines aimed the light into Stony's eyes. "Are you wearing *contacts*?" Stony didn't know how to answer. The cop said, "Take off the toilet paper, kid."

Stony looked at Kwang, but his friend only stared back, eyes wide, perhaps as frightened as he was. Stony reached up, pulled a clump of tissue away, then another. One of the boys in line said, "Jesus Christ."

The cop leaned forward. "You kind of overdid it, don't you think?"

"He's from France," Turk or Torque said.

"Shut up," Tines said. Then to Stony: "Where now?"

"He means Wisconsin," Stony said. "It just sounds French."

"La Croix?"

Stony blinked. Of course, La Croix! That almost made sense. "Yes sir."

"Right." He stared hard at Stony's face. "Go stand over there." He pointed to the patch of grass near his squad car. "The rest of you—any of you been drinking?"

Stony walked over to the car, still stunned that the cop hadn't pulled out his gun. He looked back. The cop was studying each of the licenses in the light of his flashlight, then asking questions. Behind him in the brightly lit neighborhood, a group of kids had gathered to watch the excitement. On the other side of the road was a row of three houses, and beyond that, a wall of darkness: fields dense with tall October corn.

Officer Tines glanced back at him. Stony looked at his feet.

"Officer?" Kwang said loudly. "Officer!" He stepped up to the man, one arm raised. "I think I'm drunk." And then he pitched forward into Officer Tines's arms.

Stony stared at them for a long moment, then realized what Kwang was doing for him.

Stony crossed the road in five strides, then leaped across the ditch to the front yard of the first house. He listened for cries of alarm, for gunshots, but he heard nothing but the sound of his own feet. He aimed for the space between the house and the garage, moving faster than he'd ever moved in his life. When he reached the edge of the field he kept running.

He did not become winded, because he did not breathe. He did not tire, because he was too frightened to remember to be tired. But he did become completely lost.

At some point he slowed to a walk. He stripped off the last of the crêpe paper and tissue, leaving behind a fluttering trail of faux bandages. He didn't know what time it was, but it seemed very late, three or four in the morning. He came upon another gravel lane—he crossed over several of them—and this time decided to follow it to his left. He walked on gravel now, between two barbed-wire fences.

Kwang had saved his life. Even though it meant he might be arrested, or crucified by his mom and dad. But if he hadn't distracted the cop, Stony would be in jail right now. They'd know who he was, what he was: a ghoul whose bite could kill. Who could make you into a monster just like him. They'd put him down like a rabid dog.

His mother was right. He never should have left the farm. And now he could never leave. Kwang would go on without him, into the world of football games and college classes and cities and oceans, and he would burrow into the basement. His own personal Deadtown.

In the distance, a pair of headlights crossed the horizon, moving right to left. The lights brightened, as if the car had swerved in his direction for a moment, and then he heard a faint thump. The car squealed to a stop.

Stony stood still, watching. Half a minute later, the car moved forward again, slower now. The red taillights receded into the dark.

Stony resumed walking, and eventually came to a paved, two-lane road. He turned left, following the path of the car. A few minutes later he saw something thrashing in the high grass beside the road.

A deer. A small whitetail, only fifty or sixty pounds. It lay on its side, one eye staring wildly at him, glossy black. Its front legs churned the grass, but its back legs did not move. He looked for blood but didn't see any.

He knelt next to the animal and stroked its neck. It lurched in a fresh frenzy, and he tried to soothe it.

The deer was going to die. If not in the next hour, then when a cop or farmer came to put it down. He sat with it, and gradually the animal settled, though its side rose and fell in quick breaths.

Stony leaned down, put his face to its neck, and inhaled. The scent was dense, peppery. He wondered if all deer smelled like this, or only dying ones. He pressed his nose and lips into its fur for nearly a minute. And then he opened his mouth, and pressed his teeth against its flesh.

He didn't think that the walking dead could pass the disease to animals. Nothing he'd read suggested it. But nothing said it was impossible, either. Did the animal need to be dead first, and then bitten, before it could rise again? Or did he need to kill it himself, the wound and death occurring simultaneously, for the curse to be transmitted? The Easterly Public Library had been silent on the questions that most concerned him. Did he carry the disease? Should he fear himself as much as others feared him?

He lifted his head. He closed his mouth, wiped a hand across his lips.

It wasn't disgust that stopped him. He thought he could bite into that furred neck. He just didn't think he could bite it a second time, and a third, then *keep* biting until it died or turned. Maybe somewhere inside him there was a monstrous beast waiting to devour living flesh, but if it was there, it wasn't coming out tonight. As a creature of evil, he was a washout. As a human being he wasn't so hot, either. He should at least try to strangle the animal to put it out of its misery— that was the *humane* thing to do—but he didn't think he could follow through on that, either.

"Shit," he said to the deer.

He sat there until the sky began to lighten. A tall shape resolved out of the dark: the Easterly water tower. He knew where he was, then, and how far he had to go by morning. There was a slim chance that his mother still didn't know that he'd slipped out.

He touched the animal a final time. It had stopped moving some time ago, and its big eye stared at him. He'd never been able to produce tears, but he wondered if doing so would have made him feel better. "I'm sorry," he said.

CHAPTER FOUR

1982
Easterly, Iowa

ou may have overdone it, kid."

"Alice!"

His sister had a talent for gliding silently into a room, and into town, like a tall-masted sailing ship in heavy fog. She stood just inside the basement door, one hand against a paneled wall, regarding Stony's handiwork—the refinished planks, the painted cement floor, the yards of handmade bookshelves—most of it new since the last time she'd come down here, at Christmas. In those five months he'd also wired the room and installed new lights, moved his entire book collection onto the shelves, and dug a new drain for the dehumidifier.

Stony shrugged, smiled. "It kind of got away from me."

"I can't believe you got Mom to pay for it."

"It didn't hardly cost anything. The planks came from the old barn on Mr. Cho's farm. The furniture's all secondhand. The cement and the paint cost some, and, well, the drywall and two-by-fours. But we didn't have to buy that all at once."

She went to a bookshelf, ran a hand across his complete

set of Deadtown Detective Adventures. "Think you could make a couple of these for my apartment?"

"Really?" There was no one else in his family he more wanted to impress.

Alice looked amused. "I'll pay you," she said. "Maybe I'll smuggle you out of here, and you can deliver them." She lived only six hours away, but her visits had become rarer. It was only lately that Stony realized that she was probably never coming back home. After medical school she'd go on to her residency, and then on to a hospital or some specialist grad school. She'd already escaped, as completely as Crystal had.

"Come on," Alice said. "Mom's got supper ready."

He turned out the lights and followed her up the stairs. In the yard she looped her arm through his. She was still taller than him, but just barely. "Maybe Junie's right," she said.

"About what?"

"Never mind." She nudged him toward the back door. "Go on, you first."

They yelled surprise! and he made a surprised face, but of course he'd heard the floorboards creaking above his head as they filed in, the hushed voices. Junie and his mom, as well as the three Chos. A store-bought graduation banner hung along the kitchen wall.

"But we already had Kwang's party," Stony said, mock mystified.

His mother kissed him on the cheek. "Quiet now. Go sit down."

There was enough food to feed a real graduation party, instead of this tiny circle of coconspirators. Mrs. Cho had made *Dak bulgogi,* which he'd told her once was his favorite, and set out a dozen side dishes: two kinds of kimchi, five varieties of noodles, a couple of potato dishes, chili peppers, and two bowls of vegetables that he couldn't identify. Alice had brought from the city a potful of something called Italian beef: thinly sliced beef marinated in a spicy juice everybody said smelled wonderful, so Stony assumed it did. She showed them how to dip the big French rolls into the hot juice, then pile on the beef with tongs, and top the sopping mess with Giardiniera hot peppers.

Mr. Cho had finished two sandwiches, and Kwang stood up to get his fourth. "This is the best thing I've ever tasted, Alice."

"I'm glad you like it," she said.

"No, I'm serious. Seriously serious."

"I can put it in an IV drip," she said. "You can carry it around with you."

Mrs. Cho said, "Any word from Chelsea?"

And with that the room went quiet. Stony's mother frowned.

Junie said, "She said she was coming."

"I'm sure she's been very busy," Alice said.

Stony laughed, and Mom gave him a warning look. Crystal—Mrs. Cho and Mom were the only two who still called her Chelsea—hadn't been home since last summer, missing even Christmas, which was a high crime in the May-hall family. The last Stony had heard, she'd been in Costa Rica with her latest boyfriend, whose name escaped him. Her original kidnapper, Alton, was long gone.

"Why don't we clean up?" his mother said. "Then presents."

Alice assigned them jobs, and of course no one argued. She may not have lived there anymore, but she was still second mother. So while Stony washed, Alice dried and put away, and Junie cleared the table. "So you and Kwang," Alice said, "still good friends?"

"Yeah, sure." The past couple of years, though, he'd felt like they were pulling away from each other, a movement too slow to track with the human eye. Continental drift. Kwang was busy with school and sports and friends who could do amazing things like leave their house or walk into a restaurant. And Kwang had no interest in the books Stony was reading, and very little curiosity about science or technology or the world. He wouldn't even be going to college if his mother weren't forcing him. In some ways, Stony felt like he was the one leaving Kwang behind.

Alice said, "You're still the same height."

"I suppose. I think the growth spurt is over."

"I mean you've always been the same height. Ever since that first summer. About the same weight, too, month after month. How about shoe size?"

"That's an awfully personal question," he joked. Though it was true, he and Kwang had always been able to wear each other's shoes, even the summer after seventh grade when they both shot up into the adult sizes. It came in handy when they spent the night in each other's houses. Stony said, "You don't think it's just coincidence?"

Alice frowned at him, disappointed in his dimness, and he laughed as if to say, Of course it's not coincidence, who could think that?

Alice said, "You have anything you want me to repair this weekend? Kwang shoot you with a shotgun or anything while I was gone?"

"Just small stuff I can't reach. Junie's tried to help, but she doesn't have your skill with a fishing line."

"Okay, then. Full checkup in the morning."

"You're looking at me weird. You have some tests you want to do?"

"Maybe."

Alice had always been the one most interested in his condition. Once when he was fifteen she'd had him put a clear plastic bag over his head, just to see if he really could go without breathing. (He could.) They also found out that he didn't exhale carbon dioxide.

Junie came in and set down a stack of plates. "Less talk, more wash. We've got a cake to eat."

"Hey Junie, what is it that Alice said you were right about?"

Alice chuckled. "She thinks you need to get laid."

"Oh that!" Junie said. "Yes, definitely."

"What?"

"We're not sure, though, if you have sexual feelings."

Alice said, "Have you ever masturbated?"

"I really don't see the point."

"What?!" June said, giggling.

He'd been thirteen, sleeping over at the Cho house, when Kwang magically produced a worn copy of *Oui* magazine. Kwang had told him about jerking off, but this time his friend pushed down his underwear and with some pride showed him his erection. Stony dropped his pants, but his own penis didn't move. Kwang told him to spit on his hand and rub. Stony didn't know what effect the motion was supposed to have, but judging from Kwang's pained expression, it should have been either much worse or much better than it was. When Kwang came, Stony was amazed. Vaguely worded phrases from biology textbooks abruptly became specific; an entire class of dirty jokes suddenly became both funny and disgusting.

"Are you attracted to girls?" Junie asked.

"*What* girls? The only ones I get to see are you guys."

"Speaking of guys—" she said, and shut up as the kitchen door swung open.

Mom swept in and picked up the cake plate. She'd made German chocolate, one of his favorites. "Junie, unplug the Mr. Coffee when it's done; it's been overheating lately."

She walked out, and Stony said, "I'm not queer, either."

"It's okay if you are," Alice said.

"I'm not going to—this is not . . ." He shook his head.

Junie put an arm around his waist. "We're not trying to embarrass you. We just want to help. You haven't exactly had a normal childhood. And with your condition, well . . ."

Alice said, "We didn't know what your sex drive was like."

"There is no sex. There is no drive." That night, Kwang had nonchalantly wiped himself clean with a tube sock and put his pajama pants back on. Stony just stopped rubbing. Since then, every time Kwang made a joke about jerking off, or loaned him a porn mag he'd found, Stony would laugh conspiratorially. But Kwang never again did it in front of him, and Stony never made a second attempt on his own. His penis remained quietly in its place.

"Can we stop talking about this now?" he said. "And why am I doing the dishes at my own party?"

In a break with protocol, Mom decided that they should eat dessert in the living room, all the better to watch Stony unwrap his gifts. The Chos had bought him a Skilsaw, something only Mr. Cho would know to buy. Alice presented him with a boxed, two-volume set of the *Oxford English Dictionary* (abridged) that included a magnifying glass in its own drawer. Junie gave him a twenty-five-dollar gift certificate to Ace Hardware, as well as a handmade certificate for messenger services, promising to go back to the store as many times as it took to get the right screws.

His mother went to her bedroom and came back with a JCPenney garment bag. Alice frowned. Stony took the bag, unzipped it.

The jacket and pants were navy blue. Inside were two shirts, one white and one blue, and two paisley ties. He looked at Junie, whose eyes had gone wide in surprise. He couldn't look at Kwang—he'd crack up.

"Wow, that's . . ."

"A young man needs a suit!" his mother said angrily.

"That's true," Mrs. Cho said.

"What for?" Mr. Cho said. "He going to a funeral?"

Kwang lost it then. He collapsed sideways on the couch, hooting in laughter. Stony stood up and said, "I'll try it on."

Mom snatched the garment bag from him. The pants slipped from the hanger and fell to the floor. "Never mind."

"Mom, I like it! Let me try it on."

She stormed out of the room. Alice stood up. "Mr. Cho, would you like more coffee?"

His mother didn't return from the bedroom. The Chos left soon after, with Kwang carrying a Tupperware bowl full of Italian beef.

Junie hung around for a while, then announced she was going to another graduation party for some burnout named Tony. She still went to her youth group meetings, and she still wore a gold cross around her neck. But she also maintained a separate and nonoverlapping circle of friends, mostly big-haired seniors who partied hard, listened to heavy metal, and smoked pot. In the Venn diagram of her relationships, Junie was the point where the two circles met, the intersection of Jesus and Judas Priest. She always told him not to wait up, but of course he was up every night, and knew exactly when she sneaked back into the house. He'd never told Mom about her comings and goings, and Mom had never asked—all of them complicit in maintaining the force field of Everything Is Fine.

Stony tried to do some work in the basement, couldn't get into it, and finally went back up to the dining room and sat down across from Alice. She'd covered the surface of the table with books and papers, and was pecking at a portable electric typewriter.

He picked up one of the books, *Human Virology.* "Mom's still pouting."

Alice didn't look up. "Don't worry about it. She'll be over it soon."

"I should have acted happier."

She grunted, kept typing.

He dropped his voice. "I just don't get it. A suit? She might as well buy me dance lessons."

Alice kept working. It was like this every time she visited, even at Christmas: relentless cramming. He wondered if she ever wished she could be like Stony and go without sleep. He would have had a huge advantage in college.

"So do they study me in medical school?" he asked. "The walking dead?"

"They talk about what you did," she said. "Not what you are."

"What do you mean?"

She looked up from the typewriter, then took a breath and leaned back in her chair, allowing him to interrupt her for a while longer. Alice and Crystal both took after the Mehldaus, Mom's side of the family: black hair, deep brown eyes, Cherokee-quality cheekbones, strong noses. At a casual glance you could take them for twins. But in Crystal those features added up to a kind of dark beauty, a mystery that drew you in. In Alice what you noticed first were the angles of her face, the severity in every expression, the certainty in her gaze. One sharp look and you'd rethink your next step.

"They teach us about the outbreak. How many died, how many were bitten, how many were transformed. The world should have ended that night, John. We don't know how the hell they transmit the disease, but it doesn't make much of a difference. The math is scary, John. One living dead person, biting and transforming one other person per hour—that's all you need. In three days all the humans are dead or turned into walking dead."

"*What?*"

"Those are raw numbers. Let's say you manage to quarantine people as they're bitten—say ten or twenty percent. That cuts down on the spread rate. But the world still ends in five days. Six billion people, dead or undead."

"But the world didn't end. They stopped it once."

"The only way the model works out for human survival is if you kill off almost every single undead in the first two days. A ninety-nine-point-four-percent kill rate. Not ninety-eight, not ninety-nine-point-three—ninety-nine-point-four. And that's what happened on the East Coast. Everyone who could carry a gun organized into gangs, and they went door to door shooting anything that moved. If that didn't happen, we wouldn't be here today." She shrugged. "Well, I wouldn't."

"Shit," Stony said.

"You're a walking threat to national security, John. You're smallpox. You're an ICBM."

"They have to find a cure," Stony said. "Somebody's got to be working on a cure, right? A vaccine or something."

"Sure they are. But there's a problem. The living dead break all known rules of biology and common sense. There's no virus that works like this, we can't find a pathogen, and it's certainly not caused by space radiation or whatever the government tried to tell us it was. All the corpses that were examined after the outbreak, the ones they rekilled? They were just that—corpses. No one's found anything to tell us what the disease was, or how we can prevent it. So the medical people threw up their hands. There was no way to study it with the normal tools of science, so they booted the whole subject down the road to the theoreticians. All a young doctor can do is pray that it never comes back."

"But it hasn't gone away," Stony said. "I was reading a newspaper article about a sighting in Indiana in 1971—"

"Stragglers, kid. Some of the infected were smarter than the others and tried to hide once the cleanup gangs came out. And some were hidden by their crazy relatives."

"That *is* crazy."

"In the early seventies there was a lot of hysteria, a lot of paranoid books being written. You had Dennis Wenger on television talking about the 'hidden dead,' and antiwar activists claiming solidarity with them. People were seeing the living dead everywhere, turning in sick people, the elderly. New hunter gangs formed, though that was mostly rednecks looking for a reason to walk around with guns. I thought Mom was going to start drinking."

He didn't remember any of that. All he remembered was playing with Kwang and his sisters.

"So if they're stragglers, why aren't they biting people? The disease should be spreading. You said all it takes is one victim."

"Not all the victims were homicidal a hundred percent of the time. We don't know why. Some of them could talk. Well, at least form words. Residual brain function."

"That wasn't in anything I read. None of the magazines or books."

She shrugged. "I've looked at all the newspaper stories,

and even went back to the original incident reports. I wrote a couple of papers on it, before my advisor told me to drop it." She leaned forward. "People *are* studying the outbreak, John, just not the people at my level. And sooner or later, somebody is going to have to study you."

"Great."

"You grew up, John. How you did that is a complete and utter mystery. There's not a whiff of this in the literature—at least the stuff I've been able to get access to. I don't know how it's even possible. Somebody needs to figure out how you did it."

"Somebody like you," he said. "You want to be one of those theoretical people."

"I've got to get through med school first," she said. "Then pay off my loans. But yes, I'd like to be that person. Does that scare you?"

"Scare me? Are you kidding?" He laughed. "Alice, there's nobody else I'd want doing this."

She seemed taken aback. "John, you don't have to—"

"Nobody else. And I want to work with you."

"Of course."

"No, I mean really work with you. I want you to train me. Teach me. I want to take college courses. By correspondence, I guess—I haven't thought through this yet. But I don't want to be just a test subject, I want to be one of the investigators."

"John—"

"Just tell me what to read, I'll read it. Tell me what to study, and I'll pass the test."

She regarded him for a long moment. "All right, Brother John. I guess you *have* graduated from high school." She tapped the virology textbook. "Read the first two chapters, then write me a two-page essay on bacteriophages—what they are, their different types, et cetera."

"Do you want it typed?"

"I'm using the typewriter, thank you. Now get to work."

He worked for an hour and got halfway through chapter two. He learned pretty quickly that a bacteriophage was a virus that ate bacteria. But there were just so many new terms and concepts to track down. What was a lysis gene? What was RNA replicase? He wanted to know it all, *now*. Alice refused to answer questions. "Work through it," she said.

He realized he'd have to find an introductory textbook, something at the level of Alice's undergraduate courses. There was no such book on the shelves downstairs; he'd have to ask Mom to get one from Des Moines. Just like he had to ask her for everything. He was trapped here, in this farmhouse, his own personal Deadtown. Kwang was leaving for college at the end of the summer, Junie would be gone in a year, and Alice and Crystal weren't ever coming back—at least not to stay. It would be just him and Mom. He was the retarded kid who could never live on his own, the crazy lady in the attic— the vicious dog you could never let off the chain.

Alice typed away, concentrating so hard she looked angry. Eventually she noticed he was staring at her. "Yes?"

Take me with you, he thought. Get me out of here.

"Still confused?" she said.

"Kind of. But it's cool."

"Good. Struggle is part of the process."

Mom came out of the bedroom sometime after nine. She still wore her green dress—her only party dress. "Doing homework, John? I thought you could take at least one day off."

"I've enrolled in the University of Alice," he said.

"I see." She placed a hand on his shoulder. "How about we go for a drive?"

Stony looked up from his page of notes. "What?" One of the cardinal rules was to never leave their farm or the Chos'.

And as far as they knew, he'd never broken that rule. He hadn't been caught the night of the deer, and he'd never told anyone in his family about it.

"It's not far." Her eyes were tired, but her mouth was set, exactly like a woman who'd been crying for a long time and then had decidedly stopped crying. He'd seen that look a lot over the years.

"We'll hide you in the back," Mom said.

"Okay . . ." He got up to put on his gym shoes, then realized something. "Would you like me to wear the suit?"

"Yes, as a matter of fact." Then, "I also bought you dress shoes. And socks. I put them in your room."

He got dressed, choosing the white shirt and the most colorful of the two ties. He had no idea how to tie it, though. Jack Gore always wore a tie, but of course he never explained how he knotted it. Stony carried it out to the kitchen and his mother told him not to worry about it for now, but that he'd have to get Mr. Cho to teach him. She buttoned the middle button of the jacket. "You look handsome," she said.

He knew it was a lie. He looked like a corpse in a funeral suit. But he also knew his mother would never say so.

He lay down in the very back of the station wagon, on a fresh blanket to keep his clothes clean. She spread another blanket over him. "If we get pulled over," she said, "act like cargo."

He turned on his side and watched the lights of the town scroll past the windows. Then they were leaving town, and his mother began to speak. "It was so cold the night we found you," she said. "You should have been stiff as a board. But your mother had you wrapped up in her rabbit fur coat, with her arms around you. She was trying so hard to keep you warm that she spent all the heat in her body."

He could barely hear her over the sound of the engine and the wind coming through the windows, but it didn't matter: He'd heard this story countless times. He used to beg her to tell him about that night, and she used almost the same words every time. He used to lie in his bed at night thinking of his mother—his first mother—burning down like a candle to protect him.

Mom told him about trying to resuscitate him, and how she had bathed him in warm water at the kitchen sink, a "low-rent baptism." She laughed. "The girls were so excited. Junie thought you were her pet."

The car slowed, turned, and came to a stop. It had been twenty minutes since he'd seen any houselights. "We're here," she said.

She opened up the back of the wagon for him and he climbed out. They were in a cemetery. The gravestones stretched out into the dark.

His mother turned on a flashlight and led him back into the rows. She seemed to know where she was going. After a minute she stopped and aimed the beam at a patch of grass.

"Hello, Jane," Mom said. "I brought your boy this time."

The stone was about ten inches high. She raised the light so he could read the inscription: *Jane Doe. Died 1968*. Then in smaller print, a line at the bottom: *At Home Now.*

"I'm sorry about the marker," she said. "I couldn't afford a big one, or many words. I wanted to mention you somehow, but I was afraid to even hint. I hope you aren't—"

"Mom, it's fine. It's more than fine." He had no idea she had been coming out here.

"She would have been so proud of you," his mother said. "How hard you work, how much you study."

He crouched down, plucked a weed. He didn't know

what to feel. He knew he should be having some moment of communication with the woman who gave birth to him— one dead person to another—but what saddened him was the thought of his mother coming out here over and over, beating herself up for raising the woman's son without her, and not getting a big enough gravestone.

"They never found out her name I guess," he said.

"There's a detective I call every few years. Detective Kehl. He says he's still looking, but no one's ever reported a missing girl that matches her description. He thinks . . . well. He's still looking."

Stony looked up. "He thinks what?"

Even in the dark he could see his mother take a breath. "Oh Stony, he believes she was murdered."

"You told me she died of exposure." He got to his feet. "She was hitchhiking."

"That probably is what happened. But he's pretty sure she was also robbed, because she didn't have a purse or ID. Plus, the autopsy made it clear that she'd been pregnant and had given birth recently."

"So they're looking for a baby? For me?"

"No, no. Detective Kehl thinks it was a miscarriage, or a . . . well, an abortion that went badly. He thinks maybe she was weak from internal bleeding."

"But nothing about the walking dead."

"Don't you worry, you're still safe. No one's looking for you."

Together they stared at the grave. For years he'd imagined meeting her. He daydreamed about walking along the winter highway, and coming upon her walking the other way, a young woman with long brown hair, wearing a rabbit fur coat and yellow rain boots. Her skin would be as cold and gray as his own. She'd reach down to touch his cheek, and she'd say, There you are. I've been looking all over for you.

He put his arm around his mother's shoulders. They were almost the same height.

"I should have brought some flowers," Stony said.

"You're here," she said.

CHAPTER FIVE

1982
Easterly, Iowa

rystal didn't show up the night of graduation, or the next day, or the next week. She finally called from somewhere out west and said that her travel plans had gotten "complicated." Then one night in mid-August she called Mom at work, saying that she'd be home for supper next Saturday. "She says she has a surprise for you," Mom said to Stony.

"The only surprise would be if she showed up," Junie said.

On the appointed night, Junie, Stony, and Mom sat around the kitchen table, staring at empty plates, enveloped in the smell of the lasagna warming in the oven. Crystal always loved lasagna, though maybe not enough to make her show up on time. Mom was trying hard to stay positive, but her kids weren't making it easy. Junie kept staring at the clock and sighing, because she had a party to go to. Stony was supposed to spend the night at the Chos', because Kwang was leaving in three days for Iowa State and it was probably the last sleepover they'd ever have.

Mom told them to sit.

At 6:30, when Crystal was already an hour late, Mom let

them eat the garlic bread. At seven she let them have their salads. At 7:30 she said, "To hell with it." She pulled the lasagna out of the oven, and told them to serve themselves if they were in such a rush.

Stony waited until she was out of the room before melodramatically whacking his forehead against the table. Junie cracked up. "You know what the great thing about Crystal is?" she said. "She takes all Mom's attention off us."

"She's like Jupiter," Stony said. "Sweeping all the killer asteroids out of the solar system with her massive gravitational pull."

"Right. Jupiter." Junie took one bite from a square of lasagna, then called her boyfriend to pick her up at the end of the lane. Stony wondered if any of his sisters' boyfriends ever wondered why they weren't allowed to approach the house. Probably they were happy about it.

Kwang was outside, watching the fields for Stony's approach. He jumped when Stony appeared behind him. "Jesus, what did you do, teleport?"

"I'm working on my ninja skills. Here, Mom made lasagna. I figure you were starving over here." The Chos were visiting Mrs. Cho's sister in Philadelphia. Kwang took the full plate inside.

"It'll be good to have something in our stomachs," Kwang said. He paused. "Until it isn't."

Kwang had decided several weeks ago that before he went off to college, he needed to teach Stony how to drink. "You're going to miss the most important thing about college," Kwang had told him. "And I can give that to you."

Stony wouldn't admit this to Kwang, but he was touched. Things had gotten so distant between them that he was pleased that Kwang wanted to share this with him. With Mr. and Mrs. Cho gone, Kwang and Stony would have the run of the house for the next two days—plenty of time for Stony to recover.

The bar was set up on the dining room table. Ten different bottles, most of them less than half full. "I borrowed from people," Kwang said. "I wanted you to get a good sampling. Like this one, Southern Comfort. That'll kick your dead gray butt, my friend."

"This one smells good," Stony said.

"That's peppermint schnapps. It's a girl's drink, but that just means it'll kick your butt without you knowing what's happening."

Stony said, "You haven't tried any of this, have you?"

"Of course I have. I had a shot of Wild Turkey just last weekend."

"Right. This is about you wondering if you can hold your liquor with the frat boys."

"Hey, do you want me hurling on my first night out? Look, I bought mixers. I'm thinking we start with rum and Dr Pepper."

Kwang declared this an awful, awful combination. Vodka and orange juice was tolerable, practically sophisticated in comparison, but bourbon was terrible no matter what they mixed it with. "It tastes like ass," Kwang said.

"There's certainly an assy quality," Stony said. As with food, he followed Kwang's lead. "With notes of burnt rubber."

After a couple of hours of sampling, Kwang thought everything tasted like aluminum siding. The night quickly became a contest to concoct the worst-tasting combination possible.

"I call this the Gay Nazi," Stony said, and handed him a mixture of schnapps, gin, and Mello Yello. "It's the perfect drink right before you commit suicide in a bunker."

"Gah! It's like a Christmas tree threw up in my mouth. Try this. Tequila, Jack, and a dash, a dash, a dash . . ." He reached for the rum, and Stony saved a row of bottles from tumbling off the table.

"Captain José Daniel's," Stony said.

"Yes!" Kwang said. He handed the glass to Stony.

Stony took a sip and shook his head. "Wretched. Truly abominable."

"Abobida—abob—shit." Kwang took the glass from him. "You're not even buzzed, are you?"

"Did you really think this would work on me?"

"But you've had twice as much as me! You should be, I don't know—"

"Dead drunk," Stony said.

Kwang barked a laugh. "You know what? We should light the next one."

"No. Definitely not. No fire, Mr. Cho."

"Don't be an old woman. You know I made out with Junie once?"

"I don't want to hear this."

"I think she wanted to see what it was like with a man of the Asian persuasion. That's why I have to go to college—to get some pussy! You know how many girls I've dated in this town?"

"You do not want to compare scorecards with me."

"*One.* For two weeks!"

"Sherry was a nice girl," Stony said. "Dumb as a box of rocks, though, and that face . . ."

"Shut up, you never met her."

"Oh, you still have feelings for her."

"Yeah, I got a feeling. A deep, deep feeling." He stood up suddenly. "I have to piss."

Stony retrieved a rag from the sink and started wiping up spills. He didn't think the alcohol was having an effect on him, but something was churning. One moment he was happier than he'd felt in a long time, and the next he was almost floored by sadness. Maybe Kwang's state was contagious. In the old days it had been. Whatever Kwang wanted, he wanted. Whatever Kwang loved, he loved. Only lately had he realized how simple that had been, how wonderful. And Kwang had saved his life. When police brought Kwang home that Halloween night, his parents grounded him for a month. He'd taken the fall for Stony, and he never squealed, never complained, and never held it against him.

Kwang came down the hallway carrying a shoe box. "I found something," he said. "I was cleaning out my closets the other day, and—well, here." He handed Stony the box.

"You shouldn't have," Stony said. "You know how I love cardboard." Inside was a clump of red knitted cloth. He picked it up.

It was a ski mask. No, *the* ski mask. The black *U* was still sketched on the front.

"I can't believe you still have this," Stony said. At some point he'd traded the Unstoppable for Jack Gore, the invincible dead boy for the Deadtown Detective.

It looked much too small for him, and he pulled it onto his head anyway. The bottom of it came down only to his lips.

"You look like Mushmouth," Kwang said.

"Wuss ubba, Fabba Alba."

The phone rang. Kwang collapsed into laughter.

"I think I should get that," Stony said.

"Wait, it's my mom." It came out *isssmamom*. "If we answer it too quick, she'll know we were up."

Stony glanced at the kitchen clock, a big gold sunburst above the cabinets. It was nearly 1 a.m. "I don't think your mom thought you'd be in bed by nine." He pulled off the mask and picked up the receiver. "Hello?"

The voice on the other end was crying. "Kwang?"

"Junie, is that you?"

"Stony! Oh God, Stony. I have to get out of here."

"Where are you?" All he knew was that she'd gone out with the hair metal crowd.

"You have to come get me. Please don't tell Mom. You can't tell Mom."

"Junie, what happened?"

"I'm at Sarah's house. Do you know where she lives?"

"Sarah Estler?" Stony turned to Kwang. "Do you know where Sarah Estler lives?"

"I think so. Yeah. Northdale."

"Okay, we'll be there—Kwang will be there in ten minutes, okay? Will you be okay for ten minutes?"

She hung up. Stony stared at the phone. He wanted to call her back, but he hadn't gotten the number. "Can you drive?" he asked Kwang.

"I'm fine. Let's go." He grabbed car keys from a hook by the door and went out to the garage. He walked very carefully, got into the car, and put the keys in the ignition.

"We should open the garage door first, don't you think?"

"Good idea." He put his head down on the steering wheel. "Just gimme a second."

Stony pushed open the garage door, then went to the driver's side of the car. "Get out. I'm driving."

"You don't know how to drive."

"I taught myself."

"When?"

"When I was thirteen." He'd made up a list of skills that he needed to learn, and driving had been top of the list. "Just get in the passenger seat. You navigate."

Despite the feeling of urgency, he drove slowly. He didn't want to give the cops any excuse to pull them over; this time, Kwang was too drunk to pretend to be a drunk, at least in any well-timed way. The boy was already passed out with his head against the passenger window. Also, Stony had never driven on a road before. He'd only lurched up and down the lane of the farm, at night with the lights off. He hadn't practiced much since he was thirteen, but he thought he still knew how to do it.

Keeping the car between the lines was more difficult than he thought. When he came to a turn—the farm lane didn't have any turns—he swung wide and nearly struck a car in the opposing lane. He slammed the brakes and the car squealed to a stop. Kwang didn't even wake up.

Stony began to talk to himself, becoming his own driving instructor, giving himself encouragement.

He knew the streets of the town from the maps he'd studied, and he knew how to find Northdale, but he didn't know the Estlers' address. As it turned out, he didn't need it. On the first road he turned down, cars were parked along both sides of the street. The party house was obvious. Music blasted from the windows, the front door was open, and teenagers stood on the lawn. Was Junie watching for him? He stopped the car and laid on the horn. The teenagers looked at the car, then ignored him. He hit the horn again, but nobody walked out of the house.

Stony drove a little farther, then pulled in at a neighbor's driveway. "Kwang, you have to go in there and find Junie." He punched him in the shoulder. "Kwang!"

Kwang didn't move. His eyelids didn't quiver.

Stony got out of the car, went around to the passenger side, and opened the door. "Come on, man. Now." He shook Kwang by the shoulders, slapped his face. But he was unconscious, inert. Dead drunk.

"Fuck." Stony shut the door, turned toward the house. He'd have to go inside. Maybe everyone would be too drunk to notice his dead skin, his black gums, his milky eyes.

Sure.

He started across the lawn, stopped. The red ski mask was still in his pocket. He pulled it out and tugged it over his head.

Nobody on the lawn paid him any attention, but as he stepped onto the porch a kid in a Motörhead T-shirt looked at him and laughed. Stony said, "I'm looking for Junie Mayhall. Do you know where she is?"

"I don't know, inside?"

He didn't want to go through the door. The place was crowded.

"Can you go get her?"

"What are you going to do, rob her? And what's wrong with your face?"

Stony pushed through the people clogging the door. In the living room he grabbed a girl by the arm and she yelped. "Where's Junie Mayhall?" He had to yell above the music. She pulled her arm away and he asked someone else. Then someone else. Someone thought she was in the family room downstairs, so he headed toward the stairs.

Three boys—teenagers, probably, though they looked older—started up as he started down. "Is Junie Mayhall down there?"

"She's fine," one of them said.

That stopped him. "What's wrong with her?"

"Nothing's wrong with her." The one in the middle stepped around his friend. He wore a sleeveless T-shirt and two leather wristbands. "Who the hell are you?" He reached to grab the mask.

Stony brushed his hand aside. "Get out of my way."

"Fuck you," the boy said, and pushed Stony in the chest.

"No," Stony said. "Fuck you." He put two hands on the boy's shoulders and shoved. He fell into the boy behind him and they went down in a heap. Stony stepped over them. The remaining kid, a boy not older than thirteen or fourteen, grabbed Stony by the shirt. The arm was pale, skinny. Not much flesh at all.

For the first time in his life, Stony felt it. It ran like a hot wire, up from his spine, to the base of his skull. His mouth opened on its own.

He wanted to bite. He wanted to bite hard.

The boy jerked his hand back.

"That's right," Stony said. "I'm smallpox. I'm a fucking ICBM."

He turned away from them, went the rest of the way down the stairs. The room was dim and hazed with cigarette smoke. Pot, too, he guessed; he recognized the smell from his sister's clothes. Perhaps a dozen people sat on couches or on the floor. He finally spotted Junie curled up on the carpet in a corner of the room, between a lamp and an armchair.

"Junie? Junie?"

She looked toward his voice. Something was wrong with her eyes. Her pupils were so large, making her look excited as well as scared.

Something struck him in the back of the head, something solid and thick. He felt no pain. He half turned, seized an arm—he didn't know if it belonged to one of the boys from the stairs or someone new—and yanked. The person screamed and fell aside. Someone else stepped forward and punched him in the jaw. Once again he felt nothing. It was no worse than getting shot in the chest.

He turned his back on the attackers and reached out a hand to his sister. "Can you walk?"

A blow to his back made him take a half step forward. Then someone yanked the mask from his head.

He turned. It was the boy with the wristbands.

Stony grabbed him by the throat. The movement was so

fast, the boy didn't have time to flinch. With his other hand, Stony reached out behind him. "Come with me, Junie."

She grasped his hand and Stony stepped forward, still holding the boy by the throat. The boy backpedaled awkwardly. Stony walked him back to the doorway, then up the stairs. When he stumbled, Stony held him upright. His face turned cartoon red.

When they reached the top of the stairs, Stony pushed the boy away from him, into the bodies of the onlookers. Only a few people seemed to understand that there was some sort of fight going on.

Stony led Junie outside. Halfway across the lawn he glanced back. Figures filled the open doorway, staring at him. The wristband boy broke through their ranks and shouted hoarsely.

"We have to hurry," Stony said to Junie.

She was babbling about being sorry. He didn't know what she'd taken, but it must have been strong. He opened the back door for her and told her to lie down. Then he jumped into the front. Kwang was still passed out.

He started the car, put it in gear, looked over his shoulder, and pressed on the gas. The car lurched forward, and he slammed on the brakes. Reverse, reverse! He changed gears and backed out. At the end of the driveway he spun the wheel—the wrong way, but he quickly corrected and got the car pointing in the right direction.

He heard shouts, and someone slammed the trunk of the car. Oh God, he thought, please don't dent Mr. Cho's Buick.

He put the car in drive and gunned it. He turned at random, zigzagging through the residential streets, sure that they were going to follow him. Then suddenly the street he was on ended at a T-section with a two-lane road. He couldn't remember if he'd come in this way, or if he was on the other end of the neighborhood. He turned left and floored it, driving with one eye on the rearview mirror. So far, no lights were following him.

Junie was crying. He said, "You okay back there?"

She sobbed harder. "Don't tell Mom."

Stony knew he'd blown it. Why did he fight with those boys? Why did they have to keep attacking? They'd seen his face. They'd seen him with Junie. And now they'd be calling the police, reporting one of the living dead.

It was an accident, he thought.

A light in the rearview mirror caught his eyes. Headlights, moving up fast. He crested a hill, too fast. The car seemed to float for a moment, not quite airborne, then slammed down on its suspension. Junie shouted.

"Whoa," Kwang said. "Where are we going?"

"Not now," Stony said.

A sign flashed past. The junction for Route 59! He knew where he was. The entrance to the road was at the bottom of the hill. He braked, but he had too much mass, too much momentum, and he stomped harder. The car began to skid. Kwang yelled. Stony tried to correct the skid—and then they were spinning.

Kwang slid into the passenger door with a thump. Another thunk might have been Junie hitting the back of the seat. Stony gripped the wheel, willing the car to stop, but the vehicle seemed to move in slow, heavy motion, spinning and traveling at once, like a planet revolving as it glided through its orbit. Through the windshield he saw an open field, then a patch of highway, then a line of trees . . . and then headlights. Too close, too bright.

The windshield turned white.

CHAPTER SIX

1982
Easterly, Iowa

He'd read that people in car accidents sometimes lost all memory of the event. He wasn't that lucky. Each moment had been captured as a vivid image, then set running in his head, a series of educational slides. Here is the windshield exploding. Here is the dash, suddenly curled over them, a solid wave. Here is Kwang's body half swallowed in plastic and metal. The pictures kept coming—click, click, click—so that he could barely see the room in front of him. He tried to concentrate on the closet full of clothes, the half-filled suitcase on the floor. With his working hand he grabbed a jacket from a hanger and threw it into the pile. Still the images flickered, every moment of the crash and after.

Only the sounds, the words, had been erased. He knew that he must have heard Kwang's voice first, but he couldn't remember what his friend had been saying. Something about the pain, probably. Or an appeal to God. Stony tried to open the driver's-side door, but there was something wrong with his left arm. He twisted in his seat, managed to pull the handle, and half fell, half crawled out of the car.

The vehicle that had struck them—a blue pickup—sat a dozen yards away, its grille crumpled, its windshield crazed with white impact webs. A man with silver hair stared at him through the starry glass. Stony couldn't tell if he was injured.

He turned to the back door of Mr. Cho's car. He couldn't see Junie, and thought that she must be on the floor. He yanked at the door with the arm that was still working. The metal squealed and popped, and the door opened. The back-seat was empty, the floor was empty.

He could not process the impossibility of it. She was gone. Raptured.

Then he noticed that the rear window had been blown out. They'd been hit in the front, but the car had been spinning. Had she been thrown clear? He began to call her name. He walked to the trees beside the highway, crossed back to the fields on the other side, then back again.

A car stopped, then another. At some point someone must have driven to find a phone, or neighbors had called to report the accident, because an ambulance arrived, and then a fire engine. The banks of strobing lights helped him find her.

She was curled up under a tree, twenty or twenty-five feet deep in the woods. He knelt next to her and put a hand on her shoulder. She didn't move except to blink at the ground a few inches from her face. Her cheeks and forehead were puffy and white, as if she were suffering from some allergic reaction. He remembered talking to her, pouring words over her, but he could not remember what he said.

Someone had spotted them under the trees. Flashlight beams lit up the surrounding grass and leaves. Perhaps they called out to him.

Junie was talking, too, or trying to: Her mouth moved, but no sound came out. He bent over her and felt her breath on his skin. He must have asked her what she was saying; that was

the natural thing to do. He flattened onto his belly, his forehead touching hers. She inhaled, a quick sharp breath, and
said, "Run."

An orange-jacketed man, a fireman or paramedic,
appeared next to him. Stony didn't remember what he said;
he was studying his sister's face.

"Run," she said again. "Run. Run. Run."

But he failed her again. He didn't move—couldn't
move—away from her. And then the man in the orange jacket
played his light across Stony's face. He started to say something, and then stepped back as if he'd been punched. He
called for other men in a thin, barely controlled voice, but the
panic was rising in him like a siren, clear enough even for
Stony to hear. Maybe he knew what he was seeing. Maybe he
wasn't sure. But finally, finally, Stony obeyed his sister.

He closed the half-filled suitcase with his good hand. He
was forgetting things, he knew. He'd been imagining this
moment for years, picturing it as clearly as the escape from the
Deadtown prison in book 5 of the Jack Gore series, *Bad
Brains*. But now that the moment was upon him he realized
he hadn't prepared at all. There was no one here to help him.
When he'd made it back to the house, after twenty minutes of
frantic running through pitch-black fields, he'd found the
lights on in the kitchen and living room, but his mother gone.
A quick check of the driveway confirmed that she'd taken the
car.

They must have called her. She'd be at the hospital, with
Junie. And soon enough, they'd be coming for him.

He opened the trapdoor to the basement, tossed the suitcase below, and jumped down. He went to one of the shelves
and reached up to bring down a thick book. When he was ten
he'd stolen an idea from the Hardy Boys and carved a hiding
place out of the pages. Inside was $220. His life savings, his

emergency fund, his ticket out of Easterly. And also, he knew, completely inadequate. The plan had called for getting to Chicago and hiding out with Alice. He'd planned on driving there, but that was out now. He didn't think he'd ever drive again.

He had only a few hours until daylight. By then he had to be miles away.

He walked to an expanse of wood-paneled wall covered by his old Kiss poster, put a finger into the small hole next to Paul Stanley's star-painted eye, and pulled. The panel slid out from the wall. Behind it was a thick metal door that Mr. Cho had rescued from salvage for him. He pulled open the door to reveal a narrow closet lined with sheet metal. There was just enough room for a pallet of old blankets and a small bookshelf that held his favorite books and two flashlights. It was his secret vault. His fortress of solitude.

Jesus, what had he been thinking?

Hanging from a hook above the pallet was a long over-coat with high lapels, and a broad-brimmed hat—a costume straight out of Jack Gore's closet in Deadtown. He put the hat into the suitcase. Then he shrugged into the coat, forcing his dead arm into the sleeve.

He heard the distant sound of helicopter blades. From the floor above him, a door slammed open, and a voice called his name.

He didn't climb up through the trapdoor—he didn't want anyone to know about that route—but went out through the cellar door. Outside, the sound of the helicopters was thunderous. A chopper had passed over the house and was flying in the direction of the hospital. He hurried around to the front of the house and saw the lights of a second helicopter, a few hundred yards away, rising up out of the dark. It had set down in the yard in front of the Chos' house and now it had nosed forward, heading toward him. He pressed himself against the wall of the house—and miraculously, it passed overhead, barely clearing the roof. He watched the lights of the two aircraft disappear in the distance.

A motorcycle sat in front of his house, a Triumph with a bottle-green gas tank. He edged up to the front door and leaned in. In the living room, a man in jeans and a brown leather jacket stood with his back to Stony, a black motorcycle helmet still on his head. He was listening to someone in the kitchen. There didn't seem to be anyone else in the house.

Stony pushed through the door. The rider turned at the sound. The helmet had a full, black-tinted visor, masking the face, but something in that movement made him realize it was a woman. Behind her, a taller figure stepped out of the kitchen.

She was dressed in white painter's pants, and a black, formfitting top, and a purple, frayed scarf. Her hair was longer than he'd ever seen it, frizzed out, wild, windblown and electrified.

"Stony!" Crystal pushed past the motorcyclist and threw her arms around him. "Oh my God, we thought you'd been hurt." A crazy thing to say. He was the last person who could be hurt. She told him she'd called home, but the phone was busy, and then when she called back Mom was leaving for the hospital. Junie and Kwang had been in an accident.

"Are they okay?" Stony asked.

"I don't know. Mom was going to find out. Were you there?"

He told her what had happened, but rushed and jumbled,

and without detail: Kwang drunk, the accident, the fight at the party, Junie high on something. How the firemen saw him. How he'd run.

The motorcyclist had gone into the kitchen and returned carrying a blue metallic helmet. "Crystal," she said. "We've got to go."

"Who the hell are you?" Stony said.

"This is Delia," Crystal said. "You can trust her. There are other people looking for you, Stony, government people. We've heard them on the radio. Delia will get you out of here."

Stenciled on the front of her helmet in small type were the letters LDA. She flipped up her visor. Stony blinked at her, amazed.

"See?" Crystal said. "You can trust her."

"They're already at the hospital by now," Delia said. "Two teams of fast responders. It won't take them long to figure out where your sister and your friend live and send a team here. Five, ten minutes tops. You have to come with me. Now."

Stony couldn't stop looking at her face.

"It's either us or them," Delia said. "And trust me, you'd much rather ride with me than burn with them."

"Go," Crystal said. "Go with her."

"I have a suitcase, some things—"

"No fucking time, Stony. Are you getting on the bike or not?"

He turned to Crystal. "Tell Mom. Tell her I'm so sorry." She bent and kissed his forehead.

Delia put the helmet in his hands. "Safety first," she said.

He followed her to the front yard. She started the motorcycle. He climbed behind her and tugged on the helmet with his good hand. "I'll call as soon as I can," he said to Crystal.

Delia looked over her shoulder at him. The left side of her

face, from temple to jaw, was exposed bone. Her lidless left eye seemed to pierce him. "Welcome to the Living Dead Army," she said. "Hang on."

He'd never moved so fast. His experience was limited, of course, but the speed seemed crazy, even on the empty road. He gripped her waist with his good arm and bent his head into the buffeting wind. With his mouth next to her helmet he yelled, "Where are we going?"

She didn't answer. They were heading north, or mostly north, along back roads, avoiding the highways. The sky to his right glowed faint pink. His mother used to sing a hymn called "I Will Meet You in the Morning." Junie liked to sing harmony, in a low, soft alto he loved. He knew that she was dead. She'd been dying beside the road. He thought, I should have given my heart to Jesus. It didn't matter if he didn't believe. It would have made Junie so happy to save him.

After twenty minutes he saw a town in the distance. He guessed it was Effington, or else Manchester. Then Delia abruptly slowed and pulled up behind a white van that was parked along the edge of the road.

Delia cut the engine and said, "Hop off. We should be—"

The back doors of the van swung open and a figure leaped out at them. Stony shouted and pushed himself backward off the bike.

Another ghoul—this one in a brown three-piece suit and a dark gray homburg. The man landed, looked at Stony, then at Delia. "You found him?" He sounded shocked and happy.

He was shorter than Stony, and his face was pocked with dozens of tiny dark holes that went bone deep. Under his suit he wore a French blue shirt and a striped tie of brown and yellow, firmly knotted. He wore thin black gloves over large hands.

"We got lucky," she said. "No problems here?"

"None. A few cars passed us, but none of them gave us a second glance."

Delia said, "John Mayhall, Mr. Blunt."

He pulled back from Delia. "My boy, it's an honor," he said. "I've heard a lot about you, most of it unbelievable." He pulled off one glove and extended a hand. The entire hand was carved hardwood, polished and gleaming. The knuckles were wooden ball joints.

Stony hesitated, then put out his own hand. The long wooden fingers closed around him, sliding with the faintest sound. He did not squeeze, though Stony felt the prosthetics could crush his bones. He could see no springs or wires that made the contraption work.

Meanwhile, Delia had single-handedly lifted the Triumph into the back of the van. "Nothing on the scanner?" she asked someone inside.

"They traced the car and went to the Cho house first," a male voice called back. "They went to the Mayhall house next and questioned Crystal. No mention of you or a motorcycle."

"Wait," Stony said. "They're in my house?"

Mr. Blunt looked at his shoes. Delia said, "Don't worry, they're not going to do anything to your family."

He pulled off his helmet. "You're lying."

"Yes," she said. "But we don't have time to talk about this now, and it doesn't change a thing. Get in the van, John."

"No, not until you tell me how you met Crystal, how you found me—"

"Ah, you think maybe that we're part of a *conspiracy*," Mr. Blunt said, drawing out the word. "And we most certainly are."

Delia looked annoyed. "We have nothing to do with the government, Stony. There's an underground network out there, made up of the living dead and breathers who are sympathetic to us. We try to contact those people, though in this case Crystal found us."

"But where? I thought she was in New Mexico. You got here so quickly."

"Stony, we've been driving in this direction for two days. Crystal said you'd be at home. Nobody thought you'd be—" He was sure she'd been about to say "stupid enough." She said, "We were thirty miles out when the first report went out, from the scene of the car accident. By the time we got into Easterly, they were already reporting your escape. We just got to you first. Happy? Now get in the van."

"Where are we going?"

Delia stared at him. "How the *fuck* does it matter?"

"I'm not going until you tell me where we're going."

Mr. Blunt lifted a squeaking arm. "The boy's staying here," he said. "In Effington."

"You don't understand what I've done," Stony said. "I can't let them arrest Crystal, or my mom. I have to know I can get back."

"Then you're an asshole," Delia said.

"You can't—what?"

"Your sister and your mother risked their lives to save you. We risked *our* lives. People you don't even know put their necks out to save you. And you, you're going to go do what, *surrender*? No, John. No. You do not have a choice. Get in the fucking van."

A bench seat had been set against one wall of the van, opposite the motorcycle and a pile of blankets. Near the front, a bucket seat that looked as if it had been ripped from a sports car had been bolted to the floor.

The man in the driver's seat turned and waved. He was a round-faced black man with a thick beard and a high fore-head. And he was alive. "That's Aaron," Mr. Blunt said. He pulled the van doors closed. "The beard." Stony sensed that the title was some kind of joke, but he didn't know what it meant.

"Glad to have you," Aaron said. He didn't seem that glad—he seemed nervous.

Delia reached up to the shower curtain rod that hung just behind the front seats and spanned the cabin like a roll bar. She tugged the blue vinyl curtain across, cutting them off from Aaron and the morning light shimmering through the windshield. "Keep to the speed limit," she said through the curtain.

"I know, I know," Aaron said.

Stony looked at the bench seat, then decided to leave that to Mr. Blunt. Instead he sat on the pile of padded moving blankets and leaned back against the motorcycle's front wheel. The interior of the van smelled of stale cigarette smoke and something earthier, like the dense, worm-rich soil he exca-vated from the basement.

The van lurched into motion, and Mr. Blunt put a metal hand to the low ceiling to steady himself. "Is it true what Crystal said? That they found you as a baby?"

Stony didn't answer.

"And then you—and this is the part that we all find hard to believe—you *grew up*?"

"Enough questions," Delia said. She nodded to Stony's arm. "It looks like you hurt yourself."

Stony glanced at his shoulder. His shirt was torn above his bicep, but of course there was no blood. He hadn't been able to move his arm since the accident. *Dead Weight,* he thought. The title of the fourth Deadtown Detective novel.

"You could move it if you wanted to," Mr. Blunt said. "As the Lump says, 'Integrity is all.'"

"It happened in the accident. I think I ripped a muscle or something," Stony said.

"Doesn't matter. If it's still attached, you can move it. Still belongs to you, doesn't it?"

"Give it," Delia said. She squatted beside him and circled his wrist in one cold hand. She moved the fingers of her other hand along his bicep, to the top of his shoulder. He looked at her face, looked away. The gray flesh of her cheek stopped at her bare jawbone, like a thin slice of old meat on a china plate.

Her fingertips dug deep into his flesh. She frowned. "No pain?"

"No," he said.

"Hold that thought." She yanked down on his wrist, and at the same time slammed the palm of her hand against the top of his arm. He yelped, more from surprise than discomfort.

"It was only dislocated," she said. "You're fine now."

He flexed his fingers. He was afraid to lift his arm.

"I *said,* you're fine." She turned back toward the curtain.

Stony raised his arm a few inches, then lifted his hand to the ceiling and back. "See?" Mr. Blunt said. "Integrity was not compromised, and so the self persists."

Once they reached a highway, the van accelerated and the interior became a rattling, thrumming tin can, making conversation nearly impossible. Thank God. Stony was free to stare at the metal floor. He knew he should be paying attention, trying to figure out where they were going, but he couldn't bring himself to care. His mind raced but he couldn't focus on anything. His mother had to be crazy with grief and worry. Kwang could be hurt, maybe dead. And Junie—he couldn't think about Junie. He craved sleep. He was jealous of that blankness, that thought-erasing void that he'd watched his sisters and mother fall into, that he'd read about in a thousand novels. He ached for it, just eight hours of mental silence.

They rode over rough back roads and uneven highways, and the air grew thick with the smell of cigarette smoke: Delia, Mr. Blunt, and even Aaron seemed to be chain-smokers. About an hour in, Stony heard the chop of helicopter blades, but the van didn't stop or speed up. Aaron had a CB up front with him; he spoke into it a few times each hour, and a staticky voice answered. He seemed to be talking to a car ahead of them on the road. After three hours or so, Aaron, Delia, and the person on the CB agreed that they needed gas. When they rolled to a stop, Stony got to his feet.

"Where the fuck are you going?" Delia said.

"I need to call my mom."

"You can't do that. The Diggers are probably waiting for your call."

Diggers? he thought. "My sister Alice, then. I have to tell them about Kwang, about—I have to tell them where I am."

"You're not anywhere yet," Mr. Blunt said.

Delia said, "Later, Stony. We'll get a message to your family when we can. We have three hundred miles to go today. Now, do you eat?"

"Do *you*?" He meant both of them—Delia and Mr. Blunt.

"I don't, but some of us never got out of the habit. Aaron can get you a snack if that would make you feel better."

"No, I mean—" He stopped himself. What was the polite way to ask, Do you eat brains? "Everything I've heard about you. The hunger, the rage—"

"The taste for human flesh," Mr. Blunt said.

"No. Yes."

Mr. Blunt laughed. Delia fixed Stony with that bulging,

milky eye. "There's no *you* here, Stony. Just us. The faster you drop all that mass-media bullshit they've been feeding you, the healthier you'll be. Do you know anything about yourself? What you are?"

"Amnesia's not uncommon among us," Mr. Blunt said.

"I don't know what you're talking about."

"See?"

Delia said, "Everything you need to know, you already know. Do you have an uncontrollable urge to kill? Are you trembling with desire to bite into warm flesh and eat their organs?"

He thought of the party, the boys on the stairs. Only a few hours ago, when Junie was alive, when Kwang was unhurt. "No," he said. He didn't feel like killing now, and he'd never felt the urge before tonight. Still, he felt like he was lying.

"That's right, Stony. Once the fever passes, you can control it."

Aaron came back to the vehicle, then opened the curtain a few inches. "Okay then." He seemed calmer than he'd been when Stony climbed in the van. "Everyone ready?"

They were living dead: They could have driven all day, all night. But Aaron was human, and eventually he needed to sleep. Near midnight he pulled in to a motel outside of Rawlins, Wyoming. The other car, Stony learned, would be stopping fifty miles from here. Delia said that Stony would meet the rest of the crew when they reached home.

"Which is where?"

"Need-to-know basis."

"I just want to know where we're going."

Mr. Blunt said, "Did you choose that name, or was it given to you?"

"Pardon?"

"It's an appropriate nom de mort," Mr. Blunt said.

"You mean, like 'Delia'?" Stony said. She didn't answer. "In the first Deadtown Detective book, Delia's the name of the girl who tries to sell Einstein's brain. And in book three she's caught smuggling guns to the prisoners."

"I never read them."

"*Stone Dead*," Mr. Blunt said. "*Stone Cold. The Gravestone . . .*"

Aaron pulled around to the rear of the motel and backed the van up to the building. "I'll check it out," he said. Mr. Blunt had put on a wide-brimmed fedora, chocolate brown with a black band. Delia grabbed a straw sun hat from a bag on the floor and handed Stony a Cleveland Browns ball cap. He couldn't wait to get out of the cramped vehicle.

A knock on the back of the van door: all clear.

They hopped out one by one, crossed the short stretch of sidewalk, and then entered the room. In that brief moment in the open, Stony got the impression of vast emptiness surrounding them. The motel felt like the only building in a hundred miles of dark prairie, a lone ship at sea.

Delia was last in. She shut the door and Mr. Blunt said, "Another mission accomplished."

"Jesus Christ," Aaron said. He looked both exhausted and relieved to be out of the van. "I'll be in the next room. Wake me at five."

After he left, Mr. Blunt said to Stony, "He likes to sleep alone. He's a good man for a breather, but he can't quite bring himself to close his eyes when we're around."

The room was bigger than the interior of the van, but not by much. Two double beds, a green carpet, a tiny TV, pressboard dressers. Mr. Blunt turned on the TV and began flipping through channels filled with snow. Delia sat by the window, keeping an eye on the van through a gap in the curtain.

Stony perched at the end of one of the beds. Mr. Blunt found a clear channel, then sat beside him. He crossed his legs with a squeaking sound. One pant leg had ridden up, exposing a length of gnarled wood where his leg should have been. Mr. Blunt saw him staring and laughed. He rapped on the wood and said, "Shin splints."

"That's a terrible joke," Stony said.

"I'm a warped man."

"Please, stop it."

Onscreen was a black-and-white movie, a comedy with Katharine Hepburn and Cary Grant chasing a baby cougar around a big house. Mr. Blunt kept up a running commentary on Howard Hawks and Grant's homage to Harold Lloyd. "Grant famously ad-libbed here. It's the first time in film anyone used the word *gay* to refer to homosexuals."

"Uh, okay," Stony said. He could not get over the fact that he was sitting in a room with other dead people, people like him. He'd grown up thinking he would be alone the rest of his life—whatever a life counted for in his case—hiding in basements and barns. He'd convinced himself that the world of Jack Gore was a fantasy. But here he was, on the run with the Living Dead Army.

"So what do we do now?" Stony asked. "Sit here all night?"

"The life of a fugitive is not easy, my boy," Mr. Blunt said. "In '68, I spent five weeks in a dump. An actual dump! I dug my own bunker deep into the garbage pile. I could have lived there forever if it weren't for the dogs. They knew I was in there, and it drove them crazy."

"I dug, too," Stony said. "I dig. I do a lot of digging."

"A common urge," the man said. "The Lump says that we struggle between two desires, to rise"—his fingers splayed like the spines of a wooden fan—"and to return." They clacked back together.

"What's the Lump?"

"It's a who," Delia said. She tossed Stony his baseball cap. "Walk with me." .

"Outside?"

"I think we can risk an excursion." She pulled on her big sun hat and led him into the parking lot. They walked quickly . to get out of the light. At the edge of the lot she looked around, nodded toward an area of deeper dark, and said, "That way." They marched over uneven ground. A rancid odor drifted in on the wind, slipped away, then returned, stronger. "What is that?" Stony asked. "Something die out there?"

"You can smell?"

He knew farm smells, and some summer days they'd catch a whiff of the hog plant outside Easterly. "I think it's a slaughterhouse," he said.

"This is a cattle state," Delia said. "Plenty of big processing plants. Humans have a gift for large-scale murder."

Stony thought, *Humans?* After a few moments he said, "I just realized that I haven't said thank you yet. For rescuing me."

"It's what we do," she said. "About the only thing we *can* do."

"I'm still kinda in shock. Back at the house, when you took off your helmet?" He shook his head. "I'm just having some trouble adjusting."

She looked at him. "You thought you were the only one, right? All those years, the only living dead boy in the world."

"I thought they killed us all."

"Almost all. Just shy of a hundred fucking percent. Some

of us who escaped the cleanup gangs were protected by family, though God knows why, after the things we tried to do to whoever was nearest. But mostly it was blind luck. Every one of us has an amazing story—waking up after the fever in a cellar that the humans had missed, or in the bottom of a pile of bodies that hadn't burned all the way through, or managing to climb out of the fucking grave too late for the party. That's because all the ones without an amazing story were shot, decapitated, burned, or sent to Deadtown."

Stony jerked to a stop. "Wait—what?"

"I said, or sent to—"

"Deadtown is *real*?"

"It's just a prison, kid. Really, a couple of prisons—they keep moving it. Some of our people nicknamed it after those books, not the other way around."

"Okay, you're blowing my mind. There's a prison, and there are undead people . . . but are you saying we didn't kill any humans? I mean, you and Mr. Blunt are like me, you're not . . . crazy. But everything I've read—"

"Don't trust the media, Stony."

"But they couldn't make up all those deaths. Seventy thousand people?"

"They could," Delia said. "If they wanted to, they could." She paused. "It just so happens that in this case, they didn't."

"What?"

"Yes, we killed a lot of people. But it wasn't our fault."

"You're talking about the fever."

"It lasts twenty-four to forty-eight hours. During that time, you're exactly what you've read about—a mindless carnivore. But the fever passes. You wake up. You may not remember who you were, or what the hell happened, but you're sane. You're not homicidal anymore."

"The government has to know this."

"Sure they know, Stony. They've captured enough of us."

"In Deadtown."

"Right."

Stony stepped away from her, shaking his head, then turned back. "We have to tell people."

"Really. Tell them what?"

"Get the word out. Go on TV. We can show people that we're not the monsters they think we are."

"That's sweet."

"Why are you making fun of me?"

"You ever hear of Eli Cohen?" she asked. They resumed walking. "Antiwar activist, bit of a whack job, but his heart was in the right place. In '69 he met some of the LDs and tried to talk about it. He's still in prison. Then in '71 a reporter named Hockner managed to work his way into a safe house—turned out he was working for the government, and ten of us were captured. After that, we stopped talking to reporters. We were a fucking national security threat, Stony, and still are. They've killed every one of us who've stepped out into the open, or else black-bagged us and hauled us off to their secret medical prison. They can't afford to have even one LD out in the wild, because we're still a danger. We *can* still bite, Stony, even if we choose not to. And because of that, we're the scariest disease carrier they can imagine. We can wipe them out. We can end the world."

ICBM.

They'd walked in a wide arc, keeping the motel to their left. Delia turned to take them back the way they'd come, well outside the glow of the parking lot lights. They were silent for a long time, and then Stony said, "How many of us are there? This army of yours?"

"You'll never know. You'll only meet a few of us at a time.

And when you do, you can't tell them that story about being a baby and growing up."

"But it's true."

"It doesn't matter. The only ones who know the truth are Aaron and Mr. Blunt. Everyone else, you tell them you were bitten two years ago by an LD you didn't know, and you've been hiding out at your mom's house since then, okay?"

"I don't understand."

"You don't have to. Just trust me."

"Trust you? I just met you."

She grabbed his arm and spun him around. Stony was stunned by her strength.

"Listen, bucko, I saved your fucking life. There are political situations in the LD world that you do not understand. This miracle baby crap? Some of our people are superstitious—hell, some of them are bone stupid—and there are factions that will use that magic fundamentalist shit to make them do stupid things."

"What kinds of stupid things?"

"Shut up. You *will* be educated, and your eyes *will* be fucking opened, and on that day you will thank God that I found you first and not some asshole like Billy Zip. But until that day, you'll keep your mouth shut. Are we clear?"

Stony stared at her. After a long moment, she released her grip on him.

"Okay," he said.

"Okay?"

"Okay!"

"Okay."

Stony watched Delia march off. He thought, *Miracle Baby*?

PART
TWO

CHAPTER SEVEN

1988
Los Angeles, California

A young brown-skinned girl, perhaps eight years old, rode down the sidewalk on her bike, a purple and pink two-wheeler with a white basket. She seemed to pay no attention to the van pulling up behind her. It wasn't until she heard the doors of the van open that she put out a leg to stop herself, and looked back—and then gaped as two clowns hopped out of the vehicle.

Strange, colorless clowns: Their white faces were outlined in black, and they wore black shirts, black pants, and white gloves. The shorter one (who wore black sunglasses, which didn't seem right, either) slammed shut the van's sliding door. On it, in white letters, were the words "Goes Without Saying."

The clown in the sunglasses hurried toward the front door of the house they were parked in front of, but the taller one turned toward the little girl. His eyes went wide, and his mouth formed a surprised O. Then he crouched and held a finger to his lips. One black-rimmed eye closed in a slow-motion wink.

The girl dropped her bike and fled. The man stood and watched her run down the sidewalk. Then he slumped his shoulders and dropped his chin, the very picture of disappointment.

Delia called back, "Are you fucking coming or not?" Then she opened the door without knocking and went inside. Stony sighed—silently—and turned to follow.

A dead man in a black toupee met them in the hallway, looking distraught. "The mailman's in the bedroom," he said. "I didn't know what else to do with him."

Roger was an Oldy, one of the Original Living Dead from '68, his face as gray and mottled as a cardboard egg carton. He wore a bathrobe over a yellow Tweety Bird T-shirt and blue sweatpants.

"I don't know what you were doing with him at all, Roger," Delia said. She took off her sunglasses. "You know better than this."

Roger pulled at the neck of his robe, looking insulted. He was one of the fifty-two in her parish scattered throughout safe houses in the Los Angeles area, and this was his third placement.

Stony said, "On the hotline you said he'd surprised you?"

"He walked right in the door without knocking! I think he was delivering a package, but still, you don't just walk in like that, do you? I was sitting right there on the couch. I'd come up to watch *The Pyramid*. I know I shouldn't have, but the reception's so much better up here. The curtains were pulled, and I thought the door was locked. Bob always locks the door on the way to work." Bob was the breather who owned the house.

"The mailman saw you?" Stony asked. "He recognized what you were?"

"I saw it on his face. He was going to run. So I had to . . . well, grab him."

"Jesus," Delia said. "Did the neighbors see anything?"

"I don't think so."

"Show us where he is," Delia said. Roger stumped down the hallway—one leg was a few inches shorter than the other. She asked, "Did you hurt him?"

Roger hesitated. "Maybe."

"Maybe?" Delia said.

"We were rolling around a lot. He was fighting, yelling. In all the ruckus, I may have, uh, bit him."

Delia grabbed Roger by the shoulder and spun him around. "Did you kill him?"

"No! It was just a bite, a little, tiny bite. I didn't even mean to!"

If you bit him, Stony thought, you've already killed him.

They reached the back bedroom door. There was no sound. Stony said, "Did you knock him out or something? Gag him?"

"I tied his hands with my belt! Then I just, well, sat on him. When I heard you come in, I told him not to move, or *else,* and I locked him in here."

Stony tried the door, but the knob didn't turn. He looked at Delia.

Delia said, "Roger, you do know that bedrooms don't lock from the outside?"

"Oh," he said. "Right."

Stony stepped back and kicked. The door banged open. There was no one in the room. The blue-green belt from Roger's robe lay on the bed, next to a red blot the size of a half-dollar. There were two windows in the room, one filled with an air conditioner, the other wide open.

"Where is he?" Roger yelled.

"Gee, I don't know," Delia said. "It's a fucking mystery."

Stony went to the open window. They were in a single-story bungalow, and the brown September grass was only five feet below. He leaned out and saw a blue-shirted figure dart between the houses and disappear.

"We've got a runner," Stony said. "Delia, go back to the van, see if you can find his mail truck on the next block—he's probably heading for that. I'll try to grab him before he gets there." She didn't answer. "Delia?"

"Fine," Delia said. "Roger, you're coming with me. You've burned down another fucking safe house."

Stony dove through the open window, landed hard on one shoulder, and rolled to a standing position. Undead Advantage No. 12: throwing yourself around like a rag doll, without worrying about concussions or torn muscles. Number 13? The trick he'd learned years ago: relentless, tireless running.

Stony sprinted in the direction the man had taken. He came out between two houses, and he'd closed the distance to within fifty yards. The mailman was running flat out, with a canvas bag flapping at his side. You had to admire him for hanging on to the mail.

Stony shouted, "Wait!" The man glanced behind him, then looked a second time, and stumbled.

Stony thought, That's right, you thought we were shamblers, didn't you?

Thanks to Romero's endlessly replayed documentary of the outbreak, everyone thought the living dead shuffled around like geriatric patients. But those were the fevered dead, brain-damaged and confused, at the mercy of recalcitrant limbs jerking to their own rhythm. After the fever passed, a sane LD only had to tell the muscles to move, and they moved.

Jump, and they jumped. Free will, or its compelling illusion, was restored.

The man stopped running, turned to face him. His chest heaved, but he looked merely scared and confused, not terrified. Then Stony thought, Oh, right. I'm dressed like a mime.

He slowed to a stop about ten feet from the man. "I just want to help you," Stony said.

The mailman looked Hispanic, perhaps forty years old. His shirt was untucked, and there was blood on his neck and his arm. Roger really had bitten him, maybe more than once. The mailman pointed back toward the bungalow. "Something—" He breathed deep. "Zombie. Bit me."

"You don't have to use the Z-word," Stony said.

The man stared at him.

"Why don't you come with me," Stony said. "We can get you some help."

He nodded slowly. Stony stepped forward, and the man suddenly slung his bag behind him and bolted for the nearest house. It was a two-story modernist cube with large square windows, surrounded by a chain-link fence.

Stony swore and started after him. The mailman reached the fence, planted two hands, and vaulted over without breaking stride. The move looked so practiced that Stony wondered if he'd learned it in postal school. Advanced Canine Escape Techniques. Stony's hurdle was less graceful; he was moving so quickly that he was able to clear the fence, but he landed awkwardly and covered the last twenty feet in a stumbling, headlong rush. He barreled into the man, mashing him against the door with much more force than he'd intended.

The mailman squawked and began to slide to his knees.

"Sorry!" Stony said. He stooped, then lifted the man into a fireman's carry, and the mailman yelped in pain. "Sorry, sorry." Stony carried him to the fence, nudged open the gate with his hip, and walked into the street. Behind him, the door opened and a voice yelled in Spanish.

The blue van swung around the corner. Delia was driving, and Roger, thank God, was out of sight in the back. Stony struck a pose: hip cocked, head tilted, thumb raised. The van stopped with its bumper only a few inches from his left knee.

Stony pivoted to face the house. A dark-haired woman in an aquamarine pantsuit pointed at him and yelled, "Police! Police!"

Stony swept his free arm back and bowed to her. The purity of the gesture was marred only by the thrashing captive on his shoulder.

"We're never doing that again," Delia said.

They hauled him out of the van like a roll of carpet; Stony held his feet and Delia gripped under his arms. During the trip from Mount Washington to Venice they'd secured his wrists with plastic zip ties, mostly to stop him from trying something stupid, and duct-taped his mouth.

Stony said, "Do what, kidnapping?" But he knew she wasn't talking about that.

"And then you take a fucking bow? Are you insane?"

"That was great," Roger said from behind them.

Delia's safe house was actually two houses, Yellow and Blue, a back-to-back pair of run-down bungalows several miles from the beach, fenced off and partially shielded from the neighbors by overgrown trees. They'd parked the van on the cement patio between the houses, and so only had to carry the mailman in the open for a few seconds before they reached the back door of Yellow. Still, Stony could not help but glance up at the house next door, at the single window that overlooked their backyard.

Delia caught him. "Quit looking for an audience, farm boy." She stepped backward through the kitchen door, and then they were inside. "You *like* dressing up, don't you?"

"I thought maybe she'd think it was performance art and wouldn't call the cops." Stony shrugged. "I mean, it *is* Venice. Watch your head, Thomas." They maneuvered around a corner and entered the living room. Thomas Sandoval was the name on the mailman's driver's license. He was still sweating and scared, but part of that was due to the fever coming on.

"I'm not letting you talk to Mr. Blunt anymore," Delia said. "He's a bad influence."

It was true, the disguises had been partly Mr. Blunt's idea. If you can't hide it, he'd said, paint it red. He'd suggested Mardi Gras masks, but Stony decided that makeup was the better choice, especially if they needed to drive themselves. He was pretty sure it was illegal to drive with a mask on, and it certainly couldn't help with your peripheral vision.

"Next time—" Stony said.

"I said never."

"Well, we can't use *that* outfit, now that the cops are looking for Shields and Yarnell." Delia backed down the basement stairs, with Thomas's head braced on her shoulder, cheek to cheek. Stony felt bad about losing the traveling mime troupe gag. They'd worn the costumes for several rounds of visits to the people of the parish, and perhaps because no one wanted to engage a mime, they'd been aggressively ignored. Then again, they'd never chased down a postal worker in broad daylight. "I'm thinking of something even better," he said.

"Better."

"Three words: Kiss tribute band."

She abruptly stopped. Thomas folded between them and grunted.

She wouldn't smile—Delia wasn't the smiling type—but he'd managed to loosen the line of her frown. She wasn't really mad at him; she was furious with Roger, and with herself for allowing Roger to live on his own with the breathers. She looked at him over the tops of her sunglasses, her lidless eye like a full moon.

"One more thing. *Go get the car, Delia?*"

"Oh, that."

"Next time you give me an order, outside this house or in, I will kick your dead gray ass."

"Yes ma'am," he said.

They set the mailman on the floor in Stony's room, and Delia left to call the chain of answering machines and voice-mail systems that connected the cells. The other cell leaders had to know about a new bite, especially one to a government worker who'd be missed soon. The risks were too great. It was an article of faith among the LDA that a single victim, let loose on the world, could start a new outbreak.

Well, yes and no. The numbers and infection models he'd learned from Alice were true, but only in the purest theoretical sense, a physics problem that required a perfect vacuum. Every real LD knew that if they were seen walking the streets, much less biting someone in front of witnesses, the Diggers and every other arm of the government would sweep down and burn every LD in sight—and probably anyone without a tan. The United States had been caught unawares in '68, but they wouldn't allow an outbreak to happen again.

The other eight LDs living in the houses converged on Stony's room. The space was already crowded with equipment tables, filing cabinets, and computer desks, but they cleared a spot in the middle of the room, set down an old mattress, and

laid Thomas upon it. The man was growing delirious. He
thrashed at his bonds, and moaned through the tape that covered his mouth.

"Can I do anything?" Roger asked. "I somehow feel
responsible."

Stony stared at him. "Just stay out of the way." Roger
would be busy enough in the next couple of hours surviving
Delia. He'd broken Rule No. 1. She would have to take disci-
plinary action; she had no choice. Stony said, "We need sheets,
at least five. We're going to have to mummy-wrap him to stop
him from hurting himself." Two residents hurried off into the
tunnel that connected the two basements. "Valerie, could you
find me surgical thread and needles? Oh, and towels and
water."

Valerie, a sad, graveborn woman who was his best friend
in the house, brought him the things he asked for. He also
assembled what he needed from his own supplies in the room:
syringes, Petri dishes, sealable vials. Then he crouched next to
Thomas.

"I'm going to remove the tape, okay?"

The man's eyes flicked back and forth, and he seemed not
to hear Stony. But then his head jerked in what could have
been a nod. Stony peeled the tape from his mouth.

The man gasped, then said, "Please don't kill me."

"I'm going to help you through this, Thomas."

"I have a wife. You have to—somebody has to—" He
took a shaky breath. "I can't think straight. There's something
wrong with me."

His shirt was drenched in sweat; his breaths came fast and
light. So many autonomic processes in the living body, Stony
thought. Nerves fired, muscles twitched, adrenaline pumped;
uncountable systems and subsystems churned and contested
with one another. Thomas's conscious mind was being pushed

along on a flood of chemicals and electricity, not riding the wave but swept up in it, trying to make sense of what the body told it: You are under threat. The monsters surround you. The poison is already inside.

"It's going to be all right," Stony said. "You'll be going through some changes in the next twenty-four hours or so. You may feel afraid, or angry. You might even scare yourself. But I want you to know that I'm going to be here with you."

However long it takes, Stony thought. The folklore of the LDs was that the sooner a person died after a bite, the sooner he came back. Instead of waiting for the bite to shut off his heart, Stony could kill Thomas now, even make it painless. But that was folklore. Stony wasn't about to experiment on the man. He doubted he could kill Thomas even if he knew the rumor to be true.

Thomas said, "Am I going to die? I feel like I'm going to die."

"I promise you," Stony said. "Soon you're going to feel a lot better."

"It's not fair," Valerie said. She stood behind Stony as he gazed into the microscope. On the floor, Thomas groaned and thrashed. He was wrapped neck to feet in several layers of bedsheets, a makeshift straitjacket. Leather belts were cinched around his ankles, waist, and upper arms. He chewed at the towel they'd wedged into his mouth to protect his teeth and jaw from his frantic gnashing.

"I know, I know," Stony said absently. He rotated the slides again. Here was Thomas's blood before he died, six hours after the bite: perfectly normal. And here was Thomas's blood after he passed, at the 6:12 mark: dark, viscous, waxy. The transformation had occurred between observations, like the state change in a quantum particle. Like death itself. "I wish we could explain to him what's happening."

The bitten did not die as normal humans did. In a normal death, cells would begin to starve, and acidic carbon dioxide would build up, rupturing cell membranes. Digestive enzymes would spill into other cells, and the body would begin to eat itself from the inside out. As muscle cells stopped pumping calcium ions, rigor mortis would set in around the jaw and neck. Blood cells would begin to settle and congeal.

But the bitten did not break down, they did not stiffen. They entered the fever, which could last anywhere from 24 to 48 hours. Thomas was only on hour 10. If they let him loose now he'd attack any human in sight. Stony had often marveled at how specific the hunger was: The fevered dead didn't attack animals, or invade butcher shops. They craved human meat, human and nothing but, as if taking revenge for being kicked out of their former species. The Payback Diet.

"He didn't choose this," Valerie said. "We should have let him decide."

Stony looked up from the eyepiece. "What? Let him die?"

"If that's what he wanted."

He swiveled to face her. She must have been a handsome woman when alive. Her bearing was erect, and she wore her plain, secondhand dress as if it were an evening gown. But she was graveborn, one of the LDs who'd already been dead when the outbreak swept through the East, and so her appearance had suffered even before she'd joined the others aboveground. Unlike most of the LDs, women and men alike, she refused a wig. She was perfectly bald, and her eyes were sunk so far that they seemed to be excavated from the gray stone of her skull.

Stony said, "But we can't just let him *die* die."

She looked down at Thomas. "This one had a chance to

get away. He could have been in heaven by now. And now, he's here."

"Being LD isn't that bad, is it?"

"You're young, Stony. Fresh. You were bitten what, seven years ago?"

"Uh, about that, yeah." Valerie was his closest friend here, the one he could talk to most honestly, but he'd never told her about his birth. Delia's orders.

"You've just begun. You'll begin to realize that we're not supposed to be here—we're not part of the natural order. We're in limbo, cut off from life, from God, even cut off from hell."

"Come on, Valerie . . ." He said it lightly. "Even if we are all spawns of hell, I couldn't make him *choose,* not under duress. It would have been cruel."

He felt a little guilty making this argument; if there was one way to win a point with Valerie it was to appeal to her kindness. When he first arrived, it was Valerie who saw how lonely he was, how much he missed his family, and began to pull him into the life of the community. When she discovered how much he enjoyed building things, she convinced her sister, the breather who owned the house, to purchase materials and tools, and assigned him renovation projects that would please the other residents. It was Valerie who detected his hidden competitive streak and set him up with Tanya and Teddy, two Scrabble fiends who'd alienated everyone else in the house with their cutthroat style of play. And soon he discovered something he would never have imagined: He felt comfortable around dead people. At home he'd been so self-conscious about his dead skin, his inability to sleep, his fundamental difference from his sisters and his mother. But here he was hardly the most decayed person—in fact, he was downright attractive. He felt shallow comparing looks, but he had to admit that he was in better condition than anyone else in the house.

And he was safe. Well, more safe. In Iowa he'd been almost constantly on edge, because he felt as if his security rested entirely on his shoulders. His mother might mean well, but she couldn't really protect him. A circle of baking flour wasn't going to keep the government troops at bay. But here, Delia and Mr. Blunt were so competent, so sure of themselves, that he could do something he could never before afford to do: relax. Hell, he could even be goofy if he wanted to.

He owed so much of this new sense of comfort to Valerie. She made everything easier for him. He knew that in some ways he was making her into a proxy for his sisters, or perhaps, more disturbingly, his mother. Lately, however, he'd become worried about Valerie, and their roles had begun to reverse. She had always had a melancholy nature, but in the past year she'd been talking more and more about the wrongness of undead existence. There was a strong self-loathing streak in the LDs—Delia said it was because they'd bought into the mainstream's portrayal of them—but many of the graveborn had started calling themselves the Damned. All LDs were going to hell in an inescapable handbasket. The graveborn said they understood more because they'd gotten closer to the other side than anyone—they had a better idea of what was spiritually at stake. The bitten LDs argued that they'd *all* died, and the graveborn were putting on airs.

Thomas arched his back, then flipped himself onto his front. He raised his head and then bashed his face against the floor.

"Thomas!" Stony yelled. He jumped down from the chair and grabbed the man by the shoulders. "Thomas, stop it!"

The man suddenly went still. Stony turned him back onto his back, and the man stared into his eyes. Thomas was gone, lost in fever, but something glimmered behind his eyes.

"How did you do that?" Valerie asked.

"What?" Stony began checking the buckles on the leather straps, cinching them tighter.

"He listened to you. The fevered don't listen to anyone."

"It doesn't last long." Stony adjusted the strap keeping the gag in place, and Thomas shook his head like an angry child. "See?" he said. Valerie frowned, thinking, and Stony said, "Look, I know nobody would ask to go through this, but he was already bitten, the fever was already coming, and he wasn't thinking straight. Even if he'd begged for death, I wouldn't have killed him, because already he wasn't in his right mind. He'd just been *attacked* by us, why would he want to become us? But in a few hours he gets a chance to really choose."

"He won't be the same person in a few hours."

"Okay, maybe not," Stony said. Many of the bitten lost their memory or emerged with altered personalities. "But at least he'll be alive. Or moving at least. 'The dead stick moves in the wind.' "

"Don't start quoting the Lump to me," Valerie said.

"I'm sorry, it's just that—" He looked up at her, then back at Thomas. "Look, I haven't told anyone in the house about this, but I had a chance once. Someone I loved was very hurt, and I—I didn't do anything. I ran away before I even realized I could have saved her."

Valerie looked appalled. "Are you talking about biting someone? On purpose?"

"She was dying. If I could have—"

"Not even then. Not ever. No biting. That's our one rule, our most important rule."

"Valerie, sometimes—"

."Think about that girl who lives next door. Would you want her to die?"

Stony grimaced in frustration. Why was she bringing up the girl next door? "Never mind," he said. Every day he thought about the accident. Maybe Junie wouldn't have wanted to be converted; maybe she would have thanked him. But even if she hated him for it, at least he'd be able to ask her forgiveness now.

Valerie tilted her head. "I'm worried about you, Stony." She touched his head. He still had all his hair, smooth and brown. It never grew, but never fell out. "I would pray for you, if I thought God listened to us." She stepped away from him, then stopped in the doorway. "We'll talk about this more when Thomas's fever breaks."

"That's right," Stony said. "All three of us can talk about it then."

He tried to get back to work, but now the slide show of the accident was firing behind his eyes. He saved the VisiCalc sheet where he'd been recording Thomas's stats, then copied it to his backup floppy and ejected it. Then he crouched and touched the man's shoulder, and Thomas twisted his head in a vain attempt to bite his hand. LDs didn't hunger for other LDs—this was just an automatic response. "I'll be back in a few minutes," Stony said to him. "You're almost done." A lie. It might take another day and a half for the fever to pass.

Stony went to the bathroom, washed the last of the clown white from his face, and went upstairs. The two houses were small, falling down on the outside, but well tended inside, thanks largely to Stony's renovation efforts. Every window was covered with heavy drapes. It was 8:30 p.m. but could have been 3 a.m., or noon. Most of the residents were in Yellow's living room, smoking cigarettes and watching *Head of the Class*. Roger was laughing louder than anyone. LDs didn't need to sleep, but most of the ones Stony had met spent all of that extra time smoking and watching TV.

He found Delia in the kitchen, at the end of a phone cord stretched across the room. He was surprised to see Mr. Blunt at the table with her. Blunt lived in Aaron's split-level in Culver City, where they sheltered four LDs. Aaron drove him over to Delia's house once a week, but he wasn't due for several more days.

"You have mail?" Stony asked him.

Mr. Blunt smiled, dipped into his briefcase with clacking fingers, and produced two envelopes, one thick and one very thin. "Stony" was written on the front of each: in elegant cursive on the thick envelope, and in blocky capitals on the other. Neither had a return address, but in the upper left corner of the thin envelope was the Hangul pictogram for "friend": 동 무. Upside Down Man and Legless Man, as Stony thought of them.

"I hear you've recruited someone to replace me," Mr. Blunt said.

"I thought we should hire a professional," Stony said. He tucked the envelopes into his back pocket and sat down. He nodded toward Delia. "How are the higher-ups taking it?"

This thing with Roger had to be an embarrassment for Delia. He knew that she was more than a cell leader; she was some kind of troubleshooter in the LDA hierarchy. Once a month, on average, she hit the road to inspect other safe houses. Other times she was constantly on the phone, and messages were left for her almost every day. The LDA used a system of voicemail dead drops. Cell leaders called a number that changed every week to leave messages for the group. Stony had offered to set up an electronic bulletin board, but Delia nixed the idea: most of the LDA didn't know how to use a computer.

"The reaction has not been good, by the looks of it." He leaned forward, creaking. "We have other problems besides Roger. We lost an entire house in Nevada."

"What? How many people?"

Delia shushed him. Mr. Blunt lowered his voice. "Five LDs, two breathers. You ever hear about the Scanlon Sisters? Two lovely women in their seventies. They've been helping us since the outbreak."

"Who turned them in?"

He shrugged. "We're not sure. We wouldn't know about the raid at all if one of their friends hadn't contacted us. The Diggers sent in almost a hundred agents, sealed the entire block."

"A *hundred*?" Stony said. LDs feared even a small squad of Gravediggers. But this was an army of them.

Delia carried the handset back to the wall and hung up. "They want to call a meeting," she said. "Another fucking *congress*. All the cell leaders at least, and more delegates besides. I've tried to tell them it's a mistake. It's a fucking security nightmare."

Stony looked from her to Mr. Blunt. "They've done this before?"

"Only once," she said. "In '76."

"But isn't it dangerous?" Stony asked. "I mean, for all of you to be together like that?"

"Desperate times," Mr. Blunt said. "People are scared. We lost a dozen people in the past year, and now five in one blow."

"And two of the living."

Mr. Blunt shrugged.

Delia said, "The Big Biters are lobbying for action again."

"That's crazy," Stony said.

"Even the Perpetualists are getting antsy. They're afraid if we don't change course soon, then the Big Bite becomes our only option."

"How about you?" Stony asked her. "Is that what you think?" In front of the residents, Delia toed the line of the Abstainer majority, but he knew that she was privately sympathetic to the Perpetualist agenda. It was suicide to keep to a strict no-bite policy, the Perpetualists argued. If the LD race was to survive, the community needed to recruit at least as many members as they lost. Not one Big Bite, but a measured conversion campaign, slow enough to fly under the radar of the government, quick enough to keep their community viable.

Mr. Blunt smiled. "If we're running low on converts, we can always set Roger loose on them."

"What did they say about him?" Stony asked Delia. "Did the leaders agree on a punishment?"

"He's to be grounded," Delia said. "Grounded and disarmed."

"Shit," Stony said.

"Better than burning," Mr. Blunt said.

The back door opened. Elizabeth, the owner of the house, came in carrying a bag of groceries. She was a middle-aged white woman, perhaps twenty pounds overweight. Valerie was her sister, but Stony had never been able to detect a resemblance; the dead tended to resemble one another more than the living they'd left behind.

"Oh, we have company," Elizabeth said. "Good to see you, Mr. Blunt." She noticed something in their faces. "Is there something wrong?"

If LDs could cry, Roger would have been bawling. He pleaded with Delia, but she wouldn't be swayed. She pronounced his sentence in the living room, witnessed by the other residents of the house, as well as Elizabeth. Some of the LDs seemed nervous about doing this in front of her, but Delia said that everyone, even their partners among the living, had to understand what was going to happen, and why.

"Roger, you will be bound and blindfolded, then moved to a high-security house," she said. "You won't be told the location. You won't be permitted to go outside or see the outside. If after ten years you haven't broken any rules of the residency, you may be allowed more privileges. Do you understand?"

"I didn't mean it!" Roger said.

Stony thought of Junie. *It was an accident.*

"Yet we can't allow it to happen again. Mr. Blunt?"

Mr. Blunt raised a wooden hand. He held a pair of pliers. The LDs in the room stepped back, as if they were vampires and somebody had just whipped out a cross. Valerie shook her head and left the room. Elizabeth looked confused.

Delia said, "You can do this yourself, Roger, or I'll do it for you."

"Don't I get an appeal? There's some sort of appeal process, right?"

She put a hand on Roger's shoulder. "You or me, Roger?"

The man took the pliers from Mr. Blunt. He stared at the device for a long moment. "All of them?" he asked.

Delia didn't bother to answer. Roger lifted the pliers and opened his mouth. Half his teeth were missing, and the rest were black. He fastened the pliers on one of his remaining front teeth . . . and froze. Perhaps thirty seconds passed.

Delia said, "Roger?"

He shrugged and pulled. The tooth popped free. There was no blood. "I really like my teeth," he said.

"You can keep them," Mr. Blunt said. "Just not in your mouth."

CHAPTER EIGHT

1988
Los Angeles, California

The bite. Everything in LD life politics came down to the bite.

Think it's a sin? Then you were an Abstainer. Did you believe some biting was necessary to maintain the LD population? Ah, a Perpetualist. And if you believed it was high time to stop hiding and rain down the apocalypse on the breathing oppressors—well then, welcome to the Big Biters. They wanted an orchestrated attack on every continent, an outbreak that would spread too far, too fast to be shut down. Millions of humans would die, millions of LDs would be destroyed, but in the end, the dead would rule the earth. An undead utopia built on the bones of untold innocents—until the dead began to fall apart. Yippee.

As Delia tried to tell him the night after she'd rescued him, some of those factions would seize on the weirdness of Stony's birth and childhood—"that magic fundamentalist shit"—and use it to their own ends.

After his first two months in the safe house, Stony still didn't know what that meant. "*Why* should I be keeping this secret?" he asked her. He'd already gotten to know Valerie and a couple of the other residents. Lying about his life made him feel like a spy, an imposter: un-undead. Delia told him to keep his voice down—and to keep quiet for a little while longer. "Somebody wants to meet you," she said, as if this explained anything.

"Who?"

"Someone who'll make this clear." That's all she would tell him. Then one afternoon a few days later, Aaron backed up the van to the Yellow house, and Delia and Mr. Blunt hustled him into the back.

"Okay," he said. "*Now* will you tell me?"

"You're a lucky boy," Mr. Blunt said. "You're off to see the Lump."

Later, he would learn that the six hours in the van had taken them to a house in San Jose, but at the time they refused to tell him where they were going. When they climbed out of the van at 10:30 p.m. they were in a stunningly clean four-car garage, empty except for Aaron's van and a gleaming black Chevy Suburban with tinted windows. He and Delia and Mr. Blunt started inside the house; Aaron shook his head and said he'd rather wait out here, thanks. They'd be here for less than an hour, and Aaron would have them back to L.A. by morning.

The door from the garage was unlocked and they entered a large space—living room or den or lounge, Stony didn't have a name for this kind of room—with absurdly high white walls that bounced their voices against their ears. The white furniture and silver floor lamps looked like they'd been placed here solely for photographic purposes.

A tiny black woman, just over five feet tall, entered the room from a far door and closed it carefully behind her. She strode toward them, threw open her arms to Mr. Blunt, and said "At last!"

"Ah, sweet Rose, my riveting Rose," he said. "As lovely as ever." He removed his homburg and nodded at Stony. "I want you to meet the most polite dead boy of his generation. Stony Mayhall, this is—"

"Rose?"

"Excellent guess," she said, and extended a small, thin hand. She was beautifully preserved. Only the gray pallor of her skin and the black of her fingernails signaled that she was LD. "I've heard a lot about you."

He glanced at Mr. Blunt. And next to him, Delia, watching. "I'm too polite to ask what he said," Stony said.

"I'm not too polite to say." Hanging from her neck on a silver chain was a nobbly gray rock the size of a marble. She said, "Have a seat. He's finishing up a letter."

Delia and Rose did not hug, or even shake hands. Delia said, "Could you tell him to speed it up? We're on a tight schedule."

Rose laughed, not unkindly, and said, "You know nobody can hurry him." Stony couldn't decide if the women liked each other or not. They might have been enemies, or they might have been friends who'd known each other so long, and saw each other so frequently, that they didn't need to demonstrate their affection.

Stony sat in a chair of white leather and chrome, in front of a glass coffee table the size of a shuffleboard court. Blunt and Rose sat together on a white love seat, conferring, while Delia paced the perimeter of the room, eyeing a line of small framed photographs. The one closest to Stony was of a dark-haired woman, evidently naked, sitting backward on a triangular-backed wooden chair, crossed arms coyly covering her breasts. The other pictures, also in black and white, seemed to be of the same woman and chair, in different poses.

Stony was suddenly sure that this colorless house had never been inhabited by a living person. It had been built, furnished, and abandoned, and Rose and her crew were squatters. Maybe they were staying only for the night. They'd shut the door behind them and the whole place would collapse into a box the size of a Chinese food container.

"You all right, my boy?" Mr. Blunt asked.

"I'm fine," Stony said. "It's been a while since I've been in a room that didn't smell of cigarettes." In his experience, that was the smell of the dead: cigarettes and old clothes. "I'll be right back."

He went back out to the garage. Aaron sat in the front seat of the van, with the door open, pulling at his beard and reading a copy of *Omni* magazine. Stony said, "We're just sitting around in there. There's some nice couches."

"I'm fine," he said.

"I feel weird that you never come inside," Stony said.

Aaron looked at him.

Stony said, "I mean, I don't want you to think . . . that *I* think you're just some chauffeur. Because you're not. Not to me." Aaron didn't say anything. "I think what you do for us is so important. Because really, the LDs and the breathers—the living people? There's not really any difference between us."

"You don't think there's a difference?" Aaron asked. He put down the magazine.

"Not a *fundamental* difference. We're all people."

"Kid, *your* people are *dead*. And you creep me the hell out."

"Then why do you—? I mean, how can you keep helping us if we . . . ?"

"Would you like a persuasive backstory? A two-minute anecdote that explains my personal motivation for joining the cause? Maybe something about a beloved family member shot in the head by cleanup gangs that makes a man question his values and prejudices."

Stony thought about this. "That would be good. Sure."

Aaron laughed. "Your appointment's ready, kid."

A shriveled, dark-skinned LD man, wearing a shiny green tracksuit with white stripes, stood in the doorway. Stony thought, The great and mysterious Lump wears a tracksuit? The man nodded at Stony and said, "This way."

Stony followed him back inside. In the living room, Rose took his arm and they walked toward the far door that Rose had come through earlier. The man in the tracksuit went through the door, and Stony realized that Delia and Mr. Blunt had made no move to follow; he was going in without them.

Stony and Rose went inside. In the moment before Rose shut the door he made out a king-sized bed crowded with pillows and a couple of end tables. Then suddenly the room was dark, illuminated only by a green Lava lamp glowing on a side table. Stony looked at Rose, thinking, Lava lamp? Really?

The man in the tracksuit crawled onto the bed and sat down, facing them. From somewhere he produced a game board that he unfolded across his lap.

Rose sat on the foot of the bed and patted the space next to her. "Stony, this is Rajit, and of course the Lump. He's been wanting to meet you."

Stony said, "I'm sorry—what?" Did she mean that Rajit was his name, and the Lump was his title, or—

Then something next to the man moved. Stony sat back, startled, and nearly slipped from the bed. What he'd taken in the dark to be another pillow was a mass of tissue and bone: an eyeless skull without a jawbone; a left shoulder; a torso. It had no right arm, no pelvis, no legs.

The arm reached out to the board on the man's lap. Only

two fingers remained on the hand, an index finger and pinky. The index finger came down, and the man—Rajit—quietly said, "Enn." The finger bobbed up and down, and Rajit murmured, "Oh, ess, ee, eye."

Stony whispered to Rose, "Is that a Ouija board?"

"We'd tried to get him to use a Speak and Spell," she said. "He likes Rajit's voice better."

"Nose itches," Rajit finished.

"Oh!" Stony said. He glanced at Rose. "Does he want me to . . . ?"

The skull and shoulder swayed left and right, creaking.

"The Lump jokes with you," Rajit says. "He has no nose."

"Oh, right."

Rose said quietly, "You're supposed to ask, How does he smell?"

The Lump's hand moved, and Rajit spelled "T, E, R—"

"Terrible!" Stony said, and laughed. Rajit looked annoyed to be interrupted. The Lump swayed and creaked. Stony couldn't imagine how the Lump managed to move at all. He seemed to be a collection of bones held together by scraps of skin as dried and wrinkled as beef jerky. Was Rajit moving him somehow? Was this an elaborate puppet show?

It seemed to take forever for the next sentence to make its way down the Lump's arm to his assistant's lips. Rajit seemed in no hurry to jump to the end of whatever word was being spelled, no matter how obvious. After a torturous three or four minutes, the Lump said, "I hear you are a scientist."

"I wouldn't say that," Stony said. "Though I do like science. I'm just . . . curious."

"Show me your hands," the Lump eventually said.

"My hands?"

The Lump's arm gestured toward him, and Stony held out both his palms. The torso shifted, and the skull dropped forward with a crack! Stony thought that the head had snapped from the neck and was about to drop into his hands, but no, it stayed attached, bowed in an attitude of close inspection, studying him with those empty sockets.

This is ridiculous, Stony thought. How the hell can it see? What would the photons bounce off of?

The Lump's arm reached back, and Rajit began to spell again. Stony looked at Rose, thinking, This could take forever.

"The dead stick moves in the wind," Rose said.

"Pardon?" Stony asked.

"It's something the Lump said once—you don't mind if I repeat it, do you, Lump? 'The dead stick moves in the wind, and believes it moves itself.' I think we all suffer under that illusion, LDs and the living alike."

Eventually Rajit said, "I hear that in Iowa you did a lot of digging."

Stony smiled, out of nervousness he supposed. How much did the Lump know about him? Was it okay for him to talk about his past here? "Yes, I suppose I did do a bit more shoveling than most kids my age," he said. "It turned into a kind of hobby." He faltered, because the arm was moving again, but he decided to keep talking. "I excavated my entire basement and a little extra besides. I had a lot of time on my hands."

Several minutes passed as the Lump said, "Sounds like you worked your fingers to the bone."

"You could say that," Stony said, then suddenly realized, he should have worked his fingers down to the bone. He looked at his palms again, and his smooth, unmarked fingers. All that work with the shovel, all that friction. In a living body, skin blistered, cells died and flaked off, and had to be replaced with living tissue. But Stony's hands were fine.

"This doesn't make any sense," Stony said.

Rose said, "We're all impossible."

"Bee," Rajit intoned.

Stony sat still, spelling along with the assistant. *Be you,* he said to himself. *Bee you tee. Beauty.* The long gaps between sentences seemed to stretch his thoughts. Why were his hands so beautiful? If he was dead—and despite what Alice had told him the day Kwang shot him, he *was* dead, at least metabolically speaking—why wasn't he decaying? Why weren't any of them rotting? Given that, was the Lump's bizarre persistence in the world, despite the absence of 80 percent of a body, any more unlikely than his own?

Finally the Lump stopped moving his arm, and he spoke. "But some of us," he said through Rajit, "are more impossible than others."

They talked for two more hours. Measured in words, it was a short conversation, but Stony began to feel as if the slow-motion unfolding of the sentences was an essential part of the content. This halting speech, telegraphed through the droning Rajit, should have been the opposite of eloquence. Instead, perhaps because he was listening so carefully, the words struck home like poetry, or commandments. The Lump described the demographics of the community, how LDs aligned themselves based on geography and religion and especially origin: graveborn separating themselves from the bitten, Oldies from the newly bitten, and those who believed they'd died from those who believed they still lived and were only infected. Then of course were the political divisions based on the bite: the Abstainers and Perpetualists and Big Biters. People in all these groups, the Lump said (without any evident pride in Rajit's voice), looked to him for guidance.

"Everyone is waiting for a messiah. Someone to bridge the gap between the living dead and the merely living."

Stony didn't know what that meant, "bridge the gap."

Someone who'd make the LDs into something not quite dead? If this were a normal conversation—whatever passed for normal in the undead world—Stony might have started asking questions. Instead he waited as Rajit continued to spell out words. The Lump described how people longed for the Big Bite, but they were waiting for a sign from the Lump that the messiah had arrived.

"It seems to me," Stony said slowly—he wanted to choose his words as carefully as the Lump did—"that a messiah is the last thing you want. Once he—or she?—arrives, then all bets are off. The moderate LDs will finally believe a Big Bite is possible, and the apocalypse begins."

The Lump rocked, creaking—the cackle of a jawless man. His hand moved. "That is generally the problem with advents."

"Why did you invite me in here?" Stony asked. "What do you want from me?"

Stony watched the shriveled finger trace a pattern across the board.

"We would like you to pass on a message," the Lump said. "If you see the messiah, tell him to hide."

Stony couldn't watch the rest of Roger's extraction: One tooth was enough. He knew the risks to the community if Roger continued to act out, but he didn't have the stomach for enforcement. Despite his adventuring in greasepaint, his larking about in a mime suit, he knew he wasn't Delia or Mr. Blunt. He knew he wasn't a true LDA *soldier.* Very few of his people were. They weren't freedom fighters: They were TV watchers and Scrabble players.

He went down to the basement and back to his room. Thomas, still chained, had thrown himself off his pallet. Stony helped him back into place and then took his stats. Pulse: zero. Breaths per minute: zero. Temperature: room.

"Almost done," he told Thomas. To distract himself from the sounds coming from upstairs, he took out the two letters Blunt had given him. Letters and packages were passed from hand to hand through the network of volunteers, activists, and cell leaders, sometimes taking weeks to reach their destination. Stony was one of the lucky ones; most of the LDs didn't have anyone who knew they were still in the world, but he received a letter or two almost every week. Each of these envelopes had been opened and taped shut; no one was trying to disguise the fact that correspondence was being scanned for information that could hurt the community if it fell into the wrong hands. He assumed that his outgoing mail was also being read and possibly censored. In fact it was doubly censored. The first time he'd written a letter to Alice, Mr. Blunt told him to not mention his life in Iowa, or his miraculous childhood—and somehow Blunt had gotten that instruction to the people who wrote Stony.

Stony opened the envelope from Kwang first. Like his previous letters, it was less than a page long, and composed of 15 percent weather and 85 percent farm news. What else could Kwang talk about, if not their shared past? So, Stony learned that it had been very rainy lately, and Kwang was thinking of switching seed vendors, and in the spring he was going to try an HTF ethanol hybrid—whatever that was. Stony wondered if the LD censors suspected Kwang of encoding secret messages in his agro-jargon. But alas, there were no ciphers to be found. Kwang had become an Iowa farmer, and he wrote like one. He never talked about his feelings, how difficult or rewarding it was to wring a living from land his father had never succeeded in getting to produce, or what it was like to do all the work of an able-bodied farmer while stomping around on two prosthetic legs. The letters were stunningly boring, highly repetitious, and dry as kindling. Stony loved them.

The last line was, "Hope your doing okay. K."

He set the letter aside, then opened the remaining envelope. Four pages on lined paper, filled with Alice's dense, slashing cursive, and an eight-page photocopy of an epidemiology article. More predictions of the next outbreak. He decided to read the letter first. Alice didn't talk about her feelings, either, but she was never boring. The letter was dated three weeks ago.

Mr. Blunt knocked on the door frame. "I'm on my way out, but I wanted to see your post human."

"And there he is," Stony said. "His name is Thomas."

Blunt leaned over the man and shook his head. "Still in his swaddling clothes. And still in the thick of it, it seems." He glanced at Stony. "I noticed you skipped the second act of our little performance of *The Tooth of Crime.*"

"I didn't think I needed to see any more of that."

"You need to see everything, Stony. You're a scientist."

"I'm a dead boy in a basement with a computer."

"And a new patient." If Valerie was the mom of the house, then Mr. Blunt was the bachelor uncle, always dropping by to entertain the kids. His position in the LDA was nebulous. Sometimes Stony thought he was Delia's lieutenant, other times her superior. He was insistently vague on the nature of his responsibilities, but liked to hint darkly of his adventurous past. The joke was that Blunt had no past, at least before 1968. The fever had erased his memory, and when he dug himself from the garbage heap (if that story was true, and while Stony doubted many of Blunt's tales, he believed that one), he remade himself into the vivid outline of a man, not so much a person as a persona. His mood was too constantly light, his voice always pitched to carry beyond the footlights, his appearance as persnickety as a period costume. There were a couple of other people in the house who also seemed too consistently themselves, and Stony wondered if this was one of the side effects of the fever's amnesia. Forced to instantly invent a personality from scratch, they seized on an image of themselves, and became that. Or maybe that's what everyone did. Think of his sister: What else was *Crystal* but Chelsea's deliberate act of reinvention? Who did Kwang become when he joined the football team? And what the hell was Stony doing whenever he went out with Delia? In his head he was slipping on the red mask of the Unstoppable, or shrugging into that Jack Gore trench coat. So Mr. Blunt had adopted the dress and dialect of a 1960s British TV spy—at least he was fun to be around.

Mr. Blunt stood up, brushed some nonexistent dust from his knees. "And how are your investigations proceeding?"

"They proceed nowhere," Stony said. "Just like every other time. Stop smiling."

"I like to see you throw yourself against this particular brick wall," Mr. Blunt said. "You're bound to knock a few chips off it eventually."

"It's just that what's happening to Thomas doesn't make any sense. *We* don't make any sense. And you're the worst of all. You're, what, sixty, sixty-five percent wood?"

"I've never measured. Do I look like I've gained weight?"

"Both hands and most of your arms are artificial. Both legs up to your hips are carved wood. Your chest—"

"Stipulated. I am composed of a large amount of building material."

"Doesn't it bother you how crazy that is? You can walk around, move your hands and your fingers—with what? When I met you I thought there were wires or electrodes or something that allowed you to move them."

"Ooh, that sounds complicated."

"Complicated does not mean unexplainable. Complicated is how the world works. It's how nature works. But we're—never mind."

"Come come, my boy! It's okay to use the S-word."

"There's no such thing as the supernatural. If we're in the world, then we're part of nature—super doesn't enter into it. So there *has* to be an explanation for us."

"Nonsense," Mr. Blunt said. "Have you learned nothing from the Lump?"

"And if there's an explanation—"

"There has to be a cure. Yes, yes." They'd had this discussion many times over the years. "I only wish that you weren't so unhappy with yourself that you were pining for one."

"Don't tell Delia," Stony said. She was fanatical about LD Pride.

Mr. Blunt nodded toward the envelopes on the desk. "Any word from Crystal?"

"She's due any day now. She may have already had the baby. Alice is going to be there for the birth."

"My conditional congratulations, then! And your mother?"

"Still in 'quarantine.' Alice thinks she's still in Georgia, but they might have moved her." The Calvette Medical Prison, outside Atlanta, was her third facility since she'd been arrested two nights after the accident. She'd never been allowed to see a lawyer or been given a chance for a trial. The quarantine was a sham, of course. No disease carrier could still be alive days later, much less six years.

"I'm sorry, my boy. We live in a police state. This is what they do—burn the dead, lock up the living. At least your sisters are free."

"You don't feel very free if the government's got a gun to your head." Alice and Crystal hadn't been arrested after Stony escaped, but they'd been told not to talk to the press or they'd be prosecuted for terrorism. "Alice still can't get hired at a real research facility. Every time she applies to a lab or a university she gets turned down, no explanation. They've blacklisted her."

"Yet she is still—"

"If you're going to tell me that I could have destroyed their lives even more thoroughly than I have, I get it, Mr. Blunt."

"Ah. Well." He clapped his hands against his thighs—clack!—and then tucked his arms behind his back. "I wanted to tell you that I'll be taking Roger with me when I go, so you and Delia don't have to worry about watching him. You did a fine job today, a fine job. I wish I could have seen your performance. A mime is a terrible thing to—"

"Stop! Please don't," Stony said.

"Say no more." He started down the hallway, then stopped again. "And if I'm not here when Thomas awakes, may I be the first to say, mazel tov."

There was a small room at the top of Blue house, just under the eaves. It was less than ten feet long and was empty except for a few storage boxes, and a metal folding chair set up in front of the single narrow window. The window was covered by a blanket. No one from the houses went up there much because of the low roof and the lack of electrical outlets. A room without TV, after all, was no room at all.

Stony sat down on the chair, and after a moment, pushed the edge of the blanket a few inches to the side. They lived in a neighborhood of tiny boxes built in the 1940s for returning GIs, now populated by their white widows and the mostly nonwhite people who moved in when the widows died: legal and illegal immigrants, claiming or denying citizenship from every country in the Americas and a few Asian nations as well.

Next door, the front porch light was on, but all the windows of the house were dark, of course. It was 3:30 in the morning. In two hours Sherry would be getting up, to take the 6:40 bus to the restaurant where she worked. He didn't know the name of the restaurant. He didn't know anything about her, really. She'd moved in with her family almost two years ago. She was in her early twenties, and had a preschool-age son that she left with her mother while she worked. She spent too much money at convenience stores rather than going to a real grocery store, and she never seemed to have vegetables in her plastic bags. She liked orange soda. When she'd had a particularly tough week she'd go to the store and bring back expensive ice cream. Sometimes she went out with girlfriends, but as far as he could tell, she did not date. In the summers she filled up a wading pool for her son, and she'd sit in it with him. He'd never heard her voice.

"You know that's creepy, right?" Delia. He closed the shutters, and the room was fully dark.

"What?"

"Your girlfriend." The floorboards complained as she crossed the floor to him. "It's not healthy to lust over a breather, Stony."

"I'm not lusting, I'm just—"

Delia laughed. "I'm kidding, farm boy. I've never known a stiff who could get a stiffy." She paused, and he was glad he couldn't see her face in the dark. "You don't, do you?"

He thought of Kwang, trying to teach him to masturbate. "You sound like my sisters," he said. "They were always trying to figure out my sex life. They wanted to get me laid."

"Someone should have told them that necrophilia's illegal." She leaned over him and lifted the blanket up over the curtain rod. Pale light washed her face. This was her good side, almost unmarked.

"I watch them, too," she said. "Sometimes." She scanned the street, alert, as always, for police and Diggers. "That black girl next door—she's pretty."

"I guess."

She chuckled. *"I guess."* She took a pack of menthol lights from her jacket pocket, offered one to Stony. He shook his head, and she said, "Come on, I know you sneak smokes up here."

"Do I have no secrets?"

"I can't figure out why you're hiding them. We all smoke, Stony. We're already dead, we'd be crazy not to."

"My mom would kill me if she found out," he said, and took the cigarette from her. She lit it for him with her plastic lighter, then squatted with her back to the window.

A while later she said, "You still love them, don't you, Stony?"

"Who?"

"All of them. The breathers. You want to be one of them again."

"I was never one of them," he said.

"You may know that now," she said. "But I bet it didn't feel that way when you were growing up with them." He didn't say anything. She said, "We were worried about you that first year in the house. You were pretty depressed. Blunt put your odds at fifty-fifty."

"Fifty-fifty of what? Killing myself?"

"You've been here long enough now to see it. Some people can't take the constant hiding. They don't see any end in sight, so pretty soon they start making one. They start checking out. Doing crazy things."

"Roger's not your fault," he said.

"Yeah? Whose fault is it?"

He'd known her for six years now. He'd watched her hold the house together, and knew that other houses were depending on her. But even though he talked with her almost every day, even though they'd shared thousands of hours in the same house, he still didn't know if she considered him a friend. She held something in reserve, as if preparing to burn down the house at a moment's notice—or burn herself to save them.

"They're going to hold the congress," she said. "Sixty, seventy delegates, from all over the country."

"Wow."

"And I need you to go with me."

"Really?"

"Settle down. We could all die if we don't do this right."

"Right. But I thought it was just cell leaders."

"And delegates," she said. "You're now a delegate."

"Wait, when is this happening?"

"You have somewhere to be?"

"We've talked about this. You know Crystal is pregnant—she may have already had the baby."

"We can't get you to southern Utah, Stony. It's impossible."

"I need to be there. I haven't seen any of them since I left."

"You want to risk one of the volunteer's lives to drive you there?"

"No, but—"

"We all want to be somewhere else, Stony. But I'm sorry. The congress is risky enough. We just can't afford casual trips for weddings and bar mitzvahs."

"This is not *casual*, this is important."

"Important to you, Stony. But the community's needs come first. Plus, the Lump suggested you go."

"What? Why?"

"Consider it part of your education. There are people you need to meet—people who can affect your future."

"You're talking about the benefactor!"

She took a suspiciously long drag on her cigarette before answering. "There's no such thing," she said, and exhaled a stream of smoke. "That's just house gossip."

Gossip and cigarettes were the only currencies available in the LD world, and trading was heavy. Rumors of a millionaire backer for the underground circulated constantly. The candidates fell into three broad categories, the most popular of which was the Celebrity with a Heart of Gold, the talk show host/sitcom star/supermodel whose undead sibling cried out for justice from the Hollywood basement. Less popular, but more doctrinally pure, was the benefactor as Hometown Boy, the billionaire LD who'd died but somehow managed to hold on to his money, unliving proof that LDs didn't need breathers to bail them out, no siree—the corpses were doing it for themselves.

And then there were the rumors of the Evil Masterminds. No one would *really* help the living dead, the thinking went; the money *had* to be coming from some political group or foreign power or multinational corporation bent on using the dead for its own ends. It could even be the U.S. government itself, its cash flowing into the community like CIA-purchased heroin, lulling them into dependency so that they could be rounded up in one fell swoop.

Stony thought *someone* had to be bankrolling them. He wasn't seeing any of the money here in the house, but there had to be a reason the LDA had lasted twenty years in the wild.

Delia stood up, then toed her cigarette into the floorboards. "And if there *was* a benefactor? He wouldn't be there. Way too risky."

* * *

In the morning, Stony led Thomas up the stairs, guiding him with an arm around his shoulders. Stony had cleaned him as best he could, replacing his sweat-drenched shirt and soiled pants with a UCSD sweatshirt and a pair of nylon track pants.

Stony called out, "Everyone? Could you come out here?"

Delia and Elizabeth came out of the kitchen. Valerie and the other residents drifted in from their rooms.

Thomas stared at each of them as they appeared, his mouth open. He was shaky and weak, and had no memory of how he'd come to be here, no memory of his own name. Perhaps some of that would come back in time.

"Everyone, I want you to welcome Thomas."

Teddy, an LD with a golden, hard-shell toupee that might have been stolen from a Sears mannequin, stepped forward. "Happy birthday," he said, and hugged the man. Thomas accepted this awkwardly. The other residents embraced him in turn. Even Valerie welcomed him, though she seemed sorry to have to do so.

Elizabeth, the only living person in the room, wiped tears from her cheeks. "I have to go," she said. She touched Thomas on the arm, then quickly left the house. The man looked frightened.

Delia stepped up and took his hand. "Don't worry, she'll be fine." She pulled him close. "Welcome to our family, Thomas."

CHAPTER NINE

1988
Los Angeles, California

They watched from the trees as Aaron the Beard walked to the back of the semitrailer, fiddled with the lock, and finally pulled open one of the doors. A cloud of cool mist puffed into the dry air and evaporated.

"You've got to be kidding," Stony said.

"Is there a problem?" Delia asked.

"Yes. It's a freezer truck. Inside it's going to be, what's the word? *Cold.*"

"That's right, just a word," she said. "A little cold won't hurt you."

"Then why did we bring blankets?"

"So we don't stick to the floors."

Delia and Stony walked briskly across the parking lot, carrying their small travel bags and blanket rolls. Aaron was turned away from them, scanning the empty parking lot as they scrambled up into the back of the trailer. The interior was stacked to the ceiling with white cardboard boxes, all stamped with the familiar line drawing of Commander Calhoun's face. Evidently they were traveling with fish sticks—

strike that, *fishstix*. Delia edged into a narrow gap between two walls of boxes and inched sideways toward the front of the trailer.

Aaron came up to close the door, and Stony said, "When did you learn to drive a truck?"

"Just try to keep it down in there," he said, and slammed the door. The compartment went dark, but not completely; after a moment he realized that a light from the other side of the boxes was playing off the aluminum ceiling. Voices he didn't recognize greeted Delia happily. Stony squeezed into the gap Delia had taken, and soon emerged into a cleared space at the front of the trailer, just under the rumbling air conditioner. Two white men reclined on furniture made from arrangements of white boxes and luggage. A big flashlight was propped up and aimed at the ceiling.

Delia said, "Stony, meet Stitch and Stitch."

Stony laughed. "I thought you two would be joined at the hip." The Stitch Brothers were two of his favorite characters from the Deadtown Detective books.

"Ah, a connoisseur of fine literature," the first Stitch said. The truck lurched into motion and the air conditioner roared louder, forcing him to raise his voice. "A good sign."

Stony sat on a box, hunched against the cold. Stitch and Stitch, he learned, ran a parish in New Mexico, and had been the first on Aaron's "bus." They'd be picking up more people on the way to the congress. The LDA was using only the most loyal and trusted humans in the organization to do the driving.

Stony still had no idea where they were going. Mr. Blunt had disappeared a week earlier "to make preparations," but they hadn't trusted Stony with the information. Well, fine. He wasn't about to ask now.

As the frost accumulated on their skin and clothes, the

Stitch Brothers told appalling and hilarious stories about narrow and failed escapes, about LDs who had outfoxed the Diggers or had been captured by them, about violent deaths and accidental maimings, stories with lines like, "So now the rebar's sticking all the way through him." Stony laughed along with them. After six years in the community he'd adopted their sense of humor. The only LD comedy was black comedy.

"Stony, tell us about old Roger," one of the men said.

"And stop acting like a breather," Delia said.

"What do you mean?" Stony asked.

"Are you really cold? Or do you just think you're supposed to be cold?"

He straightened up. "Okay, fine." He told them the story of Roger and the mailman, and they all laughed some more, but Stony felt bad making fun of the old LD. Yes, a number of their people were a bit slow, addled by the fever, or brain-damaged by death, but that wasn't their fault.

"Well at least you got a new recruit for the house," one of the Stitches said, and the other said, "What *do* you think about recruiting?"

"What, me?" Stony glanced at Delia, but she was offering no clues. "I don't think we ought to go out biting people, if that's what you mean."

"Why not?" one of them said. He said it lightly, as if only making conversation. "If we don't replenish our numbers, we'll die out."

"Or people *think* we're dying out, and they get desperate," the other said.

"Clearing the way for whackos like Zip," said the other.

Delia and Mr. Blunt had told him all about Billy Zip. He was the prime advocate of the Big Bite. "You make some good points," Stony said.

The men laughed, and one of them said, "So you *would* bite humans, to keep us going?"

"No. I mean—"

"What he *means*," Delia said, "is that he doesn't know what he means. He's here to learn."

In other words, Stony thought, shut up and listen.

Nearly twenty-four hours after leaving the parking lot in L.A., the truck slowed, then stopped and backed up. Someone cheered, though not loud enough to be heard from outside the walls of the trailer. The compartment was standing room only, packed with thirteen delegates that they'd picked up along the way, and as the truck began to back down the ramp and the floor tilted beneath their feet, the LDs swayed and bumped each other like slabs on meat hooks. Despite the cold, a festival mood had held during the hours of travel, but Stony was glad to be getting off. Much longer, he thought, they'd all have frozen solid, and how embarrassing would that be? A carton of LDs dumped clattering into the second living dead congress like giant gray fishstix.

They listened as Aaron—or someone—detached the trailer and lowered the jacks. The tractor rumbled away. Delia edged her way to the trailer doors and found them unlocked. "I guess we're here," she said.

The trailer had been backed up to an internal loading dock. They stepped out into a cavernous warehouse, a massive open space with a ceiling two stories above them. Up ahead, LDs wearing name tags were checking off the names of the new arrivals, and a few were opening luggage. Beyond them, the floor of the warehouse looked like an indoor camp-ground: Over two dozen RVs were parked near the sur-rounding walls, noses pointed inward toward a central area set up like a park, complete with Astroturf carpeting, potted trees, benches and picnic tables, and a large central tent.

Stony stopped short. There, in the park, were sixty or seventy figures, all living dead. More seemed to be inside the tent, which made for how many: A hundred? Two? More LDs than he'd ever seen.

A voice at Stony's side said, "The security check is standard, my boy."

"Mr. Blunt!" The man had appeared out of nowhere. He could move silently for a giant marionette. "This is—I mean . . ." Stony didn't know how to explain it. He felt excited, yet *afraid*. He nodded toward the park. "*All* those people LDs, right?"

"Every one of them. No breathers allowed, my boy—they're all outside with the trucks." Mr. Blunt frowned. "Are you all right?"

The sight of so many of his people paralyzed him. For most of his life, he'd thought that he was alone. And then he'd met Delia and Mr. Blunt, and he'd gotten to know the LDs at the safe house and perhaps a dozen others. He'd known intellectually that there were many more of them out in the world. But *this,* this blatant display, flew in the face of everything he felt about the world.

We could be a *real* army, he thought. We could be a nation.

One member of the security team marked off his name, another unzipped his bag and ran a hand through his clothing, and another asked him questions: Was he carrying any weapons? Was he carrying any radio or communication device? Had he talked to anyone about the location of the congress?

"I don't even know where we are," he said.

"Then welcome to the congress."

The melting frost was running off him like sweat. He removed his damp jacket and followed Mr. Blunt and Delia into the park. The Stitch Brothers and the rest of his mates from the trailer had already scattered.

Delia seemed to know everyone, at least by name; he gathered that this was the first time that most of the LDA had met in person. He shook hands with a dozen people as they made their way slowly to the central tent, as Mr. Blunt and Delia made introductions. From the air temperature—much warmer than in the freezer truck, but much colder than Los Angeles—he guessed that they'd traveled north. In twenty-four hours they could have driven halfway across the country.

"Who's this pretty boy, Delia?" a man said. He was a short, stocky white man who wore a porkpie hat pulled low on one side of his head. The skull on that side was alarmingly concave, the gap large enough to cradle a bowling ball. The hat, rather than disguising the absence, accentuated it.

"Stony, this is Billy Zip."

Ah, Stony thought. The Big Biter.

"You must be the boy from Iowa," Billy said. "I heard about Delia's *daring* rescue several years ago." He held out a gloved hand whose fingers were too short; each seemed to have been broken off at the second knuckle. It felt like shaking a dog's paw.

"She saved my life," Stony said.

"Then you should put it to good use," he said. He nodded to Mr. Blunt—somewhat warily, Stony thought. "Keeping 'em sharp, Blunt?" He moved off, and a small group of people followed him.

"What an asshole," Delia said.

"I liked his hat," Stony said.

"As in heads," Mr. Blunt said, "not all hats are created

equal." A woman on the security team caught Blunt's eye, and he said, "Much to do. Enjoy yourselves, my dears."

Delia said, "There are some people you need to meet—one guy in particular." They dropped off their bags at their assigned quarters, a silver Airstream trailer near the middle of the warehouse, then weaved their way back to the main tent. Round plastic tables and chairs were set up as if for a reception, and there were LDs at half of them, and stacks of paper on all of them. Clouds of cigarette smoke formed an atmospheric layer under the tent roof. Once again he felt that thrill of seeing so many of his people in one place, but already he was relaxing into it, embracing it. Yes, they were horrors. Black tongues and yellow teeth, gray skin and exposed bones, gaping, never-healing wounds, and everything that *wasn't* there: the missing hands and feet and eyeballs. But they were his people. What did he have to fear from his own?

At the far end of the tent was a raised stage with a podium and microphones, where a man whose left jacket sleeve was pinned at the elbow read announcements from a clipboard. The secretary of the congress, Delia told Stony. Then she commanded him to sit tight, and waded into the center of the tent, moving from table to table, shaking hands and exchanging hugs. Stony picked up a packet from a pile of mimeographed blue and white sheets. The blue sheets contained a schedule for the next three days; the white sheets seemed to be agenda items and proposals.

Resolution: That the terms "zombie," "living dead," "walking dead," and "undead," being not only inaccurate but offensive to our people and prejudicial to the attitudes of noninfected humans, shall be banned from all official documents as well as discouraged from casual use, in favor of the term "Differently Living."

Stony laughed, then looked up quickly, hoping nobody was paying attention to him. No one had noticed. He sat, and began to flip through the pages. He was starved for information. He'd spent years with Delia, most of it in the same dozen, dim rooms, but she'd been withholding information from him—for his own good, and for the good of the community, she told him—and he had so many questions. How many of his people were still at large? What kept the organization functioning? Did they have spies in the government? How many of their people had been captured?

On stage, the one-armed secretary announced that 162 delegates, from fourteen states and one Canadian province, had made it to the congress. A cheer went up. Stony thought, Canada? We're in Canada?

"There are others we believe to be still on the road," the secretary said. "Our thoughts and prayers are for their safety." This sobered the crowd. After a moment of silence the secretary said, "On to the first order of business. That would be . . ." He looked down at his papers. "Rose from the San Francisco parish."

Rose, the Lumpist he'd met years ago, walked to the podium, but she was so tiny that she had to step out in front of it and hold the microphone. "I'm Rose," she said. "And the Lump says . . ." She lifted one arm and waved slowly.

Laughter erupted. Stony turned and saw scores of arms in the air, waving back.

"I'll relay your greetings back to him," she said. She talked about the number of residents her parish was sheltering, and the generosity of the volunteers. "I want to tell you that things are changing," she said. "Attitudes are shifting. I've met people who are not cowed by the government's fearmongering. They are not afraid. They're committed to helping us. They realize that they must stand by us, because any one of them could be the next outcast, the next target, the next victim."

The crowd liked the sound of that. Rose finished her talk and left the stage to applause, which Stony supposed was more for the Lump than Rose herself. The next speaker struck a more pessimistic note. Bonnie, a woman sporting a white Cleopatra-style wig, made a plea to recruit volunteers from among the living. The number of supporters, she said, was dropping rapidly. Most of the original volunteers had been relatives and friends of the victims in the '68 outbreak, and now twenty years of life in the underground had taken its toll. Some volunteers, like the Scanlon Sisters, had been arrested; some had dropped out when their relatives had been captured; others quit because of the stress; others had simply died. The LDs needed to identify breathers who might be sympathetic to the cause, and reach out to them in a way that wouldn't get both parties killed or captured.

Not for the first time he wondered how Crystal had managed to win the trust of the LDA. Delia had told him that his sister had met Aaron first—at a party? a concert?—but it was a mystery how each had sussed out where the other stood in regard to the walking dead. Crystal was beautiful and gregarious, a charmer, but wouldn't that have made them suspicious? He couldn't imagine all the delicate steps in that negotiation, the dance of suggestion and hint. *How 'bout those dead people, huh?* Everyone knew that the FBI was on the lookout for necro-symps, and that fear of a second outbreak ran deep. Every breather was a potential Judas. The human drivers who'd brought them here were supposedly the most trusted volunteers. But what if the government got to them somehow? Suppose Aaron's brother wasn't dead, but captive in Deadtown. How hard would it be to pressure Aaron into turning over LDA secrets?

Other parish officers stepped up to make their reports. They all began with statistics—the count of houses and volunteers, the number of new members, the larger number of residents who'd fallen to the police or committed suicide—but none of them could stick to the dry facts; they were there to tell stories. A woman from Maryland talked about how the breather who'd owned one of their houses had died at the hospital, and the owner's sons had shown up unexpectedly, and the four LD residents had been forced to hide in a tiny attic space above the garage for two weeks until another parish could rescue them. The story was told lightly, and drew sympathetic laughter, but the event had clearly been terrifying for the four involved. A parish leader from Columbus, Ohio, spoke about a group suicide: All three members of a house decided together that they couldn't go on, and had walked to a parking lot and doused themselves with gasoline. Another representative told how his safe house had been discovered by a neighbor, and how their breather volunteer had managed to talk the neighbor into meeting the LDs, eventually recruiting him.

The stories rolled on, and gradually Stony realized there was something wrong with the census numbers. Delia had told him that there were eight to ten thousand LDs in hiding across the country. But he'd been keeping a running total in his head, and so far, with many states reporting, the counts of LDs were in the hundreds, not the thousands. Was there a secret, massive community of his people somewhere?

Delia said, "What's the matter, Stony? You look like you're in shock."

"No, I'm—fine. Where have you been?" She'd been gone for over an hour. Beside her was a man wearing a red-orange Afro wig and large aviator sunglasses. His face was impassive, and Stony couldn't tell if he was angry or merely bored. Delia said, "This is the kid I was telling you about. Stony, this is F.M."

"Oh, hi," Stony said, and they shook hands. "Is that F.M. as in—"

"Fucking Monster," he said without expression.

Delia laughed, and something in the adjustment of F.M.'s lips suggested he was yanking Stony's chain. Stony said, "Pleased to meet you, Mr. Monster."

Delia said, "F.M.'s the coordinator of Oswog. I told him you were a scientist."

"What? No, not really—"

"Okay then," Delia said. "I'm going to leave you boys to it."

Stony thought, leave to what? He didn't even know what Oswog—Ozwog? OSWOG?—was.

"This way," F.M. said, and led him toward the edge of the tent. "Cigarette?" It was a Kool. All the LDs smoked either menthols or, worse, clove cigarettes.

"I really shouldn't. I'm watching my health."

F.M. halted, extended the pack to Stony, and they lit up together. "Thanks," Stony said.

"Thank God for *smokes,*" F.M. said. "We can't drink, least not enough to get a buzz on. Yeah we can eat and maybe get a little taste in our mouths, but then what? Just fills you up and doesn't do a damn thing for you, and then you got to move that shit *out.* Pain in the ass."

"Literally," Stony said. "I was wondering, this OSWOG—"

"But smoke, that gives you something to move in and out of your lungs, a little warmth, a little flavor. We all need a way to pass the time. Hell do we need it. Sitting around arguing about what to call ourselves. Did you see that proposal?"

"Right, 'differently living'—"

"You know what word I use?" He was interrupted from feedback from the speakers. *"Test, test. Sibilance. Sibilance."* On stage, LDs milled about carrying guitars and banjos.

"I use the word *human,*" the man said. "Forget dead, forget *un*-anything. We're just as alive as anybody else. Do we not move? Do we not think?"

"Yes!" Stony said. He'd been thinking along these lines. "And we reproduce, too."

"The holy bite," the man said, nodding. "Not exactly screwing, but it works."

"The problem is, how do we reproduce in a safe way, without violating the rights of others?"

"That's easy," F.M. said. "Make it a religion."

"What?"

"Start a church, and make it a sacrament. People will line the fuck up."

"Hi ho!" said a voice from the speakers. An LD with a gray beard and a wild head of hair had stepped up to the mike. He held what looked like a sawed-off banjo. "We're the Stump Thumper Jug Band, and we'd like to do a few tunes for you. This one's called 'Resurrection Breakdown.'"

F.M. groaned. "Jesus Christ, they're trying to kill us. Come on, Stony."

He marched off, and Stony struggled to keep up. "Tell me what you meant by sacrament," Stony said.

"The *host.* Instead of taking a bite out of Jesus, he takes a bite out of you. Everlasting life. Me, I had diabetes before I got bit, and my blood pressure—" The Stump Thumpers cranked up into a high whine, and F.M. had to raise his voice. "My blood pressure was through the *roof.* If it wasn't for getting turned, I'd be dead right now. Deader."

They passed beyond the banjo's kill radius, and were

crossing the warehouse floor toward a line of RVs. Stony said, "So, this OSWOG you're the coordinator for—"

"It's not that formal, anybody could run it, and anybody can join. Delia said you studied a convert as he was going through the change. You should write that up, present it to the group."

"But I didn't find anything out."

"Then you'll fit right in," F.M. said. "We cover a lot of issues. The fever, amnesia and memory recovery, outbreak epidemiology. But mostly we're after the big question, Stony. The origins of undeadness—what the fuck we are, and where the hell we come from. Somebody's got to work on this shit, right? Certainly not *those* damned LDs." He nodded toward a group of a dozen graveborn sitting on the ground, all listening to a man preach to them. Oh, Stony thought, the *Damned*— Valerie's fellow-believers. What could the sermon be about, then? If all LDs were doomed, then self-improvement was a waste, and Evangelism was right out.

F.M. led him to a circle of LDs sitting in camp chairs in front of an RV. The three men and two women were in various states of frozen decay. One of them, a man with a yarmulke resting on his bone skull, was reading from a paper when F.M. interrupted him.

"Everyone, this is Stony. Stony, meet the Ontological Studies Working Group."

Oh, Stony thought. OSWoG.

"In summation," said Chuck, the bony Jewish man, an hour and a half after Stony had joined the group, "the government's original claim that the outbreak was caused by radioactivity from an exploded space probe has no support in the scientific literature, and in fact can be traced to a deliberate attempt by government-paid scientists to *obscure* the cause of the outbreak; by assigning blame to an 'accident,' the government hoped to mask the true cause, which we now know, from the epidemiological data, must have originated from either (a) a security breach within the government's biological weapons program, or more likely, (b) a deliberate test of a bioweapon that—Yes, mister . . . ?"

"Stony."

"You don't have to raise your hand, young man," Chuck said.

"Right. Sorry." He lowered his arm. The other members of OSWoG regarded him with varying levels of interest, humor, and annoyance, and F.M.'s expression behind his aviator glasses was unreadable. "You're saying that the outbreak is due to some virus?"

"Or bacteria, yes. The infection, passed through the bite, attacks the victim's system—"

"But it doesn't."

Chuck blinked at him. "Just because we have not yet identified the virus, does not mean that we cannot infer its existence."

"But what does it live on?"

"Pardon?"

"We're dead. Our cells are dead. There's no material for viruses to feed on. They have nowhere to replicate." He looked to the other members of the circle, but they didn't seem inclined to support a new guy. "Bacteria doesn't even grow on our skin—I've tried it. We don't even decay."

Chuck said, "All the more reason to believe that this is an *experimental* bioweapon, manufactured by the government, operating through alternate mechanisms that we haven't yet—"

"What alternate mechanism would that be?" Stony asked. He wasn't being sarcastic—okay, he was being a little sarcastic—but he was also curious. He'd been reading some things about artificial life, so maybe they were thinking of a Von Neumann–style copier and constructor. He could imagine an inorganic virus that operated through mechanisms similar to crystal growth.

One of the women in the group spoke up. "As a matter of fact, Reichenbach's odic force will explain—"

Chuck made a guttural noise of disgust, and Stony thought, Wow, I've just witnessed my first *harrumph*. "Vitalism?" Chuck said. "Again, Wilma? Why don't you just save us time and call it magic?"

The others groaned; this was an old argument, evidently. Stony grinned. "Maybe it's not so magical," Stony said. "Have you guys ever heard of cellular automata?"

There was no night at the congress; the lights of the warehouse stayed as undimmed as a Las Vegas casino, and Stony lost track of the time. He occasionally looked around and caught glimpses of the festival bubbling around them, with delegates throwing themselves into rugby matches (ugly on cement), painting impromptu murals, singing LD folk songs, compensating for their dulled sense of touch with rough sports and high input for the remaining senses. He assumed that somewhere in the main tent the high-ranking members were debating the destiny of the community. As for Stony and the OSWoGs, they'd worked out a thorough and completely unconvincing mechanism by which a clockwork virus could replicate in dead bodies, dead bodies could move, and the dead could think via solid-state information transfer. It was the most fun Stony had had in years. Though he felt a bit guilty not telling them about his own background. What would it do to their theories and hypotheses if they knew an LD could grow from a baby?

The talk turned to politics. Stony knew before he left L.A. that the LDA was at a crisis point—that was the whole reason for the congress—but he hadn't grasped the severity until one of the OSWoGs casually mentioned the census number: 1,700 "give or take."

Stony must have looked shocked, because F.M. said, "What's the matter?"

Stony said, "I knew there was something up with the numbers, but . . . Delia told me there were eight to ten thousand LDs in hiding across the country."

"Oh, Stony, no, I'm sorry. Maybe five, ten years ago, but every day there are less of us."

Stony said, "I didn't know the Diggers had gotten so many."

"They're not *that* good," Chuck said. "We're doing it to ourselves. Our people are suiciding. They're burning themselves, or deliberately turning themselves in. They're giving up, and the ones who are left are getting desperate. The Big Biters, they want to end the world now—"

"Fucking terrorists," F.M. said.

"—and the Perpetualists think they can save the world for LDs one bite at a time and somehow not kill us all, and the Abstainers want to wither away—"

"And the Lumpists? What do they want?"

Chuck looked at Wilma. Stony then noticed that she was wearing a necklace like Rose's, a nobbly hunk of metal. Lumpist, Lump. "The Lumpists are just trying to keep hope alive," she said.

Chuck said, "I thought you were just waiting for the Zombie Jesus to save us."

Wilma frowned disapprovingly at his use of the Z-word. "We're waiting for a leader, a *bridge*. Someone to bring the living dead and the deadly living to some kind of . . . rapprochement."

It was the first time he'd heard anyone use that word out loud. He had no idea it sounded so French; in his head it had always rhymed with *encroachment*.

"Oppressed people are always pining for a savior," Chuck said. "How long can you keep them waiting?"

"Two thousand years," F.M. said. "And counting."

"That's the purpose of a messiah," Stony said. The words of the Lump had stuck with him. "You have to keep our people waiting, because what's the alternative—Armageddon? The Big Bite?"

An air horn sounded, and the OSWoGs stood up. A late-arriving vehicle pulled into the warehouse, lights flashing and horn honking. The gleaming red-white-and-blue coach bus descended the ramp to the floor of congress, where they lost sight of it. Stony and the group walked a short distance, where they saw the bus roll to a stop at the center of the warehouse floor, scattering the Ultimate Frisbee teams.

The OSWoGs looked at the bus and one another, and Stony was sure they had no idea who it was, either. Then Stony saw Delia running toward the bus from the main tent, Mr. Blunt following briskly behind her. Even from this distance he could tell that Delia was furious.

Stony said, "I'll be back in a minute, guys." He jogged off toward the bus. Delia reached it well before him and began knocking at the vehicle's door. A crowd began to gather. Stony moved up to her and asked, "What's going on?"

"Not now, Stony," she said, and banged on the door again. Stony couldn't see through the tinted glass to the driver or the cabin. Porthole windows, also tinted, punctuated the side. The paint job was metallic flake, the hubcaps so shiny they seemed to be constantly spinning. A flashy ride, but not full-on rock star. More Kenny Rogers on an up year.

Mr. Blunt pushed his way to the front. Several tough-looking LDs—a couple of whom Stony recognized as guards who'd checked him on the way into the congress—came with him, forming a picket. "Please!" Mr. Blunt said to the crowd. Half the congress was converging on the vehicle. "Everyone back." He placed himself beside Delia and said in a low voice, "I thought you spoke to him."

"I *told* him not to do this," she said. "He's risking every-thing."

The door swung open. A figure in a gold-trimmed navy uniform and white skipper's hat stood on the bottom step, and Stony's first thought was that it was Commander Cal-houn, straight from the front of one of the Commander Cal-houn FishStix boxes he'd stared at for twenty-four hours on the way up here.

Stony's second thought was, My God, it really *is* Com-mander Calhoun.

His tanned face was wrinkle-free and disturbingly shiny, as if he'd been sealed under plastic wrap. His teeth were bril-liant white. He didn't look like the average LD, but he defi-nitely wasn't a living person. The Commander was one of them. "Ahoy there!" he shouted, and the crowd roared back.

He held up a hand, and when the applause and talk had died down he said, "I can't wait to meet each and every one of you. With the secretary's permission, I would like to immedi-ately address the congress and announce—" He looked down. Delia had grabbed his forearm, and for the briefest moment his smile dimmed. Delia said something to him, and Calhoun addressed the crowd again. "In one hour!" he said. "The main tent in one hour, and I promise you, you do *not* want to miss this news."

Calhoun turned and stepped up into the bus, and Delia hopped up after him. The door closed, to more applause. The members of the congress didn't disperse. It was as if they were waiting for him to pop out for another performance, like an automaton in a cuckoo clock.

"Nothing to see here, people," Mr. Blunt said.

Stony leaned in to the man. "Let me get this straight—the secret benefactor of the LDA is Commander Calhoun?"

"Ronald McDonald was unavailable."

CHAPTER TEN

1988
Somewhere in North America

Can a man without a brain have his mind blown? Stony's skull was nothing but a can of dead meat, yet he felt as if his head were about to burst: Commander Calhoun, LD bluegrass, Zombie Jesus . . . Too much, too much.

He decided not to return to the OSWoG circle, or go to the main tent to get a good seat, as so many were doing. He thought about ducking into the film tent, where a handful of people were watching a tape of Bela Lugosi in *White Zombie,* but even those few people seemed like a crowd. He needed time by himself. He'd loved talking with F.M. and his gang, and the sheer number of strange LDs had given him a jolt, but the congress was overwhelming him. He'd grown up with half a dozen people, and lived six years in the safe house with another small group. He was not built for constant interaction. He wished he could dig. A few hours of manual labor would clear his head. Instead he walked toward the cluster of trailers and RVs, figuring he'd eventually remember which one he and Delia had put their bags in.

His mind kept circling back to the census number.

Seventeen hundred. Still large enough to scare a breather—any one of those hundreds could start an outbreak—but my God it felt tiny to him. Two thousand was a midsize high school. The Diggers could wipe them out like a Vietnamese village. Was it any wonder they wanted to hold the congress immediately? This was last call before extinction.

He walked between two silver trailers, neither of which looked quite right, and turned left in the face of a big Winnebago grille. Now he was in among a pod of RVs, boxy things like shipping containers on wheels, nothing like the sleek coach Commander Calhoun had ridden in on. Stony turned a corner and saw a group of six or seven people up ahead, engaged in some kind of argument. He recognized Billy Zip by his hat, and the man he was talking to by his missing arm; it was the secretary of the congress.

Why was the secretary giving the king of the Big Biters the time of day? The biters, as F.M. pointed out, were fucking terrorists.

Stony ducked between the next pair of RVs, then went left again. In a hundred yards he was almost behind the group, with only one vehicle separating them. He could hear Zip talking, words bouncing off the cement, but couldn't make out his words. Stony could keep edging around to the back of the RV, or he could crawl under the thing. It would be like spying on his sisters.

Suddenly hands grabbed him from behind, and a harsh voice said, "What the fuck are you doing?"

Stony looked over his shoulder. The man was huge, with green-tinged skin, as if some fungus had gotten to him in the grave. Tracks of staples held the quadrants of his face together. Behind him, a group of six or seven people were walking toward them.

Stony said, "I don't know what you're—"

The big man yanked Stony backward, spun him, then slammed him face-first against the side of the other RV. "Are you messing with our vehicle?"

"What? No!"

The group came around the end of the RV, Billy Zip smiling, the secretary of the congress looking nervous. "If you're trying to spy on us," Zip said, "you're doing a lousy job."

"Who is he?" the secretary asked.

"Delia and Blunt's boy, a convert from Iowa," Zip said.

The big man said, "He's with Blunt?"

"Exactly," Zip said. "Check under the RV for bombs. Look for anything with a wire on it." One of the group, a relatively fresh-looking corpse with a wig of black hair that made him look like Moe from the Stooges, dropped to the cement and crawled under the vehicle.

"You can't be serious," Stony said. The big man lifted him a few inches and banged him against the metal. "Hey!"

Zip said, "What are you doing here, Stony?"

Stony looked past him to the secretary. "What are *you* doing here? Are you actually talking to these guys?"

The secretary blinked. "I talk to all the delegates."

"Then could you tell Bluto here to put me down?"

The secretary said to Zip, "We can take this up later. We've already discussed—"

"No, we'll talk now, Stanley. Tevvy, put the boy down."

The big man, Tevvy, released him and backed up a step. Stony edged sideways so he could see around him. "I knew the Big Biters were crazy, but—"

"Watch it, kid," Zip said. "I'll forgive that because you're new."

But Stony was pissed now. "Your plan is insane. Tell me what happens after the Big Bite, after all the living are dead or transformed. Because that's it. That's the end of the human race."

The secretary put up his hands. "I'm leaving."

"Wait, Stanley. This is exactly the kind of person we need to educate." Zip turned to Stony. "*We* are the human race, kid. You've got to stop feeling like a second-class citizen. The Bite isn't something to be afraid of. Hell, they'll thank us. Famine in Africa? Over. Disease, old age? Done. We never die."

"No, we wear out. We can last decades, maybe a hundred years, and what then? In a century the planet is a graveyard."

"Maybe, but that's a *hundred years*," Billy said. "How many years do you think we have before they hunt us all down? How many *months*? You don't think we'd be better off with just us? We'll have the entire planet working on the problem of how to save us. We'll get the smartest people in the world—"

"Whoever's left after the outbreak."

Billy lifted a gloved hand and pointed with an index finger that seemed a couple of inches too short. He seemed to be enjoying the argument. "That's a lot of smart people! People who won't spend all their time wondering where their next meal comes from, or how they're going to keep a roof over their heads, or worrying about the bomb. You don't think we can figure out how to save ourselves in all that time? You've got to show a little faith in your own people, brother."

The man who'd climbed under the Winnebago reappeared. "All clear, Billy."

"Go on inside, Stanley," Zip said. "I'll be right in."

The secretary seemed reluctant, but then he stepped up into the RV. When the door shut, Zip said to Stony, "Give Delia a message for me. Tell her we're bringing this to a vote. And fuck the Commander."

"I don't understand," Stony said.

Tevvy grabbed Stony by the arm. "Time to go. Your hit man's not here to save you."

"It's mass murder," Stony said, raising his voice. Maybe there were other LDs in the RVs, listening. "Once you start you won't be able to stop it. Every living person on the planet will be dead or converted in four days."

Billy leaned in close. "Hey, is that what's bothering you? That we'll kill all the breathers?" The men behind him laughed. Billy said, "Don't worry, kid, we're not going to kill them all. That would be crazy—we gotta keep our numbers up. But you're from Iowa, right? You know all about livestock."

Stony marched back to Calhoun's bus—he *would not* run while Zip might be looking at him—but the only people there were a pair of Blunt's security guards. Everyone had gone to the main tent. At the tent, it seemed as if every delegate was trying to climb inside, and once inside, light up. The space was full, and several people were folding up the round tables to make room. Stony heard F.M.'s deep voice, laughing, and spotted the top of his big orange Afro. Everyone seemed energized, a machine fueled by a thousand cigarettes. Finally he spotted Mr. Blunt along the back wall of the tent. Beside him was a security guard speaking into a serious-looking walkie-talkie.

"I have to talk to you," Stony said.

Blunt held a chunk of white wood in one hand and a knife in the other, whittling with great speed. Wasn't he afraid of carving his own fingers? "You look upset," he said.

"The secretary of the congress? The one-armed guy?"

"Stanley."

"He's in cahoots with Billy Zip."

"Cahoots?" Mr. Blunt asked. "Cahoots. That's a lovely word."

"He was meeting with him. They're going to bring up the Big Bite for a vote."

"*In* cahoots," Mr. Blunt said, and kept whittling. "Not *on* cahoots. Not cahoot-*ing* . . ."

"This doesn't bother you?" Stony asked.

"Don't worry about Zip," Delia said. She'd come up behind him, and she was carrying a red backpack with the Commander's face on it. "Once the Commander gets done here, nobody's going to listen to him."

Mr. Blunt said, "I was hoping you'd be able to talk him out of it."

"I talked him out of some of it," she said. "He agreed to stop before Phase Three."

"Well, that's something," Blunt said. He held up the white length of wood. "Look, it's the Lump." Sure enough, it was a little half man, with one arm waving.

"What the hell is Phase Three?" Stony asked.

"Look at the farm boy, swearing," Delia said. "By the way, don't run off afterward. He wants to meet you."

"Who, Calhoun?"

"Trust me, not my idea."

The audience began to applaud, and Stony turned. Stanley, the secretary of the congress, climbed onstage. The podium had been moved off to one side, and the center area was taken up by a wide projector screen.

"At this time," the secretary said, seeming a little put out, "the congress recognizes special delegate Commander Gavin Calhoun."

The Commander strode onstage, waving like a politician. The crowd immediately broke into loud applause. Delia said, "He thinks he's a Goddamned John F. Kennedy."

"He looks more alive than Kennedy," Stony said.

Mr. Blunt said, "I think he's had work done."

The Commander had brought his own microphone. He walked to the edge of the stage and said, "My friends, my fellow . . ." He pretended to read something on his palm. "Differently Living Individuals." That got a big laugh.

"I don't know about you, friends, but I'm mighty tired of hiding," the Commander said. "Mighty tired. Some of you have been on the run since day one of the outbreak—twenty years! Some of you have had to live like animals to get by. Most of us have survived only because of the generosity of a few living souls. But how long can that generosity last? How long can we expect breathers to protect us?

"We need a place of our own, my friends. A place free from the government, free from the mad dogs of Dr. Weiss and the Diggers. A *place* in the *sun*. Anita?" A projector set up on a table in the middle of the tent clicked on, and a patch of green filled the screen. "I give you Phase One of Project Homeland . . . Calhoun Island!"

He sounded exactly like the announcer on *The Price Is Right,* telling the lucky contestant they'd won a Brand! New! Car! The audience cheered. Onscreen, a camera flew over the island, and the Commander began narrating in the same jocular tone he used in his commercials. "Located in international waters just forty-five miles from St. Thomas, my friends. This former naval testing site has been forgotten by the breather world, but for us, it's paradise. There's everything we could desire—beaches, mountains, hardened bunkers . . . plus a level of residual radioactivity that will keep the living off our shores and out of our hair!"

The rounds of applause were lessening in volume somewhat. Even the dead could be leery of radiation. The Commander, perhaps sensing he was losing them, forged ahead.

"I've already begun construction of housing," he said. "And the airstrip is being repaved as we speak." The movie was replaced by architectural drawings of condominiums, activity centers, bowling alleys. "As soon as the living crews finish their work, the emigration can begin."

"When?" someone shouted.

"Now that's a damn good question. There's an awful lot of work to do, and as a cautious man, I shouldn't say anything that I can't back up." He looked out over the audience. "My friends, you'll be swimming in the coves of Calhoun Island by this summer, or my name's not Commander Calhoun!"

The crowd stood up, and the shouts made the steel walls of the warehouse reverberate. Stony hoped they really were in the middle of nowhere.

When the noise had calmed down and the audience had returned to their seats, the Commander said, "This is only Phase One, my friends. Phase Two will include a clinic, where we can offer our services. The rich—and I have to tell you, I know plenty of 'em—have one thing they've never been able to buy, and that's immortality. We can sell it to 'em, people! It's our monopoly. Our little island will be *the* destination for the world's rich and famous. We'll take a bite out of their Goddamn wallets!"

"And that's the pitch," Delia said.

"Security and prosperity," Mr. Blunt said. His eyes were on the crowd, scanning like every Secret Service agent in every movie with a president.

"Is he crazy?" Stony said.

"He's not crazy," Delia said. "He's just . . ."

"How in the world are we supposed to keep all *this* secret?"

"That is definitely an issue," Blunt said. "But if we can hold off—what's he doing?"

The Commander was pointing at the screen, where it said in big blue letters: PHASE 3.

Delia said, "Oh, shit."

Now the screen showed a painting of a tall, silver rocket. It had immense fins, like a 1950s sci-fi spaceship. "The island is only the first stepping-stone, my friends. We are capable of so much more. Our *destiny* is so much more. We can withstand intense g-forces. Radiation cannot kill us. We can survive indefinitely without food or water. In short, in *short*—"

He surveyed the crowd, his eyes glittering.

"—we can colonize alien worlds!"

No one spoke. No one moved. The crowd stared at him.

The Commander seemed confused. "Space, people! We can go to space!"

Stony looked at Delia. "Okay," she said. "Maybe he's a little crazy."

Everyone in the tent began to talk at once. Mr. Blunt pointed at a figure in the crowd near the front of the stage, and Delia swore. "Stony, go turn off the damn projector." Mr. Blunt was already gone—vanished through a new slit in the wall of the tent. Delia ran for the stage, pushing through the crowd.

By the time Stony reached the project table, Calhoun's assistant, a marble-white girl named Anita, had already turned off the lamp and was shutting down a laptop. Stony had never seen a computer connected to a projector before. He yanked out the connecting cables anyway. "Sorry," he told her.

A new voice boomed over the PA. "I have an alternate proposal!" Billy Zip had climbed onstage and seized the microphone. Delia was shoving her way to the front of the tent, still twenty feet from the stage and blocked by scores of people.

"We can't live on fantasy island!" Zip shouted. "The government will never allow this thing to be built. The world will never allow it. We're running out of time, people, and we've got to get—"

The sound cut off. Zip looked at the microphone, tapped it with his hand, then looked back to where the cord ran toward the stacks of equipment. Mr. Blunt stood there, holding the loose end of the cord. A long, thin blade had appeared in his other hand. Where had *that* come from?

Zip shouted something, and Blunt slowly shook his head. Zip hesitated, then threw down the microphone and stalked from the stage. Stony was surprised; Zip didn't strike him as someone who'd give up so easily.

Stanley the secretary went to the podium and tapped the mike. This one was still working. "Two-hour recess," he said.

The Commander was not happy. "Goddamn sheep!" He picked up a blueprint from the desk, started to rip it, but it was too long and he got only halfway down its length. "Goddamn—" He crumpled the paper and tossed it down the narrow corridor toward the back of the bus. "Complete lack of vision!"

Stony stood behind Delia, wishing he were outside. The Commander had been ranting for almost fifteen minutes, and Delia had given up on stopping him.

The interior of the coach was finished like a yacht, or perhaps the theme park version of one. The outward curving walls were gleaming dark wood, inset with porthole windows. The wall decorations followed the nautical theme: fishing nets, crossed oars, stuffed swordfish and squid, a gaping shark jaw like a bear trap, a dozen old-fashioned maps in dark frames, and harpoons—lots of harpoons. Attached to the ceiling was what looked like a narwhal tusk. He reached up and touched it. It felt real, but then again, what did real tusk feel like?

The Commander was living in his own fantasy land, and Calhoun Island was more of the same. Zip was right. It was a colossally bad idea. Say that all the LDs moved there. Then what? The government could simply nuke them. One-stop shopping.

"Don't touch that!" the Commander shouted. "Who are you? Delia, who the hell is this?"

"The young man I was telling you about," Delia said.

The Commander's expression changed immediately. "This is him? Goddamn!" He lunged forward and grabbed Stony's hand. "Commander Calhoun," he said. In extreme close-up, the Commander looked even more artificial. The skin of his face looked like molded plastic. His white hair, visible now that the skipper cap had been removed, was waxy as nylon.

Stony said, "I'm—"

"Johnny Mayhall," the Commander said. "No need for introductions." Stony started to tell him that his name was John, just John, but the man was going full speed now. "God-damn, you're handsome. If we ever do a marketing campaign, your face is going right up front. I've been wanting to meet you since I heard your incredible story." He leaned close, still gripping his hand, and stared into Stony's eyes. "A living dead baby. A Goddamn *growing* baby!"

"Yes sir," Stony said. He looked at Delia. How much did the Commander know? Was there anything Stony was supposed to hide?

The man wouldn't let go of Stony's hand. He leaned forward until their foreheads touched, then threw his other arm around Stony's neck. "My boy," he said, his voice dropping, "you are the *game* changer. Forget what all those corpses out there think. You are the hanging curveball. You are, what's the word . . ." His head turned with a squeak. "You're . . ."

Don't say it, Stony thought.

"A Goddamn miracle!"

Miracle was okay. It was the other M-word he'd been dreading.

"I want you to see something," the Commander said, and abruptly released Stony. He began to unbutton his jacket.

"That's okay . . . ," Stony said.

"Just a second." The Commander pulled open his jacket, then began to unbutton his white shirt. "See this?" Under the shirt was a silvery material. "Touch it. Touch it!"

Stony touched it. It felt metallic, scaly.

"I call it the Integrity Suit. The I-Suit for short. Do you know why I wear it? Because of wear and tear! Every day, our dead bodies disintegrate just a bit more. Things fall apart. Now, cosmetic surgery can shore up the banks, so to speak, buttress the framework. You wouldn't believe what the boys in the burn units can do. But our new bodies need something to hold us together—a *body*suit. I'm going to make sure that every LD in America will be wearing one of these, as soon as I can get the costs down. Maybe we go for something that's not Kevlar. Doesn't matter. We're designing gloves and footies, and even a ski-mask thingy for those extreme cases."

"That's a great idea, sir," Stony said. Compared to Calhoun Island and the Spaceship of the Living Dead, it was completely practical. Stony didn't know if any LD besides the Commander would wear a full-metal bodysuit all day, every day, but he knew plenty who could use it. Some LDs, like Roger, fell apart faster than others. They lost teeth, hair, toes. An Integrity Suit could add decades to their existence.

"We're planning a variety of colors and styles," the Commander said. "Something for everyone. Except you, of course."

"Pardon?"

"You don't need a suit, Johnny, because you can *grow*. You can *heal*."

"Actually, sir, whenever I got hurt my mom and my sisters would—"

"Nonsense! If you can grow, you're adding mass. That's healing, son. That's a whole other world of LD existence. And we need to know how the hell you do it. We need to bottle what it is that God gave you."

Stony didn't know what to say. *Bottle it?* He looked at Delia, but her face—her half-fleshed face—was unreadable.

"Stony, I want you to come with me back to Florida. We've got a state-of-the-art lab there and the best people money can buy. Wait here! I'll show you the brochure." The Commander whipped around and headed for the back bedroom.

Stony turned to Delia and dropped his voice. "What have you done?"

Behind them, someone knocked at the front door of the bus.

"I'm sorry," Delia said. She walked toward the door and he followed her. "I didn't know about the lab."

"If he thinks I'm going down to his homemade Cape Canaveral to play Ham the Astrochimp, he's insane. God*damn* insane."

Delia stepped down and opened the door. One of Mr. Blunt's guards looked up at them. "We've got a problem outside," the man said.

"*Outside* outside?" Delia asked.

"Mr. Blunt would like you to hurry."

* * *

Stony insisted on going with her. No way was he going to stay on the bus with Commander Crazy. He followed Delia across the warehouse floor, aiming for the loading docks where they'd all entered. Delia cautioned him to not look panicked in front of the delegates. Everyone was still on edge because of Calhoun's swerve into sci-fi and Billy Zip's removal from the stage.

The security guard told them that a breather had some-how gotten through the front gates and driven up to the docks. "One of Blunt's breathers, the black guy with the beard—"

"His name's Aaron," Delia said.

"Well, Blunt sent him out to talk to the other breather, and told me to get you."

"How the hell did he get through the gates? Calhoun's company was supposed to lock down the whole compound."

"I don't know, ma'am."

"Of course you don't." At the end of the warehouse, they went up a short flight of stairs, then outside. The sunlight came as a shock. It was afternoon, the oblique autumn light throwing long shadows before the fleet of vehicles parked out front on a gravel lot. There were nine or ten semis, including the freezer truck that Stony had traveled in, a multitude of vans and moving trucks, and several cars. The warehouse squatted on a vast, grassy plain, featureless in every direction he could see except for a long paved road that led away from the parking lot. The land was flat as Iowa, the sky a pearly gray he knew from midwestern winters. Stony experienced the kind of scale shift he hadn't felt since playing the Little Big game when he was a kid. The warehouse, so huge when he was inside it, suddenly seemed as small as a toy box, and he was a plastic soldier surrounded by Matchbox trucks and Hot Wheels cars.

Perhaps a hundred yards away, a pickup truck was parked on the paved road, engine running, driver still behind the wheel. Aaron stood beside the truck, his hands on the driver's-side door. The driver was obscured by the glare of the windshield—Stony caught an impression of a fat man with a high forehead—and even though Stony couldn't hear the words of the men, he could tell they were arguing. A few of the other breather drivers were huddling around the truck, blocking the driver from going forward, and more important, obscuring his view of Mr. Blunt and the other LDs, who were standing well back.

Mr. Blunt saw Delia and Stony emerge and walked over to them holding the brim of his hat, which served both to keep it from blowing off in the cold wind (cold for breathers, that is, twenty-four hours in the freezer having obliterated Stony's thermostat) and to shield his face from the breather in the pickup.

"He's the warehouse manager," Blunt said. "And he very much wants to know what we're doing with his building."

"It's none of his fucking business," Delia said. "All the employees were told to take the week off."

"Nevertheless, he says that he's going to call the police if we don't let him inside."

"But he hasn't called them yet. Is he armed?"

"This is North Dakota. He has a gun rack in the truck."

Delia and Mr. Blunt looked at each other. Stony had seen them do this before, silently exchanging information at a baud rate he could only imagine. If the driver called the police, the congress was too large for everyone to escape undetected. There would be roadblocks. Highway chases.

After perhaps ten seconds of silence, Delia said, "Fuck. Grab him. Let him see breathers only. But if he goes for the rifle—"

"Understood," Mr. Blunt said. He gestured to one of the security guards and said, "Get the word to Aaron."

The LD security guard spoke to one of the breather drivers, and that driver walked up to Aaron. Aaron stepped away from the car, listening to the man, then stared at him for a long moment.

Stony wondered what he was thinking. Aaron risked his freedom for LDs every day—all these drivers did. They were the most hard-core of volunteers, the breathers who drove the vehicles, hosted the safe houses, kept the secrets of the undead. Without them, the LDs could not survive. And yet they were always being asked to do more, even betray their fellow humans. And for what? The LDA didn't even allow them inside the congress.

Aaron nodded, then turned again toward the pickup. Stony thought, If I was Aaron, I would tell the man to run. The place is full of monsters.

Aaron said something to the pickup driver, then suddenly lunged through the driver's-side window—reaching for the truck keys, Stony realized. The driver shouted something, and the truck lurched backward. Aaron was still halfway through the window, his toes kicking up gravel.

The truck accelerated, still in reverse, and bounced onto the paved drive. Aaron half fell out of the window, and the road kicked his legs out from under him. His arm was still thrust through the window, bent backward at the elbow. Aaron screamed in pain.

Mr. Blunt was in motion, running toward the pickup. Suddenly the truck slammed on the brakes, spun. Aaron went flying, tumbling off the pavement and onto the grass. The driver twisted the truck around, aimed it away from the warehouse.

Mr. Blunt was only thirty yards from the vehicle's

tailgate—but then the driver hit the gas and the truck peeled away from him. Blunt would never catch it.

Stony yelled at one of the security guards. "Which way did the truck come in?"

The guard looked at him, then started to look away, and Stony screamed, "Which way?" He pointed left, at a diagonal from the paved driveway. The entrance had to meet another road at the front gates. "East?" Then he pointed toward the right. "Or west?"

The guard thought for a moment, then said, "East."

The only way to beat the truck was to cut through the square. A squared plus B squared equals the shortest distance to the road. And if there was one thing Stony knew how to do it was run.

The ground was frozen, the knee-high grass brittle with frost. He ran. Then he ran faster. He glanced to his right, and saw the pickup disappearing up the drive. The warehouse manager was on pavement, and the truck could go sixty, seventy miles an hour, maybe faster once it swung onto the main road. The unknown variables in play were the lengths of the sides of the triangle, and Stony's top speed—and he had no idea what that might be. This was more than just a question of endurance, like the Halloween he ran from Officer Tines, the night he realized that dead muscles didn't require oxygen. This was an engineering problem. Muscles could tear, foot bones could break, shins could fracture—but none of those injuries had to impede him if he did not let them. The day he'd chased down Thomas he hadn't pushed himself in the slightest.

So: Go faster.

A chain-link fence surrounded the compound. He'd been aiming for a corner of the fence, or rather a spot just to the right of it, and that point was coming at him at an amazing rate. He wished Kwang were here to see this. The Unstoppable, suddenly in possession of a new superpower, running like the Flash (well, Quicksilver, maybe) to stop the bad guy.

The fence seemed to be about ten feet high, and on the other side was a two-lane highway. He looked right but didn't see the pickup. He'd beaten the manager by a huge distance—unless the man had driven in the other direction. Who would catch him if he'd gone west?

Suddenly Stony was only a dozen yards from the fence. How high could he jump, and how far at this speed? But no, maybe he should stop and climb—

His pace stuttered, and then his feet tangled, and Stony pitched forward into the metal fence. The chain link collapsed as he struck it, popping free like a shower curtain yanked from the rod. He had a moment to think, Jesus, how fast was I moving? And then he was tumbling across the surface of the highway, over the gravel shoulder. He had no control of his limbs; he ragdolled to a stop in the high grass on the far side of the road.

He lay there for a moment, stunned. Then he remembered the pickup and pushed himself up. Both legs were still working, both arms. He hadn't broken his neck, as far as he could tell. Across the road from him, the section of fence he'd struck was empty, the chain link matting the grass. In the fields beyond, a line of LDs ran toward him across the field, following his path, though none of them seemed to have his speed.

He stepped to the center of the road, straddling the dotted line. The pickup appeared, perhaps an eighth of a mile away, rushing toward him. Stony suddenly remembered that he didn't have a plan. He was the dog who had caught the car. He had no gun, no rock to throw at the windshield. His only weapon, his only tool, was his body.

Stony squared his shoulders to the road and raised one hand as if he were a traffic cop.

A pickup weighed, what, three, maybe four tons? All of it moving at seventy-five miles per hour. That much momentum would pulverize him, or else catapult his body hundreds of feet down the road. He wasn't sure which outcome was more likely.

Except—except—if the driver escaped, then everyone at the congress could be destroyed, and every breather who helped them could be arrested, just like his mom. Aaron, if he was alive, would spend the rest of his life in jail.

Stony's arm had lowered as of its own accord. He raised it again, and now the truck was almost upon him, approximately a football field away. He knew that it was too close, moving too fast, to stop in time.

He hoped Aaron was alive. The insult to the man's arm, the rude throw from the car, all of it seemed, now that he thought back on it, painful but survivable. Unless Aaron had hit his head, or suffered some internal injury. The deer Stony had found Halloween night looked as if it could have hopped to its feet and run off. What had killed it—as what had kept it alive all its life until then—was invisible, as invisible as whatever animated Stony and the other LDs, the odic force or clockwork virus or space radiation that kept this dead stick moving in the wind. How much damage, he wondered, could his body take before that spark, too, was extinguished?

The pickup screamed: a shriek of grinding brakes and squealing tires. The hood nosed down, and the truck began to slide, the bed of the truck drifting out from behind the cab. The vehicle was close now, less than a hundred feet. The driver was a round-faced, middle-aged man, perhaps sixty years old, bald on top but with a fringe of dark hair. He looked distraught, mouth open, both hands clutching the wheel.

The bed began to slide the other way, swinging like a wide baseball bat. Even if Stony tried to move—and he *wanted* to, he wanted to very much—he wouldn't know which way to jump.

The truck was spinning now, and the mass of it was suddenly beside him, the cab less than two feet from his right arm—and then it was past him. An instant later and fifty feet farther down the road, the back wheels hit the gravel shoulder and the vehicle lurched, right rear and front tires tilting into the air, and for a terrible moment he thought it was going to flip. But the forward motion had been arrested and the wheels slammed down and the truck body bounced against its suspension.

I'm alive, Stony thought. And the driver is alive. Even the truck—the Goddamn truck!—is undented.

He walked quickly to the vehicle. When he was still ten feet away, the driver pushed open his door. He was a large man, with a huge gut under a crisp denim shirt. He put one leg out onto the pickup's step, then pressed a hand to each side of the door frame, as if afraid the cab would squeeze shut on him before he could get out. He saw Stony and froze.

"Are you—what were you—?"

The man seemed to be in shock. Did he see what Stony was? Did he know now what he'd stumbled into?

He realized now that his idea—if it wasn't ludicrous to call something so impulsive an idea—had depended on the driver being too humane to run down a man in the middle of the road. Which made the breather the good guy. Stony was the supervillain playing on the hero's weakness for innocent bystanders. He'd had it all backward from the start.

"I'm so sorry," Stony said. "But I couldn't let you go."

But the man wasn't looking at Stony now, but behind him. Stony turned. Four of Blunt's security guards and three other LDs had made it to the fence. They charged through the gap and headed toward the truck.

"It's okay," Stony called to them. "He's not going anywhere."

The men rushed past him. The first of them reached the truck and pulled the driver from the cab. A second man circled an arm around the driver's neck and yanked viciously down; the driver yelped and went down, hitting the pavement on his side. His other arm flailed upward and caught the second guard across the mouth. The LD laughed.

The undead men swarmed. They covered the driver's arms and legs, though any one of them was strong enough to hold him down. The driver screamed.

Stony yanked one of the LDs away. "Stop it! What are you doing?"

The first guard, now straddling the driver's waist, ripped open the man's blue shirt. His belly was huge and white. The guard looked up at Stony and said, "You want to do the honors?"

"Please, don't—" Stony said.

The guard shrugged. He opened his jaws and bit down. The driver screamed again. The guard rose up, his mouth awash with blood. "Your ass is ours now!"

The driver screamed again. A second guard rose up with blood on his face. The LDs made a sound between a growl and a cheer. They began tearing at the man. Stony put an arm around an LD and pulled him backward. The man knocked Stony away and threw himself back into the pile.

The fat man screamed, and screamed, and kept screaming, until suddenly going silent. Someone severed an artery and bright blood sprayed into the afternoon light. Then he became a fountain.

The congress disbanded. No, that sounds too orderly. The congress exploded. News of the killing reached the warehouse, and delegates scrambled for their bags, called for their human drivers, and fled in their vehicles. They scattered. Calhoun's bus was the first through the gate.

Stony was aware of none of this. Delia found him next to the highway, sitting in the grass, staring at the blood-smeared patch of pavement where the driver's body had been. Blunt's men, when they finished their meal, had thrown the eviscerated corpse into the back of the pickup and driven it back to the warehouse. The hole in the fence, and the stain, were all that remained to mark the site of the murder. It wouldn't even look like a crime, necessarily. Some large animal, perhaps a three-hundred-pound buck, had charged through the gap in the fence and been struck here, and the driver had carried off the roadkill for his freezer. Probably happened all the time out here.

"This wasn't supposed to happen," Delia said. "They were only supposed to bite him. To turn him."

"Of course," Stony said. He felt disconnected from his body, as if he were hovering perhaps four feet above his right shoulder. "It was an accident."

The driver was beyond revival, Delia said. He wouldn't be joining the ranks of the undead, but on the positive side, neither would Aaron. He'd been battered, Delia said, and his arm had been broken, probably in several places, but he would live. One of his fellow breathers would be taking him to a hospital.

After a moment he realized Delia was waiting for a response, so he said, "Good. That's good to hear."

Delia looked at him worriedly. "Let's get going, kid." They wouldn't be going back by freezer truck, she told him. She had a separate vehicle that would be taking them someplace else. He didn't bother to ask where. And later, he wouldn't remember much about the trip. The two of them were tucked into the back of a moving van. Delia spent the first hour of the journey talking into a military-quality walkie-talkie. Perhaps he heard her say "civil war." Perhaps he only realized later what she'd been talking about. Then they were out of range of whomever she was talking to, and she put the radio back into the Commander Calhoun backpack. For the next five or eight or twelve hours neither of them said much at all that he could recall. And then the breather driver, a man Stony had never met, opened the back doors of the van. They were in a one-car garage, the cinder-block walls scuffed with red clay. A small door led to what had to be the house.

"Where are we?" Stony asked.

"We contacted one of our retired volunteers," Delia said. "She offered to put you up temporarily."

"Just me? Aren't you staying?"

The door opened. A very tall woman holding a very small child stood in the doorway.

"Crystal!" he said. He walked to her, then stopped short, afraid to hurt the baby.

She laughed and pulled him in tight. "Brother John."

CHAPTER ELEVEN

1988
Reveille, Utah

er name was Ruby. He could not stop holding her, and when he was not holding her, he could not stop looking at her. That shock of jet-black hair, the blue-gray eyes, the puffy, Pia Zadora lips. Last night they'd stayed up late talking, Ruby sleeping in the crook of his elbow, and he would only surrender her to Crystal when she needed to eat. Then, just after dawn, he heard her fussing and went in to get her before she could wake Crystal. As soon as Ruby saw him she stopped crying and regarded him silently.

"I think we have a connection," he told Crystal later that morning. "She knows me." They sat on the couch in the con-verted sunroom, Crystal at one end with a mug of green tea in her hands and her legs curled beneath her, Stony at the other end with Ruby in his arms, the baby tucked into a nest of blankets to insulate her from his cold skin. They looked out through a wall of glass at a Martian December, miles of empty red rock dotted with alien trees, pink desert light shifting across the surface. Not since Iowa had he sat in front of an open window in daylight.

He had decided not to tell Crystal about the congress,

about how he'd helped kill an innocent man. He wouldn't bring that poison into this house. He would be Crystal's little brother, and Ruby's big uncle.

"It's like I know her," he said. "Like I knew she was coming."

"Hah," Crystal said. "A tarot reader in Moab—she'd never been wrong before—told me she'd be a boy."

"A tarot reader? You couldn't just get a sonogram?"

"Would a sonogram tell me that he'd be strong-willed, impulsive, and a lover of words?"

"Or have a vagina?"

She laughed. Oh, he'd made her laugh. "I didn't see *any* doctors, Stony. Everything happened here, at home. The only doctor I let near this child was Alice. She came in, you know, for the birth."

"I meant to be here," Stony said.

"That's sweet. But you would have only gotten in the way. You know how weak menfolk are around birthin' and babies."

"I just think it's so . . . cool. I mean, I can't get over the idea that you *made* her, inside you."

"I had help."

"Yeah, but still. It's kind of amazing, isn't it?" Somehow a bundle of overeager cells had stolen a strip of chromosomes from an incoming sperm, decided to rampantly duplicate, then organized themselves into eyes and ears and fingers. Then, at some indeterminate point, the wad of tissue became conscious, a sentient being with thoughts and feelings of its own. A person. A specific, unique person.

Ruby.

The entire process seemed massively improbable, a joke. If it weren't happening every second of every day, with every type of animal on the planet, nobody would believe it.

Crystal was dozing again. She reclined against the pillows, still balancing the mug on her stomach, eyes closed. Not only had she had to wake up for the regular feedings, but she'd stayed up late last night, letting Stony ask her questions about the baby. Delia had said little, frequently vanishing into the garage for long smoke breaks. When Crystal could no longer keep her eyes open she'd set out blankets and pillows for them and told them to make themselves at home. As if they would sleep, or wanted to. As if they were run-of-the-mill visitors who'd dropped in for a visit.

Crystal was so good at playing pretend, he could almost pretend to be normal himself. He could almost ignore the corpse of the driver that he saw whenever he closed his eyes, or the ghost of their sister that hovered at the edge of every anecdote, every family reminiscence. Because of Ruby. She was a little battery of life, jamming the death signal.

"You're humming," Crystal said, her eyes still closed.

"I'm sorry. I didn't know I was doing that."

"No, it's all right. It's nice. Ruby likes it." She sat up, took a sip of tea. "When I was carrying her, she'd start kicking whenever I sang. I think she's going to be musical, like her father."

"He's a musician? You never talked about him in your letters."

"He's not a professional musician. He's not a professional anything, really. He works as a river guide in Moab, and he likes to mountain climb."

"Does he know about the baby?"

"Oh, he knows. This just isn't the kind of adventure he's interested in. Not the type to stick around the house and mix formula. Sometimes he stops by. And he sends me money for the electric bill when he remembers."

"A marauder from the land of Moab," Stony said.

"What?"

"Zombie Bible story. Your guy, he sounds like an asshole."

"No, he's just . . ." She put down her mug. "Well, he can *be* an asshole. I'm just not sure if he *is* an asshole. He's himself. I knew what he was when I picked him up, as the Indians say. And God, he's beautiful. He looks like Jesus with his shirt off, all skinny and beardy."

He heard the door to the garage open, and Delia's familiar footsteps. For the past hour she'd been in the garage, whether smoking or doing something else was unclear. She appeared in the doorway behind him, scanning the landscape outside the window. "You shouldn't be sitting out here," she said. "Somebody could have binoculars."

"We're in the middle of nowhere," Crystal said. "Sit down and enjoy the sunlight."

Stony said, "Ruby and Crystal and I are—hey, I just realized that. Ruby and Crystal."

"And Stony," Delia said.

"What?" he said. Then: "Crystal, did you—?"

Crystal burst out laughing. "I can't believe you just figured this out."

He was stunned. "I thought it was just your hippie name."

"Well, that, too. But I was trying to show solidarity with you. I thought about calling myself Igneous, but my boyfriend didn't like it."

"I'm an idiot," he said.

"Noted," Delia said. She stepped down into the sunroom and squatted on the floor against one wall, out of sight of the outdoors. "Let's talk about plans."

Crystal said, "I'd forgotten what it was like to work with you, Delia. Good morning to you, too."

Delia's expression didn't change. "Mr. Blunt is in Salt Lake, watching Zip's safe houses. He has three that we know about, only two of them occupied. Blunt says that so far Zip hasn't moved any of his people, but we have to expect that at any time."

For Delia, he thought, the murder of the warehouse manager was nothing, a blip that unfortunately ended the congress too soon. The only thing that concerned her now was Zip, and his plans for the Big Bite.

"Why would he move his people?" Stony said.

"Who's Zip?" Crystal asked.

Delia said, "He has to expect that we'd turn him in if that was the only way to stop him."

"Call in the Diggers?" Stony asked. "We wouldn't do that, would we? Would we?"

Delia didn't answer, and Crystal said, "Could *some*body tell me who Zip is?"

"Billy Zip," Stony said. "He's an LD, and kind of an extremist." He said to Delia, "When did you talk to Blunt? Just now, on the radio?"

"They don't reach *that* far. Last night I walked out to the pay phone at the gas station, called our answering service. I've been trying to figure out our next move. Aaron and Mr. Blunt are going to stay on watch in Salt Lake. We have others watching the houses of people we know are in Zip's camp. But we're worried that Zip will go after *our* houses—Blunt's house, my house, the satellites . . . basically, any parish run by a security council member."

"This is crazy," Stony said. "We can't have LDs turning on each other." Even if the LDs are murderers, he thought.

"He'll do whatever he needs to, kid. He's not supposed to know the location of all our houses, but we can't be sure of that. I've got to go move our people. When they're safe, we'll be free to take him down."

He thought of Valerie, Thomas the mailman, Tanya and

Teddy, all the other residents of the house. They were frail, and some of them were like children. "I'll go with you," he said.

"Uh, no." She'd treated him differently ever since she found him at the roadside, like he was an unstable chemical. Like he was a child. "You're staying here," she said. "If things go badly in the city, Aaron and Blunt may have to hide out here, so you two will have to—"

"Wait a minute," Crystal said. "I said I'd put up Stony, not a house full of you. Look, I like Aaron and Mr. Blunt, I appreciate what you all did for my family—but I can't do what I did before, I can't run a safe house. I've got a life now, friends who stop by—"

"Tell your friends you have the flu."

"Delia, I have a two-week-old baby. If they think I'm sick, I'll have a dozen people coming by to take care of her."

Delia stood up. "You'll have to figure something out."

Stony said to Delia, "Can I talk with you privately for a minute?"

Delia stared at him. Stony glanced at Crystal, and she held out her arms for the baby. She was angry, but she wasn't going to yell.

He led Delia out to the garage, then shut the door behind her.

"You're ditching me here," he said.

"You'd rather be somewhere else? You told me you wanted to visit."

"Not like this. Not during whatever it is that this is. I know you think I'm having some kind of breakdown."

"I don't think that."

"Then let me go back to L.A. to move the house. You go to Salt Lake—"

"Forget it," she said. "I really do need someone here. Blunt needs someone here. Does Crystal have a gun?"

"What?"

"Never mind, you should have one of your own." She went to her casket, retrieved the Commander Calhoun backpack, and pulled out a black, thick-bellied revolver. "Do you know how to kill an LD?"

"That's a gun. How long have you had a gun?"

"Answer the question."

"Everybody knows that," he said. It was in every movie about the undead ever made—including the documentaries. "You shoot him in the head."

"No," she said. "You'll miss. You shoot him in the chest"— She slapped her palm against him—"and you knock him the fuck down. Then you walk up close, about two feet away. *Then* you shoot him in the head. Then you burn him."

I'm not going to do that, he thought.

She put the pistol in his hand. "This is an S-and-W model nineteen. You hold it with two hands or it will fucking jump up and smack you in the face. Keep the safety on at all times, until it's time to take it off."

"How would I know when that is?"

"Don't ask stupid questions. I'll leave you a box of shells, but frankly, if it's not over in six bullets, fifty's not going to save you."

He thought, I'm not shooting anyone—not an LD, not a living person, not a jackrabbit. He could not even shoot Billy Zip. But if he told her that, she wouldn't trust him.

She took the gun from him, checked the safety, and put it back in the bag. "I'm going to give you some phone numbers and some instructions. I'm not going to write them down, and neither are you. Ready?"

A panel truck—for all he knew, the same one that had carried them from the congress—backed up to the garage a few hours later. Stony stayed out of sight. When the truck left, Delia was gone with it, and he was left holding the bag: Commander Calhoun's smiling face hiding a pistol, two packs of Virginia Slims, and more cash than he'd ever seen in one place. Emergency money, Delia had called it.

What he should do, he thought, is give it to Crystal. Before the baby she'd worked thirty hours a week at a public library, but now she wasn't working at all, and it was clear she was living close to the bone. Her furniture was either second-hand, or a substitute for furniture: wicker lawn chairs for real chairs, cinder blocks and planks for bookshelves, orange crates for end tables. An old-fashioned TV cabinet, not even plugged in, doubled as a banquet table, its wood veneer top crowded with candles and a southwestern-style nativity scene with wooden llamas and ceramic cacti. Fringed afghans disguised fraying upholstery, and throw rugs covered bare patches in the carpet. The whole place needed a paint job.

More worrisome, she didn't seem to have any real food in the house. Lunch was a plate of lumpy, purplish vegetables he didn't recognize, and a bowl of spiky leaves that had obviously evolved to rip apart the throat of any mammal stupid enough to eat them.

"It's a salad," Crystal said, defensively. "Do you want some?"

He'd given up eating while living with LDs, but he supposed he could resume his bulimia for old times' sake. "Sure. It looks great."

She filled a bowl and plate for him. He held Ruby in one hand and shook some ranch dressing over the greens. "So," she said. "You're a smoker now."

He looked up guiltily. "I guess you can smell it, huh?"

"Oh, yeah. I got nostalgic. I gave it up when I got pregnant."

"I promise I'll never do it in the house."

"You'd better not." After a minute she said, "Smoking, swearing. Mom wouldn't know what to think."

Ah. There it was. He poked his fork into the purple thing. "Have you talked to her?"

"Stony, nobody's talked to her in three years—not even her lawyer. Alice is spending all her free time on a lawsuit to allow access, but it's slow. We don't even think our letters are getting through to her. Certainly none of hers are getting out."

"I'm so sorry," he said. "I never meant for that to happen. Mom—"

"Mom knew what she was doing," Crystal said. "She knew what you were when she picked you up."

Stony choked down the salad and the purple things, which turned out to be eggplant. Ruby also had lunch. Before today, he would have thought it embarrassing to have his sister whip out her boob in front of him, but Crystal acted like this was perfectly normal, which of course *made* it normal. Crystal ate one-handed while Ruby sucked enthusiastically. When she finished, her head lolled drunkenly back from the nipple, her eyes half closed. Crystal quickly changed her diaper—the kid seemed to poop every thirty seconds—and then began to button her into a tiny snowsuit. Which seemed extreme, considering it was above fifty degrees outside.

"I've got to run some errands," Crystal said.

"I can watch Ruby," he said. "Look, she's already asleep."

"Stony, I can't show up without my baby; people will think I threw her in the Dumpster. Plus, people want to see her."

"Is she allowed to go out?"

"It's just going to be for a couple of hours. Just don't answer the door. I'll make sure to pull the drapes."

"Trust me, I'm used to this," Stony said.

He peeked through the front window as she walked out to the driveway to a rusting '76 Honda Civic and belted Ruby into her car seat. When the car pulled away it sounded like a Cessna taking off. A leak in the rear differential, probably. If she pulled it into the garage he could work on it without anyone seeing. Delia's money could pay for parts.

He walked around the house for a while, picking up books and setting them down, and finally ended up back in the sunroom. It was odd to be alone. At the safe house people were always underfoot, and even when he was up in the attic or down in the basement he could hear his housemates talking, or listen to the babble of the TV. He should use this solitary time to gather his thoughts, to think through what might happen with Blunt and Zip, to visualize what he'd do if someone came after them in the house. Or maybe not. Maybe he should do the opposite, and *empty* his thoughts. Meditate.

He moved off the couch and sat cross-legged in front of the big window. A living person would listen to his heartbeat, or to his own breaths. He'd have to do something else, perhaps concentrate on the sound of the wind whisking the walls of the house. He closed his eyes, and the dead man was looking at him. His neck had been ravaged down to the bone. One hand rested proprietarily on the tangle of intestines that lay beside him.

Stony jumped to his feet. He paced the house, then eventually ended up in the spare bedroom where Crystal was letting him stay, and where Ruby would sleep when she left the bassinet. The walls were covered in ugly, purple-striped wallpaper. Leaning in the corner was a cardboard shipping container the size of a door—a crib that Alice had bought.

By the time Crystal returned, he'd assembled the crib, then partially disassembled it again so that he could move the pieces into the hallway, because he'd realized that the wallpaper *had* to come off if Ruby was ever going to get a night's sleep.

"I need a real scraper," he told her.

"Why are you attacking my walls?"

"Also brushes," he said. "Your choice on the paint. You want pink? No, that's not you. Too cliché."

Crystal said, "Are you all right? You don't have to do anything. Just read a book or something."

"How about yellow? Yellow is nice." From his back pocket he produced a few hundred dollars in twenties. "Or two colors. We can alternate walls."

"Where did you get that?"

"From Commander Calhoun."

"You robbed a Calhoun's?"

"Delia left it. For housekeeping expenses. You should get some food, too—you hardly have anything in the fridge. People will think you're LD."

"I'm not using your money."

"Of course you are. Look, let's pretend we argue about this for two hours, and maybe I make you cry, and then you make me cry, and then you grudgingly admit that we can use the money—because that is what's best for little Ruby."

"Do you remember the taxi game?"

"Uh . . ."

"When you and Junie were little, I used to get you to clean my room. I'd give you something to put away, and the taxi would have to carry it to my closet, or to my dresser."

"That's child abuse."

"You both loved it. You'd beg me to play."

"You obviously wrecked my ability to distinguish work from play. So, you'll get me my paint?"

"The nearest paint store's in Moab. For now, how about I find some scrapers, and you and I finish the wallpaper?"

"Fine, except for the part where you scrape. There could be lead paint under this stuff. You can't inhale toxins and pass them to Ruby."

"There isn't any lead paint here, Stony."

"How do you know? These walls are ancient. Besides, if you helped, I might finish too quickly and start looking for more projects." He thought he was doing a good imitation of the lighthearted uncle, but Crystal was frowning at him. Had Delia told her what had happened at the congress? Had she overheard them talking?

"Okay," she said finally. She smiled to signal that she was consenting to play this game, to banter and joke and pretend everything was okay. "Just promise me you won't dig a bunker under my house."

"That's crazy," he said. "I'd need dynamite to blast through that rock."

Each night after midnight he'd leave the house and walk north. He walked parallel to the road, staying in the dark thirty yards off, tripping over rocks and roots. When a car approached from either direction he crouched and shielded his face, wary of his pale skin catching the light. This was a rare occurrence. Mostly he was alone in the dark, Halloween night again.

His first waypoint, about a mile from Crystal's house, was a double-wide trailer whose tiny windows glowed each night with blue television light. Inert vehicles, half of them up on blocks, surrounded the trailer like sleeping buffalo. He gave the place a wide berth. He would have liked to ask Crystal who lived there and why they were up at all hours, but he hadn't told her about his nightly walks.

The next mile was in the dark, lit only by the moon, until he topped a small rise and saw the light of the Sinclair sign. He never rushed toward it. When he was a few hundred yards away, he began to move in a long sweeping U that let him survey the gas station from all sides, scanning for teenagers, late-working clerks, drunks, anyone loitering under the light of that grinning, green Sinclair brontosaurus, who looked extremely happy to have his old bones fuel your car. Stony liked the corporate mascot because it was one of the few that unashamedly reminded you of exactly what had died to make your life easier. Like the El Pollo Loco chicken crazy with desire to become your lunch, or Charlie the Tuna desperate to be canned, the dinosaur was a corpse with a job. One of the undead of the ad world.

When he was satisfied the station was deserted, he would walk quickly to the pay phone on the side of the building and make his call. Delia had given him seven numbers, one for every day of the week. He'd dial the day's number, then enter his personal access code, and every night a recorded voice would tell him that he had no messages. But that, itself, was a message. No one has reported in. You are not needed. Go back to your sister.

On the fifth night, a Thursday, the machine voice said, *You have one message, delivered at eleven . . . p.m. . . . . yesterday.* Two hours ago!

He held on to the receiver, scanning the dark around the station, and then the voice came on. He'd expected to hear from Delia, but then he recognized Mr. Blunt's reedy voice, the way his T's ticked like clockwork.

Bit of trouble, my boy. I'm trying to reach our motorcyclist and getting no answer. Hopefully she'll be in touch with you. Tell her that our short-fingered boy is on the move and may be accelerating his plans. Half the people in the house just emptied, in a U-Haul. I'm having our A-1 driver follow the truck. I'm at 750 East, 400 South watching the leftovers. Tell her I'll wait for her word as long as I can, and I would appreciate a few more hands on my side. But if they start to move, I'm going to have to knock on the half-wit's door.

A car horn blared in the background of the message.

Must go. Oh! And give my love to your sister. I understand congratulations are in order.

Stony pressed the key to erase the message and hung up the phone. Suddenly it seemed much too bright under the Sinclair sign. He hurried off into the dark, but he did not head for home. He sat down behind an oil tank and tried to figure out what he should do. The "motorcyclist" was Delia. Where was she that she couldn't get to a phone? Had the Diggers picked her up? Had Zip—the half-wit—turned her in?

The whole point of a Big Bite was that it had to be big: geographically distributed, with attacks on so many fronts that it would be impossible for the government to put down. If Zip was starting the bite now, then did that mean he'd already set up a nationwide network—or global network? Or else the "acceleration" Blunt mentioned meant that they'd forced Zip to act before he was ready. He hoped that was true.

He waited another half hour and called the number again. *No new messages,* the voice told him. He hurried back to his hiding place.

If Delia wasn't captured, he might be the only link between her and Blunt. And if she was captured, he might be the only one left who knew what Blunt was doing.

He called the number again twenty minutes later. This time the voice didn't pick up. The phone on the other end rang and rang: eight rings, nine, ten. The system never picked up. Had he misremembered the number? He tried it again, and still got no answer. Then he tried Saturday's number, and Sunday's.

Was the system overloaded? Was there some security scheme in place that stopped anyone from calling three times in a night?

He dialed the Thursday number that he'd used first. The phone rang once, and then a woman said, "Hello?"

It wasn't a recording, or a machine voice. He started to hang up. He held the receiver for a long moment, then put it back to his ear.

"Hello?" the woman said again. "Who is this?"

"Who is *this*?" It wasn't Delia, or Rose, or anyone he recognized.

"Are you in trouble?" she said. "Do you need help?"

"I don't know what you're talking about."

She hung up on him.

He looked around at the dark, but no cars were approaching. He'd gotten a live person—or a dead one. He dialed the number again.

The woman answered on the first ring. "Yes?"

"I need to find out what's going on," he said. "What parish are you?"

After a pause, she said, "Ohio. And you? Are you in trouble?"

He thought of the only delegate from the state that he knew. "What kind of radio do you like?" he asked. "AM or FM?"

"Tell us where you are," the woman said, "and we'll send a car to pick you up."

"Okay, I'm . . . let me get back to you on that." He slammed down the phone and stepped back.

The Diggers had taken control of the communication system.

* * *

He resisted the impulse to burst into Crystal's bedroom and shake her awake. He opened the door slowly and let the light fall across her face. Crystal lay on her side, Ruby tucked under her arm.

He touched Crystal's shoulder, and she jerked awake. "The baby?"

"She's right here." He sat down on the edge of the bed and gently rested a hand on Ruby's legs. "I've got to go, Crystal."

She sat up and pushed the hair from her eyes. Even this tired, she was beautiful. "What? What happened?"

"A lot of things. I think the Diggers are rolling us up. The phone system's been tapped."

"Does that mean—can they trace you?"

"I don't know. I tried to get off the phone as soon as I could." He didn't know how tracing worked. In the movies, they were always trying to get criminals to stay on the line. He said, "Mr. Blunt needs me. He's in Salt Lake, and I have to drive there."

"Now?"

"I can't wait till morning. The Diggers may be rounding us up."

"Okay, okay." She looked around at the darkened room. "I'll feed Ruby, you—"

"No, you're not coming with me. You need to get as far away from here as possible. Zip is—he might be starting the Big Bite. You need to get on a bus that doesn't go through Salt Lake. I was thinking you should go to Denver, and fly out from there. Go see Alice." He lifted the Commander Calhoun backpack onto the bed. Inside was a ludicrous amount of cash. "When you get to Chicago, you can buy yourself a new car. Something safe, like a Volvo."

"You're taking my car?"

"I can't take a bus. Besides, it's a crappy car."

"You can't drive by yourself," Crystal said.

"It's the middle of the night. Nobody's going to see me."

Crystal climbed out of bed. "Makeup. I'll do your face." At the bedroom door she stopped, turned. "You're going to need a hell of a lot of base."

Ruby emitted a squeak, but her eyes stayed closed. Stony carefully slid one hand behind her neck, the other under her bottom, and lifted. Her arms jerked in a startle reflex, but he brought her close to his chest and she immediately settled.

It was a mistake to come here. Yet again he'd put his family in danger. This time it had only taken him a week to force Ruby and Crystal out of their home and put them on the run—a new record. That could never happen again. Whether or not the world ended tomorrow, he couldn't come back to them. He couldn't see anyone in his family again.

He knew he was wrong about Zip, too. Only a few days ago he thought he could not kill the man, even if it meant saving the world. But now Ruby was in the world.

He leaned down and kissed her forehead. "Take care of your mom, kiddo."

CHAPTER TWELVE

1988
Salt Lake City, Utah

he Mormons were the most disciplined of urban planners. Like all their cities, Salt Lake was laid out in a grid, each street numbered from its distance from the temple at the center of the city. The address Blunt had given him, 750 East 400 South, put him seven blocks east of the temple, and on the fourth block south of it. He didn't need to read any of the building numbers to guess which one was Zip's safe house. Or rather, which one used to be his. Four squad cars, three ambulances, and two fire trucks had formed a semicircle of strobing lights around a smoking shell of a house. The fire seemed to be out, but firefighters were still spraying down portions of the structure.

He was too late, then.

Stony made a three-point turn—easy to do in the wide street—and parked a block away. When he shut off the engine, he realized that over the hours he'd become deaf to the whine of the differential.

It was seven in the morning and still dark. He'd made it to Salt Lake in a little over four and a half hours, driving fast through Green River and Price, slowing down only when he joined the interstate at Spanish Fork, where Crystal told him the cops liked to set radar traps. It was the farthest he'd ever driven a vehicle in his life, and it quadrupled the amount of time he'd spent behind the wheel. When he'd asked to borrow his sister's car he wasn't even sure whether he'd be able to drive all that way without causing an accident or getting pulled over. That he'd been able to do it felt like an achievement. That he'd enjoyed the speed and the freedom felt like a betrayal of Junie.

He pulled on the toboggan hat Crystal had loaned him and checked himself in the mirror. Commander Calhoun had said he was handsome, which was LD code for "almost normal." Crystal had tried to take him the rest of the way to passing by coating his face in Clinique Honeymilk "City Base," turning him into an extremely tanned dead man. He told her he looked like George Hamilton in *Love at First Bite*. She told him he looked fine. It would have to do.

He stepped out of the car and walked uphill toward the burned house, his hands jammed into the pockets of a denim jacket that used to belong to Crystal's ex. It was a tree-lined residential neighborhood, a mix of wooden houses and brick apartment buildings. The only people on the street were down by the fire, a dozen bystanders standing outside the yellow tape line. He walked across the street to a spot perhaps fifty yards from the house, where he could look out over the hoods of the parked cars to watch the crews work. He leaned against a tree to project casualness.

What had happened here? Did Zip set fire to the house to cover his escape? Had Blunt tried to burn them out? Where was everyone now?

After ten minutes he had a partial answer: Some people had never left the house. Two firefighters carried out a body bag to a gurney, and that was loaded into one of the ambulances. There was no way to tell whether the body was Blunt's, or Zip's—or belonged to an LD at all.

Over the next half hour four more bodies were brought out, loaded into the ambulances, and driven away. The sky lightened, and in the distance the Wasatch Mountains coalesced out of the dark. Only one ambulance remained.

Zip and his people weren't the Jonestown type—their entire goal was to go down biting as many breathers as they could—so, it had been a fight. Sometime after Blunt had called the answering system and left his message for Stony, he'd gone into the house after them.

Was Blunt really some kind of hit man for the LDA? He and Stony were friends—at least, Stony thought they were friends—but he'd only seen the man every few weeks when he brought the mail. It wouldn't have been hard for Blunt to keep him in the dark.

And if Blunt wasn't an assassin, someone like him would be necessary. It was the only explanation for why the Big Bite hadn't happened yet. The Diggers were good, and they could swarm a safe house once they'd been tipped off, but they didn't have much of a chance to prevent a bite—that required inside information. The LDA had to police itself. Jesus, Delia had to be part of it, too. She said that they didn't kill their own people, but of course she'd lie to him if she thought that was best for the army. The less he knew—the less any of the LDs knew—the less they could tell the government if they were caught.

He watched as they loaded a body bag into the last ambulance. A voice behind him said, "What's going on?" He started to turn, and stopped himself.

"Just a fire," he said.

The woman's dog, a white poodlesque creature, sniffed his shoe, then ran away from him, straining at the leash.

"Proxy! No. I heard gunshots," the woman said. "Early this morning." He didn't look into her face, sure she'd see through his disguise. She said, "Do you think they're drug dealers?"

He shrugged, kept his eyes on the house. Finally the woman let the dog pull her away, and he watched her go. Ten yards down, she forced the dog to come away from some bits of garbage on the sidewalk. After she passed, the passenger window of the parked car at that spot rolled down, and cigarette smoke drifted out. A hand tossed out a lit butt. The smoke, when it reached him a few seconds later, smelled of menthol.

Stony looked at the house, then back at the car, a boxy green Chevy Caprice. He walked toward it, trying to see through the rear window while making it seem like his attention was on the burned house. Two men sat in the front seat. When he drew closer he caught a glimpse in the car's sideview mirror of a pale face under a dark hat, but in another step the angle was wrong. He stopped, looked at the stretch of sidewalk outside the passenger window. Twenty, thirty cigarette butts lay on the cement.

Hours of cigarette butts. Hours of watching the house burn.

The ambulance rolled past, lights flashing, but with no siren. The taillights of the Caprice lit up, and then the engine started. Stony froze. The car backed up a few feet, turning to angle out of the parking spot, and suddenly the passenger window was beside him. The passenger's face was gray, but his hair was coal black and cut in a bowl—like Moe Howard. It was Zip's man from the congress, who'd crawled under the RV to look for a bomb. The man suddenly realized someone was standing outside his window, and threw up a pale hand to shield his face. The car pulled away.

Had he recognized Stony? It was impossible to tell.

Twenty feet away, the Caprice stopped abruptly, then began to back up at an angle. Stony spun in the other direction and began to walk quickly away. Then he calmed himself. The car *had* to turn around, because the way was blocked by the fire crews. It didn't mean they'd recognized him.

The Caprice slowly came up alongside him, this time with the driver's window facing him. Stony ducked his head and kept walking.

A moment later the car accelerated. He looked up to see it stop at the next intersection behind the ambulance. The ambulance turned right, and the Caprice went straight, toward downtown. Stony ran for his car. He was thankful the car was already pointing in the right direction.

The streets were starting to fill with morning traffic, but the slope of the hill let him see the Caprice two blocks ahead and below him. At the stoplight at State Street he was able to slide up behind the car with only an El Camino between them, and after that he was able to follow the Caprice north to where it pulled into a parking garage.

He slowed as he approached the dark entrance. What the hell were they doing? Going to the mall? The sign said ZCMI, which seemed to be some kind of department store or shopping center. He sat on the ramp, unwilling to follow too closely, until a car pulled up behind them. He took his ticket and began to follow the arrows first down, below street level, then around and up. The garage was mostly empty. On the third story he caught a glimpse of the green Caprice, heading up a ramp to the next level, and he followed, keeping his speed low. This level was a bit more crowded, and there was a double-door entrance to the store here. He rolled slowly past the rows of cars, craning his neck to see whether the Caprice was climbing the next ramp—and suddenly passed the car. It had just backed into a parking spot next to a white panel truck, which had also backed in. With a start he realized that on the side door of the truck was a Commander Calhoun logo.

Keep calm, he told himself. He drove past the car without looking at it, turned the corner, and went up the ramp to the next level, which turned out to be the last. He parked next to a stairwell. He felt like Jack Gore, or one of the Hardy Boys. True, they'd only traveled four blocks. It was the shortest "tail job" he'd ever read about, outside of an Encyclopedia Brown story. That kid only had a bicycle.

He stared out the windshield, trying to decide what to do. If Zip had been burned out of the safe house, then he should have hit the road to a new safe house, or rejoined his people who'd already left. Blunt had said in his message that his breather driver, one of the men they'd used at the congress, was following a group who'd slipped out yesterday.

There was only one reason for Zip to come here, a shopping center full of security cameras: In less than an hour it would be full of people.

Stony turned off the engine. He tucked the car keys under the seat and shut the door without locking it; he didn't know whether Crystal kept a spare set. He patted the roof and thought, Thanks little Honda. Then he hurried down the stairwell to the street. It took him ten long minutes to find a working pay phone.

"Collect call to Crystal Mayhall, from John," he told the operator. When his sister picked up the phone he had to interrupt her before she asked too many questions. He told her where to find her car if she refused to take his advice and buy a new one. Then he said, "I need you to do me one last favor."

* * *

Stony emerged from the stairwell a few minutes later, then found a spot behind a cement pillar where he could lean out and see the Caprice and the panel truck. The two vehicles were parked in the first row, about fifteen spots down from the store entrance. The car was empty, but there was a figure in the cab of the truck, masked by a fog of cigarette smoke. The parking garage was filling up, and people that Stony took to be staff members were being let into the store by a security guard. Two older women in bulky coats stood outside the doors, waiting for ZCMI to open, and more shoppers were probably waiting at the other entrances. It would be a busy shopping day. Christmas was only a week away. Mormons celebrated Christmas, didn't they?

He leaned back against the pillar and checked his watch. It was 8:35, twenty-five minutes before opening. Were the men from the Caprice in the truck? Was Zip in there with them? And what about Blunt?

The big question: If Blunt *was* in there, was Stony willing to sacrifice him to stop Zip?

He leaned out again and saw the man in the truck cab looking at him. Stony jerked his head back behind the pillar—and felt something hard press against his temple.

"Holy shit. Zac was right. You're the kid from Iowa."

Stony turned his head slightly, trying to ignore the pressure of the metal. It was the man with the Moe Howard haircut. The pistol looked smaller in his hand than it felt against Stony's temple.

Moe leaned past Stony to look at the store entrance. "Here's what we're going to do," he said. "We're going to walk to the back of the truck. If you say a word, or try to signal that security guard, I *will* shoot you in the back of the head."

Stony stopped himself from putting up his hands. "Is that where Zip is?" he asked. "In the truck?"

"Shut the fuck up. Move."

Moe lowered the gun, then shoved Stony between the shoulder blades. Stony had been afraid before, but never like this. He'd grown up feeling invulnerable. Unstoppable. But now that he was a twitch of a finger from having his head blown off, he realized that he was not brave at all. He wanted to live. He wanted it desperately. So he was going to do whatever this LD man said.

They walked slowly to the truck, the man a few feet behind him. He looked toward the entrance without moving his head, but now the security guard had disappeared, and the number of waiting customers had swelled to almost twenty. None of them glanced in his direction.

Stony reached the back bumper of the truck, and Moe rapped on the panel door, three quick knocks. The door slid up and a ripe, butcher-shop smell rolled out. Inside were five LD men, in various states of decay. All carried bulky assault weapons. In front was Tevvy, the green-skinned LD who'd thrown Stony around at the congress. After a moment's hesitation, Tevvy grabbed Stony by the front of his shirt and yanked him into the bed of the truck. Then the big man threw him to the floor and sat on top of him. Another man touched a rifle barrel to Stony's forehead.

"Are you wearing makeup?" Tevvy asked.

The floor was wet beneath Stony's back. The plywood wall to his right was splattered with blood. Had they already started?

"You can't do this," Stony said.

"Oh, we're doing it all right," Tevvy said. He turned to one of the other men. "Call Zip. Tell him we've got one of Blunt's people here." They had radios like Delia's. Of course they did. Until recently they'd all been part of the same army.

Tevvy said, "Did Delia send you?"

The men loomed over him. Stony said, "Nobody sent me. I haven't been able to reach anybody. I was afraid you'd, you'd killed them. Is Mr. Blunt still alive?"

One of the men made a series of indistinct sounds, which Stony took a moment to parse into the sentence: "Blunt came after *us.*" The man's jaw was unhinged on one side, making every expression a leer. "He torched the house. Came in with a pistol and a—"

Stony couldn't make out the word. "A what?"

"A machete," Tevvy said. "It came out of his arm."

"He cut off their heads!" the leering man said. "He's a psychopath!"

"He took out four of our people before we shot him down," Tevvy said. "But he's dead now. Right, Jason?" He glanced at the one with the Moe Howard haircut.

"Five bodies, five body bags," Jason said.

Someone rapped three times on the rear door. Tevvy rolled off Stony and nodded to have them open it. Stony lifted his head. Zip and another man climbed in. They seemed to be unarmed, but as Zip stood up his coat swung open to reveal a white T-shirt soaked with blood. He laughed. "Stony Fucking Mayhall!" Someone pulled the sliding door back down.

"Are we still on?" one of the men asked.

"Shit yes, we're still on," Zip said. "Bobby's team is ready to hit the loading dock. We all go in"—he glanced at a wristwatch—"fifteen minutes."

"You can't do this," Stony said. "You can't start the Big Bite."

"Not the way I wanted to," Zip said. "Your friends made sure of that when they betrayed us. I'll tell you this, though—we're sure as hell starting something. Right, boys?"

"*You* turned *her* in," Stony said. "You told the Diggers about her houses. You told them about the answering system."

He was guessing, but Zip nodded. "Stony, I reported every house I knew about. The Diggers will be so busy today they'll never notice what's happening here."

"You betrayed everyone," Stony said.

"I'm saving us, kid. Our people will realize that soon enough." Zip looked up. "How are our two converts?"

The men moved aside, and Stony twisted his head to see. At the back of the truck, two dead women lay on their sides. The oldest had short gray hair, the other, young enough to be a granddaughter, was a curly blonde. Stony could not tell where they'd been bitten, but their clothes were drenched in blood. They'd been dead only an hour, maybe two.

Each bite had an incubation period. Stony had been collecting data on the process from everyone he'd met at the house, and he'd watched Thomas's conversion in person. The longest part of the process was waiting to die. After death, there was a short period of disorientation during which the patient could barely function, and then the fever would set in. These women were already dead. They could be up and feeding within the hour.

"This will never work," Stony said, trying to sound firm. "Once you start biting, the police will see what you're doing on the security cameras. They'll swarm you before the epidemic gets rolling. You may infect some people, but for what? Once the news gets out, they'll just quarantine every victim before they bite anyone else."

Zip squatted down and shook his head. "You're missing the point, kid. We *want* the cameras to see us. Hell, once we get started, we'll call the television stations ourselves if we have to."

One of the men said, "We'll inspire people."

"Inspire them to do what?" Stony said. "Kill you?"

"No, *our* people," Zip said. He looked at his watch again.

"Once they see us on the news, biting like the old days, they'll start biting, too. The Diggers are cracking down everywhere today. Every LD in the country will realize that now's the time. We've been fighting a war of attrition, getting picked off one by one. That ends today. Besides, those people out there?" He looked up to address his men and pointed toward the front of the store. "Those breathers want it as bad as us. They're *yearning* for the end of the world. Why do you think they make so many movies about us? It's their fucking fantasy. Every one of them wants civilization to burn, for all the rules to go up in smoke. They *want* the monsters to attack. You know why? Because then they'll have the excuse to do what they've always wanted to do—shoot people in the head. No laws, no morality. They'll *have* to do it. It'll be fucking noble. Every one of them is picturing themselves as the last man standing, a bloodstained samurai with an AK-47."

"You'll get them all killed," Stony said. "You won't even be able to get out of here alive. There are what, twelve of you to pull this off?"

"Sixteen," the leering man said. It sounded like *sihhhsteen*. "That's enough."

Zip looked at Stony curiously. "Are you pumping us for information?" He nodded toward Stony's chest. "Lift your shirt."

"What?"

"Lift your fucking shirt."

Stony opened the denim jacket, then pulled up the blue Cubs T-shirt—another item borrowed from Crystal.

Zip frowned. "Drop your pants."

"Now come on, you think I'm wearing a wire?"

"Drop 'em."

Stony unsnapped his jeans, the same pants he'd been

wearing since the congress, and pushed them down to his thighs. At Zip's look, he dropped his underwear, too. "See?"

"All right, fine," Zip said. "It'd be just like Blunt to send you in here with a mike."

"But you killed Mr. Blunt, didn't you?"

"Shut the fuck up. Our people are hard to kill, but Blunt is something else entirely. Now, before I shoot you, I gotta ask: What the fuck were you thinking? You walk in here, you don't have a wire on you, or even a gun—"

"I don't believe in shooting people."

"So what the fuck was your plan, genius?"

"I was going to try to talk you out of it," Stony lied. "Using the force of reason."

Zip laughed. "The force of *what*?"

"I'm an idealist," Stony said.

"Well, we have something in common." He looked at his watch and stood up. "Time to go shopping, boys."

"Shoot him?" one of them asked.

Zip tilted his head. "Have you ever bitten anyone, Stony?"

"No."

"But you've wanted to, haven't you? That guy you ran down at the congress—I bet you wanted to bite the hell out of him."

"No."

Zip grinned. "Liar. I gotta tell you, it's pretty damn amazing. It's what we're built for." He nodded to Mel, the leering man. "Bring him along. He can die with us." Mel slung his rifle and yanked Stony to his feet. Tevvy lifted the sliding door.

There was a loud *crack* from the parking lot. Tevvy fell backward into the truck. Another crack, and a second man fell. Stony saw gray meat splatter Mel's face.

Zip looked at Stony. "What did you do? What did you do?"

"I made a call," Stony said.

He'd told Crystal to call in a zombie sighting. He didn't know if the Diggers would get here in time, or if only the local police would be close enough. He'd only gone back into the garage to make sure Zip didn't launch the attack before *someone* arrived.

Mel smiled his lopsided smile and lifted his weapon to point at Stony's chest. "*Muh*-her *fuh*-her," he said.

Stony lifted a hand. The blast knocked him backward, into one of the dead women behind him. Pain flared through his arm and chest. He could not ignore it. He could not master it. And before he could marshal his concentration, things got much worse.

The official story, as announced by government agents later that day, was that a small group of anti-Mormon extremists had captured a single zombie, which they planned to set loose on the people in the ZCMI Store. The ten (living) men in the parking garage were all killed, and another seven, parked across the street from the loading dock, were shot before they could leave their vehicle. The identities of the extremists were kept from the public under the Emergency Powers Act of 1968, which had never lapsed since the first outbreak.

As you might imagine, conspiracy theorists had a field day with this. And as usual, what began as a terrifying secret on the fringes of culture eventually found its way into the plot of a TV movie. In 1992, ABC broadcast *Deliver Them from Evil*, starring Harry Hamlin as an ex-army colonel and Teri Garr as his wife, which proposed that experimentation on soldiers, using a variant of the walking dead disease, had driven the men mad.

In 2011, a "final" unpublished Jack Gore novel was found. *Christmas for the Dead* is a thinly disguised version of the ZCMI attack. In it, escapees from Deadtown hole up in a Walmart in Nevada. In desperation they begin killing and infecting customers in an attempt to start a new outbreak. This is the first use in fiction of the term *Big Bite*. In the novel, Jack Gore sneaks into the store and tries to talk the "DLs" (as they started to call themselves in this book) out of attacking the "breathers" outside. Uncharacteristically, Gore fails, and he is killed along with the others when government troops storm the building. It's a bit of a downer, and perhaps proof that the book was not written by C. V. Ferris. One serious reader argued that it was also better written than the usual Ferris novel. On this point reasonable people may disagree.

But where were we? Oh, yes: Stony dying.

Mel's shot seemed to uncork the guns of the Diggers. A barrage of gunfire turned the interior of the truck into a hammer of sound. Stony could only stare up at the patch of air in front of his eyes, a dust storm of flesh and hair and clothing shot through with the lightning of sparking bullets. A body, or perhaps two bodies, fell over him. Stony was struck a dozen times, his body jerking with each impact—but perhaps because he was already prone, his feet pointing toward the open door, none of the shots entered his brain and ended his existence.

Because he'd gone deaf he was unsure of the exact moment the firing ended. He only knew the attack was over when armored men leaned into the dome of his vision, men in bulky vests and gleaming helmets like beetles. Still, over so quickly? It lacked the drama he'd been expecting, the slow-motion, Bonnie-and-Clyde deaths of Billy Zip and his terrorists. Where was the music?

The Diggers quickly determined that Stony was still functioning, and stepped over him to look at the two women.

"Fresh ones," one of the soldiers said. The women twisted and lurched. One of them, the young blonde, clawed feebly at the air. The soldier turned to another helmeted man and said, "What would you like to do?"

The second man took off his helmet and said, "What a mess." He was perhaps fifty years old, with a round, kindly face, and dark hair flecked with gray. He wore rimless glasses with silver stems.

The first soldier said, "Doctor, you shouldn't—"

"It's fine, Sergeant," the doctor said. He took off his glasses and rubbed the bridge of his nose. "The newspeople will be here soon," he said, almost to himself.

"Put them down, then?" the soldier asked.

"No!" Stony shouted. The doctor seemed to look at him for the first time. "Don't shoot them," Stony said. "Please."

"You're Stony Mayhall, aren't you?"

Stony tried to sit up, but his body failed to obey him. "There's another team. By the loading dock."

"What? How many? Where, exactly?"

"I don't know."

There was much shouting into radios. A few of the soldiers scrambled out of the truck, but the man with the glasses stayed.

"Don't kill the women," Stony said. "In a few hours they'll be fine. The fever passes. You don't have to kill them—"

"They'll hardly be fine," the doctor said. He squatted to

study Stony's face. "You *are* him. Your mother's told me so much about you."

"You know my mother?"

"You've been hurt," the man said. "Don't worry, we'll clean that up. You have no idea how long I've been looking for you."

I think I do, Stony thought.

The doctor said, "Sergeant, this one's coming with us."

"Yes, Dr. Weiss. And the other gunmen?"

The doctor regarded the bodies piled up around him. "Looks like you've already taken care of them. Just make sure of it."

"And the women?"

He took off his glasses and stared at the lenses as if deciding whether to clean them. "No room," he said finally. "Put them down, and may God have mercy on their souls."

PART
THREE

CHAPTER THIRTEEN

1998
Deadtown

ell, perhaps not 1998. It could be a year earlier, or later. In Stony's memory, the chronology of events during this period is a little shifty. In prison, at least the type of maximum security prison he found himself in, there was very little to anchor him to the living calendar. The seasons passed unseen beyond the windowless cement walls. His body, in refusing to age or decompose, was no use as a clock. One thing happened, and another thing happened. Sometimes these events were years apart.

Some moments, however, remained vivid in his memory, even if he could not place them on a calendar. Shame could paint an entire day. For example, the day he woke his first sleeper. The day he stopped his best friend from escaping.

He'd been in Deadtown for ten years, more or less. Sometime after the last chimp had died, after he'd been fitted for his first prosthetic hand, but before he'd gotten his second. A guard unlocked the steel door of his cell and said, "We've got another sleeper."

Stony looked up from the book he was holding. For a

moment, he wondered if they were talking about him, because although he looked as if he were reading, in truth he'd been staring at the same page for a long time. Possibly hours. He could say that he'd been lost in thought, if he could recall any thoughts. In his recent memory, there was nothing but a brilliant white void, a hole in a strip of film where the lamp had blasted through. This had been happening more and more often to him, but for how long he couldn't say.

Two guards stood in the doorway. The speaker's name was Harry Vincent, a handsome young man with watery blue eyes, a strong Roman nose, and full lips that reminded him of Ruby. There were guards who were decent men, who treated the LDs, if not kindly, then at least as if they might still be part of the human family. Harry was not one of those guards.

Stony put down the book. "Who is it?"

"One of the old-timers. The doc's away, but he said you should examine her." Because of Stony's relationship with Dr. Weiss, and his standing with the other prisoners, he had become over the years an unofficial trustee. He helped the newly captured adjust to life in Deadtown. He talked down the most violent prisoners, before the guards felt forced to kill them. He helped the prison run smoothly. He would have done these things, he told himself, even if the doctor did not reward him with certain privileges, such as access to the doctor's library.

Harry tossed him a mask. It was metal mesh and leather, a cross between a fencer's mask and a catcher's. Stony fit it over his face, then turned his back. Harry stepped forward to buckle it tight. Then they handcuffed his arms behind his back and led him out to the elevated walkway, Harry in front, the other guard trailing. As they passed the cells, prisoners stepped to the rectangular slots to whisper hellos to Stony, or to simply catch his eye. Stony nodded, saying nothing.

The cells were set on columns inside a larger cement box, surrounded by air on all sides. No one would be tunneling out of *this* Deadtown. There'd been four facilities that inherited the name. The first had been in Indianapolis, an army barracks that had been quickly converted to an emergency holding area during the 1968 outbreak. The next Deadtown was a prison farm in upstate New York, then an asylum in Florida, and finally this place, a hundred acres in the Nevada desert that had once been, and was still publicly known as, a federal toxic waste disposal facility. Wherever the dead were held, there was Deadtown.

The guards took Stony down the central stairs to the main floor, where two other guards worked the gate that allowed access to the next cell block. There were acres of cement buildings that stored several thousand tons of toxins and biological agents awaiting disposal, and among them were three oblong buildings that held the prisoners. There was no exercise yard, no cafeteria, no weight room. Most of the prisoners never left their block for the entirety of their stay. The length of their sentence largely depended on how long they could remain sane. Prisoners who acted out were destroyed. Those who tried to escape were destroyed. But those who tried to destroy themselves, or tried to escape by more subtle means, were prevented at all costs from doing so.

Stony's entourage entered the B block. As in the other building, the prisoners here were quiet, because the guards liked them quiet. But as Stony was led past the cells, LDs again came to the doors and tried to get his attention. These prisoners saw Stony less often, and they were more insistent.

"Stony, hey. Ask them about our radios. They took away the radios—" And "You have any books with you, Stony?" And "Hi, Stony. It's me, Thomas."

This last voice caused Stony to slow. If he stopped completely, the guards would become angry, so as he passed he made a minimalist wave with one bound hand, and Thomas nodded in return. The postman had almost no memories of his life before being bitten, and he'd had little time to make new ones. He'd been captured by the Diggers only a few weeks after his conversion—the day before Zip had tried to launch his Big Bite. Delia had never made it to the safe house, and she'd evidently eluded the authorities. At least Dr. Weiss had never caught her. But every LD at her safe house had been shot or captured. They'd also arrested Elizabeth, the living owner of the house.

The farther the guards took Stony down the walkway, the more his dread grew. Soon they reached the next-to-last cell, and the guards stopped to open the door. It was Valerie's cell.

The interior was identical to his own: an iron frame cot, a toilet with a waterless bowl, and a small desk and chair. On the desk was a paper tablet and a pencil. Months ago Stony had suggested to the doctor that the prisoners keep journals, and these documents could be analyzed for psychological insights peculiar to the undead. The doctor had ignored the suggestion until enough time had passed that he could think it was his own idea. Now the tablets were collected every Sunday like homework and replaced with fresh blank paper. No one knew what they were supposed to write about, only that they had to write something. Express yourself, the doctor told them.

The prisoner lay on the bunk, eyes closed, arms at her sides.

"Valerie?" Stony said.

The figure inside the blue prison jumpsuit was almost a skeleton: completely bald, with parched white skin stretched over her bones. A thin blanket covered her legs and feet.

He asked the guards, "How long has she been like this?"

"Two days. About."

"You should have moved her to the infirmary," he said, trying to hide his anger. "That's where the doctor wants them."

"The doctor wasn't here."

"All right. Could you at least take off the handcuffs, then? I need to examine her."

"Work around it," Harry said.

Stony said, "I thought the doctor didn't want to lose another one."

Harry swore, then grabbed Stony by the back of the neck and pressed his masked face to the wall. The other guard worked the key of the handcuffs.

"Thank you," Stony said when they released him.

"Leave the mask on," Harry said. Then the two guards stepped out of the cell and pulled the bars closed.

Stony went to the bunk and squatted down beside her. He took her hand in his. Of course it was cold, but the fingers were lifeless. She had not started to decompose—at least, no further than she'd been the day she climbed from the grave. She did not smell like a corpse.

"Hey, sweetheart." He touched her face. "Time to wake up."

The first sleeper had been discovered about a year ago. He was an LD from Maryland named Lawrence who'd been in Deadtown for over twenty-five years. One night he lay down on his bunk—and never got up. The guards eventually realized he'd stopped moving. They pulled him from the bed, yelled at him, beat him. They tried sharp tools and electricity. He never made a sound, and his eyes never flickered.

The doctor examined Lawrence's body, and allowed Stony to see him as well. It was a riddle. The working definition for "walking dead" was a dead person that walked. If the corpse stopped moving, was it only a corpse? Or an LD playing possum? They watched Lawrence for weeks. He never moved. Eventually the doctor ordered Lawrence to be destroyed. Stony argued furiously with the doctor. How could he kill a man, because we don't know he's gone yet! But the doctor was fed up. The destruction was carried out in the usual way: one .38 round through his forehead, then off to the prison incinerator. But Lawrence had started some kind of trend. Over the next year, seven more prisoners entered the sleep.

"I know you don't want to be here," Stony said to Valerie. *Here* being not just this cell, or Deadtown, but the world. "You've served your time. You've earned the right to leave, if that's what you want to do. But you know I can't let you go without a fight." This last he said lightly. It was a joke between them that he could argue for days about the smallest thing.

She didn't respond. Outside the bars, Harry and the other guard were already bored. Stony tried to think of what he could say to her that hadn't been said in all the hours they'd spent together. The doctor allowed him to visit the prisoners, and he'd used that privilege sometimes selfishly. He went to Valerie's cell at least once a month, where they continued their conversation (argument, debate, competing monologues) wherever they'd left off. Sometimes they talked about trivial things. When the guards weren't watching, he would sit beside her, their hands and arms entwined. Of course they didn't have sex—that was impossible for them—but these moments seemed to be the kind of intimacy that (he imagined, after reading countless novels and watching so many films) breathers drifted into after sex, the languorous morning in bed between lovers, or settled into *long* after the last act of intercourse: the deep comfort taken by couples in their eighties. Sometime since arriving in Deadtown, Valerie had stopped being his substitute mother, his older sister, and had become something else that he'd never heard an LD describe. And now she was trying to leave him.

She'd never lost her belief that the LDs were in limbo, cut off from God. He couldn't blame her for finally wanting to cross over. If he were a good person, an unselfish person, he'd kiss her good night and wish her a safe voyage. But he wanted her to stay.

"You're setting a bad example here, Valerie. If you decide this second life isn't worth living, how many others are going to take your exit as an example?" He thought, How long until *I* decide to follow her?

He glanced behind him, and saw that the guards had disappeared. The cell block had gone silent. LD ears would be straining. Whatever he said now that wasn't whispered would be heard and passed along the block. If Valerie died tonight, this would be the only eulogy his people would hear.

Well, he had no interest in delivering a eulogy. But he did want them to hear one thing. He removed his mask, and in a normal voice, said, "Some people say we're cursed, Valerie. That we're the work of Satan. But I don't believe that. I know that we're special because of people like you. You're kind. You cared for me when I first came to the house; you took care of every new arrival. Why would the devil create someone like you?

"There's a purpose for us, Valerie. And I don't think it's done with you yet. There's work to do here. You may not know it, but people here depend on you. *I* depend on you. There's a revolution coming, Valerie, and when these walls tumble down, we're going to need the most humane of us to guide us."

There. He felt ridiculous, but he'd said what he needed to for the peanut gallery. And Valerie hadn't moved.

He lifted her slightly, and lay down beside her, his arm

around her so that she rested her head on his chest. He stroked her arm with his prosthetic hand. After a long while he turned his head and whispered into her ear, "I know you're awake in there."

She didn't answer. He said in a low voice, "There's something I never told you. I don't know why—maybe because I thought you'd be grossed out, or think I was becoming a mad doctor or something. It's about my pinky." He laughed at his nervousness. "You know when I was captured, my hand was pretty much destroyed when one of Zip's men shot it. I dragged that hunk of flesh around with me for six months before I asked the doctor to amputate it completely. But I'd already done my own experiment. I cut off—well, I guess *twisted* off is more accurate—my pinky toe on my right foot. I hid it in a hole in my mattress. I know, that's a little weird, even for us.

"Anyway, the toe didn't rot. I checked it every day, and it was the same as always, a little gray nubbin with a black nail, just like the ones that were still attached. This is one of those impossible things that drive the doctor crazy—why don't LDs rot? Why is the state of our decomposition frozen at the moment we die? Yes, we wear down, some of us lose our hair and our teeth, we get injured. But why don't our cells break down and slough away? Why don't microbes eat our flesh? Not even bacteria like our taste."

He stared at the ceiling for a minute. And then he whispered, "The point is, here was a body part that also refused to rot. I kept checking on it every day for months. Eventually I looked at it once a week, and then I forgot to check on it at all. Now the interesting part. One day I was hiding something else—I'll tell you about that later, after you wake up—and I found the toe. It had fallen into the corner behind the leg of the bunk, and it was shriveled and black and it smelled awful.

It had started decomposing. Why, though? What had changed?"

He looked down at her. "Give up? It was me. I'd forgotten about it. I'd stopped thinking of the toe as part of me. And without me to believe in it, it started to rot."

He tapped her arm with his plastic hand. "And that's how I know you're still in there, Valerie. That's how I knew Lawrence, our first sleeper, wasn't really dead. You haven't given up on your body yet."

He lay beside her for several hours, talking to her. Harry and the other guard didn't return for him. It wasn't until he heard the next shift enter the cell block that Stony moved to get up.

Valerie's hand tightened on his own. "I was almost there," she said.

"Valerie! Sweetheart!"

She sat up slowly. He offered a hand to help her up, but she shook her head. She pulled the blanket from her legs and stared at her feet.

She wore no shoes. The skin had been turned the color of charcoal.

Stony looked at her face, then back to her feet. "What did they—?"

The soles of her feet had been scoured away, exposing black bone. "I remember that now," she said.

He put a hand to his mouth to stop himself from screaming. They'd burned her. The fuckers had burned her.

He stood up, went to the closed door of the cell, and peeked out. The guards were nowhere in sight. He turned, turned again.

Eventually he went to Valerie and kneeled beside her. "I'm so sorry," he said. "I'm so sorry."

"Almost there," she said again.

* * *

When Dr. Weiss returned, he was pleased to hear of Stony's success and sent for him immediately. Guards escorted him to the administration building, and home to Dr. Weiss's office, the lab, and the infirmary, a suite of private cells housing a few of the prisoners the doctor was particularly interested in. Stony worked in the lab three or four times a week. In order to do his work he needed to have his hands free, and once the handcuffs were removed it seemed pointless to leave the mask on. Yes, it was against all protocols, but Stony was a special case. See, Dr. Weiss and Stony were *pals.* Colleagues. Mentor and mentee.

"Pleasant trip?" Stony asked politely.

"Another near miss," Dr. Weiss said sourly. "They'd been in the house not a day before." He unlocked his briefcase and began removing thick file folders. He'd been traveling with one of the capture teams, tracking down rumors of walking dead in San Diego. More and more often they were missing the LDs. The dead, who used to hunker down to hide, had turned skittish. It was nothing like the late eighties, when Zip had tipped off the Diggers to the LDA phone network. In those years the teams had rolled up two dozen safe houses, and hundreds of LDs had been captured. Captured, but not kept. Deadtown's population was capped at 120, and fewer than a dozen had been brought in to the prison. The rest had been destroyed.

In the past few years, the teams had found only a few stray LDs, and no occupied safe houses. The doctor was growing impatient. He constantly worried that they'd cut his funding and end the program.

Stony said, "I don't suppose you spoke to anyone on the civilian side?" The breathers who were suspected of aiding the undead were kept in civilian prisons and fell under the jurisdiction of the Justice Department. Deadtown was controlled, for historical reasons going back to the emergency powers granted during the '68 outbreak, by the army. Still, the two sides talked. Favors could be traded.

"It wasn't that kind of trip, Stony," the doctor said. He stooped to spin the dial on his private safe, carefully blocking Stony's view of the numbers.

Stony said, "I only ask because you'd mentioned you'd be seeing someone from Calvette—"

"I'm sorry, Stony, no." He deposited a few of the files in the safe, then slammed the door. "I'm sure your mother is fine."

"But she hasn't written back." It was against all rules, but the doctor had taken Stony's letters to his mother at the Calvette Medical Prison, and had promised to deliver any letters she wrote to him.

"Stony, we've talked about this—I can't *force* your mother to write to you. Now tell me—how did you do it? How did you get Valerie to snap out of it?"

Stony tried to keep his voice level. "I just talked to her," he said. Then he picked up a stack of remaining folders and said, "Do you want me to refile these?"

"I need details, Stony! What did you say to her?"

"She wasn't as far gone as the others," Stony said. "It was that simple."

"Huh. So early intervention . . ."

"You have a problem with Harry Vincent," Stony said.

"What kind of problem?"

Stony told him about what he'd done to Valerie. "He's abusive. He could have killed her. You're going to have to fire him."

"I think we both know that's not possible. You're overstepping your bounds, Stony."

Bounds. And what were those, exactly? Stony had made it his job to move those boundaries, a little bit every day. While Dr. Weiss studied the LDs, Stony studied the doctor. Stony tried a different tack. "He deliberately disobeyed your orders. He could have ruined one of your most important subjects. Valerie is one of the graveborn, one of the few we have in population."

"I know that."

"I'm just saying, you might want to make sure to have guards who understand what's at stake here. Professionals who don't . . . undermine you with the other staff."

Dr. Weiss removed his glasses. "Undermine me? How?"

"He's not onboard with the research goals of the organization, Doctor. He thinks that you . . ." Stony frowned as if reluctant to pass on bad news.

"What?"

"He's openly told the other guards that you should be replaced as director."

Dr. Weiss started to ask a question, then changed his mind. "You should file those."

Dr. Weiss coveted data. He hoarded files and folders and magnetic tapes and disks, and threw nothing away. When he came into possession of a particularly sparkly factoid, some juicy secret, he showed it off to Stony like Kwang unwrapping a mint-condition *Astonishing Tales*—and then told him to file it away. Sometime after he'd been in Deadtown a few years, but before he'd gotten his first prosthetic hand, the doctor had called Stony into his office and handed him a thick manila envelope. "A contact of mine at DoJ forwarded on something you might find interesting."

On the front of the envelope was scrawled, in thick black marker, MAYH70381.

The doctor said, "It's from a police detective in Des Moines, Iowa. Somebody named Detective Kehl."

Kehl. Stony remembered his mother talking about him.

Weiss said, "He's retiring, trying to wrap up some cold cases. He sent a request for a final interview with your mother. DoJ said no, of course, but they demanded all his files. Those are the pertinent bits."

Stony opened the envelope and took out a sheaf of papers. They were photocopies of manually typed reports, the text faint.

Dr. Weiss said, "This detective's been looking into the death of a homeless girl in December 1968. He finally tracked down her name."

Stony looked up. Dr. Weiss savored the anticipation; he was gleeful with it. "Bethany Cooper. From Evans City, Pennsylvania."

Stony thought, My mother—my biological mother—had a name.

"The town was practically the epicenter of the outbreak," the doctor said. "She was seventeen the year it happened, living at home. On the big night, October first, she disappeared. Her parents thought she died in the attacks. Most of the town was wiped out. Somehow, two months later, she turned up in Iowa by the side of the road."

"Where was she going?" Stony asked.

"Who knows? Maybe she was running away from home, heading west. Maybe she was in shock. But at some point between leaving home and arriving in Easterly, she delivered you—perhaps on the night of the outbreak."

"The father?" Stony couldn't say, my father.

"Both parents are still in Evans City. They moved away briefly during the evacuation, but then came back and never moved. Property values probably never recovered."

"No, who was the father of the baby?"

"Ah. I don't believe that's in the file. Another missing person. Detective Kehl, however, wanted to know what happened to the child."

"He doesn't know about me?"

"He must suspect something. So what do you think? Should we tell this retired cop the rest of the story? Solve the biggest mystery of his career?"

"I don't know, but if—"

"I'm kidding, Stony. You're classified."

Stony nodded, though he was still numbed by the news. He turned over another page in the stack and saw a wallet-sized photograph—it looked like a school picture—of a white girl with straight bangs and long brown hair. And now, he thought, she had a face.

"She's so young," he said aloud. "Can I keep this?"

"Stony." The doctor's tone was condescending. It was against the rules for the prisoners to keep any personal items. Besides: It was data, and all data belonged to Dr. Weiss.

"Right," Stony said, and slid the photo back into place beneath a paper clip. "You want me to file these?"

"I'll take them." Ah. Destined for the private safe. Dr. Weiss had gotten more careful over the years; he no longer opened the vault in Stony's presence, afraid that Stony would peek at the combination. The doctor said, "I just wanted to see if the face jogged a memory. You see, the girl died of severe internal injuries—as if she'd tried to give birth to a clawed animal. Detective Kehl didn't know what to make of it."

Stony put the file on the desk. You fucker, he thought.

"Evidently," the doctor said, sliding the file toward himself, "you weren't the easiest child to bring into the world."

Sometime after Valerie's awakening—two weeks, or perhaps a month—Harry Vincent and four other guards charged Stony's cell. They wore the usual riot gear: hockey pads, thick gloves, and the Plexiglas helmets of the Diggers.

To the guards, the undead presented a problem. The prisoners did not experience pain as the living did, and could not be subdued or intimidated as easily as normal prisoners. They were a challenge. And there was something about their resistance to pain that galled, that provoked. It was a Fuck You to every state employee with a truncheon. And so the constant struggle (easily lost) to treat them as anything but carcasses, as dumb meat on hooks fit to be punched, Rocky Balboa–style, then to be shoved around, carved up, and eventually—inevitably—thrown into the incinerator. The living dead are born out of the ground, but they rise in smoke.

Harry Vincent did not appreciate being reported to his supervisor. His supervisor did not appreciate the doctor inserting himself into the running of the prison. So Stony Mayhall would be suspected of hiding contraband, and he would resist the guards, and he would be firmly subdued.

They broke both of his arms, and ripped the prosthetic hand from his stump, and cracked his shoulder blade. They jumped on his ribs, denting his torso like a wicker basket. They shattered his right cheek and flattened his face. They seemed to find it difficult to stop hitting him. Maybe if he had made some noise, or cried out in (mock) pain, they would have stopped sooner. Or maybe that would have only egged them on. Impossible to know.

Stony did not try to bite them, though he did have an opportunity to do so. One of the men slammed his arm down across Stony's face, and his forearm pad slipped up toward his elbow. For a moment there was a rectangular patch of exposed flesh at the man's wrist, only inches from Stony's teeth. He let the moment pass. After Cornelius, he'd promised himself he wouldn't bite anyone again.

Eventually the guards exhausted themselves. Harry Vincent squatted next to him, breathing hard. "I promise you, Stony. One day I'm going to be the one to throw you in the incinerator. I'm going to light a cigarette off your flaming head and watch you burn."

Stony decided a reply wasn't necessary. Later, on the floor of his cell, he attempted the first repairs on himself, imagining Alice talking him through the procedure. The tibia's connected to the patella-a-a, the patella's connected to the fee-murrr . . . Now hear the word of the Lord.

He was able to snap a knee into place, but the rest of his attempts at reconstruction were not very effective. He had only one hand to work with, a tool that was itself in need of repair. He could do nothing for his arm above the stump, which appeared to be broken in three places. Finally he rested his damaged cheek against the cement floor and watched the fluorescent light through the slot in his cell door.

CHAPTER FOURTEEN

The Turn of the Century, More or Less
Deadtown

I've been thinking about the ship of Theseus," Stony told the doctor. He struggled to enunciate clearly. Over weeks of surgeries the doctor and his team had stitched up the tears and punctures in Stony's skin, wired his rib cage together, pinned the bones of his legs and arms, and reset his jaw. Still, damage remained. He'd not yet adjusted to the limitations of his new body.

Dr. Weiss sat beside the bed, arms on his knees, his face dour, as if he were in mourning. It was one of his daily visits, which had grown longer over the weeks, as if he were lonely, or seeking counseling. Most afternoons there was alcohol on his breath.

Stony said, "It was in a philosophy book I read once. A wooden ship is damaged in battle, so they take off one of the planks and replace it with, say, aluminum. Or plastic. Each time the ship is damaged, they remove a wooden plank and replace it with a plastic one, until years later, the ship is entirely plastic. So. Is it the same ship as before?"

The doctor frowned. He looked tired, his skin gray. Maybe it was the drink, or the stress of the job. Or maybe, after so long among the undead, he'd started to resemble them. "I'm sorry," he said. "I'm not following."

"I'd like to continue with the experiment," Stony said. He lifted his broken arm, and the damaged shoulder joint vibrated like a serrated knife sawing a pork chop bone. The arm was being held together by a contraption of rods and braces and ended in a new prosthetic hand. The new hand was lighter and more cheaply made than his previous model, but he'd adjusted to it quickly, and learned to move the fingers and thumb in the space of a few days. "I think we can go further."

"No," Dr. Weiss said, seeming to wake up. "Absolutely not."

"The whole arm," Stony said. "Right up to the shoulder. All new equipment."

"I don't understand why you keep volunteering to do this to yourself." Then, with the token expression of concern dispensed with, he said, "What purpose would it serve?"

"To find out where it ends. I can already do this . . ." The index finger flexed, like a finger puppet. A small thing, but impossible to explain with conventional science. There were no wires connecting his finger to his arm muscles, no tiny motors to move the digit. No remote control. The finger moved because Stony made it move. He felt like a novice magician demonstrating the opening moves of a master's illusion: Thank you, Mr. Blunt. He ought to write a paper for OSWoG. Stony said, "Don't you wonder how far it can go? What if I can do an entire arm?"

"I'm worried for you, Stony," Dr. Weiss said.

"This could redefine the living dead. Think about it. When they ask you, 'Dr. Weiss, how *much* of one of these creatures do we have to destroy before we know it's truly dead?' And you can say—"

"All of it. Take no chances."

Stony lowered his arm. "That's not very scientific."

"Better safe than scientific."

"If you truly believed that," Stony said, "Deadtown wouldn't exist. We're here exactly because knowledge of us is important, even if it comes with a little risk." Stony lay back against his pillow. "All I'm saying is, think about it."

The doctor had already been thinking of extending the experiment, and Stony knew it. Someday soon, Dr. Weiss would call in one of the prisoners, tie him or her down, and cut off a finger, a toe, a hand, an arm. It wasn't that the doctor was Capital-E Evil. He was haunted, not only by the victims of 1968, but by the ghosts of the future dead, the millions who would die next time. Despite the Diggers' successes, despite the record lows in reports of the undead, Dr. Weiss knew, as Stony did, that a second outbreak was inevitable. It was the Diggers' failure at finding new hordes of ravenous biters that would allow them to reappear. The government was growing complacent, losing the rabid edge that would let it strike quickly when the next surge of undead erupted. Or—and this is what kept the doctor up at night—the next outbreak would begin in some third-world country, where the government was insufficiently prepared to put down an epidemic. Dr. Weiss would stare at his bedroom wall, thinking of a tide of undead rolling through the rural provinces of China, the plains of Africa. He'd begun his career desperately searching for a vaccine or treatment, but after thirty years the impossibility of the living dead, their immunity from rational understanding, had crippled that dream. Science was failing him.

His only hope now was to apply the scientific method to the irrational. He would amputate the limbs of the prisoners, not because he wished to hurt them, but because he wanted to save them, the living and the dead alike. The limits of animation seemed central to the puzzle. The doctor had heard rumors of Mr. Blunt, and Stony had confirmed that the LD was more marionette than man, a thing of polished wood. Then the doctor had seen Stony learn to manipulate artificial limbs as if they were his own bones. How much further could he go? It was the flip side of the question of how much destruction an LD could take. How much of the artificial could be assimilated and still retain that person's identity?

The doctor stared at him for a long moment, then slowly shook his head. "You're not like the rest of them, Stony. Maybe it was the way you were born. But you're different. You're more . . . human."

What does he expect me to say? Stony thought. Thank you? From day one, the doctor assumed that because Stony had betrayed Billy Zip, he was somehow on the side of the Diggers. Stony had done nothing but encourage that misunderstanding.

The doctor stood up to leave, and Stony said, "You'd have to save all the parts we remove. So we can try the Hobbes thing."

"Oh, of course," Dr. Weiss said, but Stony could tell he didn't get the reference. Thomas Hobbes had taken the Ship of Theseus story one step further. What if, Hobbes asked, some man had saved each of the wooden planks as they were taken off, and then later built a ship out of them, putting each piece back in its original location? Wouldn't the reassembled ship be the same one we started with? Then what about the plastic ship next to it?

"We can build another Stony," Stony said. "I've always wanted a brother."

* * *

Sometimes when he lay on the bed he put his plastic hand to the metal frame and said to himself, I am the bed. Feel those sturdy legs, the hard feet against the cold cement.

If the self could embrace a plastic prosthetic, he reasoned, why not furniture? Why couldn't the self be larger than this man-shaped lump of dead material he found himself in? He was as curious as the doctor, perhaps more so. He concentrated, and made a chant of it: *I am the bed. The bed is me. I belong to you and you belong to me. I am the bed . . .*

It was a struggle to stay focused. Even before Valerie's torture, Stony had been losing time, and his thoughts darted and circled like a paper sack caught by the wind. The attack by Harry and the other guards had only accelerated the disarray. Often he thought about sleep, the Little Sleep that he used to envy in his sisters, and the Big Sleep that he envied in Valerie. That he took away from her.

Sometimes an image entered his mind that he could not shake for days. Junie, sobbing into his shoulder. Kwang, crushed under the dashboard of the car. Alice reaching down to pull him out of his cardboard fort at the edge of the fields. Bethany Cooper, bleeding to death in the snow. He tried to think of positive things, to summon a brighter future. He imagined traveling to Pennsylvania and meeting his grandparents. He imagined his grandmother reaching out an arm to him and saying, "It's you, isn't it? Bethany's boy."

But even that fantasy felt like a betrayal. His mother sat alone in a cell like his, in the Calvette Medical Prison. Dr. Weiss had promised to look into his mother's case, but he'd done nothing. He hadn't even managed to get his mother to read Stony's letters—or if she had, to write back. Years ago the doctor visited Wanda Mayhall regularly. Stony had found folders thick with their transcribed conversations. At first she'd refused to tell the man anything, but her daughters were still under threat of arrest, and the facts could not be hidden for long. The doctor learned all about how Stony was found, how he refused to grow, then how he refused to stop growing. He got everything from her, eventually. And then when he captured her son, he had no more interest in Wanda Mayhall.

Most nights Stony heard the guards—really one guard—making his rounds. He knew it was Harry Vincent. The man walked through the offices, sat at Dr. Weiss's desk, rattled the file cabinets. Each night he stood for a long time in front of Stony's cell. He never spoke, though sometimes he stood there for minutes at a time.

Of course Stony fantasized about revenge. Against Vincent, against the doctor, against the other guards who'd beaten him. The daydreams were vivid and bloody, an acid bath that burned away everything but a copper-bright circuit of hate. It was almost addicting. He tried to break himself out of these toxic spirals by willing himself to think of Ruby. She was ten now (or eleven, or twelve). He invented hobbies for her. He listened to her practice the cello, except when it was a saxophone or piano. He regarded her artwork as it hung on Crystal's refrigerator. He imagined her letters, written on ruled paper: *Dear Uncle Stony, It sure has been a busy week!*

And all other times he planned his escape. It was his duty as a prisoner. The Diggers' helicopters were just outside the administration building, their black SUVs gassed up and ready to go. He fabricated elaborate escape plans worthy of a Jack Gore book. No, stranger than a Jack Gore book. He pulled himself up and went to the door of his cell. He put his plastic fingers to the wall and thought, *I am the door. The door is me . . .*

Stony had spent years becoming one of the most reliable workers in the doctor's office. Now that he'd moved into an infirmary cell, he could be that diligent employee every day: the doctor's most important research assistant. The nurses who rotated through the facility never lasted long, and outside scientists were not encouraged to visit. Dr. Weiss did everything he could to block other researchers from direct access to the prisoners, and he only reluctantly released data to the government teams studying the undead. The doctor thought Stony posed no threat, however, either to his ego or his health: Stony was never forced to wear a mask and was never handcuffed: The doctor wanted nothing to slow down his typing speed.

And Stony could type like a fiend, nearly 160 words a minute, and spent hundreds of hours at the computer, filling databases, and writing little DOS and VB6 programs to help the doctor churn out statistics. He typed an uncountable number of reports, memos, official letters, and articles. The articles had not been published, and would never be as long as the existence of Deadtown remained a state secret. "I'm sitting on a gold mine," the doctor said at least once a week, "and I can't tell anyone." He feared for his legacy.

Sometime before, Stony had expressed concern about the archives. This was in 1995 or 1996, a couple of years before Valerie first tried to sleep. In the old animal lab there were almost a dozen file cabinets filled with documents going back to the first days of the prison. "They can take paper away from you," Stony told the doctor. "They can burn it."

Soon the office had a scanner. Stony set about digitizing the most important of the years of paper documents and saving those first to Zip disks, then later burning to CDs and DVDs. Stony made two copies of everything. "Just in case you need to take a few home." Internet access was forbidden at Deadtown, but Stony set up a VPN, a kind of private digital tunnel, between the office and the Weiss home, so the doctor could get at the files remotely.

The work beat cleaning the animal cages. Those experiments were over now, thank God. Now his most interesting task was making the rounds of the special patients in the infirmary. Some of these were sleepers, inert men and women chained to their beds, who would lie there until the doctor decided to dispose of them. Stony tried to talk to them as he had to Valerie, but he never felt that they were listening to him, or that he was breaking through. Maybe it was because he didn't know them as well as he did Valerie, or care for them as deeply. Maybe it was because he didn't want to rob them of their escape from Deadtown.

Many of the patients were headbangers. Suicide was no easy task for an LD, but a determined prisoner could bash his skull against the floor or wall with enough force to destroy himself. If he (and most of the headbangers were male) failed to finish the job, or if the guards heard the distinctive thumping and interrupted him, he'd be brought to the administration building and strapped to a bed in the infirmary. Sometimes the prisoner recovered, and went back to his cell, living for months more like a dented aluminum can on a grocery shelf. Sometimes he went back to his cell and finished the job.

Stony's most unusual, and favorite, patient was Perpetual Joe. Most of the man's cell was taken up by a sturdy, squealing treadmill that was little more than a rubber mat wrapped around a set of steel rollers. Joe ran full-out, chest up, arms pumping. A slight hitch in his step—caused, perhaps, by one leg being shorter than the other—gave him a jazzy, swinging gait. He always seemed happy to see Stony, though he never paused or slowed.

Stony checked the battery and connections, recorded the output from the voltmeter, inspected the treadmill for wear and tear, all the while trading small talk with Joe. The man had

risen from the grave during the original outbreak, been captured at dawn the next day, and had spent the last thirty years
as a prisoner of successive Deadtowns. In 1982, Dr. Weiss had
decided to test LD endurance. He started with four LDs, on
treadmills wired to generate a current. The other prisoners
had damaged themselves, or stopped in protest, or pleaded
fatigue. Joe kept going. Joe *liked* it. He spent all day, every day,
running toward the cement wall three feet in front of him.

"How much today, Stony?" he'd ask, and Stony would read
him the latest figures. He'd recently passed the 25 million-mile
mark, and had generated enough power to electrocute every
prisoner in Nevada. Part of Stony's job was to inspect Joe
himself, especially his feet and legs and knees. Joe ran barefoot,
and his feet should have been pulverized by the constant
pounding, his knees and hips destroyed. But his body was
unchanged from the day of Stony's first report. Maybe, Stony
thought (for the thousandth time, the millionth), we are
wounded only by what we expect to wound us. Anything
beneath our notice—like the wear and tear of constant running, or obsessive digging, or the daily microscopic impacts
with air and ground—cannot harm us because we forget to
allow it to harm us. Integrity is all, as the Lumpists said.

"Better check that third roller," Joe would say, or point
out some disturbing squeak or incipient tear in the rubber
pad. He was as conscientious about his equipment as any professional athlete. When the backup treadmill was out for
repairs, as it was now, he was constantly nervous. He'd been
forced to stop only three times. Stony had seen only one of
those stoppages. Joe, the most upbeat LD that Stony had ever
met, flew into a rage and had to be restrained.

"Keep up the good work," Stony would tell him. And
Stony kept working, too. Tasks kept him from losing time,
kept the white void from blanking his mind. He had a job to

do every day, and long-term goals, and people to care for. Most of the time he didn't think about going to sleep. Whole days went by in which he didn't imagine crushing his skull against the cement floor of his cell.

On Sundays, Stony's job was to go through the collected journals, summarize them and log them into a database, and set aside the most interesting entries for the doctor's consideration on Monday morning. In the first weeks of the project the doctor read every tablet, but it soon became clear that most of the LDs had nothing of interest to say: They doodled, or copied down nursery rhymes, or wrote, "I prefer not to." A few of the prisoners became memoirists, describing their lives before they were bitten, or how they'd stayed hidden during the years. Stony scanned these for mentions of other LDs still at large, or for information that might help the Diggers find a remaining safe house, and when he found these references he cut those pages free using an X-Acto knife, then ate them. Later, sometimes days later, he would sneak into a bathroom and vomit the paste into the toilet. Delia was still out there, and Commander Calhoun had not been discovered. Rose and the Lump, as far as he knew, were still free. Even Mr. Blunt might still be alive. So he swallowed the evidence, and every Sunday he unboxed a fresh stack of blank tablets to distribute to the prisoners. On some of the middle pages, he wrote messages in faint pencil. Sometimes he passed on news from the outside world. Sometimes he gave them assignments called DGCs, for Drive the Guards Crazy.

DGC #84. On Tuesday, everyone softly hum "Climb Every Mountain."

And, They are waiting for us outside.

And, Give a man a stick and he will beat you for a day. But give

*him a uniform, and he will beat you every day, then complain about
how tough it is on his rotator cuff.*

The journal entries that most interested Dr. Weiss were
the ones in which LDs talked about their feelings. If they
talked about their feelings about death, the doctor became
almost giddy. "Listen to this," the doctor said one Monday
morning. " 'We are proof that God exists. We may be the only
proof that God exists. We are dead sticks moving in the wind,
and the wind is God.' That stick thing again! Why do they
keep talking about sticks? Is that code?"

"It's something we all say," Stony said. "I'm not sure where
it started."

"It sounds like a verse. Take a note, Stony—we need to
survey the population and see which of those were most religious before they died, and compare to how religious they are
now. Maybe those who believe in a higher power are more
resilient."

"Like alcoholics," Stony said.

The doctor gave him a blank look. "I suppose."

The doctor had taken to drinking at work. Some afternoons he sat at his desk, refilling his travel mug from a bottle
he kept out of sight, and talked at Stony. Stony called it
Unhappy Hour.

He complained about the Department of Justice's
attempts to grab his funding, or other researchers trying to
steal his data. But mostly he railed against his bosses at the
Pentagon. They were undermining him, trying to shut down
Deadtown. There were even rumors of a second LD project
somewhere overseas, a black site.

"They're keeping me in the dark," the doctor said one
afternoon. "It's not just the CIA. Someone else is working
domestically. Another agency. First, every tip we get for a
zombie foxhole turns up empty, and *now*—" He lurched out

of his chair and unlocked his briefcase. "Now this. Look at these photos."

He tossed a manila folder into Stony's lap. Inside were several dozen eight-by-ten color photographs. Shots of corpses—decapitated corpses.

"Those are undead," the doctor said. "Notice the lack of blood."

Stony stared at the bodies, wondering whether he knew any of these people, but it was impossible to identify them. "When did—when did this happen?"

"Two days ago," the doctor said. "But this has happened before. Some other team is finding LDs, and they're chopping their Goddamn heads off. They take the heads, but don't bother to dispose of the bodies—they leave those for us. Every couple of years we get a call from some cop or civil servant saying they've found a room full of headless corpses."

"Maybe it's a vigilante," Stony said.

"What?"

"A lone hunter. Perhaps his family was bitten in the outbreak, or he was attacked himself, and now he's out for revenge."

"I never know when you're pulling my leg, Stony." He waved dismissively. "We're talking about a roomful of zombies. This requires *organization*. Someone at our level or higher—an FBI-level organization."

"You think the FBI is behind this?"

"I can't get anyone to tell me! And I have a higher Goddamned clearance than anyone."

Stony said, "I wouldn't worry about it, Doctor. They can't keep it a secret forever." He was already planning the news items he'd write into the fresh tablets of paper the guards would distribute this Sunday.

The civil war continues. More LDs destroyed by partisans. Mr. Blunt is alive.

Dr. Weiss stared at the photos, exhausted. "Stony, you have no idea how difficult my job is."

"Hey Joe, did I ever tell you about the time I met the Lump?"

Stony sat on the floor looking up at Perpetual Joe, who was running as hard as always. He was the true Unstoppable, Stony thought. He did not get depressed. He did not worry. He ran away from his problems, but in the most Zen-like way possible.

Stony said, "When I met him, he scared me, frankly. I'd never met anyone who . . . who was that far gone. I thought it was a trick, that he was some kind of puppet. Then he said something that floored me. He said that we were all impossible. Flat-out impossible."

Joe laughed. "Yet here we are."

"That's right—we're walking miracles. Well, running miracles." Joe liked that, too. Stony said, "The doctor is confused, Joe. We're just lumps of dead meat, yet we move, we talk, we think, we love. We *are* alive. And we're alive in a way that's much more profound than normal life. The breathers are machines that take in food and oxygen and turn it into electricity. Their muscles twitch, their neurons fire. It's an amazing process, but it's *knowable*. It's reducible to facts and processes down to the microscopic level."

Joe frowned. "Are you calling me a machine?"

"What? No!" But of course he was, in way: a perpetual-motion machine that generated electricity out of nothing. Stony said, "I'm just trying to say that the living dead aren't reducible at all. There are no sets of smaller facts to explain us. We're moving statues, tin men and scarecrows."

"I'm not a tin man," Joe said.

"I'm not saying that. We're *like* tin men, because—"

"I'm a person."

"I'm not saying you're not!" Stony got to his feet and tried to start over. "Look, you know how everybody quotes the Lump: 'The dead stick moves in the wind, and believes it moves itself.' For years I mulled that over. What I thought it meant was that I was a dead thing who only *believed* he was alive. But lately I've been thinking that I was paying attention to the wrong part of that sentence. The question is, What is the wind? What is it that's moving us? Valerie thinks maybe it's God, or the devil. That idea is spreading through Deadtown."

Joe was shaking his head. He did it in rhythm with his arms, to keep his momentum. "*I'm* moving me," he said. "I can stop any time I want to."

Harry Vincent made his rounds only once per night. Once he'd made his presence in the infirmary heard, rattling the cabinet drawers and door handles like a poltergeist, no other guard came through before the morning shift. It was in those predawn hours that Stony let himself out of his cell and set to work on the doctor's private safe. He had hours in which to work, and any number of nights to experiment. He told himself to be patient. But the night the safe opened for him, he was so surprised that he almost shut the door again by accident.

On top was the file folder from Detective Kehl: MAYH70381. Stony took it out and looked again at the picture of Bethany Cooper. He wanted to slip it into his pocket, but he couldn't risk that it would be missed. He removed other files, being careful to stack them in the order that he removed them: reports from capture teams; letters to a general in the Pentagon; and the file he'd been looking for, marked JOHN MAY-

HALL. Did the doctor think Stony would not notice that his own file was not kept with those of the other prisoners?

The folder was filled almost to bursting. Stony opened it carefully to avoid spilling the contents on the floor. The first thing he saw were a dozen envelopes, addressed in his own handwriting. The envelopes were unsealed.

If he were a living man, perhaps his hands would have been shaking in rage. Perhaps his heart would have been pounding. But Stony slowly removed the pages from the envelope to confirm what he suspected. It was a letter he'd written to his mother, dated only a month earlier. He put it aside and opened another one, and another. Dr. Weiss hadn't delivered a single letter.

Stony knew he shouldn't have been surprised. Of course Dr. Weiss had been lying to him. But to stare at the bald evidence was a fresh blow. Still think you're clever, Stony? No matter how crafty he thought himself, how much he hardened himself for survival in Deadtown, he always found a way to fool himself. He'd wasted years writing these letters. He'd wasted years waiting for a response.

Okay, he thought. Burn every damn thing in the safe. Sit here in the middle of the office until Dr. Weiss came in that morning with his fat face and smudged glasses, that BE ALL YOU CAN BE travel mug, that ridiculously self-important eight-hundred-dollar briefcase. Shove the envelopes and files down his throat until he choked. Then wait for the guards to burst in and shoot him in the face. Suicide by cop.

He began to put away the files, then noticed a fat cardboard binder with a string fastener. He unwound the string. The binder was stuffed with envelopes. Each had his name on them, written in a familiar hand. At the top of each was a date in black marker, in Dr. Weiss's typewriter-like print. He sorted through them, and found the earliest, dated 11–4–92.

My John,

I've started this letter so many times in my head and now Dr. Weiss is waiting so I can't start over. I'm sorry if this doesn't read well. You and Alice were always such good writers and I'm sure it didn't come from me. I'm out of practice, too. Dr. Weiss said he would bring this to you, and bring back anything that you write, if you do write back to me. I know it must be so hard for you. I'm so sorry. I think of you every day, and what it must be like for you wondering if anyone is still thinking of you. I am, John. I keep you in my heart and in my prayers. Do you have friends? Someone to talk with? Dr. Weiss says you talk often but I hope you have someone else to talk with, I mean someone like you. That's important. I could never give you that.

They're knocking. I know I let you down. ~~I let them~~ I wouldn't blame you if you found it too hard to write back. Dr. Weiss says you're a bright young man and a credit to your race. Be careful.

I love you.
Mom

P.S.
Please, I hope you don't have any grief about Junie. I know it was an accident.

There were many more letters, as well as Christmas greetings, birthday notes, and in one case an inspirational poem that she'd copied out for him. He read them all and then started again, more slowly, only stopping when he felt the vibrations of doors opening at the far end of the administration building: the guards of the morning shift on their way to the infirmary. He put the last of the letters away into the binder and put everything away exactly as he'd found it. Even in his anger and disgust he found that he could be careful. Patient. He considered it a small victory that he did not scream, that he closed the safe door without lighting a match, that he returned to his cell without murdering a single person.

"I don't want to live in this kind of world," Dr. Weiss said. It was the Unhappy Hour, and the doctor had wandered into one of his regular existential crises. "All I want is a *reason*. If we have a reason, that changes everything. Suddenly we're living in a rational world, a world of science, where one man, a Newton or a Leibniz, can examine the evidence, draw conclusions, and make a difference."

Stony thought: Dr. Weiss, brother to Newton.

"I want to write that sentence, Stony. 'The cause of the plague is X. Here is the vector Y, here's how it works, here's how you kill it.' I want it printed in *Nature*, damn it. Because if we never find a reason, then we're living in fantasy land, where wishes come true and unicorns eat your brains. But as things stand now . . ."

The doctor seemed to have lost his train of thought. He reached for his stainless steel mug, swirled it without drinking, proving to himself, perhaps, that he didn't have to take another drink. Stony said, "As things stand now . . ."

"It's untenable, Stony." He took a drink from the mug. "I'm in hell. I'm trapped in a prison full of zombies. You know what they are? They're an insult to the scientific worldview." He made a vague gesture. "Present company—"

"No, no. I quite agree. We don't make a lick o' sense." The doctor grunted, and Stony said, "And maybe we're never going to get an answer. Would that be so bad?" This was a grenade lobbed to the heart of the doctor's soul, and had the desired effect.

"Not bad?" The doctor's face, already flushed, closed on itself like a fist. "Not *bad*?"

"I'm just saying that maybe we shouldn't expect every little mystery—"

He was prevented, or rather rescued, from finishing this sentence by the entrance of one of the guards. Stony knew he was pushing it. If the doctor lost his temper, he could do anything to Stony he wanted to. And then Stony would have to decide what he would do with the doctor. He'd promised himself ten years ago that he would never harm another breather, but he was no longer sure it was a promise he could keep. He was stronger than the doctor and could kill him easily. When they were interrupted, both Stony and the doctor were saved.

The doctor yelled at the guard, "What is it for Christ's sake?"

"We've got another sleeper."

"Who is it this time?"

"Kind of a repeat, actually," the guard said. "That woman that we almost lost."

"Valerie?" Stony said. He thought he was masking his terror well. To the doctor he said in a steady voice, "Take me with you. I can help."

"You ain't helping this time," the guard said, but the doctor instructed him to mask Stony and bring him with them. They marched through two cell blocks. No one tried to speak with Stony. The prisoners, his people, stood at the front of their cells and watched silently as they passed.

Several guards, one of them Harry Vincent, loitered at the entrance to Valerie's cell. The doctor pushed them out of the way, and Stony followed in his wake without making eye contact with Vincent. On the bed was a gray, papery shell of something that resembled a woman.

"My God, the smell!" Dr. Weiss said.

It was the smell of rot. Of death.

Stony put out a hand. Her skin was as cold as before, as gray as before, but somehow she'd slipped from stasis—undead, unalive—to true death. She was meat again. Microbes were feasting on her, turning her flesh into energy for their little bodies. She'd been returned to nature.

At last, Stony thought. Valerie's escaped.

CHAPTER FIFTEEN

2001
Deadtown

S ome dates are easier to remember than others.

"They want to make soldiers," Dr. Weiss told him. It was September 18, a week after the towers fell. "Undead soldiers."

Stony had already read the memo—the doctor had been keeping it in his private safe—but he feigned surprise. "That's a very bad idea," he said.

"They want to bite perfectly healthy soldiers, let them convert, then use them on the battlefield. Send them into—remote regions." He couldn't just say Afghanistan? As if Stony had anyone to tell this to.

Stony said, "That hasn't been approved, has it?"

"I'm fighting it tooth and nail. It's a crackpot idea, worse than any of our existing biological weapons. I'm not saying we wouldn't get valuable data from living volunteers . . ."

"Of course." The doctor had never been allowed to experiment on humans, and paid lip service to the idea that that would be immoral. But so many times over the years he'd started sentences with "If we could monitor the transformation in a controlled setting . . ."

"But the blowback!" the doctor said. "You wouldn't be able to control them. They could start an outbreak in a foreign country that we'd be powerless to stop."

"I can run the infection scenarios again," Stony said. "Show them the spread rates—"

"Have them ready by Thursday," the doctor said. "That's when the Accountants are coming." He said their name with a capital A. "You'll have to move back to a real cell before then."

"Why? And who are these guys?"

"They're doing a full security audit. Every prisoner locked down, in masks." The doctor removed his glasses and pressed his palms to his eyes. "Just try to get all the file cabinets organized and locked by today, all right?"

"But what does that mean? What's covered by an audit?"

"When you're dealing with these people?" the doctor said. "Everything."

No one spoke to him when he was escorted back to the cell block and to a new cell. After an hour, though, a voice from the cell next to him called his name, and Stony went to the door.

"So," the voice said. "Back from the massa's house."

Stony said, "Is that you, Kerry?" Kerry was a prisoner from Peoria who'd been brought in kicking and screaming a few years ago. Stony had helped talk him down and kept him from being killed. The doctor liked to keep him around because he was one of the only Chinese in Deadtown; the doctor liked diversity in his sample.

"Looks like they patched you up some," Kerry said.

There were mirrors in the administration building bathrooms, but he'd avoided them. He didn't need to be reminded that he was no longer one of the pretty LDs. Dr. Weiss had tried to restore his face to something like his old one, but the doctor was no plastic surgeon. Stony walked with a limp now, and his torso automatically wanted to sit on a slight angle to his hips, as if his spine had been twisted. Maybe it had.

Stony sat down on the floor in front of the cell door. "So tell me what's new," he said. "How are people on the cell block?" He took off his shirt. His plastic arm was secured to his torso by a web of leather straps. He loosened one of the straps, then another, and pulled down on his arm so that a gap opened between the rubberized base and his gray skin. He thought about clenching his fist, and the fingers curled appropriately.

Kerry said, "There's a lot of talk about sleeping. Ever since Valerie passed."

"Is anyone trying it?" Stony unbuckled several of the straps completely. Now there was a six-inch gap between his artificial arm and the stump.

"What are you doing in there?" Kerry said.

"Just getting comfortable."

"Well, everyone's tried it. Nobody's gotten the hang of it. It's harder than it looks."

Stony pulled the arm free and set it on the ground in front of him. It looked like an object now, a sculpture. And that was entirely the wrong frame of mind to be in.

Wave, Stony thought. The arm didn't move. The fingers didn't even twitch.

"Wave," he said aloud.

"Wait for what?"

"Nothing," Stony said. Then: "We just have to wait them out. That's our talent."

"That's your talent for bullshit," Kerry said. "We're all going to die here. We're just trying to speed it up."

"No!" Stony said. "You have to remain positive. We can get out of here. There's always a way out."

Kerry laughed. "You really are as upbeat as you are in the *Sunday Deadline.*"

"I'm sorry, what?"

"The weekly news. Though I suppose that's over now, isn't it?"

"For now," Stony said. He didn't know they'd called his messages anything. He liked the idea that it had been a kind of newspaper.

He stared at the fake limb. *I am the arm. The arm is me. I belong to you and you belong to me.*

Consciousness was the key. The self. Experiments from the animal lab had proved that to Stony. None of the bitten animals—and Stony had bitten some of them himself—had become undead. The closest they'd come was a chimpanzee that Stony had privately named Cornelius.

It had been a horrible experience. After they'd secured the animal to a table, Stony bit him in the finger as gently as he could, though of course it had to be hard enough to break the skin. Dr. Weiss stopped the chimp's heart with 500 milligrams of sodium pentobarbital. Cornelius screamed in rage—and kept screaming. It seemed to go on forever, but later, when they reviewed the videotape, they saw that the tantrum had gone on for just over three minutes, before the chimp suddenly went rigid, his mouth stretched wide. During the entire episode, his heart had never beat. Had he briefly been undead, or was he simply one pissed-off chimp? Dr. Weiss was terribly excited, and over the next year he killed a score of chimpanzees, none of which did more than screech for a couple of seconds before dying.

Dr. Weiss concluded that the disease was a human malady, specific to the species, but that was the wrong way to think of it. It was the idea of self that animated. Lose faith in yourself as an individual—lose integrity—and things fell apart.

I am the arm. The arm is me.

The fingers curled as if stroking the keys of a piano. There we go, he thought, and waved back at himself. He had three, four days tops before they came for him. He had to be absolutely ready.

"Tell me about the Lump."

It was the first time Harry Vincent had spoken to him during one of his night visits to the infirmary. It was after Valerie's escape but before the towers fell, so perhaps winter of 2000 or spring of 2001. Stony still spent most nights with his plastic limb pressed to the bed, the wall, the steel of the cell door.

Vincent dragged a chair into the open doorway. He sat hunched over, the truncheon across his knees. Finally he said, "They say you talked to him."

Stony didn't answer. He lay on the bed as if he were capable of sleeping.

"Come on," Vincent said. "Tell me. Is he real?"

"People like to make up stories," Stony said.

"I'm not fucking interrogating you!"

Stony sat up. What was this then, a *chat*? "I don't have my mask on," Stony said. "I could bite you."

Vincent stared at him, then looked at the floor. His forehead shone with sweat, though the room was not warm. "They say he's just half a person. A chest, a head, one arm."

"That's what they say."

"How is that possible?"

Stony shrugged. "It's not."

"I sure as hell wouldn't want to turn into *that*. Shit." He pressed the billy club against his forehead. "How long do you think he's been alive?"

"He's not. That's kind of the whole trick."

"Right." Vincent stood up, pushed the chair back into the office. He looked around at the cell. "Right." He shut the door and locked it.

The visits would go on. Eventually Vincent would tell Stony that he'd been diagnosed with late-stage peritoneal mesothelioma, a rare cancer usually caused by exposure to asbestos, but also linked to other toxins. It was incurable. Surgery was not an option. Treatment with chemotherapy was available, though it was strictly palliative. He'd decided to keep his condition secret from his employers. Yet for some reason he confided in Stony.

This was in the future. That first night, Stony didn't know what Vincent wanted, what violence he might be planning. As the guard walked away, Stony thought, There goes one damaged human being.

Three days after Stony's expulsion from the infirmary, Harry Vincent and four other guards burst into his cell and quickly masked him.

"I always knew you were up to something in there," Vincent said, loud enough for the prisoners in the nearby cells to hear. "And now you're going to burn." He yanked Stony to his feet. Vincent had lost weight recently, but he was still strong.

Stony's prosthetic arm lay on the floor. There was some debate among the guards as how to shackle a one-armed man, and finally they chained his arm to his waist and padlocked it shut. One of the guards carried the prosthetic arm with him.

Dr. Weiss was nervous and distraught. "I can't believe

you'd betray me like this," he said. "I thought we had a *relationship.*" Strangers were there, four white men in their mid-thirties, hair longer and arms more muscled than what you'd expect from brainy desk jockeys. They wore jeans and sport shirts, and one of them even wore sandals. Casual Friday for the Accountants.

They'd found everything: the extra accounts, the stash of encrypted email, the secret VPN. Stony knew they would. There was no way to hide the evidence, if you knew what you were looking for.

The man who was clearly the leader of the Accountants was as blandly handsome as a Lands' End catalog model. He folded his arms and said, "You've been doing some tunneling."

The challenge of a military network is that, with a few notable exceptions, it only talks to itself. Computers within the network—say, the ones in Dr. Weiss's office, and the file server that kept the HR files—can be compromised with a little work. But getting out to the public networks, the Internet, is another level of difficulty. The wires leaving the building are owned by the government, and most of the satellites carrying traffic are dedicated solely to it. A network of the military, by the military, and for the military.

What is required to jump from the private network to the public one is a machine connected to both (never allowed), and a program to ferry the packets of data through the firewall. These programs aren't difficult to write. The difficult part is finding an illegally connected computer, then tricking the owner of it to install such a program.

Stony had simply handed Dr. Weiss a floppy disk and said, run this.

Stony thought about claiming that he'd done it all under the doctor's orders. (Prescription: Treason!) But if anyone would be able to figure out the truth from the electronic evidence it would be the Accountants. Besides, the doctor was so hurt, Stony almost felt sorry for him. *Relationship.* What an overloaded word. Of course they had a relationship. It just wasn't the kind the doctor thought it was.

When Stony first began to work for the man, he didn't know whether he had the stomach for duplicity. He didn't think of himself as *wily.* He was from Iowa, for Christ's sake. But it turned out that he had a talent for it, and lying could be improved with concentration and diligence. Craftiness was a craft. And it helped that much of the work he did to get into and stay in Dr. Weiss's good graces was work he wanted to do anyway. He kept his fellow prisoners alive. He studied the history of his people, and how they worked, and the workings of the prison. And he was doing science. Though he had no formal training, and no education beyond what Mrs. Cho could teach him, he was discovering things that—

There, you see it? The ego. The knife edge to pry open the locked box.

Over the years that he became Dr. Weiss's trusted assistant, his confidant, Stony began to fear that he and the doctor weren't so different. Stony wanted to learn about LDs, their limits and their possibilities, as much as the doctor did. He *wanted* to know what would happen after he bit a mouse, a spider monkey, a chimp. How long Perpetual Joe could run. How much of Stony's self he could lose without losing himself. And like Dr. Weiss, Stony was afraid that all that research, all that data on his people, would be locked away, or burned.

"Tell us where you sent the files," the head of the Accountants said. He was deeply tanned and creased, a man who'd spent a lot of time outdoors. He was not in his thirties, as Stony had first thought, or even his forties. He might have been an extremely fit sixty-year-old. "Who received them?"

Stony had been moved to the animal lab, where there was enough room for the Accountants and several of the Deadtown guards to gather around him. They'd chained him to a metal chair and padlocked the chain. Stony shook his head. "You're going to have to torture it out of me."

"That's on the table," the handsome man said.

Dr. Weiss barked an ugly laugh. "Don't even bother. He doesn't feel pain. He's been beaten to a pulp by guards. He's been shot. I've *sawed off his arm* and he didn't feel it."

The man frowned. "What's he afraid of?"

Dr. Weiss thought for a moment. "Death?"

"Life or death. That's awfully binary," the handsome man said. "Still." He reached behind him and produced a small gray automatic.

"How did you get that in here?" Dr. Weiss said.

He put the pistol to Stony's forehead. "In my experience, this is pretty much the only thing that kills you folks."

"Pretty much," Stony said. "Is that loaded?"

"Wouldn't do much good empty," the man said. "Now. Who have you been in contact with? My team will know all that in a few hours, but you could save us a lot of time."

"You're not really an accountant, are you?"

"It's more of a nickname. I'll count to three."

"Let me think." Stony closed his eyes.

"I *will* shoot you," the man said. "Legally, you're not even a person. Ethically, it's my duty to find out what you know. Morally, you're a threat to human life."

Jesus, Stony thought, an accountant *and* a philosopher. "Could you stop talking for just a second?" he asked. "I'm trying to decide whether I'm going to comply with you or not."

Another lie. But one more couldn't hurt. He kept his eyes closed and tried to concentrate. He was just a dead stick—a stick that moves in the wind and believes that it moves itself.

He'd told Perpetual Joe that the question was, What is the wind? Maybe it was God. That would have made Valerie happy. But the more he'd learned, and the more he'd experimented, the more he came to believe something different. It's *because* the dead stick believes that it moves itself, that it moves. Joe was right: *I'm* moving me.

His body was a dead thing tied to a chair, which was itself another dead thing. The chain was made of inert metal and secured by mechanical devices whose gears and pins could not turn by themselves. Where one dead thing ended and another began was largely a problem of perception and definition.

I am the lock, the lock is me. I belong to you—

He flexed his tiny metal fingers, and the locks clattered to the floor. He shrugged, and links snapped apart and the chains clattered to the ground. Then he leaned forward, the first motion in his attempt to stand, which pressed the barrel of the pistol more forcefully into his skull. The handsome man fired.

Later, LDs would turn this moment into folklore: *Stony's Release.* Painters and graffiti artists made it a frequent subject, with Stony's expression variously determined, sad, angry, beatific. Was he ready to die the final death, or was he placing his faith in some future resurrection? Was he trying to escape, or trying to kill himself? The debate lent each painting a political weight. Curiously, none of the artists portrayed Stony as *surprised* when the locks opened—pleasantly surprised, but surprised nonetheless—an expression that was undoubtedly still on his face when the trigger was pulled.

Oh, but the damage to that face, that body. None of the paintings tried to capture what happened when you fired a .38 into a man's head at point-blank range. The bullet went through Stony's forehead and blew a large chunk from the back of his skull. Stony's body bent backward from the force, then fell back against the chair and tumbled to the floor.

The head Accountant, as well as every living man in the room, was stunned. After a long moment of silence, Dr. Weiss pointed at the handsome man and said, "What did you do? Do you have any idea how valuable he was?"

"Shut up," the leader said. He put his gun back in the holster at the small of his back and said to the Deadtown guards, "Who secured the prisoner?"

"I did," Vincent said. "And no one's ever gotten out of them before. That's Superman shit."

The leader turned to the doctor. "You didn't say he was that strong."

"I didn't know—"

"This facility is mine now," the leader said. "And you are under arrest, Doctor. Put him in a cell."

"By whose authority?" Weiss said.

The man frowned as if he were surprised at such a stupid question. "Mine. And somebody dispose of this body."

"My pleasure," Harry Vincent said.

"Go with him," the handsome man told one of his men.

Vincent wheeled out a gurney and they heaved Stony's body onto it. "How about the arm?" Vincent asked, and nodded toward the prosthetic and its leather straps.

"We'll donate it to another needy corpse," the leader said.

Vincent and the assistant spook loaded Stony's body onto a gurney and wheeled him outside. There were three incinerators on the site, but now that the facility was no longer an active disposal site, only one was kept working. It was housed in the main physical plant, a building a hundred yards from the administration building and attached to it by a covered walkway. The walkway had been added when the facility became Deadtown, perhaps because someone was nervous about satellite pictures.

Vincent pushed the rattling gurney and the spook trailed him. "So," Vincent said, "you guys are from what agency?"

The man didn't answer. Vincent said, "What's the matter, can't tell me or you'd have to—"

"That's right. And then burn your body. Standard procedure."

"You think I'm one of them?"

"Can't be too careful."

"Fine. Keep fucking with me. I'm just trying to make conversation. I mean, Jesus, we both work for top-secret organizations, you'd think . . . never mind." He stopped to unlock the double doors leading into the physical plant. Three cement rooms were set aside for garbage disposal: an outer room to hold the Dumpster of nonhazardous garbage that was hauled away twice a week; another, larger room to store hazardous materials and medical waste generated by Deadtown and the doctor's labs; and one to house the incinerator. The garbage room smelled ripe—not nearly enough air-conditioning. Vincent crossed the room and stopped before the door to the hazmat room. He unlocked it, leaving his keys in the lock. A thick suit hung on a hook beside a full mask. He started to pull on the suit.

"I hate this shit," Vincent said. "Two guys I used to work with died of cancer—the exact same *kind* of cancer. You think that's an accident?"

"I don't care."

"They're trying to kill us, man. Half the time the suit doesn't even fucking seal." He pulled on the mask and zipped up. He pushed open the door. Inside were dozens of red barrels marked with the yellow and red hazmat stickers.

The spook leaned in. "Where's the incinerator?"

"On the other side of this room. You coming?" Vincent had to raise his voice to be heard through the mask. "Didn't think so." He pushed the gurney inside and kicked the door shut behind him.

He wheeled past the red barrels, then went through the next door into the incinerator room. He could have gotten to the furnace from the far side of the plant and skipped the hazmat room altogether, but then the spook would have wanted to come with him.

He shut the incinerator room door and flipped on the lights, but only one of the fluorescents above sputtered to life. The furnace was a gray steel box with a thick door and a long, double-hinged handle. A metal rake leaned against the wall next to a steel table. The table could be tilted to slide the body into the mouth of the furnace, and the rake was there to finish the job. Vincent turned and began to unfasten his mask. Already he was sweating.

In every horror movie, there's the scene in which the next victim, sure that he or she is alone in a room, suddenly knows that someone or something else is there in the dark. The camera glides in for a close-up, which cleverly heightens the tension because the shot narrows what the audience can see. The victim's eyes shift left. The mouth frowns in concentration. We seem to be inside the character's mind: Is that the sound of breathing? Did that shadow move? And why did the background music stop?

The victim waits for a second, perhaps two . . . and nothing happens. Then—and this is mandatory—the victim breathes in and begins to relax.

That was the moment Stony tapped Vincent on his shoulder. The man jumped, spun around.

"Jesus Christ!" he said.

"Shhh," Stony said. "And don't look so surprised."

Vincent backed away from him. "I thought you were dead. Really dead."

"I told you to trust me."

"You didn't stick to the plan! You were going to escape, then *I* was going to shoot you in the head."

"I didn't know he had a gun," Stony said. "I had to improvise."

"But point blank? Jesus."

"I had to force his hand." He touched a finger to the edge of the hole in his forehead. It felt ragged and slightly . . . crispy. "I have to admit I was a little nervous about that."

"Shit, don't *poke* it," Vincent said.

Stony hadn't been completely sure he could survive a direct shot. It was a measure of his desperation that he would have been all right with it going the other way. Yet here he was, moving and talking and thinking, no worse than Winnie the Pooh with a little stuffing knocked out of him.

Vincent said, "What the fuck are you smiling about?"

"Winnie the Pooh. A bear of very little brain."

"What?"

"Nothing. Better get back to your friend out there. You didn't find out who they are, did you?"

"I thought maybe you'd know," Vincent said.

"Weiss called them the Accountants. There've been rumors of another group out there," Stony said. "Running black sites overseas, hunting LDs in other countries. They want to make undead soldiers to fight terrorists. Or something equally idiotic." He sat down on the metal table. "Doesn't matter. The rest of the plan is still intact. It's three-thirty now. Garbage pickup is four or four-fifteen, and they deposit at the dump by six at the latest. You come pick me up as soon as it gets dark, say seven, and then we'll—"

"No," Vincent said. "Do it now."

"What? You're at work."

"You run off without me, or get crushed by the compactor, I'm fucked."

"Come on, we've already proven that I'm indestructible. One of my best friends spent months being crushed by garbage."

"You could still ditch me."

"I'm not going to do that," Stony said. "I gave you my word. Plus, I still need your help to get out of town."

"Or they catch you—what do I do then? No. Do it now. You said I'd have six hours."

"More or less. It's not guaranteed to—"

"Do it or the whole thing's off."

Stony stood up again, walked toward him. "You can't make it on your own, Harry. Even if you make it through the conversion without me, you'll need me to lead you to the underground. Without our help, the Diggers will find you. Probably they'll shoot you immediately. If you're lucky, and the doctor gets interested in your case, you might earn a cell. Maybe mine. But I wouldn't count on it. The doctor's not going to be keeping his job for long."

"Here," Vincent said. He unzipped the top of the suit and unbuttoned the top two buttons of his uniform. "In the shoulder. They won't see that."

"You can't take this back," Stony said. "You have to be sure."

But of course he was sure. Vincent was desperate, running for his life—his next life, anyway. This one was over. The cancer was eating through his abdomen, churning tissue into tumors.

"Do it," Vincent said. He turned his head and pulled down his shirt.

Stony had promised himself that he would never bite in anger. But this was the man who'd burned Valerie, who'd maimed Stony, who'd abused a dozen other prisoners. Stony could rip him apart now, and to hell with his resurrection among the living dead.

But then Stony would never get out of Deadtown. They'd find him and burn him.

Stony put one hand on Vincent's neck and another on his shoulder. He could be gentle, as gentle as he'd been with Cornelius. Just a nip to start the infection.

"This is going to hurt," Stony said, and chomped down.

Everything had been going so well.

The Dumpster had been picked up promptly at four. He'd tumbled undetected into the truck and had managed to keep the metal rake perpendicular to his body as the big compactor blade moved back. The rake had bent under the pressure and Stony had been pressed deep into the already compacted garbage—but his bones had not been crushed.

The trip out to the dump was almost pleasant. Then the truck had tilted up and spilled him out. He was knocked about, but that was okay. He huddled in the bag to wait first for the garbage collectors to leave, and then for dark. Then he heard the beeping of a second truck backing up nearby.

No, not nearby. On top of him. He winced as a shushing rumble of a load emptied on top of him.

The weight flattened him in his bag. His one good arm was trapped beneath him. His legs were completely immobile.

This was much worse than the truck; he felt like he'd been buried in concrete.

He panicked then. He bucked and twisted, screaming. Somehow he managed to make a small space beneath his body, and he brought his hand up to his face. He tore through the black plastic in front of his eyes and saw no daylight. He faced a solid wall of compressed garbage.

Sometime later—an hour? Two? In some low-rent Einsteinian process, time had been distorted by the mass above him—he began to talk himself down. *Come on, Stony. You've been tunneling since you were twelve. You can't suffocate, you can't even get tired. And didn't Mr. Blunt tell you that he'd spent months hiding in the dump, in mounds just like this?*

Move, he told himself. *Make like a worm.*

He stopped his thrashing. He anchored his feet, bowed his back, and shoved his one good arm forward. The effort gained him a couple of inches. Then he pulled his legs up and shoved again.

As he worked, he thought of the myriad other ways his plan had failed him. Yes, he'd made it out of Deadtown. But that was a ticket for one. There were 119 souls still behind bars in the prison. How could he ever explain to someone like Thomas—kind, dim Thomas—why he'd left him? And even if he escaped this heap—*shut up, Stony, of course you'll escape*—he wouldn't yet be safe. He was only thirty miles from Deadtown, and dependent on a sociopath to take him to safety.

A sociopath who was infected.

Vincent would be able to hide the symptoms for a few hours, but soon he'd be sweating and anxious, and then he'd start hallucinating. Six hours after the bite, give or take an hour, he'd be dead. And then the transformation would begin.

Stony planted his feet, bowed, and shoved again. And again.

* * *

His arm punched through into air. He forced his head through the opening. He was midway up the slope in a hill of refuse.

It was still dark, but the moon was low and dawn seemed close. He saw no one, heard nothing. A few more minutes of struggle and he was able to pull the rest of his body from the mound. He was naked, coated in grime. His thin jumpsuit had been shredded by the effort.

He was late. So late.

But instead of going down he climbed higher, up to the peak of his little knoll. In the faint light the dump was almost pretty. He was in the outer precincts of a vast hilly landscape, black mounds stippled with gleaming plastic and slivers of metal that winked in the light. A dirt road wound through the valleys of the dump like a dark seam. In the distance, a cluster of lights marked the front gate.

He'd made it, then. Out of an early grave. Out of Dead-town. He'd been imagining this moment for thirteen years. He'd thought he'd be happier.

He followed the winding road toward the lights. He walked around a curve and then saw the entrance to the dump: Two light poles, an expanse of blotchy cement, and a small shack with yellow vinyl siding. A light shone in the single window he could see. The gate, chain link on a metal frame, was slightly ajar, kept open by a dark lump.

He stopped, looked at the shack, then back at the thing by the gate. He felt the last scraps of his plan—let's call it a fantasy, hey?—slip out of his hands and blow away.

He walked forward. When he was perhaps thirty feet away he realized that it was the body of a dog. It was darkly furred, perhaps a German shepherd. Then he heard a growl from inside the shack—but not a dog's growl.

He went around to the front of the shack. The door was open. On the floor, Harry Vincent squatted over the remains of a man. Blood coated the linoleum floor and had spattered across the walls and furniture: a pine desk and the white computer monitor, a TV on a stand, a beige leather armchair with a duct-taped headrest. It was alarming how much was inside a living man when you started to turn him inside out.

Vincent looked up, still chewing. His face was painted in blood. His eyes were vacant. He growled again, then turned back to his meal. The dead had nothing to offer the dead.

"Oh Harry," Stony said. He'd come to find Stony as planned. His pickup was probably just out of sight of the gate. And then the fever hit, and he'd come hunting.

Stony did not try to pull him off the man. It was much too late for that now. Stony forced himself to go into the room. He stepped around Harry and his victim and went to the desk. The monitor was on, showing a Windows screen. The computer under the desk was connected to a phone jack in the wall. Stony found the AOL icon, and then he typed out an email with his location. "Bring restraints," he typed, "and two sets of clothes." He clicked send. The email address was hosted in Canada, but the person monitoring the inbox should be close by. Hopefully very close.

The sky beyond the doorway had turned silvery. A new day.

Let's go, Stony. Keep moving.

The use of the third person, he found, gave him much-needed perspective. It was almost like not being alone.

He went back outside (he did not look at the floor) to pull the dog from the gate, to find Harry's pickup, to do whatever it was that Stony told himself to do.

PART
FOUR

CHAPTER SIXTEEN

2009
Calhoun Island

o you remember doing the dead man's float? Every kid tries it. Facedown in the water, arms drooping. After thirty seconds, a minute, your chest begins to burn but you don't move: You hold out, staring at the blue cement of the pool floor, letting the waves rock your body like a rudderless raft. The shouting voices above mute to a low roar, and your ears tune to odd clicks and thumps, the whoosh of your pulse in your ear. Oh, how your mother will wail when they find your waterlogged body. Your father will fall to his knees, wondering why he didn't appreciate you more. Imagine the funeral! And then almost against your will your feet come down and you pull your face out of the water. You gasp and ask your best friend, How long was that?

Or so I've been told; I've never tried it. Neither had Stony. He'd never learned to swim, and he wasn't much good at floating—he kept listing to the side like a ship taking on water. But he was very good at being a dead man. He could drift for hours in the crystal clear waters of the island as huge tropical fish, bright as cartoons, coasted beneath him. He'd learned some of their scientific names, but he preferred the ones he'd given them: Orange Killjoy. Blue Church Lady. Li'l Frenzy. He drifted and thought of nothing.

Or tried to. His mind, wherever it was located, kept yammering like the only guy on the bus with a cellphone. For example, in the past ten minutes, his mind had repeatedly been asking, Why can't they just leave me alone for a single hour?

Someone on the beach was calling his name. Stony had pretended deafness, but then the intruder started tossing pebbles at him—they plopped into the water near his head. Then finally something heavier slapped the water a few inches from his left ear.

Stony stood up—the water was only five feet deep at this spot. He picked up the chunk of driftwood that had nearly hit him and tossed it farther out to sea.

The figure on the beach seemed to find this amusing. He was fabulously overdressed in a dark suit and homburg, holding a black rain umbrella over his head—as if he had anything to fear from sunburn.

Stony began to slog through the surf. When he was a few feet from the beach Mr. Blunt said, "My apologies for disturbing your swim. If that was what you were doing."

"Zombie snorkeling," Stony said. "It's like snorkeling, but without the snorkel." The skin of Blunt's face had been blackened to a tarry, waxy substance. He'd been burned, perhaps several times, but not consumed.

They regarded each other for a long moment. They'd talked many times via email, but they hadn't seen each other in person since the congress, twenty-one years ago.

Mr. Blunt looked him over. Of course Stony wasn't pretty to look at, either. His skin was crisscrossed with thick stitches. The holes in his head, front and back, had been sealed with hard plastic and stitched closed by the Commander's doctors, but he was conscious that the skin tone did not match, and that his forehead bore a slight indentation like an intimation of a third eye.

"You're leaking," Mr. Blunt said.

Stony laughed, stretched out his arms, or rather one arm and one stump. Water seeped from seams in his skin. "I'd hug you . . ."

"Quite all right," Blunt said. "Perhaps you'd like to put on some clothes?"

Stony wore only a pair of torn khaki shorts. He shrugged, then nodded at a red-tiled roof several hundred yards down the beach, just visible behind the dunes. "My hut's over there."

"Oh, I know," Mr. Blunt said. "I met Chip, your guard dog."

"You didn't hurt him, did you?"

"Of course not. He was very helpful."

They walked along the white sand, skirting the incoming waves. Half a mile in the distance was the Commander's estate, a white palace perched on a cliff that jutted into the ocean. The water was brilliant blue, the sky clear but for a few clouds that would carry the afternoon rain to them.

"So this is heaven," Mr. Blunt said.

"The closest we'll get to an afterlife," Stony said. "The trip went okay, then? You're here three hours early."

"The Commander's people were very efficient," he said. "Though I suppose that's largely your doing."

Stony shrugged. "And Calhoun's money. Thank you for coming."

"You know I prefer to stay in the field."

"You have to come in from the cold sometime," Stony said.

They climbed a set of wooden stairs to a long, unfinished

beach house. The walls were unpainted, and one corner was a rectangle of bare studs covered by flapping plastic. Chip sat cross-legged on the patio, naked except for a web of hemp netting spread across his lap. "Cool, you found him!" he said.

"I did indeed," Mr. Blunt said. "Thank you for the directions."

"No problem," Chip said. He was a very pretty dead man, blond with full lips, his body unscarred but for the half-moon of a deep bite on his shoulder. He'd been trying to finish the hammock for days now, but the knots kept confusing him.

"Did anybody call?" Stony asked him.

Chip thought hard. The conversion had hit Harry Vincent hard. After the fever passed he didn't recognize his own name and had no idea where he was or what had happened to him. His new mind remained as sunny and empty as this beach.

"Never mind," Stony said. "I'm sure voicemail picked it up."

"Oh yeah," Chip said. "Sure." He turned his attention back to the ropes on his lap. Stony let Mr. Blunt into the house and closed the door behind them.

"How do you stand it?" Blunt asked. "Keeping him around like that?"

"Stop it," Stony said. "He's got nowhere else to go."

"You're a better man than I." He looked around at the front room. "Though not much of a decorator."

The inside of the house was more incomplete than the outside: bare drywall, some walls open to the plumbing, wiring taped to the wood. Stony had been meaning to finish, but dozens of other projects had distracted him. Every flat surface was covered by books, magazines, blueprints, and printouts. A long drafting table, stacked high with drawings and engineering manuals, braced one wall. The glass top of the dining room table was crowded with equipment: two computers, a printer, a scanner, several flat-panel monitors. A tangle of blue and black cables connected them to the power and to a huge Océ 7055 blueprint printer squatting in front of one of the windows. Vertical tubes of rolled blueprints made an arsenal of one corner.

"It's a look," Stony said.

"You do it all from here?" Mr. Blunt asked.

"The communication stuff? No, no. There's a real data center at the Commander's place, with a bunch of smart people. This is just for . . . my projects. I'm going to get dressed. Make yourself at home."

Stony was nearly dry from the walk back, but he could still feel the water sloshing under his skin, and he'd be weeping salt water for the rest of the day. Coming apart at the seams, he thought. His body was wearing out, the damages adding up. When he was younger he would have ignored injuries that he now worried over, and that worry kept the wounds from closing. Maybe that was the secret of youth: willful ignorance.

But not all wounds were forgotten. He ran his fingers across the place where his heart should be and found the stitches. There. The place where Kwang had shot him, where Alice and his mother had sewn him back together. He was still himself. Still Wanda Mayhall's boy.

He stripped off his damp shorts, then pulled on an identical pair from a pile on the floor. The bedroom was more of a disaster than the front rooms. Stony should probably do a little house cleaning, he thought. Or at least allow the maid to come in.

He picked up his prosthetic arm from its spot on top of the dresser, pressed it to his stump, and wiggled the fingers to make sure he had a grip on it. Then he pulled on a white bamboo shirt and returned to the dining room, where Mr. Blunt had unfolded a map.

"Is this Deadtown?" Blunt asked.

"It's nothing." Stony took the map from him and began to fold it.

"It looks like you're planning an attack," Mr. Blunt said. "You're not going back there, are you?"

"It's a pipe dream," Stony said. "I know how to get in. I just can't figure out how to get them all out without everyone being shot."

"I noticed the names," Blunt said. Taped to the wall were over a hundred index cards, grouped into three sections that roughly represented the cell blocks. Each card bore the name of a prisoner still in Deadtown when Stony had escaped. No one knew whether they were still alive. "You can't save everyone, Stony."

No, Stony thought, just me.

Mr. Blunt gestured at the other stacks of paper. "The rest of this—I suppose these are the reports you make us all fill out?"

"Some of it's my own writing," he said. "A few papers for the OSWoG journal, that kind of thing. But the reports are important. If we don't keep track—"

"Your own writing? You realize your newsletters are already turning into scripture."

Stony picked up a printout of a spreadsheet with the latest figures. "It's not good. In '88 we had seventeen hundred in the census. We're down to less than three hundred people who are still in contact, not counting Deadtown prisoners. Almost fifty of those live here."

"Three hundred?" Mr. Blunt seemed surprised. "I knew it

was low, but . . ." He skimmed the sheet. "The civil war has cost us perhaps thirty people, tops. And thanks to you we haven't lost a house in years."

"Not to the Diggers, no." Mr. Blunt frowned, and Stony said, "Sleepers and suicides. One of our houses in Rochester went silent because all five people in the house decided to go to sleep together. The police found them before I could send someone to check on them."

"You can't be blaming yourself for this," Mr. Blunt said. Stony didn't answer, and Mr. Blunt said, "Most of those people are alive only because of the work you did in Deadtown, and what you're doing now. They follow you, Stony, because they believe in you." He smiled. "And because you have magical powers."

"Don't I know it. They send me *prayers*, Mr. Blunt. They ask me to do all sorts of impossible things. I got an email from a woman asking me to please stop their basement from flooding."

"Can you blame them?" Blunt asked. "Ever since the Release—" Blunt raised a wooden hand, put a pistol finger to his forehead, and let the thumb clack down like a hammer. "When *that* got around, my boy, the proles got very excited. The Lump is our John the Baptist—and not just because he'd do fine as just a head on a plate—and you, my friend, are—"

"Stop it." Stony didn't want to hear the word.

Blunt shrugged. "Most of our people are anxious to do whatever you say."

"But they're not listening. I ask them to hang on, but they're checking out, Mr. Blunt. We're on the edge of extinction."

Blunt walked to the window, looked out at the sea. "There must be others, living off the grid."

"Sure," Stony said. "But we can't find them. The ones who do talk to us are growing desperate. Every day I get messages asking me when the bite will start."

Mr. Blunt slowly looked back over his shoulder. "Messages from biters. Do you know where they are coming from?"

"Yes, I do."

"But you haven't sent them to me."

"No."

Mr. Blunt turned and smiled. "I wondered why you called me here. You've lost faith in the mission."

"You've saved the world a dozen times over," Stony said. "If it wasn't for you—"

"No, if it wasn't for *us*. You, me, Delia. It's you who have ferreted out most of the Big Biters. My team and I are merely soldiers. The deliverymen."

"I know the blood's on my hands," Stony said. "I think about that every day."

"And *now* it's bothering you."

"The killings have to stop, Mr. Blunt."

"Done."

Stony was surprised. "I . . . wasn't sure you'd—"

"You think I've *enjoyed* my work?"

"No, of course not. But I thought—"

"In thirty years I've arranged the destruction of forty-one LDs. I've personally assassinated twelve of them. No one should be asked to do such a thing."

"I know you didn't ask for the job. But I thought you, well . . ."

"Believed? I did once. But lately, lately . . ." He shook his head. "The irrationality of my position has become more difficult to reconcile. How many LDs must I kill to save them?"

He removed a thick three-ring binder from one of the wicker chairs by the window and sat down, crossing his legs. Stony remembered the night he met Mr. Blunt, how surprised he'd been to see a man made of so much wood.

"Three hundred," Mr. Blunt said. He sounded tired.

"Not counting the hundred and nineteen in Deadtown."

Blunt removed his homburg and held it on his lap. "Have you ever considered . . . just letting us fade away?"

"I think about it all the time," Stony said.

"Really." Mr. Blunt's charred face could barely express emotion, but his voice communicated his surprise.

"The world would be safer with us gone," Stony said.

"The *living* would be safer."

"The living *are* the world. They breed. They evolve. We just exist."

"Oh my," Mr. Blunt said. "Envying the breeders? You've become a self-hating zombie, Stony. Is this some kind of mid-death crisis?"

Stony smiled. "Maybe."

"Which reminds me, how is your mother?"

"Still in prison. Ever since the Accountants busted Dr. Weiss, they've made her even more inaccessible—Calhoun's lawyers can't get to her, can't even get the government to acknowledge that they have her. She's still a terrorist."

"I'm so sorry. But your sisters, Crystal and Alice, and your friend Kwang—they used to write to you all the time. Still keep in touch?"

"I promised myself I'd never see any of them again. It's too dangerous for them. Besides, I'm supposed to be inciner-ated." Mr. Blunt either didn't realize or chose to ignore the fact that Stony hadn't answered the question. He sent emails to Alice at least once a month, through various anonymizer services, always using a different account. It was the smartest way he knew to do such a stupid thing. "I try to keep track of them from afar," Stony said.

"It's only natural," Blunt said. "Crystal's daughter, what was her name?"

"Ruby."

"Ruby! She must be what, eighteen by now?"

"Twenty-one. She's graduating from college next year."

"They grow up so fast. And you haven't even talked to her, not once?"

"You're interrogating, Blunt. Don't worry, I'm not risking our security."

"You misunderstand me. I think it would be a mistake to *not* contact them. If I had family, I would want to see them, now, before the Diggers burn us all."

"I'm not going to let that happen," Stony said. "*We're* not going to let that happen."

Mr. Blunt regarded him. Against the bright window he was nearly a silhouette. "So," he said finally, "you're going to let it happen. The Big Bite is here at last. Even the Lumpists will be relieved."

"No," Stony said firmly. "Not the bite. We're going with Calhoun's plan."

"Calhoun is insane."

"Maybe. But the idea isn't. At least, it's the least insane option we have right now."

"Have you talked to Delia about this?"

"Delia is onboard," Stony said. Actually, that wasn't quite true. Delia had serious doubts, but she said that she'd follow him.

Blunt uncrossed his legs, straightened the crease at his knees, then crossed the other leg. "I see."

"She wanted to be here for this conversation, but she's on

her way to contact the leadership in person. I'll be joining her as soon as I can."

"You realize we could all be destroyed."

"Maybe. I don't see any other choice."

Mr. Blunt stared into the middle distance. After a time he said, "Okay then." He looked up. "What day is the coming-out party?"

"We have eleven months to lay the groundwork," Stony said. "We go public on June first next year." He smiled. "We're calling it D-day."

"Of course you are."

"I also have a new job for you—one that doesn't involve killing."

"I'm listening."

"I've got to meet some people on the other side of the island," Stony said. "Let's talk about it on the way. Wanna see the spaceport?"

They walked out to a narrow paved road, where a yellow golf cart was parked beneath a palm tree, guarded by a trio of wild chickens. "The place is overrun with them," Stony said. They shooed the chickens away and got into the cart. "Usually I walk everywhere, but since you're a guest . . ." The island was only seven miles long and two and a half miles wide at its widest point; it was often faster to walk over the ridge than follow the switchbacks in the road. The undergrowth could get dense, but at least the mosquitoes didn't bother with the dead. "Hang on," Stony said, and punched the start button.

"What, no chauffeur?" Blunt said.

"I gave him the day off." He drove north, up toward the green ridge that divided the island. The air turned warmer as they pulled away from the shore, but then cooled again as they climbed the ridge. The road was walled by thick foliage, so Mr. Blunt could see nothing until they came to a break in the greenery, usually at the elbow of a switchback, when suddenly the island fell away beneath them and sky and ocean rushed in to fill the eye.

"How do you get anything done?" Mr. Blunt asked.

Stony laughed, and jerked the wheel into the next turn. "What do you mean?"

"This is completely unmotivating. There's nothing left to do here. What are you supposed to do—*improve* it? The only proper response is to lie on the beach like a clam."

"The Commander's not into lying on the beach. Just wait."

A few minutes later they crested the ridge. Stony nosed the cart into a gravel overlook. "See?"

Beneath them lay a vast plain of cement shimmering under a lens of heated air, a white beach before the blue water, like the footprint of an evaporated city.

Mr. Blunt looked at Stony.

"Yeah," Stony said. "He kind of overdid it."

At the far end of the spaceport was the gantry, three hundred feet tall and still unfinished. Steel and cement buildings huddled around its base. There was no rocket ship in sight, but several of the buildings were large enough to hide one.

"He's serious?" Mr. Blunt said. "He's really trying to build it?"

"I know, I know," Stony said. "It's kind of Howard Hughes-y."

"No, it's kind of L. Ron Hubbard. This is insane."

"Come on," Stony said. "We're supposed to meet at the Command Center." The way down was quicker—much. Stony zipped down with the engine off, nursing the brakes and leaning into the corners, and several times Mr. Blunt had to grip the aluminum frame to stay in his seat. "At least three wheels, please," Blunt said. Stony laughed. Between them they'd survived multiple gunshots and knife wounds. Blunt had outlived *burning*. One golf cart crash couldn't hurt them.

Stony rolled onto the surface of the spaceport. The tropical sun turned the treeless expanse into a frying pan, and Stony knew that the heat lingered long into the night. Fortunately heat, like cold, was something only breathers had to worry about.

It took almost fifteen minutes to reach the base of the gantry and the buildings there; the huts they'd seen from the top of the ridge grew to be warehouses and offices the size of municipal buildings. The cement buildings looked like gun fortifications, or perhaps bomb test bunkers, with thick walls and long, narrow, glassless windows. Most of the buildings were empty, built in preparation for the Commander's great project.

They parked next to one of the finished buildings, a four-story tower with blue glass windows. Mr. Blunt climbed out of the cart, straightened his tie, and looked around. "So how far along is it?" he asked.

"The spaceship?" Stony said. "He's a decade away." It had taken that long just to get the facilities in place: the gantry, the support buildings, the underground manufacturing facilities. As far as the public—and any government officials watching via satellite—was concerned, Calhoun, Inc. was investing in the commercial spaceflight industry. Zombie colonization of other planets was never going to get into a press release.

Stony said, "They do have a ship prototype, but it's one-third scale."

"You're going to need some tiny astronauts," Blunt said.

"Naw, we're just going to send the Lump." Stony laughed again. He hadn't laughed this much since . . . well, since he'd arrived at the island eight years ago. Chip wasn't much to talk to, and Calhoun was always performing the role of the Commander, and the staff at the data center thought of him as a boss. Everyone else he communicated with online. Blunt reminded him of life in the house in L.A.—before Deadtown, before everything became so serious.

He thought, not for the first time, How the fuck did I get here?

"Come on," he said. "The Commander's waiting."

They entered a large, granite-tiled lobby with empty display cases and large blank spots where the TVs would display commercials for the wonders of space travel. Etched into the polished cement walls were icons mixing the nautical with 1950s science fiction: great-finned rockets, elaborate compasses, ringed planets, tall ships. Probably the wrong message to send to investors looking for high tech (and despite Calhoun's cash, they would need outside funding to get past the prototype stage), but the Commander was a slave to his own branding, as committed to his personal style as Tom Wolfe or Leon Redbone.

They took the middle elevator (the only one in service) up to the top floor of the tower. The room looked like a half-sized version of NASA's Houston control room. The mandatory giant screen was in place, but the rows of desks were empty of computers and screens. By the western window was a small group of LDs. The Commander stood with his arms crossed behind him, gazing out at the empty gantry while he delivered his "promised land" spiel. Two of them were on Calhoun's staff, but the other six listening to him were new arrivals: LDs who'd been evacuated from Pennsylvania when their safe house sponsor—a man in his early eighties—had been hospitalized. Stony had sent a team in before the sponsor died and his relatives tried to go into the house.

One of the newly arrived LDs saw Stony enter the room and gasped; the others turned.

Mr. Blunt looked at him. "I've been wanting to see this in person," he said.

The group came for Stony, arms out. The first to reach him was a decrepit LD with a missing eye and a mouthful of brilliant dentures. "It's an honor to meet you," he said. "An honor. A real honor." Stony shook his hand, then greeted each of them in turn. Were they shocked by his appearance? He was always afraid of disappointing them. He'd been handsome once. The bandanna covered the most grievous wound to his forehead, but the prison beatings had taken their toll on his face.

But no, they didn't seem to be shocked. They didn't seem to be seeing him at all. They wore the same glassy, awed expression that all the newcomers wore. He could have shown up in a floral print dress wearing Kabuki makeup and they would have looked at him in the same way, manufacturing their own vision of Stony Mayhall to match their desires, like conjuring the Virgin Mary out of a water stain.

"I'm so happy you made it here safely," Stony said.

"Thank God you rescued us," one of them said. "It was only a matter of time—"

Stony noticed Calhoun staring at them. He was too much of a performer to show jealousy—and his surgically maintained face could convey only a limited range of emotions—but Stony could sense his annoyance. "You should thank the Commander," Stony said. "It's his vision and organization that makes all this possible."

One of the women had her hand on Stony's arm. She wouldn't let go.

"It's coming, isn't it?" she asked. She was bald, with a gray-blue face that looked like it had been flattened by an anvil:

crushed nose, broken front teeth, cheekbones pressed into planes. "The Big Bite?"

Stony drew away from her. "No, ma'am. No."

"But you're *here*. It's time."

"No! There will be no Big Bite. We're not going to attack all those people. They're just as human as us."

The one-eyed man said, "But they're killing us."

And the woman said, "We've been waiting for you!"

Stony held up his hands: one plastic, the other dead flesh. "We've got another plan. And soon we'll be able to tell you about it. But right now—" He nodded at Commander Calhoun. "Someone will show you to your new homes. You'll be safe here. Right, Commander?"

"Damn straight!" the Commander said. He strode forward and put a hand on the distraught woman's shoulder. "You won't have to worry about the Diggers here. Now, Stony and I have to go, but Anna and Rafael here will show you to your new accommodations. Welcome to Calhoun Island!"

Stony and Mr. Blunt took the cue and followed the Commander to the elevator. The Commander held out his hand: "Damn good to see you, Blunt." The hand was gloved. Calhoun wore at all times a full Integrity Suit, from toes to fingertips, leaving only his face exposed.

"Very good to see you, too, Commander. Quite the place you have here. A veritable Nassau NASA."

The Commander squinted at him. "That's right, you like words."

"Yes," Blunt said slowly. "I do."

Several seconds of uncomfortable silence followed. Stony said, "I was telling Mr. Blunt that you were making progress on the ship."

"Three years," Calhoun said. The door slid open, and he

strode into the lobby toward the front doors. Stony and Mr.
Blunt quickly followed. "Three years till first launch. I guarantee it."

"Do you think we have three years?" Blunt asked.

Calhoun stopped, turned. "What do you mean?" His plas-
ticene face managed to create a frown.

"The numbers don't look good," Blunt said.

"Goddamn it," the Commander said. "Our people have
been trying to write us off for twenty years. We will *make*
three years if we have to."

Outside, an SUV was waiting. A living man in khakis and
a white short-sleeved shirt stood holding the passenger-side
door. Franklin was one of the dozen breathers on staff on the
island. He collected an astronomical salary, and his retirement
benefits included immortality.

"Mr. Blunt, it was a pleasure to see you. Stony said that
he'd been needing to see his old friends, and I'm glad to
oblige. We're doing great work here. Important work. You
need anything, any Goddamn thing, you let me know."

"Will do, Commander."

"And Stony! Don't forget about the VIB flying in tomorrow. Franklin's got the room all set up."

"I've been looking forward to it my whole life," Stony
said.

The SUV rolled away, and Stony and Mr. Blunt climbed
back into the golf cart. Mr. Blunt asked, "Let me guess: Very
Important Breather?"

"You got it," Stony said. "Someone who can help us with
D-day. You'll meet them tomorrow."

"You also haven't told me yet what my new job is."

"Right. That." Stony started the cart and they zipped
away from the command center, back the way they had come.
He raised his voice slightly. "So you know those immigrants

back there?" Blunt nodded. Stony said, "Sometime in the next few weeks, one or two of them—usually the smart ones—will disappear."

"You eat them? No, we taste horrible. Eaten by sharks then. Again, same problem—"

"Blunt, please. Calhoun sends them away, by ship and by helicopter. He says they're going to Florida for 'advanced training.' Computers, logistics, blah blah blah."

"From your tone—and I'm just guessing here—you don't believe him."

Stony laughed again. "They don't come back, Mr. Blunt. I never talk to them again. I think Calhoun's building his own team, loyal to him, without my influence."

"Maybe he's training astronauts," Blunt said.

"Please. I need you to help me. I've never figured out how you do what you do, how you get through borders, how you avoid the police, especially now when—"

"I look like this. Point taken."

"Well frankly, yeah. We're monsters, Mr. Blunt. None of us, except maybe Delia, can move around like you do."

"And you want me to find out what Calhoun is doing with these people," Mr. Blunt said. "Where they're going, what they're doing."

"Your mission, should you choose to accept it."

"*Choose?*" he said in pretend shock. "I get to choose?"

"Not really."

A day later, Stony and Commander Calhoun sat in a room of the Commander's mansion watching a video monitor. The screen showed the interior of an empty room two doors down. The Commander sat with his arms crossed, and his face had turned to stone. It was only when all the visitors and staff were gone that the Commander stopped performing, stopped being the icon. It had taken years before he allowed Stony to see this offstage version.

"Do you think this will work?" Calhoun said.

"I don't know," Stony said. "I think she'll go for it."

"I meant all of it," Calhoun said. "The whole plan. Do you think this can possibly work?"

Stony looked up. Calhoun was staring at him, hollow-eyed. His skin was glossy, his teeth perfectly white, but his eyes were ancient and terrified. Calhoun was more afraid of death than anyone he'd ever met. While so many LDs were becoming sleepers, throwing themselves into the abyss, Calhoun was doing everything in his power to pave over it, seal it up. He was going to the stars, damn it. He was going to be immortal. Stony understood this, but sometimes the depth of Calhoun's fear shook him afresh.

"It'll work," Stony said. And now *he* was performing. Stony the confident, firm leader. The visionary. "Have a little faith," he said.

"In *what*?"

There was movement on the screen. Franklin, Calhoun's breather assistant, came into the frame first, followed by a white woman dressed in pastel yellow and green. "Please sit down, Ms. Stolberg," Franklin said. He'd positioned himself so that there was only one available seat. "The Commander will be with us in a minute. Can I get you something to drink?"

Gloria Stolberg stood a couple of inches over five feet tall and carried perhaps forty extra pounds on a stout frame. Her red hair—dyed, teased, sprayed—had lost that morning's battle with the island humidity. She was dressed for the tropics in a light cotton short-sleeved blouse and capri pants that looked like they'd been bought as a matched set at Target. She looked younger than her age.

She was sixty-three years old, one of many facts Stony had memorized. Resident of Passaic, New Jersey. Twice divorced and currently unmarried. Three children and seven grandchildren. Favorite book: *Angels Fall*, by Nora Roberts.

"I have to tell you," Gloria said. "I think there's been a mistake."

The mistake, Stony thought, was wanting to meet your idol.

Onscreen, Franklin said, "I assure you, the Commander is a huge fan." Gloria sat in the offered chair, which was well lit from the window, and faced the hidden camera. "Perhaps you'd like a piña colada?" Franklin asked her. "You might as well enjoy the Caribbean."

"Oh no! A Diet Coke would be fine." When Franklin left, she put her large handbag on the floor next to her, then picked it up again and took out a small black notebook and a pen. They'd taken her camera and cellphone before she'd landed on the island. The Commander wants no photographs, they'd told her. Which wasn't hard to explain. He was ninety-six years old. The Commander had stopped making public appearances in 1985 and had not spoken to anyone at his corporation, even by phone, since it was sold to R. J. Reynolds in 1992. His family deflected all PR requests.

But in one way—perhaps the most important way, in the eyes of the American public—the Commander never left. His likeness remained stamped on every Calhoun Family Restaurant sign and every box of fishstixs. His hearty voice—"Now *that's* a good one!"—was still heard at the end of each ad. He'd become a cartoon, as immortal as his nemesis, Colonel Sanders, or that creepy dead girl, Wendy. Most people thought he'd died years ago, others assumed that he was hooked up on life support on his island, and the rest—mostly those under twenty—had no idea he'd ever been a real person. No wonder he didn't want pictures—the real-life Commander Calhoun could only damage his image.

Franklin returned with the soft drink, a plate of crackers and cheese, and a bowl of jumbo shrimp. "We have a few minutes before the Commander gets here. I suppose you have a lot of questions."

"Yes. Why me?"

Franklin smiled. "I told you that he was a fan of your work."

"He reads romances?"

"Pardon?"

"I mostly write Regency romances. The Consort series? The Chatelaine?"

"No, I'm sorry. I was referring to your other books—"

"The westerns, then. Of course. Men love the westerns. *Wagonmaster, The Wagonmaster's Son*—"

"No."

"True crime?"

"I believe these books involved the living dead."

"Oh! The zombie detective books!"

Franklin winced. "Yes, those. He's a very big fan of C. V. Ferris."

"Those stopped selling in the eighties. I liked writing them, though. They're mostly dialogue, and the pages just fly by."

In the room down the hall, Stony put his face in his hands.

Franklin said, "The Commander thought that because you'd expressed an interest in the living dead, and in Deadtown in particular, that you might be interested in writing more about them."

Comprehension dawned on Gloria's face. "Oh! I'm afraid I completely misunderstood. I thought he was interested in me writing his biography, but this makes *much* more sense. I've never written a privately commissioned novel before, but I'm sure we can work something out." She laughed. "He's already spent thousands of dollars just flying me down here!"

"Ms. Stolberg—"

"Call me Gloria."

"Gloria. This would be a nonfiction book."

"About zombies?"

"We prefer the term *living dead. Or differently living.*"

"We?" Gloria asked.

"The Commander was interested in hiring you because you already seemed to know a great deal about Deadtown."

Gloria blinked. "I should hope so. I made it up."

"I mean the *real* Deadtown."

She smiled, then shook her head in confusion.

"The prison, ma'am. The maximum-security facility that holds living dead prisoners."

"That's an urban myth."

This, Stony thought, is not happening. "Please, stay here," he told the Commander. "Let me talk to her." He marched down the hall. Why would she lie to them? Had the Diggers gotten to her? The Accountants? She obviously knew the truth—the details were too specific. She knew that the fever passed, that the LDs became conscious again. She'd obviously changed some of the facts—Deadtown was no prison the size of Elkhart, Indiana—but the psychological details were dead on. How the prisoners lived on the edge of despair, how they tried to commit suicide, how they both feared and envied the breathers. She must have had a contact in the community, or maybe with someone on the staff at Deadtown. It was time to drop the masks and misdirection, Stony thought, and tell the truth.

He barged through the door, turned toward the window—
and Gloria Stolberg screamed.

Stony walked toward her, arms open. "Please, please.
Nobody here's going to—"

Gloria jumped up from her chair, and the table tipped.
Red cocktail sauce splattered across the white carpet. She
backed up to the only other exit in the room, a small door.
"Get away from me!"

"Ms. Stolberg!" Franklin said.

"Jesus Christ," Stony said.

At that moment, Commander Calhoun stepped in and
bellowed, "Ahoy there!"

Gloria spun to face him. Up close, the Commander
looked like an unconvincing wax effigy of himself: a shiny
mannequin in a naval uniform. She opened her mouth, her
head tilted back . . . and then her knees folded and she
crashed onto the floor.

Holy shit, Stony thought. We just killed C. V. Ferris.

But no, not dead. She was breathing, and in a few minutes
her eyes fluttered open and she tried to sit up. Stony stepped
back out of her line of sight.

"Are you all right, Ms. Stolberg?" Franklin asked. "Have a
sip of water."

"Goddamn! I haven't seen anyone faint in years," the
Commander said. He was in performance mode again.

She stared at the old man. "You startled me," she said. "I
thought I—" Then she remembered Stony and looked around
wildly for him.

Stony lifted a hand tentatively. "I'm so sorry," he said.

Gloria did not faint again. Franklin helped her from the

floor and she managed to get back to her chair without turning her back on Stony or Calhoun.

"I think it's time for me to leave," she said. "Now."

Stony said, "Please, Ms. Stolberg, if you just let me explain—"

"Of course you can leave," Calhoun said. "Franklin, go bring the car around."

"No!" she said. "Franklin—stay!"

"You really haven't met another LD?" Stony asked.

"You're—both of you are, aren't you?"

"You can tell?" The Commander sounded hurt.

"But you can talk!" she said.

"Please, Ms. Stolberg," Stony said. "I know you've met some of us. You wrote the Jack Gore books."

"What does that have to do with anything?"

The Commander said, "It's the eyes, isn't it? They said the eyes give it away."

Stony said, "Because the books are so, so . . . incredible."

"Oh." She pursed her lips. "You've read them?"

"I've *memorized* them," Stony said. "They got me through high school. If it wasn't for Jack Gore, I don't know what would have happened to me."

"I should have worn sunglasses," the Commander said.

Gloria said, "Both of you"—she pointed to Stony, then the Commander—"sit down over there. Franklin, you're human, aren't you?"

"We're all *human*," Stony said.

"Living human," she said.

"Yes ma'am," Franklin said.

"Give me your word that you'll let me return home."

The Commander drew himself up. "Mrs. Stolberg, as captain of this island, *I* give you my word."

"'Cross my heart and hope to burn,'" Stony said. "It's

what one of the Stitch Brothers promised, right before he shot Jack."

"You *are* a fan," Gloria said. "Franklin? Your word?"

"I promise," Franklin said.

"Good. Sit here next to me."

Franklin looked at the deepening red stain on the carpet as if longing to put down some wet towels, and sat beside her.

"All right then," Gloria said. "Why don't you tell me why I'm really here, Commander. You're not writing a biography, and you're not commissioning a Deadtown Detective novel. So what is it you want?"

The Commander took his seat. "I defer to Stony. This is his idea."

Stony sat as well. "It's a nonfiction book," he said. "The true story of the living dead in America."

"And it needs to be on store shelves in nine months," the Commander said.

"That's impossible," Gloria said.

"I know how to move product," the Commander said.

"Even if you could find a publisher, and get it printed, I have three books to write before June."

"I can make it worth your while," the Commander said.

"We need you for this," Stony said. "The book can't just be a dry history. It's got to engage people. It's got to show everyone what life has been like for us for the past thirty-five years."

Gloria frowned. "Why nine months? What happens then?"

"We go public," Stony said. "It will be a multimedia PR campaign. TV, radio, Internet—"

"And celebrities," the Commander said. "Besides myself, of course. Living celebrities. We believe we can get Bono. It'll be the Goddamn Super Bowl of publicity events."

"Your book will be the centerpiece," Stony said. "No one else will have your access. I've already written hundreds of pages of background material. We'll tell you how we survived, what the government has done to suppress us, how they've kept us from talking, and what we can offer the world."

"Freedom from disease," the Commander said. "Increased life span, space travel—"

"A lot of things," Stony said, cutting the man off. "The important thing we want to get across is that our people don't want to harm anyone. In fact, we've worked very hard to keep the world safe."

"Safe? From what?" she asked.

"Well," Commander Calhoun said. "*Us.*"

"I don't think that's going to earn you any points," she said.

"It's like in your books," Stony said. "You've got your good LDs and your bad LDs."

"And you're the good ones."

"Of course!" the Commander said. "Franklin, bring Ms. Stolberg another drink."

"Another Diet Coke?" Franklin asked.

"And put some rum in it," she said.

"Now that sounds like C. V. Ferris," Stony said.

"I don't think so," she said. "For this one I'm going to need a whole new pen name."

"Nonsense!" the Commander said. "No pen names, no masks. We're all walking into the sunshine, and Gloria Stolberg is coming out with us. I'll get the contracts."

The Commander walked out, and Stony and Mrs. Stolberg were alone. She seemed uncomfortable, but he was encouraged that she no longer seemed terrified of him.

This was his chance. Now, however, *he* was nervous.

He leaned over to her. "I really shouldn't ask this," he said. "But I was wondering if you would do me a huge favor."

She regarded him suspiciously. "Yes?"

"I'm just looking for your honest, professional opinion."

"About what?" And then: "Oh no."

"It's kind of a thriller slash autobiography slash detective novel. See, when you stopped writing the Deadtown Detective books, I thought someone should—"

"Good Lord, you're writing Jack Gore *fan-fic*?"

"If you could just take a look at it," he said, "I'd really appreciate it."

CHAPTER SEVENTEEN

April 2010
Evans City, Pennsylvania

He'd promised himself that he'd never try to see anyone in his family again. And now the promise was on the edge of being broken, a porcelain teacup balanced on the arm of a chair—as good as broken already.

Stony sat leaning forward in the passenger seat of a Ford delivery van, parked and lights off, staring out through a foggy and rain-smeared windshield at a stretch of dark road. He hummed some church song his mother used to sing. They'd been hiding out here for nearly an hour. A little ways off from the road was a small brick house, the light from one of its windows gauzy in the heavy rain.

He palmed some of the moisture from the window and rested his arms on the dash. The fogging windshield was the fault of the breather with him in the driver's seat, a heavily tattooed white woman named Nessa, who was one of Calhoun's island staff. She was his chauffeur and bodyguard and beard. One of her responsibilities, he was sure, was to report on him to Calhoun. He didn't hold it against her. She seemed like a nice woman, though she was probably the most boring conversationalist he'd ever met—and he was from Iowa. It was as if the gaudiness of the tattoos removed any need for her to have a personality.

"So . . . ," she said. When that didn't spark a response, she said, "Are we going in?"

"Not yet," he said. Thinking: We're not going in at all.

"It's really hard to be in the dark like this," she said. "You haven't told me anything. I don't even know whose safe house this is. It wasn't on our list."

"It's not a safe house," Stony said. "I'm sorry, I sort of misled you about that."

"Oh, then . . . ," she said. Perhaps thirty seconds passed. "Stony, I know you can't tell me everything, but it's just that we were supposed to be in Michigan tonight." They were on a tour of safe houses, traveling by night between cities. Stony's job was to spread the word about D-day and buck up the troops. Calhoun had been against it, but Stony insisted. Everyone had to be ready, he told the Commander. Everyone had to know that they just needed to hang on until June 1.

"I'm sorry," he said. "We're not going to get to Grand Rapids."

"I know, it's like seven hours. Six if we don't make any stops. I don't think I could stay awake, though." Stony didn't say anything. She said, "I've never even heard of Evans City."

"This is where the outbreak started in '68," Stony said.

"Really?"

"You've seen the Romero documentary. The cemetery where he filmed the graveborn coming up is just down the road."

"Oh, so this is . . . sightseeing?"

"Kind of." He nodded toward the house. "This is where my grandparents live. Their first house that was on this lot burned down during the outbreak. They were evacuated.

After a year, though, they came back and built this place. A lot of the survivors came back. Now I bet hardly anyone here thinks about the LDs."

"Your grandparents are in there? Right now?"

"I've never met them." He smiled again. "That's weird, isn't it? I mean, I'm not even sure what they look like."

"But isn't it a risk to even—oops. Better duck." Headlights were coming toward them. Stony had spent most of the time on the road ducking or hiding in the back of the van. This time, however, he didn't move. The car slowed, and before it reached them it pulled over to the side and doused its lights. It was parked directly across from his grandparents' house.

Nessa said, "You were waiting for that."

He smiled again. "Maybe."

"And are you going to tell me who's in the car, or is that a secret, too?"

"Just a minute." Inside the car, a Toyota Prius, a dome light flicked on. He could not make out the face of the person inside—he could barely make out any shape at all within the vehicle—but he knew then that he'd break his promise.

"So who is it? Your grandpa? Your cousin?"

"My sister," he said finally. "Her name is Alice."

Nessa seemed to process this. "You're not going to talk to her, are you?"

"Why not?"

"You're in hiding. I thought—I heard you weren't in contact with your family."

"I haven't seen any of them since I went to Deadtown." It was too dangerous for them.

"But . . ." She hesitated. Even though they'd been traveling together for weeks, he'd kept a certain formality between them. Maybe if they hadn't run out of things to say on Day 2 he would have let his guard drop. But as it stood, he was the leader of the LD community (or depending on her loyalties, second in command, after Calhoun) and she was the assistant. "It's just that—at least I don't think so—she's not in the network?"

The network. The Commander's people were always worried about who could be trusted, who was in the network of trusted LDs, and who was working against them.

"It's okay," Stony said. "I'm just here to watch."

"But she's just sitting there."

"I think she's waiting for the rain to let up." Or to decide whether to go inside. He couldn't imagine Alice nervous, but he could certainly picture her annoyed at him. He'd been sending Alice emails for several years, and he'd recently made an unreasonable request. She'd told him no, absolutely not. But he kept asking. Months later, here she was.

And there she goes, he thought.

"She's getting out of the car," Nessa said, stating the obvious. Suddenly the car door was slamming behind her and Alice was running for the front porch of the little house. She wore dark slacks and a nylon raincoat. She moved fast for a woman in her fifties. Stony laughed out loud.

"What's she doing?" Nessa asked. "Is she going inside?"

"Just a second," Stony said. A tree partially obscured his view of the front door. He leaned to the side and saw Alice still on the porch, waiting. Had she knocked? She must have already knocked.

The door opened. A man stood in the doorway, and he beckoned Alice inside. The door closed behind her. A moment later, a side window lit up. Perhaps that was the living room.

I owe you, Alice, he thought.

She didn't know he was there, so close. He'd asked her to

schedule the trip for sometime in April, when he knew he'd be on the mainland. And then he'd begged her to tell him the exact day she was going. So he could call her afterward, he said. He even mailed her a calling-card-enabled cellphone to keep with her—a one-use phone that she could throw away afterward. But when he suggested that maybe she could turn it on during the interview so he could listen in, she told him to go to hell.

He watched the house, burning to hear what they were talking about.

"I'll be right back," he said.

"But Stony!"

He unlocked the door and jumped out. The rain drenched him, hard and cold, and he allowed the sensation in and it felt good. He ran toward the house, angling toward the side window that had lit up. When he was a few yards from the window he crouched and crept up to it. This side of the house was protected from the wind, and the glass was speckled with drops but mostly clear. Through a gap in the drapes he saw Alice, sitting stiffly on a green cloth armchair. Her dark hair was shot with gray. She was no longer rail thin, but her face still looked like something carved, all high cheekbones and strong nose and sharp chin. Still beautiful.

The man who'd opened the door sat on a floral-print couch, talking. Charles Cooper was gray and jowly, with dark bags under his eyes. A face for talking about soy futures. Beside him sat a woman in a wheelchair, his wife, Mavis Cooper. She was white and shrunken, and looked a decade older than the man. An oxygen tank was fastened to the rear of the wheelchair, and a plastic tube lay across her shoulder, the mask dead on her chest. She stared at the blocky, country-style coffee table in front of her and at the plastic flowers in a small wicker basket at its center.

Stony thought, These are my grandparents? These trolls?

He watched for fifteen minutes, letting the rain soak him thoroughly. Mr. Cooper did most of the talking, his expression never changing. Alice asked a few questions, and Mrs. Cooper never spoke at all.

This was all wrong. For years he'd imagined this moment. He would walk up to the white farmhouse (in his mind, his mother had grown up in Dorothy's house in Kansas) and slowly knock. His grandmother, a regal-looking woman with bright blue eyes, would open the door and hesitantly say, "Yes?" He'd be wearing a slouch hat to hide his face, and a long raincoat like Jack Gore's. He'd search for the right words, and then his grandmother would say, "It's you, isn't it? You're Bethany's boy." He would pull his hat from his face and she'd gasp. "I'm sorry," he'd say. "I'm one of them." He'd turn to leave the porch, his heart breaking. The orchestra would swell in the background. Then his grandmother would grab his arm. "No," she'd say. "You just surprised me. We've always known. Please—come inside."

But of course that wasn't possible. He was a monster and a fugitive. So he called his adopted sister and begged her to meet these people, strangers she wasn't even related to, and ask them all the questions he'd never been able to ask. What happened to their daughter, Bethany? Did they know she was pregnant? Why did she run away? Where was she going? Did they ever look for her? Did they ever wonder what happened to the child?

Difficult questions to answer, but impossible to ask. What right could Alice claim to come here and ask them these things? She could not tell them about Stony, or how they'd raised the dead boy as their own, how her own family had suffered to protect him. So she'd found their daughter beside a road forty years ago. That made her a tardy witness to a death, nothing more. No wonder Alice had told him to go to hell when he asked her.

Inside, Alice handed Mr. Cooper a photograph. Stony couldn't see what it was of. The man stared at it for perhaps half a minute, then he leaned over and held it out to his wife. She didn't look at it, but the man seemed to be explaining it to her. Then he abruptly pushed himself from the couch and left Stony's line of sight.

Alice remained seated. She said something to Mrs. Cooper, who didn't look up. Alice moved beside her on the couch and spoke to her again, studying the old woman's face as if looking for symptoms. Ah, Dr. Alice. Always on duty. Mrs. Cooper, however, seemed as inert as the plastic flowers.

Alice stood as Mr. Cooper returned to the room. He held a book, which he gave to Alice. She turned it in her hands but did not open it. Mr. Cooper stood before her, looking uncomfortable. Alice asked him a question.

Mrs. Cooper raised her head. But instead of looking at Alice, she'd turned toward the window where Stony crouched. Her pupils seemed huge and black. He backed away automatically, then turned and ran back toward the delivery van.

Nessa shook her head. "What was that about?"

"Do we have any towels?" he asked.

Alice emerged from the house fifteen minutes later. The rain had slackened, but Mr. Cooper followed her out to her car holding an umbrella over them both. Alice got into her car.

"Follow her," Stony said to Nessa. "But not yet. Not till he goes in."

Mr. Cooper watched Alice drive away, and then he turned

back to the house. When the door closed, Stony said, "Okay, now."

Nessa started the van and rolled forward. She didn't turn on her lights until they were past the house, a tactic he approved of. He got out one of the three cellphones he carried, the purple one he thought of as the family line, and thought about calling Alice. It wasn't safe to talk on the phone when you drove. But maybe she could use the speakerphone.

"We're stalking your sister," Nessa said. "I feel like a criminal."

"We *are* criminals," Stony said. He saw the Toyota's taillights perhaps a hundred yards ahead. "Not too close," he said. He dialed Alice's number.

"Who are you calling?" Nessa said, but Stony held up a hand; the phone was ringing.

"Hello?" Alice said.

"It's me. How did it go?"

"I just got finished. I'm driving back to my hotel now. It was strange, but sweet."

"Sweet? Really? Even Mrs. Cooper?"

"Yes, sweet. Why? Did you think they would be mean?"

"Did they give you anything?"

"What?"

"I was just wondering if they—"

"Where the hell are you, Stony? You're behind me, aren't you? Damn it, you're right behind me."

"Oh!" Nessa said. "She just hit her brakes."

Stony sighed. "Pull up behind her. It's okay."

"What are you going to do?"

"Break a promise."

He climbed down from the van, and then Alice stepped out of her car and marched toward him through the rain.

They met in the space between the cars, lit by headlights. Her jaw was set, her lips pulled into a thin hard line.

"Alice," he said, "I know I shouldn't be here, but—"

She grabbed him with both arms and pulled him into her. He was shocked. He couldn't remember Alice hugging him. Hugging anyone. That had been Junie's specialty, before Crystal took on the job.

Her arms tightened into a fierce squeeze. Then she abruptly pushed him back and stared into his face. "You've been hurt."

"Hadn't I mentioned that?" he said. "I'm fine now."

She touched the bandanna that covered the dent in his forehead. "Let me see."

He laughed. "It's raining, Alice. Can we talk? How far is your hotel?"

"Fifteen minutes. Who's in the van?"

"My handler. Just a sec." He went to the driver's-side door and Nessa rolled down the window. "I'm going to ride with Alice."

"But I'm not supposed to—I don't think you should—"

"Just follow us. Thanks, Nessa."

On the passenger seat of Alice's car was an old-fashioned diary: pink and green cloth cover with a tiny lock.

"Why would he give you this?" he asked.

"I really don't know. I think when I gave him the picture of Bethany's grave he wanted to give me something back."

"I wondered what you'd handed him."

Alice gave him a dark look. "So you watched the whole thing?"

"I was standing by the window. The Coopers looked . . . creepy."

"Said the dead boy."

"The way she just stared at that table. Weird."

"They're just *old,* Stony. Mrs. Cooper had a stroke a few years ago, and she can't speak. Mr. Cooper, though, was eager to talk. He even got a little choked up."

"Really? He didn't look like he had any emotion at all. What did he say?"

"Not much that we don't already know," Alice said. Mr. Cooper had told her that Bethany had sneaked out that night to meet up with her boyfriend. He was found the next day, shot. Nobody knew if he'd turned undead, or if he'd been shot accidentally. The Coopers were forced to evacuate, but Bethany never showed up. They thought that she'd been killed, too. People were panicking, and it wasn't unusual for bodies to be burned before they were identified. It wasn't until a police detective had contacted them—this was in 1997 or 1998—that they learned she'd been found in Iowa.

"I told him about finding Bethany," Alice said. "And about finding you."

"What?"

"I said that you were dead in her arms. Which is true."

"Maybe you shouldn't have said that. Mom never told the police about finding a baby."

"Mom's in prison," Alice said. "I'm not too worried about the police."

He stared out the passenger window. They were entering a town—Evans City proper. He supposed he should be ready to duck if anyone pulled up next to them.

"We don't blame you, Stony," Alice said.

"That's okay, I do." He managed a smile. "Crystal said you've got a new lawyer working on her case."

"Not that it will do any good."

"Did you get the check?"

"What check?"

"It was an anonymous donation. I think you would have remembered it."

"That was you? Where did you get that kind of cash?"

"I know some people." He'd had Calhoun send a check to her for two hundred thousand dollars. Pocket change for him, but maybe enough to restart the case against the government.

"I was afraid to touch it. You know what that kind of thing does to your taxes? The first thing I had to do was form a nonprofit to hold it. The Wanda Mayhall Legal Defense Fund."

Alice pulled into the parking lot of a new-looking Marriott. Alice reached for the door handle but Stony said, "I can't go in there. They have lights, cameras—"

"Action?"

"That's what I'm trying to avoid." He looked left and right. There were a few cars in the lot, but there didn't seem to be anyone moving about. Nessa pulled into the row behind them.

"I have to tell you something," Stony said. "We're going public."

She raised her eyebrows. "Public."

"We're holding a press conference and everything," he said. "A book's going to come out to tell our story. We're going to set up television interviews with LDs."

"You can't do that," Alice said.

"Well, we're going to."

"That's crazy."

"We have to. Alice—we're dying off. There's less than five hundred of us in the whole country. If we just keep hiding, they'll pick us off one by one. We'll go extinct."

"Maybe you should go extinct."

"What? How can you say that?" And he thought: I said the same thing to Mr. Blunt. Why did it sound so much more awful when a breather said it?

"Stony, I love you, but think what's going to happen—it'll be like Al Qaeda going on TV and saying, here we are, right in downtown Des Moines. Come and get us. They'll turn the country inside out to find you. And then what happens? The police attack, and someone on your side bites back. Then it's the next outbreak."

"You've always overstated the danger," Stony said. "You scared me to death with those mathematical predictions when I was a kid. Yeah, one bite can start an epidemic, but that's just theoretical. In the real world, my people don't want to bite any more than the living want to murder everyone just because they can."

"Don't lie to me, Stony. Crystal told me about the Big Biters."

"They've lost, Alice. They've been killed off. They found out that as soon as one shambling, fevered LD shows up in town, the police swarm the area. They shoot and burn *everybody*. I've seen it happen, Alice. Thanks to '68, the government will never be unprepared again. So this time, we show up on TV, but we're not attacking. We're not the monsters they're afraid of."

"You're being naïve, kid."

"Alice, I'm a forty-year-old man."

"Forty-one. Forty-six if you're still pinning yourself to Kwang."

"Pinning—what?"

"Never mind. I'm asking you not to do this, Stony."

"But Alice, this is genocide."

"No it's not. You're not a *race,* Stony. You're human beings who have a disease. An incurable disease. You think people with cancer get together and say, 'We have to make sure we keep the right to have cancer. We have to maintain cancer as a lifestyle choice'?"

"The government's not hunting down cancer victims and shooting them in the head. The government's not torturing them in secret prisons. And we're not just people with a disease—we have our own culture. We have something to offer the world, a point of view that no one else has. Capabil-ities no one else has. Life is richer with us in the world."

"Now you're sounding like a marketing brochure. You've practiced this, haven't you? This is the speech you give your huddled masses."

If he was capable of blushing, he would have. Of course it was the speech. Alice was so damn sharp.

She said, "Here's what I'm afraid of, Stony, what keeps me up at night—Ruby."

"What do you mean? What's the matter with Ruby?"

"You're what's the matter, Stony. The living dead."

"I don't know what you're talking about."

"You put Ruby at risk. You put all future generations at risk. I think about Ruby, and her children, and her grandchildren—all the people who'll never get to live if one of your LDs fucks up. Crystal's tried to prepare Ruby, and I've done my part, but another outbreak could end all that."

"Future generations are always at risk," Stony said. "Nuclear war, global warming, multidrug-resistant tuberculosis—pick your poison."

"Don't be flip."

"Alice, my people are being killed, they're committing suicide, they're being experimented on. I can't just stand by and do nothing."

"What about your family? What about Mom? You're will-ing to trade her in for your 'unique point of view'?"

"That's—" He couldn't speak. *She* knew where his heart was. She could drive a stake straight into it.

"What about the rest of the fucking planet, Stony? All the living, breathing people that you're gambling with?"

He took a breath. "I think about that all the time, Alice."

Alice studied the rearview mirror. Watching Nessa? After a minute she said, "Okay. When is it happening, this public hanging?"

"We're calling it D-day," he said. "June first."

"That's in two months. You couldn't have told me sooner?"

He thought, Would it have made a difference? But instead he said, "I'm sorry. But you can't tell anyone."

"The hell with that. I'm calling Crystal and Ruby tonight."

"You can't do that! Crystal's phone is probably tapped."

"Then I'll send her one of the TracFones you sent me."

She was so angry. This wasn't the way it was supposed to go. Nothing tonight had gone as he'd expected.

"Can I call you in the morning?" he asked.

"I'll be driving back."

"Tomorrow night then."

"I thought you said it was too risky to call."

"I'll send you a new phone as soon as I can," he said. "Two phones." Then he lifted the diary. "Can I keep this?"

"Mr. Cooper didn't have the key, but I don't imagine you'll have too much trouble."

She was right; it looked like he could snap it with his bare fingers. "Alice, I can't thank you enough. For everything—this trip, talking to the Coopers, taking care of Mom—"

"Stop it," she said. "You don't get to be the nice one. Not when you're about to blow up the world."

* * *

Later, Stony would think of these weeks as the Farewell Tour. Stony and Nessa circled back to Michigan, then worked their way back east, stopping at safe houses in Ohio, Indiana, Pennsylvania, and New Jersey. On the Tuesday of the last week of April he was in a basement den, talking to four LDs, all of whom had been in hiding since the original outbreak, and their breather sponsor, a man in his late seventies with ropy muscles and a sarcastic laugh. His motivation for protecting the LDs had something do with his antigovernment, antitax belief system. He'd proudly shown Stony the automatic rifle he kept in the living room for the day the Diggers tried to break into his house.

"No one is asking you to come out in the open right away," Stony told the LDs. "First will be the television campaign. I can't tell you the exact date, but you'll know it when you see it. Then the book will come out. Then we're going to have blogs and videos, an entire website to put a human face on our people. We are going to be *so* public, so open, that the Diggers won't be able to attack us without looking like Nazis."

The three men and one woman stared at him, hollow-eyed. The people had been like this in so many of the houses they'd visited. Forty years of hiding had taken its toll. Yes, they were still LD, but the split seemed to be 20 percent L and 80 percent D. Most of the people were Lumpists—or at least wore the Lump pendants.

"Once the first phase of the public relations campaign is over, we'll be able to bring you to Calhoun Island. No more hiding in basements! I've been there, and I can promise you, it's paradise. Sunny beaches, crystal clear water, and fresh air."

One of his cellphones vibrated in his pocket—a short buzz that meant a text message. That wouldn't be Alice, then—she never texted.

"Why not now?" one of the LD men said. His voice was a thing of scrapes and rasps, an engine that had not been started in ages. "Move us now."

"The logistics are complicated," Stony said. The cellphone buzzed again, another text. "We've been able to move households to the island in cases of emergency, but it's not easy, and right now, in the current environment, it's extremely risky. Once things loosen up—once we feel more secure—we'll be able to move anyone who wants to go." The phone vibrated again and he dug it out of his pocket. It was the red phone— and only two people had its number. "Excuse me," he said. "I know this is so rude, but I really need to take this."

He walked to the other side of the room, near a stone fireplace that looked like it hadn't been fired in decades. The message was from a number he didn't recognize, but that wasn't surprising; Delia and Blunt changed phones as often as he did. There were three messages, and from the time stamps it looked like they'd been queued up and sent at once. They were all picture messages. He opened the first one and saw that it was a photo of a computer monitor, and the monitor was showing a document. There were two columns of text on the document, but the picture was too small for him to make out the characters. The caption said only "b." Mr. Blunt.

He zoomed in on the picture close enough to read the top three lines:

elena gomez bog
eric haslett mad
terry alsup iad

He looked at the other pictures, and they, too, were of documents on a screen. None of the others had captions. He wrote a one-character message in reply: "?" When that was sent, he forwarded the pictures to Delia.

"I'm so sorry," Stony said, returning to the group. The LDs were talking among themselves. The woman looked at him and said, "What if they don't care?"

"Pardon?" Stony said.

"What if they don't care about looking like Nazis?" she said. "It hasn't stopped them before."

"Then we're no worse off than we are now," Stony said. "Those of us who appear in public may be in danger, but you'll be as safe here as you've always been. It's not until it works that you have to risk anything. You'll be safe."

A lie, or almost one. Alice could be right, and the publicity would create a frenzy for finding the undead that would rival the hunts of '68. Or it could be that only the leadership—Stony, Calhoun, Delia, and the others—would be decapitated, leaving the houses without a central organization, a communication system, or Calhoun's money. And that would be an end as final as if each house had been burned to the ground.

But he couldn't tell them that. Just as he couldn't tell them that they had no choice. They were dying here.

"My message to you is to hang on," Stony said. "Change is coming." He shook each person's hand. "Just hang on."

The raspy-voiced man gripped Stony's hand. "Is it true?" he asked. "You grew from a baby?"

"Yes," he said. They always asked this. "I was found by the side of the road, just after the outbreak of 1968. I was raised by a kind family who kept me hidden."

"And at the prison?" the man said. "Show us."

"Yes," the woman said, and suddenly the other LDs seemed to grow more alert. "The Release."

"Show what?" the sponsor asked.

Stony glanced at Nessa. She'd watched this scene a dozen times by now. He reached up and began to untie the bandanna. "The shot came at close range," he said. "Only a few inches."

"Because they had you chained," the woman said.

"That's right," he said. "They'd tied me to the chair with chains."

"But the chains fell away," she said.

They all wanted this, the miracle story. "That's what frightened them," Stony said. "When the locks opened, the chains dropped, and the prison guard raised his pistol and fired." He pulled aside the cloth so they could see the indentation. "Right here. I've patched it up since then. But the hole went straight through. To here, at the back."

They stared at him, at full attention now. "It's okay," he said. "You can touch it."

One by one they put their fingers against the skin of his forehead. They were always gentle, as if afraid of poking through the plate. In his pocket, the phone vibrated again, this time repeatedly—a phone call coming in. He ignored it; he could call Blunt back in a few minutes.

The rasping man was touching his forehead now. "How is that possible?" he said. "A shot to the head . . ."

"It's not possible," Stony said. "It's flat-out impossible. But as the Lump said, we're all impossible. And so that means *anything's* possible. We have the power to survive even terrible things. We will get through these dark days."

That was usually his final word, the last bit of inspirational fluff to keep them from killing themselves before D-day. The first time he'd said it to a group in a safe house, weeks ago, he felt as if this were some essential truth. By the third time it had taken on the tinny echo of a slogan. Now, after dozens of repetitions, the words were noise and he felt like a fraud, a bad actor droning his lines. A politician.

"I'm afraid we have to say good night," he said. "Nessa and I have to—"

"This is awful!" the rasping man said. He looked distraught.

Stony said, "I'm sorry?" The other LDs turned to the man, confused.

"What if we can't die?" the man said. "What if we can never die?"

Stony looked from the man to the other LDs. He could see it in their faces: the question taking root, and behind their eyes the first blossom of fear.

"I . . . I don't think . . . ," Stony said.

"What an interesting question!" Nessa said brightly, and tugged Stony toward the door. "But we're way behind schedule."

From *An Oral History of the Second Outbreak*:

> *. . . No, we didn't know what we were protecting. Could have been the Commander's secret recipe for all we knew. But it didn't matter. We had a job to do, and we were prepared to hold the compound as long as possible, and the most important part of the compound was the Kitchen. I don't know why they called it that. Maybe because of the fail-safe. It was fifty feet underground, only one way in, with two doors big as bank vaults and a no-man's-land between them, you know, like an airlock. The whole place was locked down. It was a transmission dead zone, no network connections at all. Only four or*

five LDs had permission to work down there, and everyone under-
stood that if the Kitchen was breached those people were toast.

But nobody was supposed to get that far, ever. We were trained
to kill anything and everything that moved. Diggers? The Army?
LD hordes? Bring 'em on. But Mr. Blunt . . . They never covered
Mr. Blunt in the course materials.

I still don't know how he got down there. All of a sudden he's
in the security cameras, walking right behind one of the Kitchen staff,
like he's got a gun to the guy's back. There's a long corridor between
the two doors, about thirty feet, that's the only part of the basement
covered by cameras. At the end of the hall is the second door, and
behind that is the Kitchen itself—nobody topside ever gets to see
what's in there. So we've got this intruder onscreen, with no ID. All
we can see is the suit and half a face beneath that weird hat. I should
have guessed then—of course I'd heard of Mr. Blunt—but I didn't
put it together. None of us did.

Anyway, they send us down, Me and Devon and Sal and
Mick, to check out what's going down and shoot the fucker if need
be. The first door locks behind us—only the topsiders can let us out
now. I go in first, covered by the rest of them, guns out, full drill. And
when I swing around the second door, the guy in the suit is just
standing there. He's got his back to me, standing in front of one of
the computers. The Kitchen staffer is on the floor, flat on his stomach,
arms spread, as if he's afraid to move, which he probably is.

I shouted at him to get the fuck down, but Blunt, Blunt didn't
even move from the computer. He's standing up, and taking a picture
of the screen with his phone. Then he puts up a finger and says, "Just
a second, almost finished," and takes another fucking picture. Then I
see that wooden hand, and shit, I know who it is.

I fired my weapon. I think I hit him. I must have hit him.

I've never seen anyone move like that, living or dead. He spun
away from the computer and then there's this sword in his hand—
pop, like a magic trick, like that guy in the movies—and the next

thing I know I'm on the floor and looking up at everybody. I can't move my feet, and Blunt is whirling around the room like a fucking Dervish. I see Devon lose his gun arm, the finger still pulling the trigger. Then Blunt cuts down through Sal's leg and she falls on the floor. And I think, Oh, that's why I'm down here. I look down at my legs but my legs aren't there. They're about five feet away, one boot leaning into another.

And I can't believe it. It's hard to get your mind around something like that. Oh, I've been cut in half. By a wooden guy with a sword. By fucking Pinocchio.

Now Mick is down, too, and that's all of us, laid out on the floor. Nobody's dead, but every one of us is missing parts, and some of us are handling that a little better than others. Me, I figured out early in training how to turn off pain, but that's not a trick everyone can hold on to.

Now Blunt's looking at his phone again. I tell him, You're not going to get any bars down here. And he says, I'm aware of that. He plays with the phone a bit more, then he strolls over to me and points the sword at my neck and says, You almost made me break my promise. And I say, Yeah, what promise is that?

He flicks his arm and the sword is gone. Up his sleeve I guess. He crouches down where my legs should be and he says, I don't suppose they're going to let me walk out of here. He says it like he already knows the answer. Because of course they're not going to let him out. I tell him about the fail-safe—the aerosolized kerosene, the white phosphorous igniters. The whole Kitchen, I tell him, is designed to go up in a flash.

And he laughs. If you can't stand the heat, he says.

But I'm not fucking laughing. I tell him that in about sixty seconds they're going to open the jets and hit the WP and we're all going to die. And he looks at me and says, but you can't die, I took a vow. I can't tell if he's fucking with me or not.

*He thinks for a minute, then he cinches up the bottom of my
uniform so my guts don't spread out all over the floor. I was damn
glad I couldn't feel anything down there. Then he starts dragging me,
right out of the Kitchen and down the hallway. He stops in front of
the vault door and says, Do you have friends up there? I don't say
anything. I'm not about to be used as a hostage. Then he looks up at
the camera and says, This woman doesn't have to die. None of these
people have to die.*

*At this point, topside is seeing everything on the cameras, and
with me and the rest of the team down, the protocol is to hit the button. Burn everything. I lay on the floor waiting for that smell, that
Apocalypse Now smell. But nothing happens.*

*See, I did have friends up there. And no LD wants to die in
fire. It was stupid and it was sentimental, and if they didn't hold off
on hitting that button I wouldn't be here now in this fucking chair.*

*Anyway, Blunt shrugs, then goes back down the hallway, and
he and the Kitchen staffer pull the rest of the team to the door. Their
torsos, anyway. They left a lot of limbs behind. The Kitchen staff guy,
though, he's fine, just a couple of bullet holes.*

*Then Blunt says to the cameras, I'll be waiting in the Kitchen.
And he just walks away. When he gets past the second door he shuts
it behind him. I start yelling up at the cameras, hit the button! Hit
the button! Because I know Blunt is up to something. Somehow
that second door really isn't locked, and soon as the main door opens
for us he's going to come sprinting down that hallway with his fucking samurai sword. But topside isn't listening to me. They didn't see
what happened in the Kitchen. They didn't see how fast he moves.
They don't know anything except that they can pull their buddies
out, then torch the bastard who did this to them.*

*I hear the clunk of the vault locks opening. Then the B team is
yanking me through the door, they're pulling us all through, and in
about five seconds we're all on the other side, my three guys and the*

Kitchen staff guy. Then somebody topside hits the Big Red Button.
I thought we'd hear something. An explosion or something. But the
vault door didn't even get warm.

It wasn't until ten minutes later, when we were back topside,
that one of the B team said to me, Hey Sheila, did you just beep?

When they were fifteen minutes out of the safe house, onto the highway, Stony's red phone rang again. It was the number Blunt had used to send the text messages. "What's going on?" Stony said.

"Who is this, please?" a male voice said. It was not Mr. Blunt.

Stony clicked off the phone and stared at it. A few seconds later it rang again. He rolled down the window.

"What are you doing?"

He broke open the back of the phone, pulled out the battery, then snapped the flash card. He rolled down the window and tossed the pieces, one by one, into the dark beside the highway.

"Who's been calling you?" Nessa asked. "Is it the Diggers?"

"How could the Diggers have this number?"

"You just look so worried, I thought—"

"I don't know who it is," he said. Mr. Blunt had contacted him first, with the text messages. Then someone else had gotten the number and called him. Unless it had never been Blunt at all. He dug out his second phone and began texting Delia.

"I would really like to know what's going on," Nessa said. "I can't do my job unless you let me."

"Sorry about that," Stony said. He watched the phone's screen, waiting for an answer.

"You know, you say sorry a lot when you don't mean it."

"I'm—" He looked up, smiled briefly. "Two miles ahead, take the next exit."

"Where are we going?" He didn't answer. "Then how far are we going? Because I have to pee."

"Not too much farther," Stony said. And it was the truth: A few miles later he directed her to pull into an Exxon station and park away from the lights.

"Can you tell me now why we're here?" Nessa said.

"I need to make some calls," Stony said. "In private."

"What?"

"Why don't you go to the bathroom, get a snack or something. I just need a few minutes."

She looked hurt. "Fine." She grabbed her cloth shoulder bag, a huge colorful thing made in India, and stalked toward the gas station building. There was only one car at the pumps, and one other car parked in front of the building. He decided he could stay in the passenger seat.

He checked his phone again, but as he expected, there was no new message from Delia. He'd lied to Nessa, a bit. He didn't need to make any phone calls, but he did need to wait here for a while.

He wished he hadn't destroyed the flash card from the red phone; he wanted to look through those names in the pictures while he waited. Well, Delia would have a copy, and they'd look through them together.

He had recognized one of the three names he'd seen. Eric Hamm was one of Calhoun's "employees," an LD plucked from a group of immigrants to the island. Mr. Blunt had spent months tracking these recruits. All of them left the island by ship or helicopter, made their way to a Calhoun-owned compound in Pensacola, Florida . . . and never came out. As far as Blunt could determine they were still inside. For some time now Blunt had wanted to break into the compound, but Stony had talked him out of it. They couldn't risk Blunt's life, and they couldn't risk alerting the Commander.

As soon as the strange voice had called him from Blunt's phone, Stony was sure that Mr. Blunt had done something extreme to get these names—and gotten caught. He wouldn't have allowed the phone to be taken from him without a fight.

So, they probably had the names of Calhoun's recruits. But what did the words after their names mean? Eric Haslett was mad. Elena Gomez was in a bog. Terry Alsup was . . . whatever iad was: in a ditch? They seemed too short for passwords. Too short even for code names. Abbreviations, then?

Nessa's head appeared in the window of the station—she had a phone to her ear. She looked toward the van, then turned away from the window. He supposed she could be calling family, but doubted it. She'd be complaining to her boss.

He thought: Gomez is bogged, Haslett is mad, Alsup is I.A.D.—.

IAD. Dulles International Airport.

He opened his phone again. Even though Delia wouldn't read the message for a while, he had to tell someone.

They r airport codes, he typed.

A minute later Nessa was walking back to the van, still holding the phone. She walked up to the passenger door and held up the phone to him. She looked like she was keeping the lid on some strong emotion: anger, maybe. He opened the door.

"The Commander?" he said.

She put the phone in his hand. He checked out the parking lot again, then scanned the road in front of the station. No one else was outside, and no headlights were coming this way. He glanced at his wristwatch, then lifted the phone. "Hello?"

"Stony my boy!" His voice, bouncing a thousand miles over satellites and cell towers, boomed as clear as if the old man were standing beside him, shouting into his ear. He was using his stage voice, which meant that there were people around him, listening in.

"Good evening, Commander," Stony said.

"I've heard you've had a Goddamn barnstormer of a trip. Vanessa says that the people admire the hell out of you. You're like a Goddamn Bob Hope!"

"That was the goal." Nessa stared at him with that same tense expression on her face. Her hand was inside her Indian bag.

The Commander said, "I just wanted to tell you, you were right and I was wrong. You've done a great service for our people. You've reminded them that we're a community, a community that cares for each other."

Stony made a vaguely affirmative noise and glanced at his watch again.

The Commander said, "I also wanted to say that I don't have any hurt feelings about this."

"What?"

"I didn't trust you, and you didn't trust me. That's regrettable. But I think you'll agree that the blame goes both ways."

Stony said, "Would you like to tell me what we're talking about?"

"Don't do this, boy. I know about the spying. I know about those messages he sent to you—I'm holding the phone. Had to clean it off, but I'll give him this, he was clever."

"Where's Mr. Blunt, Commander?"

"Jammed the damn thing inside Sheila's body cavity! I don't think we'd have found it for hours if you hadn't called back."

"Where is Mr. Blunt?"

"I'm sorry, Stony. Had to be done. In the navy, they shoot spies."

"You were never in the fucking navy! You worked on a fucking *dock*!"

"Stony, get a hold of yourself."

"You *shot* him?"

"Well, with Mr. Blunt we had to be a little more thorough. You know his history. We just couldn't risk a comeback."

Nessa had stepped back, and now the gun was out, a little black pistol. Her hand shook, and she looked stricken.

"Put that away," Stony said. "Put it to hell away!"

Nessa took another half step back, then steadied the gun with her other hand.

The Commander said, "You won't be able to act on those names, Stony. It's too late. They're scattered across the globe, and they've already received the signal. I sent it as soon as we discovered what Mr. Blunt had done."

"You—you can't. Why would you do that? On D-day—"

"I was willing to give D-day a chance, Stony! But I was also pretty Goddamn sure that when we went public, the breathers would cut down any LD who dared step into the light. The backup plan was always in place. It had to be. What choice did we have?"

"Blunt was right. You're insane."

"I never expected us to see eye to eye on this. But what I'm doing is for the best interest of our people."

Nessa said, "I'm supposed to take away all your phones now." Her voice quavered.

"You're aiming a gun at me?" Stony said. "Have you not listened to a single thing I've said?"

The Commander said, "Give her the cellphones, Stony. We'd like you to avoid calling the Diggers for a while. Then

Vanessa will take you to an airport, and if it's at all possible, we'll fly you out here to the bunker. You know better than anyone else that this is the safest place to be. I'm going to hang up now, okay?"

Stony clicked off the phone and handed it to Nessa.

"And the other one?" she said.

He dug into his pocket and fished out the silver Nokia he used for talking to Alice and Crystal. "There," he said. From the road came the sound of an engine. Stony glanced through the windshield. A single headlight swerved into the parking lot.

Nessa started to turn toward the noise and Stony said, "What about my guns?"

Her eyes jerked back to his. "You have—?"

"No, I don't believe in them. Motorcycle."

"What?"

The bike flashed past, and a black boot caught Nessa under the ribs and catapulted her sideways. She hit the pavement, then bounced, tumbling, and came to a sudden rest, facedown. The pistol had disappeared—sent flying.

The motorcyclist braked hard, whipped back toward Nessa. The bike slowed, rolled forward, and stopped with the front wheel touching the woman's head.

"Wait!" Stony said. "Don't kill her."

The cyclist pulled off the black helmet and set it on the gas tank. "She had a gun on you," Delia said. Her jawbone gleamed in the reflected lights of the gas station. "Does this mean Calhoun knows about Blunt?"

"He killed him," Stony said. "But it's worse than that."

"How can it possibly be worse?"

"He's starting it," Stony said. "The Big Bite."

"Jesus," Delia said.

Nessa moaned, started to lift her head. Delia looked down

at her, then said, "You need to tell me how to get onto that fucking island."

"You won't get to him," Stony said. "He's in a bunker. A whole series of bunkers. A city of them."

"What did you do, Stony?"

"The spaceport was a decoy, something to fool the spy satellites. We needed the time to build something nuke-proof."

A man—the clerk?—stepped half out of the station door, holding it open. Then he saw Nessa on the ground and started to jog toward them. Delia reached inside her leather jacket, withdrew an automatic, and fired two shots, well over the head of the man. He ducked and ran back into the building.

"You know, it's almost a relief," she said.

"Don't talk like that," Stony said. "It's the end of the world."

"For them, maybe," Delia said.

CHAPTER EIGHTEEN

April 28, 2010
Chicago

Those who were transformed during the outbreak know everything they need to know. Even the fortunate amnesiacs, their memories scoured by fever, have since heard a hundred stories they can substitute for their own. She (or he) was bitten. Sometime later—a day, two days—she awoke to a strangely quiet world, the streets silent except for the moans of the still-hungry dead, the skies empty of planes. There was a taste in her mouth.

Ah, but those few who lived through it, who survived still breathing—they don't talk about it much. When they do, someone inevitably says, *It was just like a movie.* Perhaps it's because they saw the opening days of the outbreak through television screens. When the ghouls finally threw themselves against the door, when it was finally time to act, it felt as if they were being called in front of the camera, ready to recite their lines, to scream, to run.

But we're jumping ahead again. It's Ruby's story we need to tell.

She was just twenty-two that April of the Big Bite, finishing her first year of law school at Loyola University. She was living in a tiny, third-floor apartment in Lincoln Park. One window overlooked a slice of West Altged, a tree-lined street that had recently burst into full spring gorgeousness. The other window was semi-blocked by a semi-functional air conditioner.

Thanks to the rules drilled into her by her mother and aunt, Ruby was better prepared for the zombie apocalypse than most. She maintained a three-day supply of bottled water and canned food. She kept a 9-mm Heckler & Koch USP (a gift from Alice) in a gun safe in her bedroom, and an aluminum baseball bat by the door. Her front door was metal and could be secured by two deadbolts and a chain lock. She kept a backpack ready with clothes, antibiotics, ammo, and tampons.

When she heard of the outbreak that morning, she did not panic. The cellphone transmissions were jammed, and she could not get through to Alice, who lived on the other side of the city. But she was able to get a text message to her mother in Utah. Crystal told her to stay put. Do not answer the door, do not let anyone in, and do not leave the apartment. If she tried to flee the city, if she risked the highways, they might never find her.

Ruby had never been the most compliant of children, but in this instance her mother seemed to be making sense. She closed the windows and pulled the drapes. She sat on the floor of the living room, out of sight of the windows, with the HK beside her. She opened her laptop and was relieved to find that her Wi-Fi was on and the cable modem was still up.

Well, she thought. Facebook has certainly taken a dark turn.

The Internet was awash in second-by-second horrors: pictures, video, and eyewitness reports. Twitter had turned into an unrelenting stream of exclamation marks and bad advice. Friends and acquaintances across the country and overseas reported various levels of infection. In some places no LDs were in sight. But in the largest cities, especially those in America, the streets were filling with undead. New York, Philadelphia, Newark, Pittsburgh, Cincinnati . . . Chicago.

Outside, sirens blared, and gunshots cracked like slamming car doors, and car doors slammed like gunshots. Whenever she heard something particularly close—a scream, a car alarm—she went to the window, careful not to move the drapes. Most of the time she saw nothing. As the day wore on, slow-moving figures appeared in the streets. When darkness fell she did not turn on her lights, and opened her laptop only when she was covered by a blanket. She typed with one hand now. The other gripped the pistol.

She could admit to herself now that yes, she was terrified. Afraid of dying, afraid of—could she use the word?—the *zombies*. And God help her, afraid of turning into one.

She was disappointed in herself. She'd grown up knowing about LDs, thinking about them, advocating for them. When she was ten years old, Crystal had told her about her uncle, and where he was being held (secret emails from Deadtown had begun to arrive by then), and why her grandmother was also in prison. Ruby did not freak out. Quite the opposite: She was thrilled. By thirteen she'd become something of an undead ally, an activist who picked schoolyard fights whenever her classmates played Humans vs. Zombies. In eighth grade she went door to door with a petition demanding that the government give amnesty to any undead in hiding (she got five signatures). When she was seventeen she joined Amnesty International and started a blog, Dead to Rights. The amount of hate mail she received—and answered—was stunning. When people told her about the coming apocalypse, she called them bigots.

Bet they're laughing it up now. As they get their arms bitten off. Fuckheads.

But it wasn't just the undead she needed to worry about; the living could kill her, too. What if one of her fellow tenants tried to fight LDs with a torch—the whole building could come down. She would have to flee the building and take her chances on the street. Even if she managed to stay in the apartment undetected, eventually she'd have to leave to find food, and risk being shot by a survivor.

Alice had taught her that the outbreak, when it came, would not be over soon. The fever lasted only forty-eight hours, but that didn't mean everything would be over in two days max. It was a rolling infection, so even as some of the first to die recovered their sanity, others were dying, or in the throes of the fever.

Near 11 p.m. she got a text from her friend Gina: *Where r u? Help.*

Ruby stared at her phone. Gina lived two blocks away, on Lincoln Avenue. Another message from Gina popped up: *Zs in my building.*

Hide, Ruby typed. *Don't make a noise.*

A minute passed. Two.

Gina?

She couldn't tell if her texts were getting through. None were coming to her anymore.

She sent again: *Gina? Are you there?*

Months later, long after the cell networks had gone silent, Ruby would not throw away her phone. She had a vague idea that someday the electricity and the satellites and the cell towers would all come back online. Someday, Gina would call her.

*   *   *

Sometime later—this must have been two or three in the morning, after her cell battery had died—she lurched awake, blinked at the dark room. Her hand still gripped the gun. She didn't know she'd been asleep. She didn't know what had awakened her. There'd been a huge noise—an explosion, from somewhere outside.

She pulled the blanket from her. Her laptop screen was dead. The clock above the microwave had gone out, too. A blown transformer, then?

She went to the window. The street was dark: street lamps out, not a window lit. In the distance was the faint orange glow of a large fire. Were there shapes moving on the street? She could see nothing, but imagine everything.

She thought she heard a voice, calling thinly like a drawn-out note on a violin. She leaned her head against the window, but the sound slipped away. She walked to the center of the room and stood in the dark, straining to hear. Yes, someone crying. She let the sound pull her to the apartment door and she heard it more clearly. It was Hernán Trujillo, she realized. A third grader who lived with his mom only three doors down, a boy Ruby had babysat for half a dozen times. She'd heard him cry before, but this was different. He'd been hurt, or perhaps pushed by fear into a sound that was both smaller and more primitive than a scream, the whine of a trapped animal.

Or maybe it's not Hernán, she told herself. Maybe the sound wasn't even coming from her floor, maybe it was winding up the stairwell. That high voice could have belonged to one of a dozen children who lived in the building, someone she didn't know at all. It could even be a woman. There was no reason to leave the apartment.

Ruby moved closer to the door and looked through the peephole. She saw nothing.

She went back to the living room and felt around for the flashlight. She didn't turn it on. She made sure the gun's safety was on, tucked the pistol into the front waistband of her jeans, and went back to the door.

The crying had stopped. This only made her feel worse.

She put her hand on the deadbolt. The Trujillos' door was only what—twenty, thirty feet away? She could yank open the door, and run to their door. Hernán might even be wandering in the hallway. She would scoop him up and bring him back to her apartment, slam the door.

Or she could wait until he started screaming as the dead things ate him.

She slowly slid back the bolt, the scrape as loud in her ears as if it had been amplified. She waited, listening. After half a minute (or perhaps only ten seconds—time slowed when you were panicked) she unlatched the chain and bent to look again through the peephole. Nothing but black. The butt of the pistol grip was hard against her belly. Ruby moved the flashlight to her other hand and dried her sweat-slicked palm against her pant leg. She reached for the last lock and twisted it.

Clack.

In her mind, twenty undead swiveled at the sound.

She didn't have enough hands. She wanted the baseball bat, the pistol, *and* the flashlight. She withdrew the gun from her waistband, pulled open the door a few inches, and stepped back. She aimed the gun into the gap.

The crying had started again. Or it had never stopped, but had grown too faint to penetrate the door. The child—she was sure now it was a child—was nearby.

Fuck me, she thought, and switched on the flashlight.

* * *

She stepped into the hallway, then jerked the beam of light left, then right. The corridor was empty. A smell like burnt rubber hung in the air.

The crying came from her right, toward the Trujillos' apartment. Their door was ajar—not a good sign. She knocked on the door, causing it to glide open farther, and played the light across the tiny foyer. "Vivi? Hernán?" The crying suddenly stopped. Ruby needed to go inside and turn the corner before she could see into the rest of the apartment.

Go on, she thought. Turn the corner.

"Vivi, Hernán, it's me, Ruby. From down the hall?" There was no answer. "I'm coming in, okay?"

She took a breath, then swung around the corner, gun and flashlight aimed in front of her. A body lay facedown on the floor. It was a small woman, in khaki pants and a dark T-shirt. No: a white T-shirt with dark stains. Her back was hunched, as if she were praying, or holding her stomach. It looked like Viviana.

She swung the light around the room. The little breakfast table had been overturned. The bookshelf was still standing, but the shelves were half empty, and many of the books and CDs and knickknacks—Vivi loved porcelain Precious Moments figurines—had been dumped to the floor.

Something moved in the bedroom doorway. Ruby shouted and jerked the light toward it.

A short, paunchy man raised one arm to shield the light from his eyes. His other arm was wrapped in a bloodstained towel.

"Stop!" Ruby yelled. "Who the hell are you?"

She couldn't tell whether he was living or dead. The man shook his head. Ruby said, "Who the fuck *are* you?"

The man said something in Spanish. His face was wet with tears.

Ruby said, "Where's Hernán?"

He seemed to recognize the name. He pointed toward the body on the floor and made a wheezing, high-pitched sound, a thin peal of grief.

Ruby edged toward Viviana's body. "Vivi. Can you hear me?" She nudged Vivi's calf with her toe. Vivi didn't move.

Ruby moved around to the side, holding the gun on her. In a zombie movie, this is the way the stupid person gets bitten. The undead, playing dead. Vivi's face was slack, staring. There was another body under the woman's.

Ruby would never describe what she saw, nor will that happen here. It was clear, however, that the mother and son were dead. Maybe Viviana had killed her son, then herself. Maybe they'd been bitten and would be resurrected as LDs in a few hours. Or maybe they'd been killed by the man in the bedroom.

Ruby pointed her H&K at the man's face. "What the fuck happened here?" She was yelling, and sounded a little crazed even to her. The man shook his head and she said, "What the fuck did you do?"

The man cried out then, and pointed behind her. His fear was so raw she didn't doubt him; she spun toward the apartment door, gun raised.

A zombie: gray face, black mouth, a dark bandage covering its head. Ruby fired and the gun kicked up. The second shot went into the ceiling. The zombie, stumbling backward, fell against the wall.

Ruby reset her aim, bracing with both hands as Alice had taught her on the firing range. She fired again and the zombie yelled, "Jesus Christ, Ruby! Stop it!"

"Who—how do you—?"

The zombie looked down at his chest, then poked a finger at a new hole there. Ruby shone the light on his face. He looked up, squinting. It wasn't a bandage he wore, but a ban-danna.

Ruby said, "Uncle Stony?"

He got to his feet—slowly, slowly. "The second shot always goes to the head," Stony said. "Didn't your mother teach you anything?"

"I'm new at this," she said, and Stony laughed. But of course Mom and Alice had taught her everything they could, and everything about Stony. She'd never talked to him, and never even gotten a letter from him. Once a year, however, she received a mystery birthday card, unsigned, always from a different address.

"You can stop aiming that at me now," he said. His skin seemed eggshell white in the glare of the flashlight. His eyes were silver dimes.

She lowered the gun and aimed the flashlight at his feet. He started to say something, then seemed to notice what was behind her. She glanced over her shoulder. Oh, right: the lump of bodies on the floor behind her, and the paunchy man still standing in the bedroom door.

"Ruby, I have to tell you something, and I don't want you to panic."

"I'm not going to panic."

"Right." He thought, Please don't shoot me again. "There are lots of LDs on the ground floor of your building, and those gunshots are going to draw them up here. We've got to go. The city's burning, and there's no one to put out the fires. Do you trust me?"

"Okay," she said, her voice unsteady. Then: "Okay."

Stony nodded past her. "Is your friend coming with us?"

"He's not my friend," Ruby said. "Yet."

Stony walked toward him, hands out. Ruby swung the light onto the paunchy man, and he stayed planted in the doorway.

Stony indicated the towel wrapped around the man's arm. "You were bitten?"

The man didn't answer.

Stony said, "Your arm. Bite? *Mordedura?*"

After a moment the man said, "Yes, bite."

Ruby was surprised he answered honestly. The man said in a thick South American accent, "My name is Oscar." He said it with great formality, though his voice shook. He was terrified.

Stony said, "Oscar, do you know what's going to happen to you?"

"*Soy meurto.* Dead. Yes."

"You're going to be all right," Stony said. "*Comprende?* I've seen people go through this. Do you want me to help?"

Ruby said, "Help him how?"

The two men stared at each other. Finally Oscar nodded, lips pursed, as if he were receiving religious instruction.

"Yes," Oscar said. He nodded toward Ruby. "Good-bye." Then he turned, went back into the bedroom. Stony followed him.

Ruby said, "Where the hell are you going?"

"Just a second," Stony said, and closed the door.

"You can't just—" But there was nothing to be gained by raising her voice. She backed up to the wall and turned the flashlight on the front door to the apartment. She was careful not to look at the bodies on the floor.

There was no noise from the bedroom.

After five minutes (no, it only seemed like five to her; in reality it took less than a minute), Stony opened the door.

Ruby did not ask, Where's Oscar? She did not ask for

explanations. The important thing to do, she thought, is to think about the next thirty seconds, and the next thirty after that. The important thing is to keep going.

"You have a car?" Ruby said.

"Here's what's going to happen," Stony said. "We're going to go down the stairs to the first floor. I have a van waiting. If you stay close to me, you should be fine."

"And then what?"

"Then we drive out of the city."

"But what about Aunt Alice? We've got to get her."

"Alice wouldn't come with me. She's at the hospital, working the emergency room."

"But she'll die!"

"No one can make Alice do anything she doesn't want to do," Stony said.

Well, Ruby thought, he's right about that. She let him lead her into the hallway. He went right, away from her apartment.

Ruby said, "Wait, I have stuff in my apartment—"

"You won't need it."

"Fuck," Ruby said, but hurried to catch up to him. When they were a dozen feet from the stairwell, the door swung open. Ruby and Stony stopped. Ruby lifted the flashlight, but kept the gun down.

It was a woman. Her head was bent sideways, lying flat on her shoulder, like a smashed pumpkin on a front porch. Her mouth opened and made a low, sad noise.

Stony said, "Stop!" The dead woman paused, then swiveled slightly so that her eyes were on them.

"Go back!"

The woman turned and pushed against the door. Ruby said, "How the fuck are you doing that?"

"You don't need to swear so much," Stony said.

"Oh, I think I do. Shit." The zombie woman suddenly fell to the ground, knocked down by someone coming out the stairwell door. Another dead person, a large man wearing no shirt. More bodies clamored behind him. The shirtless man saw Stony and Ruby and started toward them in a stumbling half run.

Stony yelled, "Stop! Sit down!"

The man hesitated, but now other zombies were charging past him: six, seven of them. Ruby shouted something—undoubtedly another curse word—and stepped behind Stony. An LD reached Stony and tried to shove him out of the way. Stony pushed him backward, into the people behind him, and they shuffled aside and let him fall to the ground.

Stony said, "Maybe we should—"

The group surged forward and Stony went down, smothered in bodies. They weren't attacking him; they were trying to get through him, to Ruby. The woman with the broken neck emerged from the pile and threw herself forward. She grabbed Ruby's right arm and yanked her toward her. The flashlight went flying, the beam bouncing crazily. Ruby screamed in pain; the dead woman's fingers ground into her.

With her other hand Ruby raised the H&K, squeezed the trigger—but the trigger wouldn't budge. The safety. The zombie woman bit at Ruby's gun hand; Ruby jerked her arm back, thumbed the safety, then shoved the barrel of the gun into the woman's jaw. She fired, and the woman's face—

But you know what happened to the woman's face.

Ruby backed away in the pitch-black hallway, shouting Stony's name. She was blind, afraid to fire for hitting Stony, and afraid not to fire. Then something grabbed her shoulder and she jerked away from the touch, brought the gun around.

"Back the other way," Stony said out of the dark. "We'll circle around—"

"No!" Ruby said. "My apartment. There's another way out."

Ruby turned and ran for her doorway. She couldn't see anything, but she trailed a hand against the wall, counting door frames. She almost fell into her apartment when she reached it; the door was wide open. For a wild moment she thought, They're inside. Then Stony pushed her inside and slammed the door.

"Open—" she said, fighting for breath. "My door was open."

"What?"

"They're inside."

"No," Stony said. "That was me. I left it open when I came looking for you."

"Would you just check the fucking living room?" she cried.

"I'm holding the door shut." As if in reply, something banged against the metal. The zombies were trying to get in.

Ruby reached past him, fumbling, then found the deadbolt and the chain lock. "*Now* check it."

"Fine. Watch the door. But please, don't use the gun unless you absolutely have to."

"Are you fucking kidding me?"

"You'll disfigure these people, or kill some of them permanently."

"Fuck you," Ruby said. "They're trying to fucking kill me."

"For now," he said. "It's temporary insanity. And I know you're stressed, but you don't have to keep saying the F-word." He slipped past her then, and Ruby stood next to the door, her hand on the surface so she would know when it started to open. The metal shuddered with each bang. The undead wailed as if frustrated.

Suddenly Stony was back. "We're clear. Now where's this other way out?"

"Just a sec." Hoping the door would hold, Ruby went to the hall closet and retrieved her loaded backpack. It was heavy with ammo, an extra flashlight, batteries, food. Thank you, Paranoid Aunt Alice.

Ruby slung it onto her shoulder and went through the dark to the back window. Wedged between the sill and the top of the window frame was a block of four-by-four that held the air conditioner in place. She felt for the block, then whacked it with the side of her fist. Then she whacked it again and it popped free. "Grab the air conditioner," she told Stony, and then pushed up against the sill. The wood shrieked. "And don't let it drop."

"You're kind of bossy," Stony said. He pulled the air conditioner from the frame and set it on the futon. In the hallway, bodies slammed against the door.

The window overlooked an airshaft. Below was a black pit. Above, the bellies of clouds flickered from fires across the city.

Ruby reached down to the floor beneath the window and found the stack of cloth and plastic that had been sitting there, unused, since she had installed it a year ago.

"What is that?" Stony asked.

"Alice said never live anyplace without an emergency exit." She tossed the rope ladder out the window. The base of the ladder was bolted to the floor.

"I—I am so proud of you," Stony said. He leaned out the window. "No LDs below. At least that I can see."

"Me first then," Ruby said.

A year after the epidemic, it still wasn't clear how many agents Calhoun had planted in how many cities. The sheet of names and airport codes that Mr. Blunt had discovered in Calhoun's Atlanta offices included over eighty locations, but many more might have been off the book.

In most of the cities, Calhoun's agents struck at retirement homes and hospitals. They worked in pairs. Two LDs would enter a facility and begin shooting, using automatic weapons and small arms. As each roomful of people were executed, the LDs would deliver a quick bite. Killing by hand was inefficient. It was certainly much too slow to bite a living person and then wait for them to die.

The old and sick were perfect subjects for conversion. They couldn't run away, they died quickly, and their age made no difference in their effectiveness when they were reborn. In some instances, the LD agents were shot down by police within an hour of the start of the attack. But in a few cities, the agents moved on to second- and even third-tier institutions.

In any case, within a few hours the police had far too many living dead to handle.

The first reported attack was on the Grand Oaks Retirement Village in Columbus, Ohio. Two gunmen entered the main building of the village at 8:10 p.m. eastern. They killed and bit over eighty residents by the time police were able to corner the men in a third-floor wing of the building. The gunmen leaped from the window. The police did not figure out that the men were undead until the first of the elderly patients began to move again, and reports from around the world began to pour in.

The attacks were so widespread that local governments could not coordinate a response. By morning, when Ruby and most of the eastern United States learned of the outbreak, the Big Bite had taken on the mathematical shape of the equations Stony had worked out years ago. The infection rate soared into a hockey stick graph. The outcome for the planet was certain; only the specifics remained to be worked out.

Chicago, for example. By dawn after the first nighttime attacks, the city was teeming with fevered LDs. By the time Stony reached Ruby's apartment at 3 a.m. of the second day, the infection had reached a saturation point. According to the models (and later, it seemed that the models fit reality reasonably well), 90 percent of the residents were dead or bitten, and of the bitten, most had already turned. The streets were crowded with fevered undead.

Stony led Ruby into the street. They were both forced to do terrible things on their way out of the city. Zombies—that is to say, people—were killed and maimed. You could tell this story yourself. You know the ingredients:

- ☑ Shadows.
- ☑ Smoke.
- ☑ Dimly seen figures shambling through shadows and smoke.
- ☑ Sudden realization that heroes are surrounded by hundreds of zombies, including the following: zombie in uniform (policeman standard, extra points for nuns, referees, and clowns), child zombie, zombie with no legs.
- ☑ Screaming.
- ☑ Screaming while firing gun.
- ☑ Recognition that adjacent zombie is a friend/relative/ loved one.
- ☑ Near-fatal hesitation to kill zombie who is friend/relative/ loved one.
- ☑ Zombie beaten back with improvised blunt instrument.
- ☑ Race to the escape vehicle. Someone trips, then is helped up.
- ☑ Fumbling with doors. Passenger side unexpectedly left locked, must be opened from inside.

- ☑ Victim saved by unexpected, off-camera shot by companion.
- ☑ Vehicle door shuts just as zombie reaches it. Window smashed in.
- ☑ Multiple zombies run over as van accelerates.
- ☑ Victim says, "I think we're in the clear."
- ☑ Victim realizes they are definitely not in the clear.
- ☑ Et cetera.

But you crave sensory detail. A vivid description of how it looks and sounds and feels to run over a human body. A simile that conveys the pattern of blood and viscera spattering the windshield. Maybe some sound effects? *Ka-thump. Bang. Craack.*

Or maybe you'd like to have described to you the peculiar beauty of the sun coming up on an interstate littered with bodies, the rays glinting off chrome and broken glass.

"Battlefield sunrise," Stony said.

Ruby was slumped in the passenger seat, eyes closed but not asleep. They were on I-88 now, heading west. Stony drove fast, slipping past stopped vehicles, slowing only when the way was blocked and he was forced to nudge and scrape past the abandoned cars. The interstate was most congested near the toll plazas. The police had tried to turn them into roadblocks, but that hadn't worked for long.

Only once did they have to leave the interstate and weave through city streets. Stony told Ruby to keep her head down, but she thought this was primarily because he did not want her to see the bodies as they stumbled in front of his van. People would not get out of the way, and Stony could not slow down for them. It was a relief to get back onto the interstate.

Ruby said, "Did Alice tell you where to find me?"

"She gave me directions," he said. "But I already knew your address."

"Yeah, I got your birthday cards."

She opened her eyes. The sunlight, even filtered through the blood-smeared windshield, was too bright. She closed them again. The air smelled of gasoline, from all the extra plastic cans Stony kept in the back of the van. She said, "How much longer?"

"Four hours if nothing gets in our way."

"No one lives there, you know. It's all boarded up."

"Even better," Stony said. "You'll be safe there."

She opened her eyes to slits. He was driving with both hands on the wheel—one hand dead flesh, one plastic—and staring straight ahead. The driver's-side window had blown out during the escape, and the wind whipped at the dirty bandanna he kept tied around his forehead. She'd never seen a dead man close up. His skin was the texture and color of concrete. There was a gash on his neck, but it did not bleed; the dry flesh lay open, revealing not blood or tissue, but a deeper shade of gray. When he wasn't talking to her, or when he thought she wasn't looking at him, his face set into an expression that looked like grief, or anger.

"What's wrong?" Ruby asked.

He forced a smile, then let it slip away. After a time he said, "I need to tell you, Ruby. I'm responsible for this."

Ruby said, "What do you mean?"

"All of it." He glanced at her, then back to the road. His eyes were milky white, blind man's eyes. "The man who started the bite—I made sure everyone trusted him. Trusted *me*. Then I let him get away with it. I could have stopped it at any time, but I thought I was the smartest guy in the room."

"I don't understand. If you didn't know what he was doing, you can't take responsibility. You didn't start the outbreak."

"Oh, Ruby," he said. "They couldn't have done it without me."

CHAPTER NINETEEN

April 29, 2010
Iowa

The road cleared, and they crossed the Illinois border without incident. He kept the speedometer pegged to 90, and even then cars zoomed past him.

He talked as he drove. He told her everything.

He started with Commander Calhoun, the island, the theory and practice of the Big Bite. She asked questions, and he told her more, going back years: The Living Dead Army, the safe houses, the congress, Billy Zip and the ZCMI attack, Deadtown. She needed to know how the undead had waited underground like a bomb, like a poisonous gas. A thousand pockets of inevitability. She needed to know the crimes he'd committed. "I wrote it all down," he said. "I've got a printout in my bag. It's about twelve hundred pages. Plus there's a diary my mom kept—my biological mom. And there's this novel—"

"You wrote a *novel*?" Ruby asked.

"It's a draft," he said.

They were making good time. The infection would be rolling west from Chicago, north from Madison, south from

Des Moines. If they could beat that wave to Easterly, Ruby might live through the day.

Then they reached the rolling hills outside Iowa City.

He stopped the van at the top of a hill. Ruby stirred, and Stony said, "I don't want you to panic."

She sat upright. At the bottom of the hill, the four lanes of interstate had become a parking lot: semis, school buses, dozens of cars. Foraging among the vehicles were hundreds and hundreds of LDs, like the graduating class of the University of Iowa on an undead field trip. Some of the LDs had noticed Stony's van and were heading up the hill.

"Turn around," Ruby said.

"I told you not to panic," he said. "You just need to go lie down in the back of the van. I'll help you get—"

"You're not going to drive through them? There are too many, Stony. They'll swarm us."

"I should have tried this earlier. I know how to get through them."

"*You'll* get through them. They're not trying to eat you," she said. "Just turn the van around and we'll find some other way."

Jesus, she was stubborn. Absolutely no doubt she was a Mayhall woman. "Please, Ruby, just trust me, okay?"

"If I get bitten, I'm going to come back and kick your ass."

"That's a given. Now please, before they get here." He got out of his seat and went to the back of the van. He pried up a section of the aluminum floor to the left of the drive shaft and showed her the coffin-like space below. It was a metal box with a bit of foam padding to dampen the noise when going over bumps.

She frowned. "You're putting me in a coffin."

"Coffins are smaller, trust me."

She got in the compartment, lay back, and crossed her arms over her chest, one hand holding the pistol. He placed the flooring over the compartment, thought for a moment, and lifted it again.

"What?" she asked.

"I just remembered that this may be airtight. Just a sec."

"What the fuck! Get me out of here!"

"Shhh," he said, and set the lid at a slight angle so the corners were open, then threw a tarp over the area. She should be fine; there were handles on the inside of the lid so she could push her way out if she needed to.

He climbed back in the driver's seat. A ragged column of fevered LDs shuffled up the hill, the nearest of them less than twenty yards away. Stony put the van in drive, covered the brake—and closed his eyes. He felt his hands gripping the steering wheel. Relax, he told himself. Feel your hands . . .

He heard a thump and glanced up. A huge white man in a Blackhawks shirt smacked the fender of the van and reached for the passenger door.

Stony shut his eyes again. He rubbed his palms against the plastic wheel. It was a part of his hands, an extension of him. He felt the steering column, the engine, then each axle like a set of limbs . . .

I am the car. The car is me. I belong to you and you belong to me.

The passenger door shook and the LD howled in hunger, but Stony kept his eyes closed. He slowly eased up on the brake, and the van began to roll forward. He rode the brake against the gravity of the hill, never letting the van get over walking speed. The road was warm and rough beneath his wheels. His skin was dented sheet metal. His eyes were shattered glass. He could see everything.

The LDs stepped aside as the car approached, and then

they began to walk away from him. The vehicle had become another dead thing. Not food, not even a container of food.

He slipped down the hill, one undead among many. As he approached the helter skelter of stopped vehicles at the bottom of the hill he was forced to pull into the grassy median, but even that did not alarm his people. He rolled past cars with sprung doors, shattered glass. He forced himself to look into the cabins of the cars, through the open door of the yellow school bus. He memorized what had been laid out on the road.

He'd done this. He'd brought this moment to them.

He did not tell Ruby it was safe to leave the compartment until they were miles past and the road was clear again. She'd seen enough, hadn't she? Awful enough to witness horrors in the dark. But in bright sunlight, on a beautiful spring day, with the wind blowing across the Iowa fields? Too much. Too much for anyone.

An hour later and fifty miles from Easterly, Ruby told him to pull over. "I have to pee like a racehorse," she said.

He scanned the scrub brush by the side of the road and decided it was unlikely an LD would be lurking here. She grabbed her backpack and stepped off the road. "Be quick," he said, and turned his back to her.

But she wasn't quick. After five minutes she still hadn't returned, and without turning around he called out for her.

"Bite me," she called back. In another minute she came out of the brush. She'd tried to wash the blood from her face, and had only partially succeeded. Still, she was beautiful. He saw Crystal in her, of course, and therefore Alice: those high cheekbones, that narrow, stern architecture of shoulder and hip and knee. But there was something in the way she walked, the way she swung her arms climbing up to the roadway, so unself-conscious, that reminded him of Junie.

"Your turn to drive," he told her. "And my turn for the box."

"Are you sleepy?"

"We're ahead of the wave now," he said. "The next people we'll see are likely to be breathers. They might be police, or just armed gangs. Who knows how crazy it'll be. I'll be back there if you need me, but it'll be up to you to get us the rest of the way. I know you can—why are you smiling?"

"You're using the Patton voice."

"I don't know what you're talking about."

"Mom does that to me all the time. And Aunt Alice, too. You sound just like them."

"I do?"

"You Mayhalls all sound like you're about to march into battle. Now, are you going to tell me how you got through those undead in Iowa City?"

"What do you mean? I just drove slow and—"

"What? No. They ignored the van."

He shrugged. "I'm dead, they're dead—"

"Bullshit. They didn't even try to get in. They were pawing through all those other vehicles for food, *hungry*, and you just sailed right through them. They walked away from you."

"You peeked."

"It's like back at the apartment," she said. "Those zombies you commanded to stop. Can other LDs do that?"

"I'll remind you that that didn't work so well."

"Tell me what's going on, Uncle Stony. What are you, King of the Zombies?"

"Don't use that word," he said. He was stalling for time. "It's just that, well, some of the newly turned LDs are suggestible."

Ruby rolled her eyes. "Never mind. If you're going to blow me off, fine. Where are the keys?"

She was mad. A little bit. But at least she'd stopped interrogating him. "In the ignition. Always leave the keys in the ignition in case—"

"Patton."

"Right."

He sat in the back of the van, next to the open compartment, ready to slip inside at the first sign of breathers, and jump up front at the first sign of LDs. He told her to exit on Route 59. The highway that led into Easterly.

"The Shell station looks closed," Ruby said. "The BP, too."

"We should have enough gas in the tank to get to Easterly."

"I'm just trying to be a good tour guide. Oops—cops ahead." He saw the flashers reflecting in the windshield. "They're blocking the road." Her voice rose slightly.

"It's fine," Stony said. "As soon as you can, roll down the window and yell something, so they know you're not a zombie," he said.

"Zombies don't drive cars," Ruby said.

"Listen to me. Tell them you're on your way to see Kwang Cho, he lives in Easterly. Keep your hands visible, you don't want them to shoot you. They're going to search the van, so for goodness sake don't even look at the floor. Also—"

He saw her face.

"Also, that is the last instruction I'll give to you." He dropped into the compartment and pulled the lid down over him.

The van rolled to a stop. After perhaps a minute he heard a door open, and Ruby speaking. He couldn't hear what she was saying.

He thought, She might want to stay with the cops. Her own people. There were other towns near here, and they'd probably armed up. She might think her chances were better with them than with her deranged undead uncle. She'd be wrong, but he could see her thinking that.

After several minutes the car door shut. The engine started and the van began to move.

Was that Ruby driving, or was a cop in the van? Maybe they were pulling it over so they could search it.

A minute later the van accelerated. Judging from the smoothness of the ride, they were still on the interstate. He waited until he couldn't stand it anymore—perhaps two minutes—then popped the lid and slid it back a few inches. All he could see, though, was the roof of the van. He really should have put a periscope in this thing. He listened, but she wasn't talking to anyone in the van, and he couldn't hear anything else.

Finally he said, "What happened?"

She said, "Nothing. I told them I was alone, and desperately trying to reach my uncle's house in Easterly. They said most of the town's evacuating, and my uncle probably had already left, but they let me through."

He slid the lid back farther and sat up. His head was still well below the windshield. "Without searching the van? Why would they do that?"

"Because they're a bunch of old white guys, and I'm a cute white girl."

"No, really."

She tilted down the rearview mirror so she could see his face. "You don't understand living people, do you? Breathers."

"Of course I do. I—no. Not all the time."

"Haven't you ever fallen in love?"

He thought of Valerie, the long hours with their arms entwined. Was that what breathers were talking about when they talked of love? Or was what he experienced some shadow emotion, some impersonation of romance? He had no nervous system, no capillaries to flush with arousal, no glands to manufacture oxytocin to bind him to his mate. How the hell could he know?

He said, "It's not really in my nature."

He climbed out of the compartment and squatted behind her seat. The way ahead looked utterly unfamiliar. Where had all these houses come from? Where did all the *money* for these houses come from? Clusters of pale, tasteful two-story homes had filled in the cornfields. At the center of town were actual fast-food restaurants: a McDonald's, a Subway, and a Wendy's.

"Holy cow," Stony said. "There's a Walmart." Perhaps a hundred cars were in the parking lot, and the people were pushing through the doors with shopping carts piled high.

"Those must be the ones who are staying," Ruby said. "Or looting the place on their way out of town."

"Iowans don't loot," Stony said.

"Oh yeah? Wait till the zombies attack."

They passed through the little downtown area, and he directed her onto a two-lane road. Out here the fields were still open, still undeveloped. And now, he thought, they never would be.

"There," he said, and pointed toward a distant barn roof.

And then he was home.

"We're not staying here, are we?" Ruby asked.

The windows were boarded up with weathered plywood, and the white paint was flaking from the wood siding, but otherwise the house looked exactly as it had the day he left it—sturdy and firm, braced for another blazing summer, another hard winter. A horde of brain-eating zombies.

"The lawn is mowed," Stony said.

"So?"

"So nobody lives here."

"Maybe you have really nice squatters."

Then he thought: Kwang. He must be keeping an eye on the place. Stony looked around. The rise in the land still hid the house from the road, if not the barn, and the Cho house was obscured by the row of trees that separated their fields. The front door of this house was locked, another good sign.

"Okay," Stony said. "You turn the van around so it's facing nose out, and leave the keys in it. I'll be back in a minute."

He walked around the side of the house. The crawl space door was still there but padlocked shut. He held the lock in his hand, smiling at it, until it clicked open.

The light from the doorway only partially illuminated the room, but he could see that it had been nearly emptied. His tool bench was still there against one wall, though his collection of power tools was gone. The handmade bookshelves were bare.

Oh. Of course his sisters couldn't hold on to this stuff. He was in hiding, their mother was in prison, and Crystal was two thousand miles away. Still, he'd imagined this basement room sealed up like a tomb, his Batcave, waiting for him.

He tried the light switch, but of course the electricity was off. He walked across the room. The cement floor was water-stained, but still smooth. On the far wall, the Kiss Alive poster was gone. Where it had hung was the clear outline of the paneling that hid the door to his little secret room. He'd thought he'd been so careful, so clever.

Above he heard Ruby banging on the front door. He

walked to the spot in the room that was beneath his bedroom, and reached up. The trapdoor popped out of the way, exactly like the lid in the van. That's right: This was his first tongue-and-groove door. He'd been reusing the design for years.

He pulled himself up into his bedroom—his bedroom closet, actually—and stepped out. There were no windows, and the only light was from the faint glow from the living room. The room was an empty box, stripped to nothing.

He went to the front door and unlocked it. The wood had swelled in the frame and he had to yank hard to open it.

"I could have been bitten by now," she said.

"Sorry."

The house was nearly empty. The sale had taken every article of furniture, even the carpets. Ruby kicked at a dark clump of something clinging to the floorboards. "I think animals have been here," she said.

"I'd be offended if they hadn't," Stony said.

In the kitchen they found a plastic patio table he didn't recognize and a cardboard box. Ruby peeled back the lid. "Christmas decorations," she said. "So we've got that covered."

"I'll get us something to sit on," Stony said. He went back to his bedroom and dropped back through the trapdoor. He was thinking he could unbolt the bookshelves, maybe improvise some benches. But unless he just smashed the boards apart, he'd need a screwdriver at least.

He went to the section of paneling that hid his room, pulled it aside, then opened the metal door. On the sheet metal floor of the tiny room were stacks of cardboard boxes, four deep and five high. He went to the nearest stack and lifted the topmost box—surprisingly heavy—and carried it out into the light slanting through the cellar door. He opened the flaps, and the rich, familiar smell of pulp filled his nose.

The top of the box was lined with faded, colorful covers and white-crackled spines.

His books. His sisters had kept all his books.

He laughed aloud and pulled out a copy of John D. Mac-Donald's *The Green Ripper*. Beneath it was Frank Herbert's *Dune*, and below that:

Head Case, by C. V. Ferris. A man in a business suit, his back to the audience, and on his left a beautiful red-haired woman in a clinging red dress, facing out. She rested her arm on his shoulder, looking devious. The man's face, gray and decayed, was half turned toward her, grimacing. His right arm hung at his side, holding an automatic.

C. V. Ferris wasn't a chubby breather woman from New Jersey. He was an LD with a Royal manual typewriter. He was Jack Gore, a hard-bitten cop bitten hard.

Still, he wished Gloria Stolberg well. He hoped she survived the outbreak. He didn't need any more Jack Gore novels, but he would love to see what she'd written about the LD community. Now, after the outbreak, her book would either be a brilliant defense or damning evidence.

No, that was the old way of thinking. Who would be alive to put them on trial? The surviving LDs would never indict their own.

He moved all the boxes out of the metal room until finally the floor was clear, with only the little pallet of old blankets on the floor (blankets intact), and the two short bookshelves screwed to the wall. He picked up a flashlight that had been left behind on one of the shelves. It wouldn't turn on. He shook it, then unscrewed the cap and tipped out the batteries. Completely corroded, as to be expected.

He shut the room, then carried a couple of the book boxes back to the trapdoor and pushed them up and through.

Ruby heard the noise and came to the hole. "Where the hell did you go? The cellar?"

"Could you carry these back to the living room, please?"

Soon they had enough boxes to make two chairs and an end table; Stony felt like they were playing house. Ruby, sweating now in the close atmosphere, sat down to eat her last protein bar. She set the pistol on the floor between her feet. "Do we have water at least?"

"We should—it's on a well, not city water." He went into the kitchen and turned on the taps. The water sputtered, then ran orange-red, stinking of rust. He let it run and walked back to the living room. "It may be a few minutes until it's drinkable."

She bit off another inch of the energy bar, then folded the foil over it and put it back into her backpack. "We're going to have to hit that Walmart," she said.

"It's almost sundown," he said. "I'll get you some food then."

"From where?"

"I'll think of something."

"You know, I'd like to know if you have any plan at all. What are we supposed to do, wait it out and hope the outbreak misses us?"

"It won't miss us. It won't miss anyone."

"You can't know that. We're in the middle of nowhere."

He shook his head. "The mobs will be moving in from the cities, especially west from Chicago. We already saw Iowa City was spilling over. It's only a matter of time till they get here."

"Like when—tonight?"

He hesitated, then said, "Tomorrow morning at the latest."

He watched her take in this information, consider it, and set it on some mental shelf—not forgotten, but in plain sight. He loved her for this, how she refused to panic. Crystal would have been so proud.

"You know," Ruby said, "an abandoned farmhouse in the middle of a flat plain is not exactly where I'd pick to make my last stand."

He smiled. "I think I need to show you something."

He supported her under her arms as she lowered herself through the trapdoor, then followed after her. "I dug out this basement when I was in high school," he said.

Ruby played her flashlight around the space. "By yourself?"

"I had a lot of time on my hands. Let me show you the best part." He took her to the secret panel and swung it out of the way. "I called this my fortress of solitude."

She leaned in, and the beam of her flashlight gleamed against the metal. "Okay then," Ruby said. Her voice echoed oddly. "Your own safe room."

Stony said, "If the undead get into the house, I want you to come down here, okay? Close the door behind you. You can bolt it from the inside."

"What about you?"

"They won't hurt me. And if things get really bad, lift up the pallet. Like this." He squatted and levered the wooden platform out of the way.

She aimed her light into the darkness. "Are those stairs?"

"Just follow them down, and then keep following the tunnel. If you go left you'll end up behind the Chos' house. If you go right, you'll end up in our barn, in one of the old stalls.

And if you go down the middle passage, it'll take you about half a mile away, near the highway."

"Half a *mile*?"

"Alice said that I had a tendency to overdo things."

"She got that fucking right."

"Come on, let's go out to the barn." He walked down first and was pleased to find out that his wooden stairs were still sturdy. "Wait, I just remembered something." He felt around under the last step, and there it was: the metal toolbox that used to belong to his sisters' father. Stony had supplemented Ervin Mayhall's tools with his own supplies. He pulled out two squat, white safety candles and a box of matches in a small plastic bag.

Ruby said, "You planted that here." Her tone was disbelieving. "When you were in high school."

"I read a lot of spy books. And at Kwang's house they let me watch *Hogan's Heroes.*"

"Watch what?"

"You're yanking my chain again."

"Seriously, I have no idea what you're talking about."

"It was a sitcom about a Nazi prisoner-of-war camp."

"You're shitting me."

"Come on, Colonel Klink? Sergeant Schultz? Hilarious Nazis. Anyway, all those prisoners had secret passages, like stairs under a bunk that flipped up."

"Did all your ideas come from TV and movies?"

"Pretty much." It took him three tries, the matchsticks practically disintegrating at his touch, but he finally managed to light one of the candles. He saw her shocked expression through the flames, then she looked away.

"What is it?" he asked. "Did I scare you?"

"Nothing, it's just—well, sometimes it catches me by surprise that you're, well—"

"A zombie."

She shook her head. "Come on. Off to the barn."

He decided to let it pass. Act normal. "So, which passage?" he asked.

"Right to the barn," she said. "Left to the Chos'. Middle to Bumblefuck, Egypt."

"Gold star," he said. The barn tunnel was the first he'd dug when he was a kid, and the passage was much shorter than he remembered, in both height and length. They walked stooped over for perhaps twenty yards, a slight breeze in their faces, until they came to a ladder. It rose only six feet and dead-ended against the wooden floor of the barn. Stony climbed up a few rungs and pushed. The floor didn't budge. He decided not to look down at Ruby to see what she thought of that.

He climbed two steps higher so that he was bent under the floorboards. Then he straightened and pushed hard. The floor rose six inches. He began to shove it aside—and the rung snapped beneath his feet. He fell to the floor of the tunnel and the candle went out.

"I was supposed to escape how?" Ruby asked.

"I'll fix that," he said. He got to his feet, then boosted her up so that she could crawl into the barn. She even managed to keep the candle lit. He pulled himself up through the hatch in the floor, a square barely three feet by three feet.

"We could have just walked over," she said. The house, visible through the half-open barn door, was a short distance away.

"But now we've tested the escape tunnel," he said.

The barn had been left largely undisturbed, probably because there'd been nothing in it worth selling or stealing. In the corner, under the hayloft, were a score of ancient seed sacks that had been there since Ervin had stopped farming.

More seed was up in the loft. He went to the stack and tried to pry the canvas bag from the top. Mold or some kind of growth had cemented the bags together. He wedged his arms under the edges of the top bag, gripped hard, and yanked. The bag tore free, and white, dusty soy seed spilled onto the floor.

Ruby said, "You have a strange look on your face."

He looked at Ruby. "I know how to save us."

"What? How?"

"I know how to save us!" He cradled what remained in the bag, nodded at the pile on the floor, and said, "Grab some of that. Come on."

"Stony, you've got to tell me what's going on. What are you doing with this stuff? It's getting dark."

"Something my mother taught me," he said. "Your grandmother. Please, just trust me."

He walked out about fifty feet in front of the house. He tilted the bag, and began to pour a line of seed on the ground. Slowly he began to walk along the front of the house, leaving a trail. "Fill in where I miss, okay?" he told her.

"No."

He stopped, adjusted the bag.

She said, "I'm going inside, and I'm going to sit there with my gun aimed at the door, unless you tell me what the fuck you're doing."

"I'm making a circle."

"You're not helping."

He looked toward the road. The sun was going down, gilding the tall grass. "It's a magic circle," he said. "Everything inside the circle is mine, and cannot be harmed."

"What the hell, Stony. Magic?"

"Look, I know it doesn't sound rational. But we're a little bit beyond rational right now."

She stared at him for a long moment. A few white seeds

slipped through her fingers. "Fuck it," she said. "Magic circle it is."

She followed behind him. He went slowly, staring at the seed as it poured into the grass. *Everything in this circle is mine,* he said under his breath. *Integrity is all.*

"Are you, uh, praying?" Ruby asked.

"It's kind of a mantra. Integrity is all."

"What does that mean?"

"See, there was a guy named the Lump who—well, it's complicated."

"All of your stories are complicated."

"It's about keeping the body intact. If an LD can hold on to the idea of a body, then he can hold on to the idea of a self. Did I tell you about Calhoun's Integrity Suit?"

"Calhoun has integrity?"

He told her how Calhoun lived in the suit, a second skin to keep himself from falling apart. "See, we all need the illusion of continuity. Your cells are replaced every seven years, without you even thinking about it. But for my people, staying intact is an act of will."

Ruby said, "So you can't die unless you want to."

"Oh, we can die."

"But you just said—"

"It's complicated."

They made several trips back to the barn, opening bags of seed, racing the falling light. Ruby kept the flashlight tucked under one arm as they worked. They'd reached the west side of the house when Stony saw headlights swing off the road and head down the lane toward them.

"Ruby."

She saw the lights and exchanged a look with him.

"You get inside," she said. "I'll take care of this."

He thought about this. As she'd pointed out before, zombies didn't drive cars. Then he said, "I'll be right behind the front door."

"Move it, for Christ's sake," she said.

He hurried inside but left the door ajar a few inches. The car rolled slowly toward the house, easing into and out of the potholes in the dirt lane. Ruby stood about ten feet in front of the door, her left hand behind her back, holding the pistol.

The car, a light blue Buick LeSabre, stopped at the end of the drive, the headlights aimed at her and the front of the house. Stony stepped back a foot, keeping to the shadows.

No one got out of the car. Ruby shifted her weight. Her fingers flexed on the grip of the gun.

Then the car door opened and the dome light lit up, revealing two figures. The headlight warning tone chimed.

Ding. Ding. Ding.

A man stepped slowly out of the driver's side but stayed behind the open car door. He was very thin and wore a white shirt. His arms stayed down, out of sight.

He looked at Ruby, tilted his head.

"This is not your house," he said. His voice was firm, the accent still there but not as thick as it used to be.

Ruby slid the gun from her waistband and Stony yanked open the door. "Ruby! Easy."

The man did not move. Stony stepped out into the light and held up a hand against the glare of the headlights. "Mr. Cho. It's me, Stony."

Mr. Cho stepped out from the shelter of the door. In his arms he held a shotgun. Ruby raised her pistol.

"Geez, hold on, you two!" Stony said. He stepped down from the porch, his arms raised. "Ruby, he's a friend."

She said, "Tell him to put down the shotgun then."

Mr. Cho stared hard at her, then turned his attention to Stony. They had not seen each other since before the crash.

The night Stony totaled the man's car and took away his son's legs.

Mr. Cho set his gun on the car seat. He said something under his breath that could have been "Mayhalls."

Ruby dropped her arm. Stony strode past her, and at the same time Mrs. Cho stepped out of the passenger seat. She wore a green pantsuit with a wide, floral print collar. Even in the near dark he could see her bright red lipstick.

He stopped, afraid of spooking her.

She walked to him and stared up into his face. She was tiny. Her face was so sad.

He said, "Hi, Mrs. Cho."

She reached up and touched his cheek. "Oh, my boy." Suddenly she threw her arms around him. It was a long minute before she let him go.

He said, "Mrs. Cho, this is Crystal's—Chelsea's daughter, Ruby."

"Oh, I know this little girl," she said. She went to her and took Ruby's hands in her own. "Crystal sends me a picture every Christmas."

Stony thought about hugging Mr. Cho, but of course that was out of the question. The man had never been hugged in his life. They shook hands and Stony impulsively escalated the intimacy by gripping Mr. Cho's bicep.

"Where's Kwang?" Stony said. "Is he home?"

Mr. Cho shook his head. "Bad luck. Up in St. Paul."

"He's got an Internet girlfriend," Mrs. Cho said. "He hasn't called since . . ." A hand fluttered. "All this."

"I'm sure he's fine," Stony said.

"Ruby should come with us," Mrs. Cho said. "The whole town is leaving before they get here. Everyone's going to Camp Dodge, in Johnston."

"You can't do that," Stony said. "That's near Des Moines. You've got to stay away from the cities."

"National Guard is there," Mrs. Cho said.

"No, listen. The open road is no place to be. You've got to stay here, with me and Ruby. Tell your friends, too—they'll be safe here."

"We're building a magic circle," Ruby said.

Stony frowned at her, then turned back to the Chos. "I've got a bunker, okay? Tell your friends it's a bomb shelter. I can keep them safe."

Mrs. Cho and her husband did not look at each other, but they seemed to be communicating. After a moment, Mr. Cho said, "They will not understand."

"Okay, right, I'm undead. I'll hide. They won't even know I'm here. But you have to believe me, this is the best place to be when the mob comes."

"Impossible," Mr. Cho said.

Mrs. Cho said, "The radio said the zombies are coming. Thousands."

"Mrs. Cho—"

"Thousands!"

Mr. Cho said. "Already in Ames. Very close." He nodded to Ruby. "There is room in our car. Your family cannot afford to lose anyone else."

Ruby ran a hand through her hair. She looked back at the house. Then she said, "I'm staying with Stony."

It was full night when he completed the circle. Eight bags of seed to make an egg-shaped ellipse about fifty feet out from the walls of the house. Above, the moon was a hair's breadth short of full. The white seed glowed.

He heard a gunshot in the distance. Then another. He turned. The sound, if he judged correctly, came from the south end of town, where Ruby had driven through the road-block. He waited thirty seconds, a minute—and then gunfire rolled like thunder.

He hefted the ninth bag and tore open its top. He started at the circle and poured a line that ran up to the porch, then to the front door. He nudged open the door with his foot.

Ruby, Mr. Cho, and Mrs. Cho sat on the improvised chairs, the candle burning on a box between them. Ruby held one of Mrs. Cho's sandwiches. At their feet, plastic water bottles gleamed.

Of course they'd heard the gunfire, too.

"I think it's time that you all retired to the basement," Stony said.

CHAPTER TWENTY

April 29, 2010
Easterly, Iowa

o you remember Officer Tines? He was the young patrolman who pulled over the pickup truck full of Kwang's friends that Halloween night in 1978. Kwang fell into his arms, mock-drunk, to allow the toilet-paper-wrapped Stony to escape. Yes—that guy. His full name was William Randolph Tines, but his friends and family called him Willie. (Drunk teenagers still called him Officer Tines, or else.) Willie wasn't born in Easterly, but he came for the police job in 1976 and never left. Just adopted the place. He was thirty before he married Nancy, an apple-cheeked girl who was way too serious about politics, but pleasant besides that. They had four children: three brown-haired boys and a tall yellow-haired girl who poked up between them like a dandelion. They moved out to the unincorporated area north of town, a bigger place on a three-quarter-acre lot. His kids played every sport imaginable, and his daughter turned out to be a hell of a fast-pitch softball player; she got a partial scholarship to Iowa State. Willie was a good father. Not to say he was perfect. He hit forty like a bad spot in the road, started drinking more, then had an affair with a certifiably crazy

woman who worked at the yarn store. But then he found Christ and straightened right up. Everyone said so. And even during the bad years he never missed a day of work or one of his kids' games.

It's important you know all this so you understand that Willie Tines was not a bad man. It's just that, like everybody else on April 29, he was on the wrong planet at the wrong time.

He'd been working the roadblock on the edge of town for thirty-six hours, ever since they'd learned of the outbreak. The barricade wasn't much: three barrels, a bunch of planks, and a pickup pulled across the road. His "deputies" weren't that impressive, either. There were only three cops in Easterly, so Willie had drafted four municipal employees, middle-aged guys who were snowplow drivers in the winter and landscapers in the summer. They'd brought their own weapons. For the first thirty-five hours there'd been nothing to do but wave good-bye to the people fleeing town, and wave through the few cars coming in. Willie was there when the pretty dark-haired girl rolled up in that big delivery van, claiming to be Kwang Cho's niece. And he was there at dusk of the second day when the first zombie shambled down the road at them.

After all the buildup, all the frantic reports on the radio, the crazy television reports, it was kind of a letdown. Willie had set up generators and big lights aimed down the road, and the thing shuffled toward them, lit up and haloed as if on a beauty pageant runway. It moved kind of sideways, as if its hip had been broken.

The city employees looked to Willie to make the first move. He put down his shotgun and asked for a deer rifle. The thing was, he'd never fired a gun in the line of duty. He'd certainly never shot at something human-looking. He sighted down the barrel, steadied himself—then lowered the gun. The municipal men looked at one another. One of them started to say something, and then Officer Tines raised the rifle and fired. Then again.

It took three shots to finally make it stop moving. The men hooted and slapped high-fives.

Willie handed back the rifle to its owner. "Get the extra barrels in place," he said. The men went to the half-dozen barrels lining the side of the road and began to wheel and walk them into place.

Willie walked perhaps twenty feet away, got out his cellphone, and called his wife. "It's happening," he said. "Are you at the school yet?" Willie and his fellow officers had designated the elementary school as the emergency shelter. The building was brick, large enough to hold a few hundred people, small enough to defend, with access to the roof so they could shoot from high ground. They didn't know how many people would stay in Easterly—five hundred? a thousand?—but the three policemen agreed it was better to be together when the attack came.

His wife told him they were leaving the house now, she and the two younger boys. Their daughter and eldest son were away at college. He'd talked to them both a few hours ago, but he could barely stand the thought of them being away from home right now.

"Okay, good," Willie said. He glanced at his watch. The house was on the north end of town, well past the subdivisions, but still only fifteen minutes from downtown. "Grab us a couple of the good cots."

Behind him, the crack of another rifle shot. He turned. Another zombie—no, three of the dead things were staggering toward the roadblock. "I've got to go," he said into the phone. "I love you, hon. Please hurry."

The men were firing repeatedly now, using too much

ammo. Willie went to the barricade and picked up his shot-gun. Not that it would do much good. What they needed was a machine gun, a flamethrower—hell, an Apache gunship. But everyone understood that there'd be no help coming from the state police or the National Guard—from anyone in the government. They were on their own.

The three zombies went down, but the men didn't celebrate this time. They held on to their guns and waited for the silhouettes to appear at the edge of the light a hundred yards away.

They felt it first. The barest tremor in the pavement beneath their feet, as if a train were passing—but the tremor persisted, grew more insistent. The sounds came next. From far away in the dark rumbled a low murmur, an engine-like noise of a thousand throats, wordless and random.

The sound grew, and still they could see nothing beyond the rim of light. The men glanced at one another, and looked away.

One of the men on the barricade said, "We're no better than them. We're already dead."

"Cut it out," Tines said. Something made him check his phone again. The phone icon was blinking. He'd missed a call from his wife's cell. He knew then that he was in the wrong place, doing the wrong thing. He slowly turned in place, like a compass needle, until he faced north. The threat wasn't behind him, it was ahead.

Someone said, "Shit."

A shape had appeared at the edge of the light. It was a wall of black, a mass distinguishable as bodies only because of the swaying and bobbing at the edge of the silhouette.

The men began to fire, round after round. They could see no effect. The mass shuffled forward, and the moans of the dead increased. The percussive scrape of their feet against the pavement rattled up through the men's bodies.

Tines yelled for the men to stop firing, and they obeyed. "We'll never hold this," he said. "You all go back to the schoolhouse. Back to your families."

"What about you?" one of them asked.

"I'll do the dump."

"Fuck that," one of the men said. "I've got no family. You guys go."

Willie said, "Ron, you don't have to do this."

"Go. Git."

The men got into the pickups, and Willie climbed into his black and white SUV. The six extra barrels were filled with kerosene. Ron had to wait until the zombies were close—ten, twenty yards—before he dumped the contents onto the road, or else the fuel would run off the pitched surface like rainwater. Even then, it was a low-probability tactic. At best it would only kill the monsters who were walking on the road. But at least it was something.

Willie drove north down 59, going fast. The flames erupted in his rearview mirror.

Stony sat on the floor in the center of the living room, a map of Easterly spread out on his lap, his hands at his sides. He was surrounded by a circle of powdery white seed, which was connected to the larger circle outside by a straight line that ran through the open door of the house. The two white candles burned inside the circle with him, so he could see the map.

His hands, one gray, one Barbie-colored plastic, rested in the powder. The circle, he told himself, was an extension of his body. His flesh, laid out in a line. He encircled the house, and he was the house. He could feel the brittle bones of the barn like the bones of his missing hand. Mine, he thought. He flexed his fingers, and felt timbers snap.

Better watch that, he thought. He relaxed his hands and went still.

Now, how far could he go? Surrounding the house and barn were the spring fields, eager with life. He felt them in his arms, his legs, his chest. He masked the new grass with his own dead nature.

He looked down at the map. He'd drawn a big O around the town's borders, and inside that a smaller O where the farmhouse was located—and within *that*, a dot to represent the circle he now occupied.

He closed his eyes. Be fractal, he thought. Larger than the town and inside it at the same time, all scales at once. Little Big.

Take it all in, Stony.

He needed the entire town. Houses and fields and fast-food restaurants, roads and cars and the thousand souls who'd refused to evacuate—all of it. He could feel the undead out beyond the borders of the town, pressing to get in, desperately hungry. But the dead would not eat the dead. The grave had nothing to offer them.

All he had to do was turn the house, the farm, and the entire town into a corpse.

But the task, the geography, was too big for him. He couldn't forget himself, this body he was in. He could feel his arms, his legs, the small of his back. He knew it was all just dead flesh—some of it was even plastic. But he'd lived in it for a very long time. He'd grown too comfortable.

Someone was outside. No, two people. He could feel them like breath on the skin of his arm.

He opened his eyes.

Standing in the front yard, twenty feet from him, were two boys. Brown-haired, clearly brothers. The oldest of them—he was twelve or thirteen—held a cellphone in one hand and his brother's hand in the other. There was blood on their clothes and arms. Something terrible had happened. They hadn't been bitten. For some reason he was sure of that.

The boys peered into the dark of the house. Stony wondered how much they could see past the flickering light. Did they recognize what he was?

Suddenly the older boy turned away, pulling his brother with him. Stony stood up, and as he stepped out of the circle it was like a circuit breaker had been thrown. Suddenly he was cut off from the house, the farm, the network of roads. He blinked in surprise. Maybe he'd gotten further than he thought.

He reached the doorway in time to see the boys run into the barn. He stared after them, trying to decide what to do, and finally went back into the house, to the back bedroom, and dropped through the trapdoor.

Ruby sat on the cement floor outside the fortress room, holding her flashlight and a book. She was dressed in a hoodie and jeans, and her knees were drawn up tight. It was pretty cool down here at night. The book she was reading was his mother's pink and green diary. He'd given it to her. He'd never been able to open it himself.

"You're supposed to be in the safe room," Stony said.

"It's a little cramped in there. The Chos are scared, which is making me scared. You're doing something. I can feel it. I can feel you."

He nodded at the book. "How is it?" He couldn't stop himself from asking.

"Bethany Cooper was a very sweet, innocent girl."

"Really?"

"According to this, she wasn't even sure how she got pregnant. But you're changing the subject."

"I need you to do something for me. There are two young boys out there, hiding in the barn."

"What? Where'd they come from?"

"I have no idea. Could you check on them, find out where their parents are? Maybe convince them to go in the tunnels with you?"

Ruby put down the book. "Are they hurt?"

"I don't think so. They look like they're in shock. I can't go check on them without scaring the shit out of them. So please?"

"No problem. As soon as you tell me what you're doing up there."

"Just one little thing," Stony said. "One impossible thing."

He pulled himself back up through the trap and went to his mother's old bedroom, which faced the barn. The window was blocked by plywood but he reached under the wood and popped it free. Ruby had already emerged from the cellar door and was walking toward the barn.

Huh, Stony thought. The cellar door was practically under his mom's window. How many nights had she watched him haul dirt out that door? He thought he was being so sneaky.

Ruby stepped through the barn door, leaving it ajar. He watched for several minutes, waiting for her to step back out, when the night was lit up by blue and red flashing lights. Stony hurried to the front of the house, keeping out of the open doorway.

The driver was moving fast, so much faster than when

Mr. Cho had taken the road in his Buick, jouncing over the potholes. A police car, a big SUV, braked to a halt in front of the house.

A man stepped out of the SUV, his features hidden by the glare of the headlights. Stony watched him through the gap in the door. He had the impression of a tall, bulky man. He carried a rifle or shotgun in his hands. He seemed to be studying the front door.

"Marc! Peter!"

Ah. He had to be looking for the boys.

Stony waited for them to answer, but nobody replied. The cop moved out of Stony's line of sight. Stony stepped back to get a view into the yard—and suddenly he was staring into the cop's face. They were two feet from each other, and for a second both of them were too shocked to move.

The cop recovered first. He recognized Stony for what he was. Then he jammed the barrel of his shotgun into Stony's gut and fired.

The blast knocked him off his feet. He crashed onto his back, into the circle. White powder puffed around him.

Pain flared across his abdomen. No, no time for that. He needed to put the sensation away. It was the first thing he'd learned after Kwang fired that arrow into his heart. How many times had he been shot since then? You'd think he'd be used to it by now.

He tried to sit up, but there was a lot of him missing in the middle now, major structural damage. Stony succeeded in executing a kind of aggressive twitch.

The cop raised the weapon again, aimed carefully, and fired from the shoulder. Stony felt his throat and face tear, and again he was knocked flat.

The cop leaned over Stony. His face was distorted by the

flickering candlelight, but he seemed somehow familiar. Stony tried to say, "Officer Tines?" But the sound came out as a cough.

Tines ratcheted the shotgun, reloading it, and pressed the double barrels against Stony's face.

The world reduced itself to a single noise.

He'd told Ruby it wasn't in his nature to fall in love. But that wasn't true, was it? He'd been in love from the moment his mother picked him out of the snow. For the first eighteen years of his life he'd been surrounded by women he loved, and by women who loved him: Mom and Alice and Crystal and Junie. And later, he'd met a sad woman named Valerie.

And what had he done with that love? He'd failed them all, betrayed every one of them. He'd killed Junie with incompetence, and Valerie with lack of imagination. He could never think of a way to save her. His mother had been arrested because of him, and locked away for decades like a terrorist. And Alice and Crystal—they might very well be dead by now, hunted down by the undead he'd helped set loose.

All he'd ever done, his entire life, was run. He was so good at it. Unstoppable.

Time to stop.

He did not move when Willie Tines searched the house. Or when the boys came out of the basement cellar, calling their father's name. Or when Willie went back to his vehicle to get the gasoline.

Ruby tried to stop him, bless her heart. Stony wished he could have told her that it was all right. He was guilty as charged. He was tired. For years he'd been holding this body together with twine and duct tape. It certainly wasn't worth saving. He could only imagine what his skull looked like. Caved-in papier-mâché, perhaps. A busted piñata.

So, he waited as the pungent gasoline splashed around his body. He'd known since he was a boy that this was the way he was destined to die. Hunted, shot, and finally burned. It was a relief to have the moment finally arrive. His only regret was that the house would burn with him, and all those lovely books.

Morning bells are ringing.

2011
Easterly Enclave

erhaps you were expecting a happy ending.

Sorry about that.

I don't blame you for hoping. Even the most hardened of people—and who isn't hard, these days—would welcome a respite from the miserable spiral into the abyss that the universe guarantees its citizens. Take Ruby, our Last Girl, who is determined to sift a happy ending from the ashes. I mean this literally. Thanks to Kwang's newly appropriated backhoe, her sweet but misguided plan is finally under way, but she is frustrated by the pace of the excavation. When the house burned, it collapsed into Stony's basement, creating an enormous fire pit. Sparks and flames inevitably crossed over to the barn. Both buildings burned through the night and cooked for days. Later, spring rains turned the pit to a swamp that refused to drain completely even through the heat of the summer. Amid the skeletal timbers, a few identifiable objects have surfaced: the barrel of the water heater, a surprisingly white toilet, a naked floor lamp like a great fishhook. Ruby fears that Stony's bones have been cremated by the fire, or else broken apart and scattered through the slurry.

"Don't worry, they'll find him," her grandmother tells her. Wanda Mayhall has taken to sitting out here under a shade tree, keeping Ruby company. Wanda, at seventy-six, can sit with the best of them. Her hyperthyroid condition, undiagnosed while she was in prison, tires her out, though now that the emergency government is delivering her medications, she's getting stronger.

Unlike almost everyone else in the enclave, Wanda has no beef with the new feds. It's not like the old ones treated her all that well. Mrs. Cho, who on most days joins Wanda and Ruby on Backhoe Watch 2011, often says (politely, somewhat formally) that she wishes Wanda would keep her opinions about the government to herself. People in the enclave are sensitive. Wanda says that if you can't speak your mind when you're old, when are you supposed to do it? Right, Mr. Cho? But Mr. Cho knows better than to be drawn into the argument. He stays near the rumbling backhoe, silently indicating where Kwang should dig next, while the ladies bicker and gossip. They do this for hours, keeping up a constant fireside chat beside a fire that's long gone out. Ruby finds this tremendously entertaining, as do many other residents. People stop by and trade stories, and sometimes they even ask about her son.

The story, after all these years, is out.

The townspeople who were living in Easterly back then can barely believe that she'd hidden an undead child from them for over fifteen years. Alice told her mother to expect a backlash from the enclave residents—they're rabidly antizombie, as you might expect—but no one has been rude to her face. There's something distinctly un-Iowan about attacking an old woman, especially one who spent decades in prison, and who doesn't give a damn what anyone else thinks.

Ruby is a different story. She's been extremely vocal about how Stony saved her in Chicago, and how he protected the Chos, and made sure the Tines boys were watched over. There have been quite a few shouting matches in the past year, and one fistfight. (Ruby held her own.)

Willie Tines came by the burned house once, to pay his respects to Mrs. Mayhall. He told her he felt terrible about destroying her son and her farm. Like most of the residents of the enclave, he is a haunted man. His wife was bitten during the outbreak, when she ran into a group of LDs coming in from the north. The two boys escaped the wreckage and the monsters and made it to the nearest house—but you know the rest of that story.

"You have nothing to be forgiven for," Wanda told him. "No more than any of us. A lot of people in town say they have you to thank for their lives."

"Ma'am, nothing I did made a damn—made a bit of difference. We all should have died." Better than almost anyone, Willie knew that the town should have been wiped out. It wasn't just that the southern barricade was breached; it was that every one of their defenses failed. The zombies marched in from all directions. The living fled their homes and headed toward the schoolhouse, and the hordes followed them.

"And then they just . . . stopped," Willie said. "They turned around and wandered away. Like they couldn't even see us anymore."

Wanda nodded. She'd heard versions of this story from everyone in town, though not everyone had played a role as heroic as Officer Tines's. It would make an excellent movie, if there were still movies.

Tines said he'd come over to say good-bye—he was leaving town. "My wife got in touch with me," he said. "She's living—well, *staying* less than fifty miles from here. She misses the boys. And the boys miss her." It was like he was asking for her blessing. Most of the town considered him a traitor for leaving the enclave to live with the dead.

"Family should be together," Wanda told him. "Period."

A few days later, a federal helicopter flies low over the enclave. It's a big green Huey, two rotors, and it lands in the old soy field behind the burned house, sending ash and debris swirling into the air. USMRA is in big white letters near the nose: United States Midwestern Regional Authority.

Ruby jams her rake into a pile of ash and pulls off her gloves. Part of the reason the excavation is going so slowly is that she wants to check every load that's removed from the pit. Kwang scoops out a pile, then dumps it on the ground, setting out pile after pile. Ruby, and sometimes Alice with her, goes through it, shoving aside chunks of wood and building material, looking for bones and teeth. It's filthy work. It would be grisly work, too, except that they haven't found any remains.

Ruby hurries over to the aircraft. She knows that the rest of the townspeople will be rushing over here any minute. It's strictly against the covenant for a federal craft to enter the town limits, and people will be pissed. They'll be especially pissed at Ruby if they find out that she's the one who called them.

The big side door opens, and three soldiers in camouflage jump out, holding rifles. Just behind them comes a woman in a blue flight suit. It's odd for the director of an eight-state area to be dressed like a pilot or a mechanic, but Delia's never been interested in convention.

Ruby and Delia have never met in person, and they've only talked on the town's landline phone once. All their other communications have been by letter, an old-fashioned medium revived by the fall of the cell towers. The USMRA maintains an intermittent postal service that they allow the breathers to use. Ruby assumes all their letters are being read by intelligence officers. Delia says, "I was beginning to think you were going to have the funeral without me."

"We're running into delays," Ruby says. "We haven't found the body yet."

"Will you?"

"I don't know, have you found my mother yet?"

It sounds like sarcasm, but there's a note of desperation to Ruby's voice. Delia's voice softens. "Sorry, kid. We're looking. Crystal was a friend of mine, and I'm not giving up. But you have to understand that it's still pretty chaotic out there."

Crystal hadn't contacted anyone in the family, and no one had seen her. She could be dead, or turned and suffering from amnesia, or . . . anything. Breathers are fighting with LDs, LDs are fighting each other, and whole areas of the country are still without power—electrical or political. Ad hoc governments—half school board, half street gang—are seizing authority in the vacuum. And that's just in the United States. Everybody in Easterly thinks it's got to be a lot worse in the rest of the world.

"After your service we'll do one of our own," Delia says. "A full state funeral. The Lump will officiate."

"Whatever," Ruby said.

"Of course, we'd like to display the body. If you find it."

Ruby is shaking her head. "Absolutely not. We never agreed to that."

"I don't think you realize what he means to his people."

"I don't think you realize what he means to his family."

Perhaps that's a smile on Delia's face—but Delia's half skull turns every expression into a leer. She says, "Your uncle had a talent, kid. He made families wherever he went."

After a moment of silence, Delia shrugs. "Just think about it."

"I'll talk to Gram and Alice."

"Tell them we're going to publish his papers," Delia said. "We've got almost a complete collection of *Sunday Deadlines*— the Deadtown prisoners kept them hidden from the guards all the way until the Big Bite. Plus we've started an oral history project, recording all the stories of the outbreak before they're forgotten, and a lot of those stories are about Stony. If you've got anything he's written—anything at all—we'd sure appreciate it." Ruby has never told Delia that she has Stony's memoir, and has suggested it was all lost in the fire. But Delia suspects she has it, and Ruby knows that Delia suspects she has it. To explain the various relationships in play—between Ruby and Delia, the living and the dead, the locals and the feds, and midwesterners and easterners—would require several economists, a team of anthropologists, and a theologian.

Delia says, "We're planning on a Stony Mayhall Library. We can build it near here, if you think the rebels wouldn't burn it down."

"I want money for a memorial," Ruby says. "Nothing big. Just something out by the highway, where they found him with his mother. Something simple, just their names maybe."

"I'll see what I can do," Delia says.

Kwang has shut off the backhoe, and he's walking stiffly toward them. And down the lane comes Alice, pedaling like the witch in *The Wizard of Oz*. Ruby, seeing that her time is running out, says, "Did you bring me the package?"

Delia calls up into the helicopter, and someone throws down a thick square wrapped in paper and tied with twine.

Delia hands it to Ruby. "Straight from Calhoun's personal collection."

Ruby looks at the parcel. It's heavier than she thought it would be. "You know, I can't figure out why the Commander would commit suicide in his bunker like that."

"Yeah, tragic," Delia says. "Very Adolf Hitler."

"Hitler was losing. Calhoun was about to win everything. But you were there on the island, right?" At her look, Ruby says, "Stony told me you were going there. You must have tried to get to Calhoun. He killed your friend, right? Mr. Blunt?"

"My best friend," Delia says. After a moment, she says, "I got to the island a couple of days after the bite. I never got into the fortress, though. No one could get inside it."

"Right, right," Ruby says. "I heard that." She frowns. "But you know what's weird?" Her voice has taken on an innocent, I'm-Just-So-Curious tone. "Stony helped build that place, and it's just not like him to leave out a secret passage. A back door or something. He was kind of OCD about that kind of thing. I mean, that's what he told me once." He'd told her no such thing. But Ruby has read Stony's memoir, several times, and has come to certain conclusions about his character. "Did he tell you about anything like that—a way to get into that bunker?"

Delia goes very still. She's ready to say something, but then Kwang huffs up. One of the soldiers steps in front of him, blocking his way. Kwang calls, "Everything okay, Ruby?"

Delia signals for the soldier to let the man pass. She says, "You must be Kwang." She pronounces it correctly, rhyming it with *swan.* She offers her hand and says, "Stony always looked forward to your letters."

Kwang says, "No offense, Director, but a bunch of angry townspeople are going to be showing up with pitchforks soon."

"I'll be on my way," Delia says. "We're flying back to headquarters in St. Louis, but I'll be in touch." She nods at Ruby. "Let me know when you find him."

Ruby and Kwang step back and watch the Huey take off. As the helicopter clears the edge of the enclave, Kwang says, "We found him."

He shows her the plastic arm he's spotted, melted almost to a blob. After a few minutes of combing through the latest pile they find a long bone, a femur, blackened but distinctly human. The hunt is on in earnest.

That night Ruby and Alice move all the bones they've found to the house that they and Gram are "borrowing." The owners evacuated during the outbreak and haven't returned. Ruby has set up two foldout tables in the basement, and there they begin the jigsaw puzzle portion of the process.

Alice is the expert here, but Ruby is a fast learner. By the third day of reconstruction Alice only has to make a shape with her hands and say, "Look for a bone that looks like this," and Ruby retrieves it from the dwindling collection. The skeleton is all but complete. The rib cage and spine and three limbs are in place, and the skull, deeply fractured, rests on one cheek, looking away as if embarrassed by his nakedness. Of the missing bones, it's quite possible that he'd misplaced those before the fire.

"I know what you're trying to do," Alice says to her.

"You do?" Ruby says.

"It's wrong. You can't make a shrine out of him. He doesn't want to be a religion."

"What are you talking about?"

"I know what Delia wants. Stony's an icon to them. They

want something to worship so they can all feel good about their undead paradise."

Ruby says, "We're not giving anything to Delia."

"Come on, what did she promise you? She had to offer you something."

"I told her I wanted a memorial. For where he was found."

"And what else?"

"Nothing else!" Ruby says. "We're not giving her the body."

"Then why are you doing this? Why don't you just let him lie?"

"Because he deserves a decent burial," Ruby says. It's the reason she keeps handy to whip out whenever anyone asks. It's all she had to say to her grandmother to get her to go along with the idea. "And because he *is* an icon. If we don't bury him, if we just leave him out there in that ash pile, then his followers will try to dig him up themselves. They'll run off with pieces of him like he's a, what do you call it—a relic. One of those finger bones of the saints."

Alice narrows her eyes, as if Ruby is the one with the religious ideas. And perhaps she is.

"We'll have the funeral immediately," Alice says.

"What?"

"Before Delia can make her move. You don't understand these people. I'll set up the chapel for Thursday."

"That's the day after tomorrow!" Ruby says. "That's way too soon. Maybe—"

"We have enough bones."

"Yeah, but not all of them. If we keep looking . . ."

Alice sets down the tiny bone she's trying to place—an ankle or wrist bone, only Alice knows—and takes off one of her work gloves. "Thursday, or no funeral at all. I'll hide the bones myself."

Ruby is angry, but she knows better than to argue with Alice when she's like this. "Anything else, General?"

"I'll ask Mom if she wants to speak at the service. I assume you're going to say something?"

"Uh, sure, aren't you?"

"The last time Stony and I saw each other it was an argument, which I won. No sense ruining my streak."

This is completely wrong, of course. Alice did not win that argument. Not completely. Besides, this is obviously an example of Alice using her gruff exterior to hide her true feelings.

"I'm going to bed," she says, and Ruby says she's going to keep going for a while. "Take your best guess on them," Alice says, meaning the bones. "I'll straighten them out in the morning. Then we'll get him into a coffin before Mom accidentally sees him."

After several minutes of fiddling with a few bits that look like chips off the old skull, Ruby goes to the cardboard box in the corner. Inside is the package from Delia, as well as a red Etch A Sketch she found in an abandoned house. She unwraps the package, revealing a shiny white ghost—one of Calhoun's Integrity Suits.

Oh, Ruby.

It's a full-body model, from head to individual toe pockets. It is padded and reinforced to support a body—specifically, Calhoun's ideal body. There are foam inserts to add superhero definition to the abs, and structural wiring to keep feet and spine and shoulders in alignment. It raises serious issues about what kind of shape Calhoun's body was in *without* the suit. It's quite possible that all Delia had to do to kill the man was unzip him.

Ruby pushes the two long tables next to each other. On one table lies the disjointed skeleton, and on the other the unzipped I-Suit. One by one, she transfers the bones into this Halloween costume. A laborious process. She's trying to be so careful, fitting each tarsal and scapula into its assigned slot, but isn't it doomed to failure? The bones are not wired together, or even glued. As soon as she tries to lift the suit, the whole agglomeration will jumble to the bottom. Bag o' bones indeed. The plan is ridiculous.

She keeps at it for hours. She gets sweaty and cranky, swearing at Stony for the condition of his bones, which hardly seems fair. Sometime late in the night she picks up the final piece. She slips the skull under the mask-like hood and zips the suit up to its bony chin. Then she lifts one of the suit's hands and places it atop the Etch A Sketch.

"I know you're in there, Uncle Stony." She is addressing the mannequin on the table. "Time to get up."

Ah. This is sad. The girl is so distraught with grief, she's delusional.

"I know you can hear me, motherfucker."

Hey now.

"Just move your hand, then. I couldn't find a fucking Ouija board, so this will have to do."

The suit does not move, the fingers do not twitch. Of course not. Stony is no more in this bag of bones than he is in the empty water bottle she keeps beside the table, or in her left tennis shoe.

"Okay, fine," she says. "You want to play hardball?" She goes upstairs to her bedroom, trying to keep quiet so as not to wake her aunt and grandmother, then quickly returns to the basement. She's holding a large stack of paper bound in a thick rubber band. And a box of matches.

"Yeah, I bet I've got your attention now, don't I?"

The manuscript isn't Stony's memoir—that's in the binder, and it's a lot thicker. Besides, even Ruby knows that there may be some historical value to that. But this—this is nothing. Stony's amateurish attempt at fiction.

She lifts the cover page into the light. "Christmas for the Dead," she intones. "A Jack Gore, Deadtown Detective Novel." She strikes a match.

A stray breeze from a corner of the basement ripples the flame, and the match goes out.

"Shit," she says. She looks around the basement. Studies the deflated suit on the table. Then she crouches, guarding the matches with her body, and lights another. The breeze whips up, to no avail. When she stands up, the cover page is aflame.

Damn it.

It's no easy thing to animate a collection of ossified odds and ends, even pieces that used to belong to me, even ones so lovingly arranged by my deranged niece. Maybe with time and effort I could persuade myself to own it. Settle into this loosely wrapped junk shop. Convince myself that I am *here* and no place else. Inside this second skin, not soaked into the soil of my hometown like rainwater.

My problem last year—my whole unnatural life, really—was learning how to forget myself. The brain eaters were coming. People were dying. All I had to do was let go of the particular arrangement of bones and skin that I'd grown up in and take on a new, larger body. I thought I could do it. I'd learned so much in Deadtown about defining my body on my own terms. What was the difference, really, in moving around a dead stick, and becoming the ground it was stuck in? Purely psychological. A mental backflip. Yet I couldn't make it happen. I couldn't let go of this body, until Officer Tines burned it down like an old house.

It was an accident.

Suddenly I was kicked out like a stubborn teenager and forced to find a new home. And once I was out . . . well, I adjusted. Now it's difficult to remember what I saw in the old place.

The page she's holding transforms from a thing on fire to fire itself, and Ruby drops it to the floor. She stamps on it—a little vigorously, I think. She's crying now, but angry tears. Is she mad at me, or herself?

I really don't want her to be angry with herself.

She sits down against the cinder-block walls of the basement, her forehead on her arms. Eventually she hears a faint sound, a scratchy squeak, and looks up. The hand of the suit isn't moving, but the white knobs of the Etch A Sketch are turning. Then they stop.

She lifts the arm of the suit and picks up the red tablet. On the gray screen is a wobbly message: PLEASE STOP

Ruby, despite the fact that she was expecting this (or only pretending to expect it? Breathers are complicated), squeals in what could be fright or surprise.

"Uncle Stony?" she says.

I think, Who the hell else?

Now she's crying in a different way. The good kind of tears? You'd think that after growing up with breathers, and spending this past year doing nothing but watching them, I'd be a little better at interpreting this kind of thing. But it does seem to me that her face is a pleasant mix of shock and happiness and pride. Oh, yes, she's proud of herself.

Stubborn girl.

* * *

I've been present at every funeral and memorial service in
Easterly, and we've had a lot of them, especially in the first few
months after the outbreak. Ruby and Wanda Mayhall sit up
front. Ruby's holding the Etch A Sketch, twiddling with the
knobs to cover the fact that they sometimes turn on their
own. She's gotten into the habit of carrying it around at all
times. Mom frowns but doesn't say anything: proof, if we
needed any, that Ruby's status as only begotten granddaughter
exempts her from behavior that would have earned a wrist
slap for any of her own kids.

Alice gives the eulogy. She tells the story about finding
me in the snow, and how they carried me home and baptized
me in the kitchen sink. It's very well written. Alice was always
the best writer.

My bones are in the casket behind her. I convinced Ruby
that I didn't need them. I wouldn't know what to do with
them if we kept them: walk around like a skeleton from *Jason
and the Argonauts*? I've freaked out enough people in my life,
thank you. I also convinced her that my persistence in the
material world—or rather, my failure to leave it—needed to
remain our little secret. What good would it do for people to
know that their town is haunted by a ghost? So of course
Ruby immediately told Alice. And then Alice and I had to
have a fight about why I didn't tell her earlier. (I think I made
a convincing argument, despite—or maybe because of—
being able to write only a line at a time.) We agreed, however,
that it would be a bad idea to tell Mom. At least for now. No
one wants to be responsible for a heart attack.

Near the end of the service, the middle Stanhoultz girl
stands up to sing the song Mom requested. Lizzie is fourteen, and her entire family, mom and dad and five other sib-

lings, made it to the elementary school the night of the outbreak. Mrs. Cho swears that Mrs. Stanhoultz is pregnant again. Lizzie sings "I Will Meet You in the Morning" like a born Baptist. She has a clear, bell-like voice, and Mom is crying by the first chorus. Let me tell you, you haven't known guilt until you've fooled your mother into watching your own funeral.

I still think about leaving for good. Checking out of this accidental afterlife I've found myself in. The door opens a crack. But I hesitate. I linger. It's not that I'm afraid of oblivion, or hell, or the absence of a promised land. Oh, I'll admit that sometimes I entertain fantasies about a very Iowa kind of heaven, a place with a big kitchen and a large table and an infinite pot of coffee, where Junie and Crystal and I can argue about nothing while the snow blows outside the windows. Some nights I open that door and gaze into the black tunnel and think about stepping through.

And then I hear Ruby waking up, bitching about the humidity, or Mom laughing dryly with Mrs. Cho over some fresh news, or Kwang firing up his tractor. And I think, not yet. Maybe stick around for a little while longer. Until Kwang has babies. Until the enclave is safe. Until Ruby finds someone to love.

Someday I'll step into the dark. But not yet. Not yet.

Read on for an excerpt from

THE DEVIL'S ALPHABET

B A A
C ACAHB AC
B AC

BY DARYL GREGORY

Published by Del Rey Books

CHAPTER ONE

Pax knew he was almost to Switchcreek when he saw his first argo.

The gray-skinned man was hunched over the engine of a decrepit, roofless pickup truck stalled hood-up at the side of the road. He straightened as Pax's car approached, unfolding like an extension ladder. Ten or eleven feet tall, angular as a dead tree, skin the mottled gray of weathered concrete. No shirt, just overalls that came down to his bony knees. He squinted at Pax's windshield.

Jesus, Pax thought. He'd forgotten how big they were.

He didn't recognize the argo, but that didn't mean much, for a lot of reasons. He might even be a cousin. The neighborly thing would be to pull over and ask the man if he needed help. But Pax was running late, so late. He fixed his eyes on the road outside his windshield, pretending not to see the man, and blew past without touching his brakes. The old Ford Tempo shuddered beneath him as he took the next curve.

The two-lane highway snaked through dense walls of green, the trees leaning into the road. He'd been gone for

eleven years, almost twelve. After so long in the north everything seemed too lush, too overgrown. Subtropical. Turn your
back and the plants and insects would overrun everything.

His stomach burned from too much coffee, too little food,
and the queasy certainty that he was making a mistake. The
call had come three days ago, Deke's rumbling voice on his
cellphone's voicemail: Jo Lynn was dead. The funeral was on
Saturday morning. Just thought you'd want to know.

Pax deleted the message but spent the rest of the week listening to it replay in his head. Dreading a follow-up call. Then
2 a.m. Saturday morning, when it was too late to make the
service—too late unless he drove nonstop and the Ford's
engine refrained from throwing a rod—he tossed some
clothes into a suitcase and drove south out of Chicago at 85
mph.

His father used to yell at him, Paxton Abel Martin, you'd
be late for your own funeral! It was Jo who told him not to
worry about it, that everybody was late for their own funeral.
Pax didn't get the joke until she explained it to him. Jo was
the clever one, the verbal one.

At the old town line there was a freshly painted sign: WEL-
COME TO SWITCHCREEK, TN. POPULATION 815. The barbed wire
fence that used to mark the border was gone. The cement bar-
riers had been pushed to the roadside. But the little guard
shack still stood beside the road like an outhouse, abandoned
and drowning in kudzu.

The way ahead led into what passed for Switchcreek's
downtown, but there was a shortcut to where he was going, if
he could find it. He crested the hill, scanning the foliage to his
right, and still almost missed it. He braked hard and turned in
to a narrow gravel drive that vanished into the trees. The
wheels jounced over potholes and ruts, forcing him to slow
down.

The road forked and he turned left automatically, knowing the way even though yesterday he wouldn't have been able to describe this road to anyone. He passed a half-burned barn, then a trailer that had been boarded up since he was kid, then the rusted carcass of a '63 Falcon he and Deke had used for target practice with their .22s. Each object seemed strange, then abruptly familiar, then hopelessly strange again—shifting and shifty.

The road came out of the trees at the top of a hill. He braked to a stop, put the car in park. The engine threatened to die, then fell into an unsteady idle.

A few hundred yards below lay the cemetery, the redbrick church, and the gravel parking lot half-full of cars. Satellite trucks from two different television stations were there. In the cemetery, the funeral was already in progress.

Pax leaned forward and folded his arms atop the steering wheel, letting the struggling air conditioner blow into his damp ribs. About fifty people sat or stood around a pearl-gray casket. Most were betas, bald, dark-red heads gleaming like river stones. The few men wore dark suits, the women long dresses. Some of the women had covered their heads with white scarves. A surprising number of them seemed to be pregnant.

An argo couple stood at the rear of the group, towering over the other mourners. The woman's broad shoulders and narrow hips made a V of her pale green dress. The man beside her was a head shorter and skinny as a ladder. He wore a plain blue shirt with the sleeves rolled up his chalky forearms. Deke looked exactly as Pax remembered him.

The people who were seated rose to their feet. They began to sing.

Pax turned off the car and rolled down the window. Some of the voices were high and flutelike, but the bass rumble, he knew, was provided by the booming chests of the two argos. The melody was difficult to catch at first, but then he recognized the hymn "Just As I Am." He knew the words by heart. It was an altar-call song, a slow weeper that struck especially hard for people who'd come through the Changes. Leading them through the song, her brick-red face tilted to the sky, was a beta woman in a long skirt, a flowing white blouse, and a colorful vest. The pastor, Pax guessed, though it was odd to think of a woman pastor at this church. It was odd to think of anyone but his father in the pulpit.

When the song ended the woman said a few words that Pax couldn't catch, and then the group began to walk toward the back door of the church. As the rows cleared, two figures remained seated in front of the casket: two bald girls in dark dresses. Some of the mourners touched the girls' shoulders and moved on.

Those had to be the twins. Jo's daughters. He'd known he'd see them here, had braced for it, but even so he wasn't ready. He was grateful for this chance to see them first from a distance.

A bald beta man in a dark blue suit squatted down between the girls, and after a brief exchange took their hands in his. They stood and he led them to the church entrance. The argo couple hung back. They bent their heads together, and then the woman went inside alone, ducking to make it through the entrance. Deke glanced up to where Paxton's car sat on the hill.

Pax leaned away from the windshield. What he most wanted was to put the car in reverse, then head back through the trees to the highway. Back to Chicago. But he could feel Deke looking at him.

He stepped out of the car, and hot, moist air enveloped him. He reached back inside and pulled out his suit jacket—

frayed at the cuffs, ten years out of style—but didn't put it on. If he was lucky he wouldn't have to wear it at all.

"Into the valley of death," he said to himself. He folded the jacket over his arm and walked down the hill to the cemetery's rusting fence.

The back gate squealed open at his push. He walked through the thick grass between the headstones. When he was a kid he'd used this place like a playground. They all had—Deke, Jo, the other church kids—playing hide-and-seek, sardines, and of course ghost in the graveyard. There weren't so many headstones then.

Deke squatted next to the grave, his knees higher than his head like an enormous grasshopper. He'd unhooked one of the chains that had connected the casket to the frame and was rolling it up around his hand. "Thought that was you," he said without looking up from his work. His voice rumbled like a diesel engine.

"How you doing, Deke?"

The man stood up. Pax felt a spark of fear—the back-brain yip of a small mammal confronted with a much larger predator. Argos were skinny, but their bony bodies suggested scythes, siege engines. And Deke seemed to be at least a foot taller than the last time Pax had seen him. His curved spine made his head sit lower than his shoulders, but if he could stand up straight he'd be twice Paxton's height.

"You've grown," Pax said. If they'd been anywhere near the same size they might have hugged—normal men did that all the time, didn't they? Then Deke held out a hand the size of a skillet, and Pax took it as best he good. Deke could have crushed him, but he kept his grip light. His palm felt rough and unyielding, like the face of a cinder block. "Long time, P.K.," he said.

P.K. Preacher's Kid. Nobody had called him that since he was fifteen. Since the day he left Switchcreek.

Pax dropped his arm. He could still feel the heat of Deke's skin on his palm.

"I didn't get your message until last night," Pax lied. "I drove all night to get here. I must look like hell."

Deke tilted his head, not disagreeing with him. "The important thing's you got here. I told the reverend I'd take care of the casket, but if you want to go inside, they're setting out the food."

"No, that's—I'm not hungry." Another lie. But he hadn't come here for a hometown reunion. He needed to pay his respects and that was it. He was due back at the restaurant by Monday.

He looked at the casket, then at the glossy, polished gravestone. Someone had paid for a nice one.

JO LYNN WHITEHALL
BORN FEBRUARY 12, 1983
DIED AUGUST 17, 2010
LOVING MOTHER

"'Loving Mother.' That's nice," Pax said. But the epitaph struck him as entirely inadequate. After a while he said, "It seems weird to boil everything down to two words like that."

"Especially for Jo," Deke said. A steel frame supported the casket on thick straps. Deke squatted again to turn a stainless steel handle next to the screw pipe. The casket began to lower into the hole. "It's the highest compliment the betas have, though. Pretty much the only one that counts."

The casket touched bottom. Paxton knelt and pulled up the straps on his side of the grave. Then the two of them lifted the metal frame out of the way.

Paxton brushed the red clay from his knees. They stood there looking into the hole.

The late Jo Lynn Whitehall, Paxton thought.

He tried to imagine her body inside the casket, but it was impossible. He couldn't picture either of the Jo's he'd known—not the brown-haired girl from before the Changes, or the sleek creature she'd become after. He waited for tears, the physical rush of some emotion that would prove that he loved her. Nothing came. He felt like he was both here and not here, a double image hovering a few inches out of true.

Paxton breathed in, then blew out a long breath. "Do you know why she did it?" He couldn't say the word "suicide."

Deke shook his head. They were silent for a time and then Deke said, "Come on inside."

Deke didn't try to persuade him; he simply went in and Pax followed, down the narrow stairs—the dank, cinder-block walls smelling exactly as Pax remembered—and into the basement and the big open room they called the Fellowship Hall. The room was filled with rows of tables covered in white plastic tablecloths. There were at least twice as many people as he'd seen outside at the burial. About a dozen of them were "normal"—unchanged, skipped, passed over, whatever you wanted to call people like him—and none of them looked like reporters.

Deke went straight to the buffet, three tables laid end-to-end and crowded with food. No one seemed to notice that Pax had snuck in behind the tall man.

The spread was as impressive as the potlucks he remembered as a boy. Casseroles, sloppy joes, three types of fried chicken, huge bowls of mashed potatoes . . . One table held nothing but desserts. Enough food to feed three other congregations.

While they filled their plates Pax surreptitiously looked

over the room, scanning for the twins through a crowd of alien faces. After so long away it was a shock to see so many of the changed in one room. TDS—Transcription Divergence Syndrome—had swept through Switchcreek the summer he was fourteen. The disease had divided the population, then divided it again and again, like a dealer cutting a deck of cards into smaller piles. By the end of the summer a quarter of the town was dead. The survivors were divided by symptoms into clades: the giant argos, the seal-skinned betas, the fat charlies. A few, a very few, weren't changed at all—at least in any way you could detect.

A toddler in a Sunday dress bumped into his legs and careened away, laughing in a high, piping voice. Two other bald girls—all beta children were girls, all were bald—chased after her into a forest of legs.

Most of the people in the room were betas. The women and the handful of men were hairless, skin the color of cabernet, raspberry, rose. The women wore dresses, and now that he was closer he could see that even more were pregnant than he'd supposed. The expectant mothers tended to be the younger, smaller women. They were also the ones who seemed to be wearing the head scarves.

He was surprised by how different the second-generation daughters were from their mothers. The mothers, though skinny and bald and oddly colored, could pass for normal women with some medical condition—as chemo patients, maybe. But their children's faces were flat, the noses reduced to a nub and two apostrophes, their mouths a long slit.

Someone grabbed his arm. "Paxton Martin!"

He put on an expectant smile before he turned.

"It *is* you," the woman said. She reached up and pulled him down into a hug. She was about five feet tall and extremely wide, carrying about three hundred pounds under a surprisingly well-tailored pink pantsuit.

She drew back and gazed at him approvingly, her over-inflated face taut and shiny. Lime green eyeshade and bright red rouge added to the beach ball effect.

"Aunt Rhonda," he said, smiling. She wasn't his aunt, but everyone in town called her that. He was surprised at how happy he was to see her.

"Just look at you," she said. "You're as handsome as I remember."

Pax felt the heat in his cheeks. He wasn't handsome, not in the ways recognized by the outside world. But in Switchcreek he was a skip, one of the few children who had come through the Changes unmarked and still breathing.

Rhonda didn't seem to notice his embarrassment. "This is a terrible thing, isn't it? People say the word 'tragic' too much, but that's what it is. I can't imagine how tough it must be on her girls."

He didn't know what to say except, "Yes."

"I remember your momma carrying Jo Lynn around the church in her little dresses when she was just a year old. She loved that girl like she was her own. So pretty, and so smart. Smart as a whip."

Pax waited for the slight, the veiled insult. Rhonda had been the church secretary while his father was pastor. She was a sharp-tongued woman with opinions about everyone and everything, including his mother's performance as a pastor's wife.

Rhonda shook her head. "And you two! You two were like brother and sister. Only three months between you, is that right?"

"Four," he said. A dozen feet behind Rhonda, a young

charlie man, broad as a linebacker and not showing any of the fat that clung to the older people of his clade, watched them talk. His hair was shaved to a shadow. A diamond stud winked from one ear.

Pax spotted the twins at a nearby table. The girls didn't seem to be eating. The beta man who'd walked them into the church—a beta man in a dark suit—sat at the end of the table, the beta pastor beside him. The man seemed to be trying to talk to the twins, but they only stared at their plates.

Rhonda half turned to follow his gaze. "That's Tommy Shields, Jo's husband." There was the slightest pause before the word "husband."

"I'm sorry—what? Nobody told me she'd—"

Rhonda lowered her voice. "Oh, hon, not the way anyone but them calls a husband."

Pax didn't know what she meant. No betas had been getting married when he left town.

He knew Tommy, though. He'd been a junior in high school when Deke and Jo and Pax were freshmen. Complete asshole. That freshman year, Tommy had beaten up Deke, evidently for standing too close to Tommy's car, a red-and-white '76 Bronco that he'd restored himself. Pax didn't remember seeing Tommy after the Changes.

"Still," Rhonda said, almost sighing. "Tommy's a help to those girls. They've got a hard row to hoe—but I don't need to tell you that, do I?" She shook her head sadly. "It just breaks my heart. I let the sisters know that the town's going to help any way it can. And of course, they've got their church to help."

Their church. "You're not going here anymore?" Paxton asked. Rhonda's grandfather had been a founder, and Rhonda had held the office of church secretary for twenty years. Pastors came and went, she'd told his father more than once, but she wasn't going anywhere. Even during the Changes, when the church had closed and her own body was bloating, she'd refused to step down. Then again, Pax's father hadn't stepped down either, not until a year after Pax had left town. Pax had never tried to get the whole story—that was his father's life, nothing to do with him now.

"Oh, Paxton, it's not like it was before," Rhonda said, keeping her voice low. "This is Reverend Hooke's church now. I go to First Baptist, though I can't be as involved as I'd like."

Paxton's father had impressed upon him at a young age that attending First Baptist was almost as bad as converting to Roman Catholic. The First was where the rich people went—as rich as anyone got in Switchcreek—and everybody knew they didn't take their scripture seriously.

"Aunt Rhonda's the mayor now," Deke said, sounding amused. He was bent under the ceiling, holding his plate and plastic cup of iced tea between big fingers. Waiting to see how Pax would react.

"Really?" Pax said, trying not to sound too shocked. "*Mayor* Rhonda."

"Six years now," Deke said.

"Well," Pax said. "I bet you keep everyone in line."

Rhonda chuckled, obviously pleased, and patted his arm again. Her mood kept changing, fast as switching TV channels. "You and I need to talk. Have you seen your father yet?"

He felt heat in his cheeks and shook his head. "I just got in."

"He's not in a good way, and he won't take my help." She pursed her lips. "After your visit, you give me a call."

"Sure, sure," he said lightly.

Her eyes, already small in her huge face, narrowed. "Don't *sure* me, Paxton Martin."

Pax blinked. She wasn't joking. He remembered a church picnic when he was nine or ten: Aunt Rhonda had found Pax and Jo misbehaving—he couldn't remember what they'd been doing—and she'd taken a switch to their backsides. She didn't care whose kids they were. Then she gave them both MoonPies and told them to stop crying.

"I'll call," he said. "I promise."

She smiled, all sweetness again. "Now you better go eat your meal before it's cold."

She turned away, and several people at the table nearest them resumed talking. The charlie man stepped away from the wall and followed Rhonda. He glanced back at Paxton, his expression serious.

Deke walked toward the other end of the room, where a group of argos, including the woman in the green dress, ate standing up, bent under the drop-tile ceiling. Pax tried to follow, but he'd been recognized now, and people wanted to shake his hand and talk to him. Some of them seemed exactly as he remembered them. Mr. Sparks, already an old man when Pax knew him, had been one of the few of the elderly who'd survived, and in his own skin. He still looked trim and vigorous. Others had become distorted versions of their old selves, or else so changed that there was no recognizing them. Each of them greeted him warmly, without a hint of reservation or disapproval, as if he'd decided on his own to leave Switchcreek for greater things. After all, every other unchanged person under thirty seemed to have left town. After the quarantine lifted, after the Lambert riots and the Stonecipher murders, who the hell would stick around if they didn't have to? The skips skipped.

He squeezed past two tables of charlies, nodding back at those who said hello to him, even when he wasn't sure of their names. The people of Aunt Rhonda's clade were as wide as he remembered from the year and a half he'd lived among them: squat, moon-faced, engulfing their metal folding chairs. Finally he made it to the far side of the room where the argos had congregated. Most stood with their slouched backs touching the ceiling. A few perched on benches at the edges of the room, knees and elbows splayed, like adults at kindergarten desks. Each of them was a different shade of pale, from pencil lead to talcum.

Deke held out a long arm. "P.K., you remember Donna?"

Like all argos, the woman was tall and horse-faced. But while argo hair was usually stiff as straw and about the same color as their skin—troll hair, Deke had called it—hers was long and red, cinched tight close to her head and then blossoming behind, like the head of a broom.

The woman held out her hand. "Good to see you again, Paxton." Her voice was as deep as Deke's—deeper maybe—but the inflection was more feminine somehow.

"Oh! Donna, sure!" He put down his plate and grasped her big hand in both of his. Donna had been a year behind them at school. She was a McKinney, one of the poor folks who lived up on Two Hills Road. Poor black folk. And now, he thought, she was whiter than he was.

"You two have been married how long again?" Pax asked. As if it had just slipped his mind. He remembered a wedding invitation that had been forwarded to him from his cousins' house in Naperville. He'd meant to respond.

"Eight years at the end of the month," Donna said.

"You guys were kids!" Pax said. "*Tall* kids, but still. What were you, nineteen? That must have been some shotgun wedding."

"Not really," Deke said.

"Oh shit, I'm sorry," Pax said, then realized he'd said "shit" in church and felt doubly embarrassed. There was no such thing as a pregnant argo, no such thing as an argo baby. "I didn't mean—"

Deke held up a hand: Don't worry about it.

Donna said. "We want to feed you supper, then of course you have to stay at the house."

"No, really, that's okay—"

"We've got plenty of room. Unless you're staying with your father?"

"No." He said it too quickly. "I thought I'd just stay at the Motel Six in Lambert."

Deke said, "Have you talked to him lately?"

Pax started to say, *Twelve years, give or take*—but then the two argos looked over his head. Pax turned. Tommy Shields walked toward them, the twin girls trailing behind him.

Tommy had been tall before the Changes, but he'd lost several inches of his height. His face was hairless, without even eyebrows, and his skin had turned a light brown that was splotched with dark across his cheeks and forehead. But he was still first-generation beta, with a broad jaw and too much muscle in the shoulders, and the old Tommy was still recognizable under the new skin.

His voice, however, was utterly different. "You're Paxton," he said softly. His lips barely moved, and the sound seemed to start and stop a few inches from his thin lips. "Jo Lynn's friend." He extended a hand, and Pax shook it and released without squeezing.

Pax couldn't think what to say, and finally came up with, "I'm sorry for your loss."

"Girls," Tommy said, "this man was a good friend of your mother's."

The girls stepped forward. Heat flared in Paxton's chest, an ache of something like embarrassment or fear. They were the same height, their heads coming up to just past Tommy's elbow. They had to be almost twelve now.

Tommy didn't seem to notice Paxton's discomfort. "This is Sandra," Tommy said, indicating the girl on his left, "and this is Rainy." They were second-generation betas—the firstborn of that generation—and their wine-colored faces were expressionless as buttons.

"Hi," Pax said. He coughed to clear his throat. "It's a pleasure to meet you." He knew their names from decade-old letters. Jo had rejected twin-ish stunt-names. No alliteration, no groaners like Hope and Joy. The only thing notable was that Rainy—Lorraine—was named after his mother. "Your mom was—"

He blinked at them, trying to think of some anecdote, but suddenly his mind was empty. He couldn't even picture Jo Lynn's face.

No one spoke.

"She was a great person," Pax said finally. "I could tell you stories."

The girls stared at him.

"I bet they'd like to hear those," Tommy said. "Come by the Co-op and we can talk about her. Before you leave."

Pax hesitated. Co-op? "I'd like that," he said. "I'm not sure if I can, though—I have to see how my father's doing. But if I can get away . . ."

Tommy looked at him. "If you can spare the time," he said in that soft voice. He smiled tightly and turned away. The girls regarded Paxton for a long moment and then followed Tommy across the room.

Pax exhaled heavily. "Man," he said.

Donna said, "Are you okay?"

"Yeah, it's just those girls." He shook his head. "I know Jo loved them. She did, right?" Before they could answer he said, "Never mind, stupid question. It's just that I can't believe she'd leave them."

There was an awkward silence, and he looked up at the argos. Deke was frowning, and Donna wore a strangely fierce expression.

⟍ "She wouldn't," Donna said.

He looked from Donna to Deke, back again. He could see it in their faces. "You don't think she killed herself?"

Neither of them said anything for a moment. Deke shook his head. "It's just a feeling," he said.

"Show me," Pax said to him. "Show me where it happened."

ACKNOWLEDGMENTS

Many people breathed life into this book. Martha Millard encouraged me to go for broke, and Chris Schluep pushed me to go for broker—nay, brokest.

A crack team of forensic readers and fellow writers poked and prodded at the first draft. Andrew Tisbert, Matt Sturges, Jack Skillingstead, Chris Roberson, Dave Justus, Gary Delafield, and Elizabeth Delafield have my reverse-alphabetical gratitude.

Ian Gregory read each chapter as it rolled out of the printer and then demanded to find out *what happened next*. His enthusiasm for this book animated every page.

And Kathy Bieschke did all of the above, plus kept *me* breathing through the writing of this book—no mean feat.

Thank you all so much.

ABOUT THE AUTHOR

Daryl Gregory won the Crawford Award for his first novel, *Pandemonium,* which was also a finalist for the World Fantasy Award. *The Devil's Alphabet,* his second novel, was a finalist for the Philip K. Dick Award and was named one of the best books of 2009 by *Publishers Weekly.* His short stories have appeared in *The Magazine of Fantasy & Science Fiction, Asimov's,* and several year's-best anthologies. In 2005 he received the *Asimov's* Readers' Award for the novelette "Second Person, Present Tense." He lives with his wife and two children in State College, Pennsylvania, where he writres both fiction and Web code.